A *LESS THAN ZERO* ROCKSTAR ROMANCE

FEARLESS

KAYLENE WINTER

A *LESS THAN ZERO* ROCKSTAR ROMANCE

FEARLESS

KAYLENE WINTER

THIS BOOK IS ABOUT SURVIVAL AND REDEMPTION. IT HAS A STORYLINE PULLED FROM THE HEADLINES INVOLVING THE #METOO MOVEMENT THAT CONTINUES TO SWEEP THROUGH HOLLYWOOD. *Just a little advance warning—*

PROLOGUE
PRESENT DAY

"Fuck my life!" Byron Angel, the pampered second-bit actor screeched just before shoving his chips over to me. Yanking his fancy mirrored-lens sunglasses off, he tossed them on the poker table, unable to mask his disdain at losing 50k to a lowly bass player in a rock band. His words, not mine.

Not bothered in the slightest, I carefully stacked my bounty of chips and assessed the situation without saying a word. I'd learned over the years that being stealthy allowed you to fly under the radar. It also came in handy to observe and learn things about the people around you. Stuff that was often quite useful.

Like winning big hands in an invitation-only poker game.

"Angel, you're out. So it's time to get the fuck out." The A-list director of *Phantom Rising* pointed to the door.

"Maybe I'll stay and just hang out for a bit?" Byron's desperate pandering was *not* endearing. It was pathetic, truth be told.

Glancing up at the other players' bemused expressions, I knew without a shadow of doubt that his failure to read the room was fatal. It had cost him a significant amount of money. Worse, it cost him respect.

Respect was always better than money. Always.

The director sniffed sharply. Probably to clear the last of the coke from his sinuses. Barely even giving Byron a second glance, he waved him off with a "shoo" gesture. "Nah. Jermaine will see you out."

And just like that, the eejit Byron Angel was booted the fuck out.

Good riddance.

The director's exclusive games were always a veritable male celebrity cock-fest. Filled with actors, directors, producers, and other industry bigwigs who felt the need to throw their power around. All it really meant was a bunch of yammering on and on about their looks, their women, and their stupid cars. Oh, how I loved to slag these boyos. To their face. My slight second-generation Irish accent made my insults harder to understand if I turned up the brogue. Easier to swallow.

Tonight wasn't my first go-round. A few months ago, I'd been in LA with my band, Less Than Zero, recording the soundtrack to *Phantom Rising*. The director found out I liked poker and invited me to his regular underground game hosted in his Hollywood mansion. Tonight, my band was in New York City for the movie premiere and to play a private concert afterward. He'd practically dragged me out of the VIP party to attend his relocated poker game, which happened to be here in his Manhattan penthouse.

In other words, an underground game that wasn't *actually* underground. This one was thirty-six stories up.

After a few hours, I'd all but forgotten about the dim-witted actor. I had a huge pile of chips. It was turning out to be a good night. Especially when I mentally calculated my winnings. Factoring in the implied odds, I was on target to strip these losers of a couple hundred thousand dollars. Give or take a few grand after subtracting the buy-in.

Not that I'd keep any of this ill-begotten money for myself.

I just liked winning. Especially against arseholes.

Jermaine's booming voice snapped me out of my thoughts. "Need a beer, McGloughlin?"

"Nah, I'm grand." Studying my cards with a covert glance at the table, I estimated I was about one hand away from shutting the director out.

"I'm all in." The director pushed his chips to the center of the table. *Boom.*

"Call." I barely looked up.

The director blanched, only for a second. Had to maintain the appearance of dignity. Or whatever. Just as the dealer was about to lay down the river card, the door burst open. Byron Angel was back, tugging a divine, auburn-haired woman behind him. I was surprised to see her but steeled my expression to keep it neutral. Waiting to see WTF was going on. The mystery was solved when the actor produced a stack of hundred-dollar bills.

"Well, well, well." The director tapped a couple of chips roughly on the table and visibly ogled the woman's ample breasts. "I haven't seen you in a while. I think you've been avoiding me."

She ignored him completely. She pointedly ignored everyone, actually.

"I want back in; my girl is staking me." The desperate actor's slick, veneered grin made me want to punch a hole in his face just for existing.

Without being obvious, I kept an eye on her. For a split second her soulful green eyes locked with mine, but she quickly looked away to study something fascinating on the floor. It gave me a prime opportunity to more openly admire her. Delicious tits straining against a snug, plain

9

black blouse that bared her shoulders. Lightly sculpted muscles. Curvy waist. Long, slim legs clad in tight jeans.

Luscious.

Licking his lips, the director leered at her while addressing me, "You in, McGloughlin?"

"Nah." My eyes snapped back to my cards and I knocked the table with my knuckle to encourage the dealer to keep it moving.

Byron whined at me, "C'mon. Stay for one more hand. A hundred grand buy-in."

The director leaned back in his chair and stared me down. I held his gaze without moving a muscle. Mentally calculating my odds. God, this guy was a tosser. So what if his movies made hundreds of millions of dollars. The way he threw his clout around was obscene. Probably to make up for a deformed, tiny dick.

Allegedly.

His entitled, disgusting ogling of the beautiful interloper? Confirmed he was a complete knob when it came to women.

Again, allegedly.

It made me want to intimidate him a bit, so I lowered my head and fixed him with my most intimidating gaze from under my curtain of long hair. The director looked away, of course.

Because *no one* fucked with me.

I knew that real power wasn't Hollywood power by any stretch. It came from within. I'd learned this the hard way at a very young age. Even now that I was rich, famous even, I never forgot where I came from. I'd worked hard to improve my station in life. To be proud of who I was. To never take anything for granted.

True power meant putting your family first.

At all costs.

This lowlife director would never, ever come between me and mine.

"Fine. One more hand. Then I'm out. I'm knackered." I fixed my gaze on my cards again but pointed to the hand lying on the table. "First we finish this."

I knew he was drawing dead and wasn't surprised when he simply threw his cards on the table. Then gestured for me to take the pot. Seemingly obsessed by the gorgeous woman in the room, the man wasn't paying attention to me anymore. He motioned her over. "Hey, beautiful. Come sit down, we need to catch up. I have a role that is perfect for you."

A shadow passed over her face. Defiantly narrowing her eyes at him, the stunner pasted on a perfect pageant smile and gracefully eased into a cushioned chair far away from the poker table. She crossed her legs and tucked them up underneath her. I was fascinated with the dynamic and couldn't stop staring. She caught me looking. A flicker of heat flashed in her eyes.

Uh-huh. Now we're talking.

"Nah, I'm all good." Crossing her arms over her chest, she looked away. Essentially dismissing him.

Undeterred, the director licked his lips. His smooth, syrupy voice nearly made me ill. "Baby, don't *tease* me. I really want to collaborate with you."

"How wonderful. If you're actually serious we can talk about it Monday with my agent." She looked down at her dark-pink fingernails and examined her perfect manicure. One eye twitched slightly. Huh. She was nervous.

"Why do you always have to be such a bitch—" The director's tone changed. He pointed at her menacingly.

"Are we gonna do this thing or what?" I motioned to the director and Byron. Distracting him. Regretting my decision to play another hand, now I just wanted to get the feck out.

With the hottie, of course. No way would I leave her with this melter.

Byron took a seat and each of us put our ante in the middle of the table. Once our hands were dealt, we engaged in requisite bravado as the dealer turned over each card. Then it was time for me to put them out of their misery.

Mr. Angel couldn't contain his toothy smile. "Three of a kind."

The director spread out his cards. "Full house."

Byron's smile was erased. He slumped down into his chair, his hands covered his eyes.

"Thank you, gentlemen." I laid out my four Jacks.

"Fuck!" The director narrowed his eyes at me.

"Call it the luck of the Irish." I pulled the chips toward my big pile. "Cash me out. I gotta go."

I made sure my winnings were wired to the right account while keeping an eye on the director, who'd sauntered over to the woman. She pierced him with a vicious glare. She moved to get up, but the director placed his hands on the arms of the chair, effectively caging her in. "Hey, baby, so glad you finally decided to join our after-party."

Jermaine dutifully stood guard to the side.

Assessing the situation, I hustled over. The director wasn't going to get anywhere near this beauty. Especially with his reputation. Not on my watch.

"Let's get more comfortable, sweetheart." He had the audacity to untuck his shirt.

She bared her teeth and spat, "Get out of my personal space. Now. And you don't *ever* get to call me sweetheart."

Her rebuke gave me the perfect opportunity to pull him back and shove him away. "Not in this lifetime. Keep your dick in your pants and your motherfucking hands off her," I growled.

"McGloughlin, take it easy. Stay for a change. This is when the night gets interesting." The director held his hands up in surrender. "Everything's cool."

Um, no. It wasn't.

The beautiful woman's shellshocked eyes caught mine. She was shivering with fear but trying to hide it. I held my hand out to her. She didn't take it. In an instant, just like a warrior princess, she transformed her energy and deftly shifted into badass bitch-mode. This was a woman who didn't want to be rescued. Probably didn't need rescuing. Her glare directed at me was an attempt to warn me off.

As if.

You could hear a pin drop in the room. The clock on the wall ticked like a metronome. Those who remained were frozen in place, equally horrified and intrigued at what was going down. In my book? All of them disgusting excuses for men. They were just going to stand by and let something happen to her. Not on my feckin' watch.

I moved toward her.

The director held up his hand to me and motioned to Jermaine with the other. "Now, Connor. If you're not in, you're out."

I felt Jermaine's big palm on my shoulder.

Bollocks.

Tucking a thick strand of hair behind her ear, the beauty fixed her big, green-eyed gaze on me then flicked her eyes to the door, which I took as a silent plea for me to leave. The tough-girl act was good. Almost good enough to work on most people. I guess that could be expected for an actress of her caliber.

I saw through it all.

And I'd seen enough.

Shaking Jermaine off me, I scooped her up and strode purposefully toward the door. Quickly side-stepping the big bodyguard.

"Who the fuck do you think you are?" The director motioned for the rest of his security goons to stop us.

"She's coming with me." I deftly evaded his crew. I shot the director my most evil don't-fuck-with-me glare. "And you best not follow."

The man was visibly shocked at my insubordination. But he smartly didn't make a move. I knew he wouldn't. He fancied himself a wise guy when he was really a scared rabbit. Besides, over the past few months, I'd planted some seeds. He had no idea I wasn't in the Seattle Irish mob. Or that there wasn't actually an Irish Mob. His hesitance gave me an opening, and I took it.

With precious cargo safely cradled in my arms.

Thank Christ she didn't acknowledge she knew who I was. Resigned, she wound her arms around my neck and kept quiet. Once we were outside the suite, I crushed her to me. Breathing in her delectable, fresh lemony scent, I strode to the penthouse elevator. Once the door closed behind us, I gently set her down and held her quivering body to my chest with one arm. I texted my driver with my free hand.

Still, neither of us said a word.

Through the floor-to-ceiling glass windows of the lobby, I was relieved to see the Town Car waiting for us outside the building. Only when we were settled into the buttery, black leather seats did I allow myself to look at Veronica Mae Miller's tear-streaked face.

She devastated me. Every. Single. Time.

"You have no idea what you've just done, Connor." Ronni nestled into my chest, her need for comfort outweighing her words.

"Of course I do," I growled. "If I hadn't been there—"

"I had it handled." She shoved off me rebelliously.

14

We stared at each other. A buffalo stance. Until she looked down at her shaking hands clasped in her lap. I got no pleasure in winning this staring contest. Not with her. Gently, I tipped Ronni's chin with my thumb and forefinger so she'd be forced to look into my eyes. "*No*. You. Didn't. This shite ends for good now. It's long past time."

A traitorous tear rolled down her cheek. "After everything I keep putting you through, why do you even care?"

"Because, my love. I take care of my own."

"But…"

"But nothing. Get it through that thick skull of yours. I'm your *husband* and it's high time you start acting like my wife."

RONNI

CHAPTER 1

EIGHTEEN YEARS PRIOR (AGE 15)

"**V**eronica Mae Miller, get your ass to the car. Right now!" My mom, the formidable Mable Miller, was on a mission of which I was the main focus. "We're late!"

I had another frigging audition.

By the time I was six, I *knew* I was destined to be an actress, Lizzie McGuire obsession aside. After pestering my poor mother for years, she finally relented and was determined to help make my dream come true.

She was awesome like that.

Of course, at the time I had no idea that casting calls were part of the process. Oh, how naïve I was. Three years later and I only had a few stupid commercials in my reel. Hollywood was a hard nut to crack. Casting agents had no qualms about telling you how wrong you were for a role and why. Simply based upon your appearance. Or what you wore. Or your hair color.

I was trying to develop a thicker skin.

My confidence was shaky.

Luckily, my determination was not.

"Coming!" I sang, running down the stairs and out the front door.

Mom was leaning against our beat-up Honda, which sputtered in anticipation of the long drive from Long Beach to West Hollywood. "Did you bring the suit?"

I couldn't help but cross my arms over my newly ample breasts. "*Maw-emm...* it's so gross to wear a bathing suit in front of a bunch of old men."

"We're late, Veronica." Mom marched past me into the house and emerged a minute later with my pink-and-white polka dot bikini. "If you want to make the audition, we need to go."

Pouting, I muttered, "You have to admit, it's creepy."

"The show is set in Hawaii, the casting notes are clear. They need to know you look good in a two-piece, and you do," Mom reassured me. "Do you know your lines or should we run through them on the way?"

"No, I'm good."

"Sweetheart, if you don't feel comfortable, just tell me."

As much as I loathed the audition process, Mom made a lot of sacrifices to keep my dream alive. Including working two jobs. If I were cast in this show, it would be the end of all our financial worries.

Plus, Hawaii.

"No, I really want the part. Seriously, I'm ready, let's go."

Like many auditions, this one was held in a rented production studio. All of us were ushered into a utilitarian room lined with fold-out chairs. Mable objected when they escorted her to the door. I shot her a look.

I've got this. Don't ruin it for me.

Thankfully, she departed with the other parents.

Clutching my backpack, I anxiously took a seat and waited. My heart pounded and my scalp pricked with fear. As much as she annoyed me sometimes, Mom always provided me with much-needed moral support.

Now I was alone.

Shutting my eyes, I breathed deeply to center myself. To calm down. To remember why I was doing this. Knowing that if I *really* wanted something I should give it my all. Knowing that if I *really* wanted to be an actress, I had to push down my deep-rooted fear that the acting profession didn't want me.

I felt something intangible take root inside me.

Conviction.

Resolve.

Whatever it was, I'd do whatever it took to win the role.

An hour passed before my name was finally called by a geeky girl in mismatched clothes with hair the color of a carrot. Scanning her crazy outfit, I noticed she was wearing purple sparkly Chucks. Obviously customized. "Your shoes are great."

The girl looked shocked at being noticed, never mind the compliment. "Th-thanks."

"I'm Veronica."

"Hannah." She gave me a smile that looked more like a wince and motioned for me to follow her.

Being nice always gave me a boost of self-assurance. I was going to own this room. Fake it until you make it. Wasn't that the old saying?

I sucked in my gut, threw my shoulders back and glided through the door like I owned the place. "Good afternoon, I'm Veronica Mae Miller."

Two schlubby guys in their forties and a younger, fitter guy in a tailored blue suit let their eyes travel up and down my body. Schlubby number one licked his lips.

Ewww.

"Are you wearing the required attire?" Schlubby two narrowed his eyes at me.

I held up my bikini.

The men exchanged glances.

"You can change there." Hannah gestured to a semi-sheer blue curtain, which hung from the ceiling but stopped short of the floor by about four feet. Her eyes held mine in what seemed to be an apology.

"Um... Sure, sounds good..." I glanced at the curtain, which didn't offer much privacy.

Well, any privacy.

Every ounce of manufactured confidence I'd conjured seeped out of me like a deflating balloon. I bit my lip to stave of the creepy feeling that took root at the base of my neck and prickled toward my scalp like icicles.

Was this weird?

Um, yes.

"In this lifetime, please," suit guy barked out impatiently.

I had no idea what to do.

Every instinct told me to run out of the room.

Except, at least twenty girls had auditioned before me and they were fine.

Right?

Right. After all, this was a professional audition. Actors and actresses had to be ready for anything. It all boiled down to one thing.

How much did I want this part?

More than anything. That was the truth of it. It was up to me to prove it. Willing myself to go into the zone, the mantra I kept on internal repeat during times of stress kicked in.

Deep breath

Suck it up.

Be fearless.

Behind the sheer curtain, I kept my back to the men and quickly changed into my bikini. All the while chastising myself for not listening to my mom in the first place. I should have just worn it under my clothes. It would have spared me such incredible humiliation. My God, these creepy creeps were probably watching me change.

Ick.

A clock on the wall ticked loudly. Reminding me that it was now or never.

I chose now.

It's showtime.

Determined not to show weakness, I pushed everything out of my mind. After adjusting my top to make sure my boobs were covered, I was ready. I strode out and looked each one of them in the eye. Thrust out my breasts. For good measure, I cocked my hip. No way were they going to see how truly scared I really was.

All three sets of eyeballs popped open. From there, my muscle memory took over, and it was like magic. The lines came to me as though I'd been born to say them.

I nailed it. In a tiny, pink polka-dot bikini in front of three pervy dudes. I friggin' nailed it.

I stood waiting for further direction. Each moment ticked by slowly. Bravado aside, it was off-putting to have grown men openly gawk at my body. Assessing me. Deciding if I was hot enough. Thin enough. Boobalicious enough.

The clock ticked.

I stared at the men with a fixed smile on my face.

Waiting. For. This. To. End.

Finally. *Finally*. Suit guy sniffed deeply and nodded toward a door on the other side of the room. "We'll be in touch."

Get outta here. Stat.

Determined to remain professional, I backed away, still smiling. "Thank you all, *very* much. I *truly* appreciate the opportunity."

Once I was out of the room, I pulled on my clothes quickly. Toeing on my ballet flats, I burst out of the building in search of my mom. She was sitting on a bench outside the door in a small courtyard. I resisted the urge to run into her arms.

"Well? How did it go?" Mable's brow was furrowed with stress.

"I nailed it. I think we'll be moving to Hawaii soon."

CHAPTER 2

SIXTEEN YEARS PRIOR (AGE 17)

"**B**oys." Ma popped her head into the garage where I was jamming with my twin brothers, Liam and Padraig. "Yer Da's home. It's time for dinner."

Our entire clan—in Ireland and the US— referred to the three of us as "Irish triplets" because only eleven months separated us. I was the oldest. Then the twins. Cillian, Brennan and Seamus rounded out the family at twelve, ten and eight respectively.

We were living the American dream.

My Da, Rory McGloughlin, loved to tell our story. Eager to get out of Northern Ireland during the Troubles, he applied for and scored a coveted green card in the lottery. He brought my mother, Maureen, and me to Seattle right after I was born. After a couple years working his ass off for other people, he started McGloughlin Construction. Fifteen years later, his company employed thirty people working on high-end projects all over the Seattle area.

Da's showpiece was our eight-bedroom, five-bathroom Craftsman mansion in the Volunteer Park neighborhood. The house was originally a tear down, but Da meticulously fixed it up to historical accuracy with high-end finishes and fixtures throughout. The house was worth five times as much now as it had been before the renovation and served as a stunning showpiece for clients.

With financial privilege came benefits. Ma stayed home with us five rambunctious boys. We enjoyed many advantages. Private school. Sports. Extracurricular activities. All because my folks wanted to give us the things they didn't have where they grew up.

Freedom.

Choice.

Oh, the irony.

Da made no secret about his plan for me. As the oldest, I was expected to take over the company. My brothers weren't let off the hook, though. All of us were highly skilled in carpentry and a multitude of other tasks like tiling, framing, laying flooring, painting.

Too bad I hated it with a passion.

My obsession was music, which I hoped to build a career around.

Da thought it was a frivolous hobby.

Needless to say, we fought all the time about my future. I was adamant that I wouldn't take over the business. Even without his support, I managed to teach myself guitar. When the twins followed in my footsteps and we started our little garage band, it was like pouring salt in his wounds.

Again, the irony.

For all his talk about freedom and choice, it was frustrating he wasn't more supportive of what I wanted for my future.

We were getting pretty good. Padraig played drums. Liam sang and played lead guitar. I stuck to the bass because it suited me. Bassists were the oft-forgotten heart and soul of the band, a role that was perfect for me. I didn't crave the spotlight, I just loved to play.

When Ma finally herded all of us to the dinner table, we dug into steaming bowls of savory homemade Irish stew. No one spoke. We were too busy sopping up the rich, brown gravy with slices of homemade soda bread lathered in creamy Irish butter. Once we finished, Padraig dutifully got up and cleared the table. Seamus brought out dessert.

Ma didn't raise heathens, after all.

We were forks-deep into a strawberry-rhubarb crumble when Da chose to drop a bomb.

"Lads, I have brilliant news." Da clapped once loudly to ensure our rapt attention. "Today, the permits were approved on the Lake Union property. By the time Connor graduates, we'll break ground on two condo buildings, a suite of retail units, and an office tower. Our legacy in this fair city will be intact."

Ma glared at him from across the table. "Rory."

"Yer grand, Maureen." Da fixed her with a look that stopped her from saying another word. In front of us, at least. "It's our destiny. You can finally have a spot for your own bakery, love."

"Brilliant, Da." Cillian loved everything about the construction business.

"Lads, I'll need all hands on deck for the next few years." He scrubbed a hand over his reddish beard. "I don't need to tell you, this will set our family up for life."

My head was spinning. The twins and I gave each other "the look." As the three oldest, we knew what was coming and what would be expected. Our dreams of being musicians were beginning to crumble before our eyes.

My mom abruptly stood and began clearing the dessert dishes. "The boys will be staying in school, Rory. Don't you be getting any ideas otherwise."

"Ah, Maureen. Connor's nearly finished. No reason he can't be my foreman." Da patted his belly and leaned back in his chair.

"I'm not missing uni," I muttered under my breath. "I've got a full-ride football scholarship at University of Washington."

Undeterred, Da ignored my comment and made a move to his recliner in front of the TV. "You're my first-born son. When we finish this project then you have my permission to do whatever you want."

My Irish temper flared. Clutching my fists under the table, I ground my teeth together as I seethed with anger. Liam shot me a warning look. Nothing good would come of me confronting Da.

But I couldn't help it.

"When am I going to get a say in my life?" I bellowed. "Fuck this."

Throwing my napkin on the table, I nearly knocked my mother over when I stormed past her on my way to my bedroom.

For the next few weeks, I ignored my impending doom and went about my regular routine as if nothing had changed.

School.

Football practice.

Jamming with my brothers.

Shagging the girls on my rotation any chance I got.

No bother.

A couple of months before graduation, I was at my locker joking with a few teammates. My coach's voice startled me. "Connor, please come with me for a minute?" He motioned for me to follow him.

The taunts of my friends followed until his office door shut behind us. I slumped down in the chair across from his desk, because was there any other way to sit in your coach's office? He squirmed in his seat, looking really uncomfortable.

"What's up?" I asked.

"Son, I'm not sure how to tell you this. Your father's been in a serious car accident. Your brothers should be here any minute now. You'll all be excused to meet the rest of your family at the hospital."

Wait, what?

Dumbfounded, I sat mute. Gobsmacked. Five minutes later, Liam and Padraig sauntered into the office. Mr. Benson filled them in and their swagger deflated. We all stared at each other, unable to comprehend.

Mr. Benson placed his hand on my shoulder and squeezed. "Will you be alright to drive, Connor? If not, I can have someone take you all to the hospital."

I snapped out of it and motioned for my brothers to follow. "Nah, I'm grand. Thank you, sir."

We arrived at the hospital waiting room to a truly grave situation. Ma looked tiny and scared. Seamus sat beside her, sobbing. Brennan and Cillian looked shellshocked. The six of us huddled around our mother protectively while we waited for news of Da.

Many hours later, the doctor gave us the horrific news. "We've done everything we can. Although Rory did very well in surgery. It's going to be a very, very long road if he's ever to recover."

Later, we learned the extent of his injuries. Broken back, shattered femur, dislocated shoulder, concussion, hundreds of contusions. Lying in the hospital surrounded by nurses, hooked up to tubes, his leg suspended in midair? He looked twenty years older.

As my brothers and mom surrounded my unconscious father, a strange sense of calm permeated my body. All animosity of the past weeks vanished. I knew exactly who I was and exactly what I was meant to do.

That day my life changed in an instant.

And so did my priorities.

RONNI

CHAPTER 3
PRESENT DAY

"Ronni."

I heard my name, but I couldn't tell if it was a dream or real until I felt a firm hand on my shoulder gently shaking me awake. My eyes felt like they were glued together. My head was filled with thick, sludgy mud. No way was it time to get up already.

Groaning, I burrowed under the 1000-thread-count linens and tucked my knees up to curl into a ball. Hoping to create my own little cocoon where no one could bother me.

It was dark.

Warm.

Cozy.

I planned to stay here all day.

"Ronni."

His baritone voice was close to my ear now, only a whisper. I didn't budge, still pretending to be asleep. I couldn't face him. Not after he refused to make love to me when he'd brought me to his hotel room last night.

Connor loved sex. And I mean *loved* sex. Which was handy because I loved sex with Connor. Over the years, I used sex to distract him from finding out about my secrets. So, of course, I'd tried it after the scene at the poker game. It should have been a tried-and-true tactic to avoid discussing the worst of my secrets. Especially since we hadn't been together since our wedding.

So, let's just say the rejection was unexpected.

Painful.

Justified.

The expanse of my husband's hand covered not just my shoulder but a good part of my back too. The only sound in the room was his soft breathing. My body zinged at the sensation of his touch; he always had that effect on me.

I loved this man with every ounce of my being.

Five minutes later, or it could have been five hours for how well my brain was working, a whoosh of air assaulted me when the covers were unceremoniously flung from my naked body. I bolted upright, trying to grab them back. "Connor, what the fudge!"

Rather than answer, he sat on the edge of the bed next to me. He was naked too. His mammoth, muscular body caused the bed to dip. I relaxed back down against the pillows, noting my nipples were on high alert. *Not* because of the cold. His amber eyes bore into mine as he reached over to trace a puckered bud with his finger.

Oooh! Did he change his mind?

"You're supposed to be over at Ty's suite in a few minutes." His attempt to stare me into compliance was funny. His gruff tactics never worked on me. My huge mountain-of-a-man scared most people. In reality, my gentle giant was the most thoughtful and considerate guy I'd ever known. Always putting me first. Always putting everyone ahead of himself.

This man believed in me.

Even when I gave him no reason to.

Flinging my arm over my eyes dramatically, I whined, "Do I have to go?"

"I don't like it, but yes." Connor's sneaky fingers were now teasing both my nipples into hard points. He lightly scraped my puckered buds with the blunt edges of his fingernails. To drive me even more crazy, he leaned over and replaced his fingers with his tongue. Keeping eye contact while he savored one nipple after the other. I felt his hand snake down my stomach and with little fanfare, he plunged two thick fingers inside my soaking channel and pressed his thumb on my clit.

A keening moan escaped my lips. God, the things this man did to my body. That I let him do to me. He was like a drug. His thumb picked up the pace and circled my swollen clit faster. He grazed my nipple with his teeth before sucking it soothingly. Then he repeated on the other side. The cadence of everything he was doing lulled me into a sex-induced haze where the only thing I comprehended was the pulsing, quivering beginnings of an incredible orgasm.

I needed this so bad.

I needed *him* so bad.

My thighs began shaking. I clenched them together, trapping his forearm in position. His soft beard tickled my breasts as he kissed his way down my belly and replaced his fingers with his tongue.

Connor really and truly had a PhD in oral pleasure.

The tip of his tongue traced through my soaking lower lips. Using

31

gentle suction, he lazily lapped up the juices all along my slit. Threading my fingers into his wavy, reddish-brown lion's mane, I held him to my pussy, guiding him so I could get where I wanted to be faster. Taking the hint, he blew on and then sucked my clit into his mouth. Hard. Grazing his teeth against it, ever so slightly.

Immediate. Utter. Detonation.

Bucking against his mouth, I couldn't stop my body from thrashing against the bed. The orgasm was exactly what I needed. Like the release of a pressure cooker, tremors rippled through my core as he nibbled, licked, and teased my entire sex until I went over the edge again. And again.

And again.

This exquisite pleasure was something I had only ever felt with my husband.

In this case, pleasure was probably my punishment. Death to Ronni. By orgasm. Every part of my sex was so overstimulated that my body shook with a flurry of jolts and aftershocks. Throughout, Connor suckled me and stroked my thighs. Soothing. Eventually, helping me settle down.

Connor's hair hung over one muscular shoulder. I marveled at his glorious body, which could have been carved in stone. Yes, he'd fit right in at the Medici gallery.

Except for one thing.

Which not only put David to shame, but other men as well.

His thick, velvety cock lay rigid against his muscled abs, stretching just past his belly button. I gripped him, stroking up and down his length.

Connor growled, "Ah, love. So feckin' good."

His slight lilt always did it for me. It always was stronger after he'd been to Ireland. The ridiculous interview I had scheduled with Ty, his bandmate, was long forgotten when Connor dipped his head to capture my mouth in a slow, torturous kiss. My pussy pulsed with need to be filled with him. I hooked my legs around his back to pull him on top of me. Caging my head with his forearms, he relaxed into our kisses.

My legs fell open wider to allow him access. Connor's cock nudged my opening and he pushed in, but also held himself back. Just the tip penetrated my wet heat. His eyes squinched shut with the effort not to thrust inside me all the way. So considerate. Always. He was my everything, I just needed to—

A sharp knock on the door snapped us back to reality. Connor pressed his forehead to mine, staring into my eyes. Our breathing was labored. He remained partially inside me.

"Connor, my brother, you're not answering your phone. I'm trying to find Ronni. Katherine is freaking out. Is she in New York yet?" Zane, LTZ's guitarist, yelled through the door. He talked so fast it always seemed like he was cramming twice as many words into any given sentence.

Connor's amber eyes bored into mine. We stopped what we were doing and listened. After a couple of minutes, it was still quiet at the door. Connor finally thrust fully into me. Grabbing his ass with both hands, I held him in place. Loving how full I was. Hungrily, I devoured his lips—

Zane pounded on the door again. "Can I come in? Dude? Shit's going down, I need to find her."

"Go away, Zane," Connor yelled back, grinding against me. "I'm busy."

Zane thudded his fist against the door. "Not cool, dude. Can you tell her she's late?"

Talk about a mood destroyer. At the worst possible time. I wanted Connor so badly that I nearly started to cry. He pulled out and sat back on his heels. His wet cock bobbed against his stomach, drenched in my essence. I wriggled out from under my gorgeous beast. Sadly, realizing that—like it or not—I had to honor my commitment.

Connor pulled me back against the warm wall of his chest, wrapping his thick arms around me. "I'm *not* sorry that I've made you late. Go get it over with, then come back to me."

"I don't want to go, you know. Get dragged into this again. It seems stupid since we both know it's going to blow over. Why your manager, Katherine, thinks that anything I say will make a difference is beyond me."

"Well," Connor kissed my temple, "aren't you curious to finally meet Zoey?

"Meh."

I was totally curious.

He stood and swooped me up from the bed. Effortlessly. It was always sexy when Connor picked me up and carried me like I was tiny. I *felt* tiny in his arms. He gently deposited me on the cold, marble tile. With a smack to my ass, Connor turned back toward the bedroom. My man of so few words. But his message was loud and clear.

Get it over with.

Crap. I was really late. Unprofessionally late. I'd been asked to give a statement to help my "ex" Tyson Rainier out. To bless his new relationship. To appease my old publicist Sienna King, one last time. It was bad enough that my fake relationship with LTZ's singer was still real in the minds of the public.

It was worse relegating Connor to being my dirty little secret.

His words, not mine.

I just needed to get this Ty thing over with. I quickly dried off. Threw some clothes and makeup on. On my way out the door, I checked on my husband. He was sound asleep. His left arm thrown over his head. The ink of his most recent tattoo began at his shoulder and wound around his arm in the most delicate yet graphic swirl of Celtic knots and spirals. So sexy.

I could look at him all day.

But duty called.

I managed to slip out without waking him, knowing that my moment of reckoning was near.

When I got back, it was confession time. Connor deserved a goddamn medal for his patience with me over these past few years. In a world where I found it extraordinarily hard to trust, he was the one person I could count on.

Yet, I'd never given Connor a true chance.

Oh, I had my reasons. I'd been burned. By so many people. People who tried to use me. Tried to *hurt* me.

Until Connor.

My Connor.

But still I couldn't let him in. Not all the way.

Which meant, in all likelihood, I'd blown up all that we'd overcome. Allowing my personal baggage and my relentless need for redemption to take precedence over everything else in our life. Especially, our relationship.

Connor deserved more. Someone who would cherish him for the wonderful man he was.

Someone who would be a true partner.

Someone who would be proud to be on his arm publicly.

Someone who would tell him the truth.

The whole truth.

My past had finally caught up to me. His expression when he saw me at that poker game? Feigned indifference, thank God. The thing is I knew this man better than anyone on the planet. It was what I saw behind his eyes that nearly stopped me in my tracks.

Confusion.

Hurt.

Disgust.

For a man who valued honesty above everything, I'd made a fatal mistake. Done to him what had been done to me. It was way past time to come clean.

Because if I didn't?

I would lose him.

For good.

RONNI

CHAPTER 4

FOURTEEN YEARS PRIOR (AGE 19)

L ooking back at my fifteen-year-old self, I wish I could have injected her with more confidence. Decisions you make when you don't know any better often haunt you. Young girls are so easily influenced by trying to fit in. To do what is expected of them. To stay silent.

Which is why after the audition, I did my best to ignore what happened and pretend things were okay.

Waiting to see if I got a part was agony.

Eight long weeks passed before I found out I was cast as the lead in *Hawaiian High*. Getting the lead made the audition worth it, that's what I told myself. When the formal offer arrived, Mom used her entire savings to hire a prominent entertainment lawyer. He was worth every penny. He negotiated life-changing money and a fully-paid-for modern condo in Oahu close to the production studio.

So, we were off to Hawaii.

Off to my dream.

Except, it soon turned into a nightmare.

My character, Melody Pierce, was a homeless surfer girl with a heart of gold. Wynn Bentley, a sandy-haired boy-next-door played my romantic interest, Kai Kinkaid. The gritty series followed the ups and downs of the kids in high school, and explored the differences and similarities between jocks, surfers, and academics.

I was in way over my head. With no experience on a television set, the learning curve was dramatic for me. As one of the leads, I was in most of the scenes but there was so much more to it. Wardrobe fittings. Acting coaches. Speech training. Running lines. Surf lessons. Table readings. Media training. On-set tutoring. Blocking. Filming.

God, it was really hard work, but I loved acting. The show was a hit. I loved that part too. All the cast became instantly famous. Wynn and I were best friends. I trusted him. Probably because he had the honor of giving me every one of my on-screen romantic firsts. First kiss. First make-out. First sex. Our acting chemistry was off the charts. The media ate it up. Everyone speculated whether the Melody-Kai romance carried over to Ronni-Wynn in real life.

It didn't. Mainly because out of the public eye, Wynn was unapologetically, enthusiastically, fabulously gay. The producers, however, encouraged us to play our relationship up for the tabloids. It allowed them to keep his sexuality secret from the public. Better the fans thought he was with me. It translated to ratings, after all.

The producers of *Hawaiian High* were "Schlubby One" and "Schlubby Two" from my audition. Otherwise known as Merv Sofer and Jared Graham. "Suit Guy" was Don Kircher, the show runner who was responsible for everything about the series.

Ruthless, sadistic tyrants. All of them.

My wide-eyed innocence was shattered within the first few weeks on the set. I noticed Merv Sofer had some sort of obsession with Wynn. He always wanted to give my costar "notes" on his performance. Alone. In his trailer.

Wynn was always withdrawn and surly after these so-called meetings.

He wasn't the only actor who was given "notes." Actors who "met" with Merv, Jared, or Don often received benefits. More lines. Better publicity. Perks. Many of my castmates vied for their attention. Those who refused were punished. Written off the show, even.

I was lucky. Still underage, I was allowed to have Mom on set with me every day. She stuck to me like superglue. After all, she also had eyes. And no intention of letting her teen daughter get exploited by grown men. While under her protection, I was the only cast member who hadn't been requested to attend a "meeting." But, as my eighteenth birthday approached, I had no illusions. My time was running out.

Which was terrifying.

My birthday happened to fall on the last day of filming season three. Mom and I were called into a meeting with Don. Instead of birthday wishes, he physically removed Mable from the set. Called her a disruption. A nuisance. The entire cast and crew heard her curse and scream as they "escorted" her off the lot and dumped her in an Uber.

My hourglass had run out. So I did what I had to do. I mentally prepared.

Deep breath

Suck it up.

Be fearless.

With only one more scene to film, I did my best to remain

professional. Immediately after we finished, I bolted off the set to get myself off the lot and out of danger. I only had one stop to make. My purse was in my trailer with the car keys inside.

Don was waiting for me. Lounging on the sofa wearing only a bathrobe. Shocked—but yet not that shocked— I tried to act like finding him undressed in my trailer was normal. My mind shifted into survivor mode. I just needed to get the hell out of there. Babbling some nonsense, I yanked my bag off the counter and bolted for the door.

I fled in tears and barely made it back to the apartment without crashing the car. When I burst through the door, Wynn and a couple of the crew were hanging out with my mom waiting for me. I barely noticed the huge lasagna and a room full of Happy Birthday balloons because I was so distressed. Mom ushered everyone out and tried to comfort me, but I sobbed for an hour.

I couldn't tell her that Don was in my trailer. It would have killed her to think she wasn't there to protect me. So, I simply told her I was scared to be on the set without her. That was all it took.

Enraged, my mom called our attorney, my agent, and my publicist to figure out a way for her to be back on set with me. Or, to get me out of the contract. Our so-called advisors gave us bleak news. If I didn't fulfill my obligation for my remaining two more seasons, the attorney's fees and potential contractual fines would bankrupt us. And then some.

If I filed a complaint. I was advised that Don and the producers would make my life a living nightmare. My lawyer flat-out said it wasn't worth it.

After learning the sad truth, Mom and I both felt defeated. No one on the set of *Hawaiian High* would protect me.

Because Mable Miller *was* formidable, she devised a genius strategy. After poring over my contract herself that night, she found a provision that allowed me to have one personal assistant on set with me at all times. By the time filming for Season 4 began two months later, my new employee was my mother. Smugly, we returned to the set.

Don was furious but shrewd. He simply found many other ways to humiliate and degrade me.

I was used to being filmed in a bathing suit. My contract even stipulated the weight I had to maintain to look the way Don envisioned Melody. Soon, my bikinis were tinier and tinier. Every day Don made a point to describe everything wrong with my body in front of the cast and crew, often reducing me to tears.

Mom went into complete mama-bear mode.

Except each time she reacted, Don's sadistic and lewd comments would become a million times worse. He was untouchable. He sure didn't give two shits about me or any of the cast.

By mid-season, Don brought in an actress to play my rival, Serena Lewis. The girl had no problem spending time with both Don and Jared. Individually. Together. It didn't matter to her. Her role increased in proportion to how mine diminished. By the end of the season, I was barely in any scenes at all.

Viewers were left with an end-of-season cliffhanger—would Kai stay with his first love Melody? Or embark upon a new journey with Serena?

My own vote was for the new journey.

When we returned for season five, the entire cast learned that Kai would choose Serena at the table read. In other words, the first show of the season would be my last. I'd been written out.

Hallelujah.

Wynn had a different reaction. He threw his script across the table and stormed out of the room to his trailer. Merv followed close behind. My heart sank. I couldn't believe how selfish I'd been. I'd be free but Wynn would now be on his own, living his own personal nightmare. After I told him what happened with Don, Wynn confessed something even more shocking. He had been caught up in the circuit of casting couch parties at Merv's house. Aspiring actors attended to fast-track their career. Plied with drugs and alcohol, it was expected that partygoers would trade sexual favors in exchange for roles.

It was how he'd been cast in *Hawaiian High*.

And how he kept his role.

Wynn wasn't alone. It made my skin crawl to learn about the cesspool Hollywood underground of prostitution and sexual abuse. Even more chilling was how pervasive it was. And the caliber of industry executives who embraced it.

Normalized it.

It was sick.

Which is why I took off after Wynn with Mom following behind. Pounding on the door, I screamed and screamed for him to open it. Not caring who heard me. A crowd of cast and crew gathered, but no one moved an inch. They just stood there watching my meltdown. Some of them filmed it on their phones.

The door remained shut and locked.

Everyone eventually dissipated, but mom and I waited. A while later, Merv left the trailer, tucking himself into his pants. Scoffing at us when he brushed past. We rushed inside to check on Wynn, not sure what we'd find.

He was sitting in his underwear on a stool smoking a cigarette. His eyes were hollow and disassociated. I took his hand, devastated that my best friend was hurting, and I was powerless to help him. "What can I do?"

"Nothing." He stubbed out his smoke.

"Quit," I begged him. "We don't need this show, it's not worth it."

"I don't have a choice." Wynn stood and pulled on a shirt. "I'm under the same contract as you. The difference is, no one gives a fuck about me."

My mom rubbed his back. "That's not true, sweetheart. I'm sick about what is happening, we just—"

Wynn shook her off. "Mable, you don't have real power. Go back home."

He finished dressing, refusing to look either of us in the eye. I could feel the air in the trailer change. It grew colder. We were losing him, I knew it.

"Wynn—" I reached for him.

"I'll be fine." He evaded me, grabbing his keys on the kitchenette counter. "Ronni, just leave me alone. On-set relationships are not real. Our friendship is not real. What I choose to do or not do is really none of your business."

Then he was gone.

I was devastated. In utter disbelief of what had just happened. Mom comforted me, assuring me that all would be okay. That we'd find a way to help him.

She was wrong. So, so wrong.

A month after we returned to Los Angeles, Wynn took his life.

He didn't leave a note.

CHAPTER 5
TWELVE YEARS PRIOR (AGE 21)

My fingers were cut up to shite, but I didn't care.

Because I was playing again. A few weeks prior, I'd picked up the bass so I could fill in on some gigs my girlfriend, Jennifer Deveraux's brother, Jace had with his college cover band. It wasn't the same as jamming with my brothers, but it was something.

For the first time in years, I had an outlet. In just a few practices, I was hooked. I needed music in my life. Playing with Jace was the only time I felt free. Fulfilled.

It was feckin' amazing.

After Da's accident, I'd been forced to give up music— along with everything else in my life— to run McGloughlin Construction. Three years later, I still had my priorities straight. Family always came first. Still, it felt good to do something for myself.

"Fuck, dude. I've gotta get outta here." Jace was in a hurry to hook up with his latest conquest. I envied his carefree college life, so I did. He was only a year younger than me, but I felt more like his dad than his friend.

I flexed my aching out-of-practice fingers. "Yeah, no worries."

Jace stood from behind his drum kit. "You're killing it, my brother. You'll be ready for the shows in no time."

"Aye."

"I'm out. A hot redhead is waiting for me." Jace waggled his eyebrows and was gone in a flash.

Jay-sus. If only I wasn't so mentally and physically exhausted. It sucked to be way too tired for my age. I set my bass in its case and wandered into the house looking for my girlfriend. I heard the shower running, which gave me a few minutes of blessed alone time while Jen freshened up. I plopped down on the worn, plaid couch and turned on the Mariners game. My eyes felt heavy, but I fought going to sleep.

Mainly, because I was hoping for my own hookup.

Jen was my respite from the daily pressure of keeping Da's business alive. When the perky, blonde natural beauty applied for a contractor position, I immediately hired her. Much to the chagrin of Da. He furiously objected, claiming no woman could handle the hard labor construction required.

Especially a woman I was screwing.

His words, not mine.

Except he was wrong. On both counts.

Jen's prowess on a jobsite was unmatched. Skills? Check. Instinct? Check. Love for construction? Check. Check. Check. Plus, she saved my ass by staying on top of the company paperwork. Until we got together, I was drowning. With her help, the business finally was turning around.

As far as sleeping together?

Sigh.

"Hey, babe." Jen settled in beside me on the couch. "Did you have fun jammin' with Jace?"

"Aye." Right now, I didn't want to talk. I needed her affection. Craved it even. Except my hopes of hooking up evaporated when she nestled into my chest and promptly fell asleep.

Sex was overrated, I tried to convince myself. Especially when everything else with Jen was awesome. She was calm. Comfortable. Our relationship was easy. We never fought. We just enjoyed being together. She was my best friend and the only person I could talk to honestly. Without judgment.

Unlike everyone in my own household.

I was essentially the sole provider for a family of eight, and I'd never felt so disconnected from them in my life.

So, yes. Jen was my safe place. I loved her. Even if we didn't have passion.

Except, something's missing.

Shut up, you bollocks. Don't blow the only good thing in your life.

Really, dude. Something's missing.

Shut the feck up.

Pushing the competing thoughts out of my head, I carefully moved her to a sitting position after the Mariners lost again, "Babe, wake up."

Jen yawned and stretched her arms above her head. "You heading out?"

I hoisted myself up off the couch. "Aye. Have you given any more thought about getting our own place?"

"Connor—"

47

"No, I get it."

I didn't really get it, but I couldn't afford to waste any brain cells thinking about it more deeply. My phone buzzed in my pocket. I'd missed several calls from Ma. My heart plummeted, I answered straight away.

In near hysterics, she screamed through the phone, "Connor, go git yer Da."

Feckin' hell.

Not again.

He was in one of two places. If I was lucky, he'd be at the Old Irishman. Sitting at the bar with a few other ex-pats. Most likely drunk as a skunk. I pulled my old Ford work truck into a prime parking place on Market Street and trudged into the bar. I was just twenty-one, but at six-six, nearly two hundred and fifty pounds of solid muscle and a full beard, I hadn't been carded in years.

Scanning the dank room that smelled of pine-scented cleaner and old, stale beer, I didn't see Da or his buddies. Sean, the bartender recognized me and waved me over.

"Sean."

"Connor."

I didn't have time for pleasantries, it was too late at night. "Well?"

Sean polished the glasses he was pulling out of the dishwasher and stacked them behind the bar. "He left about two hours ago."

Bollocks.

My next stop was the Lotus Blossom, a hole-in-the wall restaurant in Chinatown. Taking a deep breath, I steeled myself and pushed open the heavy fire door. Quickly maneuvering past the hostess through a beaded curtain, I knocked four times on a door marked "janitor." Waited a beat. Knocked again.

The door swung open. Thick cigarette smoke clouded the air and infiltrated my clothes. Sure enough, my father was there. Half-asleep, slumped over at a poker table with a short pile of chips. He was so drunk he didn't even notice me come in.

"Da." I dragged a metal chair next to him at the table, quietly speaking into his ear, "It's time to go."

His unfocused, bloodshot eyes looked in my general direction. He wiped a bead of sweat from his brow. "Feck ye."

I didn't react. My father's fall from grace seemingly had no bottom. Resigned, I knew what I had to do. Slapping a couple of hundreds down for the ante, I gestured for the dealer to deal me in.

After his accident, Da had been unable to walk. For the first year or so, he was diligent about his physical therapy and worked hard to recover. His leg just wouldn't heal properly. Four operations later, he was relegated to a walker on good days and a wheelchair on bad. Living with pain all the time broke him in more ways than one. Broke all of us, really.

His aversion to over-the-counter painkillers was honorable.

His love for whisky had become all-consuming.

Witnessing Da's descent into alcoholism was devastating. His behavior was increasingly more and more out of control. Decisions he made whilst drunk threatened to destroy everything. If Da didn't turn shite around soon, life as we knew it would be over.

My sacrifices would be for naught.

Dropping out of high school.

Foregoing my scholarship.

I'd convinced myself giving up my own life for my family was worth it. The twins were on scholarship at Washington State University. My wee brothers were getting excellent marks in public school. Ma was back to work.

But on nights like tonight? I couldn't fathom what the feck I was doing. Da risked everything that I worked for in these poker games. It made my blood not only boil, but bubble over.

Feck it.

I needed put on my big-boy pants and get us out of this mess.

Da's head lolled before he passed out in the middle of a hand. A quick scope of the room revealed, unsurprisingly, I was in a room full of losers. Within a couple of hours, I'd won the money he'd lost back plus a few hundred dollars. Once the winnings were secure in my wallet, I dragged his sorry ass to the truck. When we got home, I slung him over my shoulder fireman style and staggered up the narrow concrete staircase to the house.

Ma was waiting up in the living room with her head buried in her hands. Her pitiful, watery eyes met mine when I stumbled in, nearly dropping my father to the ground. She couldn't hide her disgust for her husband. "Put him to bed."

"Aye."

When I returned to the living room, Ma hadn't moved from where she was sitting. I fished the wad of cash from my pocket and placed it in front of her on the coffee table.

"How much?"

"Six thousand."

"Jay-sus."

I sat next to the money and placed my hands on her shoulders. "It's fine."

Ma took my hands in hers. "It's not right. I'm so sorry that you've had to grow up too fast."

"It's fine," I repeated.

She patted my knee and stood. "I'd better keep an eye on him."

I glanced at the ornate grandfather clock Da shipped over from his granny's house years ago after she died. A present for Ma on their anniversary during happier times. Something to remind them of Ireland. The hell they had escaped from to provide their family with a better life.

4:00 a.m.

Trudging into the kitchen, I cursed my fate. Ma had a point. I'd grown up too fast. For now, all I could do was brew a pot of coffee. No reason to go to bed when I had to be up in an hour. Today was going to be an absolute bitch.

Again.

Unfortunately, it was my not-so-new normal.

CHAPTER 6
PRESENT DAY

O nce Ronni left to do the stupid interview, I showered and moved the operation to the living area until she returned. With a moment to myself, the full impact of the night before hit me like a ton of bricks. Her independence and strength were sexy, but also reckless. Thank God I'd been there, or who knows what that arsehole would have done to her.

Why was she there?

I needed answers. Ronni had lied to me about her travel schedule.

Flat-out lied.

Lying was a deal-breaker for me, she knew that.

Especially after— well. Everything.

I couldn't figure it out. Why she'd put herself in such a precarious position. So soon after we made wedding vows to each other. My blood was already *boiling* at the thought of *my wife* and Ty being asked to put their fauxmance back into the spotlight. To take two steps backward in our relationship by lying to me?

Unacceptable.

No matter what her reasons.

Still, we *were* married now. I took my vows seriously. I still wanted a future with her.

Needed a future with her.

There was no other woman for me in this world. She was it. So, I had to believe there was a reasonable explanation, even though she *apparently* didn't trust me with it.

Jay-sus. I was brooding again. With no sleep and an extraordinarily cluttered, angry mind, exhaustion began to pull me under. Just as I was dozing off the door clicked open.

"Well, that was out of control." Ronni threw her bag down and sat next to me. "Zoey's a tiny little spitfire, I'll give her that."

I couldn't look at her. "I've tried my best to stay out of all of their shite."

"Yeah? Well Zoey is getting a huge dose of celebrity BS and she's not handling it well at all."

"*I'm* not handling it well," I muttered, finally looking her in the eye.

Ronni cast her eyes downward, having the decency to at least feel bad.

My ire wasn't quelled by her contriteness. "Mae, you have no idea how sick to death I am of this."

Ronni nodded. "It's over for good now. I gave my statement to that psycho, Sienna. I'll give Zoey credit. She's pretty observant; she called Ty out on things that I tried to tell him when—" Ronni caught herself. "Anyway, she rightfully called me out too."

That got my attention. "What did she say?"

"Um. Well. Just that lying to the public was stupid and completely unnecessary."

"Hmmm." I cocked my eyebrow at her.

"Shut up." Ronni slugged my arm before cuddling back against me, so we were side-by-side on the sofa. A perfect opportunity for her to come clean, and yet she made no mention of the night before. Instead, her fingers traced along the tattoo on my forearm. My dick grew stiff at her touch because I had no willpower when it came to her. Instinctively, I pulled her on my lap, banding my arm around her so my erection nestled against the crease of her ass.

"We need to talk, Mae," I whispered into her soft hair.

"That doesn't feel like talking." She wiggled her bottom against my cock.

I just couldn't feckin' resist her. Not ever. She knew it, thinking that distracting me with her pussy would shut me up. Stop me from wanting to protect her. It wouldn't. It never did. My tongue traced a line along the graceful arch of Ronni's neck and jawbone. She sighed heavily and rested her head against mine. When I cocooned her, she relaxed instantly. "I want you, Con but I'm so sleepy," she murmured before going slack in my arms.

It was for the best. As much as I wanted to be ball-deeps inside her, sex wasn't going to give me the answers I needed. Besides, having her warm body enfolded against mine relaxed me too. I started to doze off when Zane pounded on the door for the second time that day. "Open up! Connor!" he bellowed. "It's an emergency!"

Jay-sus. F.

Ronni bolted up and let Zane in. His wild, dark curls bounced around his head when he whooshed like a turbo jet into my suite. His boundless energy was exhausting at times. This was one of them. Ronni and I stared at him slack-jawed, waiting for him to spill.

"Zoey's been in an accident. I don't have details, but Katherine's on her way over. So's Jace. Security has us on lock-down up here. It's all over the news, you'll see," Zane word vomited.

Ronni, the brightest spark out of the three of us, dashed to the window and pulled back the curtains. "Holy crap, it's right below us." She motioned for us to join her.

It was hard to make heads or tails of what was happening from our vantage point, but we could see LTZ's entire security team trying to fight their way to where Zoey lay in the street shrouded by Ty. It was a mad scene. Police forcing their way through the crowd. Sirens blaring. Hundreds of mobile phones recorded the craziness.

No doubt the entire event was being live-streamed.

We were interrupted by another knock on the door. Zane let Jace and Katherine into my suite. No one was completely sure what happened, but we all shared our theories. Jace monitored social media and got to work on crafting LTZ's official message. Zane was on the phone with someone, talking in a low voice for once. Katherine was furiously texting.

I remained on the sofa, silently watching my wife.

She was buried in her tablet. The sun was setting over the Hudson, casting a glowing light on her face. From gold to red to deep chestnut, her thick, long hair cascaded around her shoulders. Her full lips were mouthing the words to whatever she was reading. Probably the script for her upcoming feature film. Christ, she was the most beautiful woman in the entire universe.

"This is pretty fucked up." Zane paced in front of the window after ending his call.

"Aye."

Zane shook his head sadly. "Ty can't catch a fucking break."

Jace rolled his eyes but didn't say anything.

Ronni chimed in from across the room. "I warned Ty about Sienna—"

For feck's sake.

I shot her a look.

She wrinkled her nose and buried it back in her tablet.

Glancing around the room, I wondered how in the hell my suite become the congregation room. Ronni and I had unfinished business. I needed to talk to her. Alone.

"I've got to get to the hospital." Katherine still had the phone held up to her ear as she made her way to the door.

Jace stood and began to pace. He furiously typed into his phone, muttering various expletives under his breath. Then he'd wait for a reply and repeat the process. Something was way off with our drummer. Usually he was Fonzie about any situation we had to deal with. Today, he was absolutely wrecked. His hair was in knots. His eyes were bloodshot. When he caught me staring, he slammed his laptop closed. "I've shut down all the fucking comments on all of our social sites until we know more."

"Now, what do we do?" Zane chewed on his bottom lip. "Shouldn't we go with Katherine?"

"No. Stay put," Katherine ordered. "I'll be back later tonight, and we'll hopefully be closer to having a plan."

Once Katherine left, my bandmates began to make themselves comfortable. Ronni's green eyes caught mine. Subtly she eyeballed the door and then looked back at me. I was glad we were on the same page. It was time for us to be alone.

Time to get to the bottom of things.

"Lads, can we reconvene later?"

"Gladly." Jace bolted up and was out the door without a backward glance.

Zane stayed back, looking a little lost. "I'll just hang with you guys, Jace is such a drag right now."

"Ronni and I have to finish something up, my brother." I nodded to the door.

Zane looked at me and then Ronni. A wave of understanding passed over his face. He trudged out leaving me, once again, with my wife.

As much as I loved her, we couldn't go on like this.

Our fate had to be determined. One way or the other.

"What a weird day." Ronni was back at the window looking down at the accident scene. "How crazy. It's completely clear. As though nothing ever happened. I thought for sure people would be putting up a flower shrine."

"Mae." I willed her to turn around so we could talk. She glanced back at me. The last remnants of the sunset lit her in a soft, orange haze.

"Con—" Ronni's vulnerability nearly broke me.

"It's time."

"I know." She turned back to the window.

I stood and joined her, placing my hands on her shoulders and resting my chin on her head. We both stared out at the busy Manhattan streets as the neon lights of New York one by one lit up the city.

"Are you going to tell me what you were doing there?" I kissed the top of her head, pulling her back against me.

"Are *you*?" she shot back.

"I was playing poker."

Ronni slipped out from under my embrace and grabbed the room service menu from the desk. "I didn't realize you ran in those circles."

"I don't know what you mean."

"That man is *horrible*." She thumbed through the menu.

"I agree. He's a world-class wanker. So, why were you there then? With that idiot actor Byron, no less?"

Ronni shrugged. "He wants me to be his beard."

Before I could stop it, my fist slammed down on the windowsill. I scrubbed my hands over my face. I was about to lose my mind. "What the *fuck* did you say?" I gritted out. "This is not the time to joke, Mae."

Ronni didn't answer, instead she handed me the room service menu. I took it and threw it across the room. Calmly, she got up to retrieve it and called in an order while I sat back down, stewing in a pot of boiling-hot oil. She hung up the phone, sauntered over and straddled me, pushing my chest so I was reclining back against the sofa cushions.

"I'm *not* doing it. You know I would never after Ty." She pressed her lips to mine. I kept mine taut. Unyielding. I stared daggers at her.

She ignored me and reached for my buckle. I grabbed her wrist. She wove her hand through my hair. I grabbed that wrist too.

"Mae, what are you at?" My anger was tempered into annoyance. "Fucking me isn't going to work this time."

Slowly she undulated against my traitorous, hardening cock, which clearly had a mind of its own. Her voice dripped like syrup. "Maybe it will, Con. It's us."

My head lolled back against the cushions, but I held fast to her wrists. Staring at the ceiling, I took a deep breath. Propped my feet up on the ottoman. I willed myself not to desire her. Not to succumb.

The molten heat of her pussy against my prick thwarted my best intentions.

Determined to take back control, I lifted my head and studied her. She blinked at me innocently. I glared. She licked her lips. God, how I wanted to kiss her. To make love to her. Except the truth of what was happening hurt more than anything I'd ever been through. And I'd been through a lot.

    We'd been through a lot.

    But her lies?

    They threatened to destroy us both.

CHAPTER 7
TEN YEARS PRIOR (AGE 23)

When we returned home to Los Angeles, I was blacklisted. Labeled as "difficult" and "unprofessional," it wasn't hard for me to figure out who was behind the smear campaign. I knew the "source" for the stories was Don and his lackeys. Each week, the tabloids were filled with made-up accounts of my so-called antics on the set. Photos of me pounding on Wynn's trailer were leaked everywhere.

There was no getting around it, I looked insane.

Then, when Wynn killed himself, the press pinned it on me. Claiming he did it because the love of his life abandoned him. He couldn't cope with my departure. For six straight months, my face graced the cover of every celebrity gossip site. Not in a good way.

Talk about a heavy burden.

Talk about a complete and total cover-up.

As far as I could tell back then, my career was over and done.

Luckily, Mable had the foresight to settle us into a small three-bedroom house in Los Feliz, paid for by my earnings from *Hawaiian High*. She went to work as a personal assistant to a tech executive to cover our daily expenses.

Thank God because I sank into a horrific depression. For months, I could barely get out of bed. Even if I were hireable, auditions were out of the question. A year after Wynn's death, Mom insisted on therapy. I was put on antidepressants. Slowly, over time, I was able to cope. Mourn. Heal.

Well, as much as it was possible.

Eventually someone else's scandal took attention off me. The tabloids forgot about Ronni Miller, but the industry didn't. I knew no one would hire an actress who'd been labeled difficult and unprofessional. It was hard not to be bitter after all I sacrificed to be on *Hawaiian High*. Only to be rewarded with sexual harassment, excruciating media scrutiny, vilification, and loss.

Somehow, when I was at rock bottom, I found strength. I became enraged at what happened to me. The anger fueled my determination to rewrite my story. I didn't want to be a victim anymore. Even though I was nervous, I enrolled in acting classes, which made me fall in love with my craft again. When I felt braver, I joined an improv group to try my hand at comedy. It was exhilarating.

Finally, I felt like a grown-up. Taking charge of my destiny. It felt good to get my head back in the game. To find my voice. After all, why should a trio of pervy men and a few tabloids stories define me?

They wouldn't.

No friggin' way.

After a few months, I caught a break. An up-and-coming

showrunner named Kris Blakely contacted my agent. She wanted me to audition for her new comedy called *She's All That*. I was thrilled. I meticulously prepared for my first audition in six years.

Deep breath

Suck it up.

Be fearless.

Of course, things didn't go as planned.

When I entered the casting room, I was *sooo* confident. I stood in front of Kris, an effortlessly chic woman wearing black cigarette slacks, a white t-shirt, and a white-piped black blazer. She smiled at me. And then suddenly the room began to spin. My entire body broke out in a cold sweat. I couldn't catch my breath.

A panic attack.

Dramatically, I swooned and fell down hyperventilating. Kris rushed to my side and held my hand until my breathing regulated. She rubbed my back while I cried hysterically. Soothed me with kind words. Which I appreciated. Greatly. Except, I was ashamed. I'd blown a golden opportunity.

She surprised me by inviting me to lunch the next day. I didn't want to go, figuring it was pointless. Mable convinced me to take a chance. So I went.

"How are you feeling?" Kris greeted me at a bistro across the street from her Wilshire Blvd. office. "You really scared me yesterday."

Mortification threatened to set in, but I decided to take the advice of my therapist and be honest. "Kris, I apologize for being so unprofessional. The thing is, I haven't auditioned for anything since *Hawaiian High"*

Kris nodded and motioned the waiter over. After we ordered lunch, she leaned back in her chair and studied me. Not in a weird way, more like she wanted to ask me something but wasn't sure how to do it.

"What happened in Hawaii?"

I guess she settled on direct and to the point. "I'm not sure what you mean—"

"I've heard some disturbing things." She was clearly uncomfortable, shifting in her seat. "There are many rumors about that set. About the people running the show."

My heart galloped out of my chest. Panic began to take root in my scalp.

Not again.

My voice sounded like someone had punctured my windpipe, "What did you hear?"

"My information came from someone I trust."

It felt like a swarm of bees invaded my head. I wasn't sure what the hell was going on. Was this a trap?

Kris leaned forward in her chair. "Ronni. I've been following your career. I know you've been dealt a tough hand. The reason I invited you here is because you're really talented. I'd like you to play the lead in my show."

Wait, what?

She grew serious. "What you experienced happens far too often in this town. Misogyny in Hollywood is pervasive, and I want it to end. The only way to do that is to elevate more women. We need power to make it possible for more of us to earn the same kind of money the men do. Then we can make our own shows and movies. Take positions of authority at the studios. Most of all, make sure sick, middle-aged white guys don't exploit the less powerful anymore."

Holy moly, was she for real? "You're amazing."

"And so are you."

"Why me?"

"Why *not* you?"

And that's how I found myself as the lead in a smart, sassy sit-com.

And Marvelous Mable became a production coordinator, complete with six-figure salary.

And how I learned that fate didn't change your life, choosing to embrace the opportunities it provided did.

CHAPTER 8
EIGHT YEARS PRIOR (AGE 25)

"Fuck off, Deveraux." I pushed Jace's camera phone out of my way. Tonight's show was the biggest we'd ever had and he wouldn't give the videos a rest. It drove me batshit. How was a man supposed to concentrate on changing a broken string with all of his carry-on?

I rolled my eyes when Ty started his pre-show pep-talk. I wasn't in the mood. Too much was riding on this gig. After two years of playing every coffee shop, house party, and dive bar in Seattle, we were *finally* playing a sold-out, headlining gig at The Mission in front of five hundred people.

It's wasn't like my entire bleedin' life would be decided in the next few months or anything.

Jace and I'd come a long way in two years. Determined to break out of cover-band purgatory, we decided to form a real band. One that wrote and performed our own songs. After hearing great buzz about Ty and Zane, we checked them out at a Vera Project showcase on the Pacific Science Center grounds one night.

Watching them play together was exhilarating. Magic, even. Halfway into their set, an unexpected optimism about the future began to seep into my pores. My scalp prickled. For the first time since I'd given up everything to run McGloughlin Construction, I was— Well, I nearly didn't recognize the feelings zipping through my body.

Exhilaration.

Possibility.

Hope

What would it be like to be part of something great?

It would be everything.

I'd never seen a guitar player with as much raw talent as Zane. His technique was flawless, but unique. And then there was Tyson. Jay-sus. On stage he resembled a mythical rock god. His vocals snuck up and grabbed you by the throat and pierced your heart.

After the show, even though I was knackered, we grabbed a coffee to chat. Zane spoke a million miles a minute. Ty was quiet. Turns out, he was incredibly shy. One thing was for sure, we all clicked. Four distinct personalities. One perfect puzzle.

I was desperate to be part of whatever voodoo magic they had going.

Of course, I didn't show it. No. No. No. That's not the way I worked. Years of bailing Da out meant I'd developed the best poker face around. The way I saw it, the dudes had to ask us to collaborate. Not the other way around.

The thing is, Jace and I had developed into an extremely tight rhythm section. We weren't flashy but were regarded as solid, stable musicians. A real commodity. The perfect backbone for these two superstars. The yin to their yang. So they needed us as much as we needed them.

Within the hour, Zane was begging us to join them. Ty nodded his assent; the faint trace of a smile letting us know he was happy. The next thing I knew we were at Zane's dad's house jamming and we formed our band, Less Than Zero.

Did I mention Zane's dad was guitar legend Carter feckin' Pope?

And now I was knocking fists with my bandmates and playing The Mission's sloping, tiny stage. Our show couldn't have been better. It was magic. Lightning in a bottle. A pot of gold at the end of the rainbow. The entire audience knew the words to our songs. I'd never experienced such a thrill.

I felt happy.

I might have even cracked a smile.

The months that followed were a whirlwind. It was overwhelming trying to record our album and get ready for tour while managing my duties at the business.

I was also facing a conundrum.

Jen and I were still very much together. I loved her. Deeply. But, with the tour looming, I was starting to wonder if we would make it. My feelings were, in all likelihood, because of Ty's new relationship. What I noticed – well, anyone around them noticed – was their intense chemistry. Even when they didn't have their tongues down each other's throats— which was rare— the energy between them crackled. Ty and Zoey's obvious emotional and physical connection stirred up feelings of longing in my own relationship.

It shocked the bejeezus outta me.

Because I knew.

I wanted something more.

Hence, the conundrum.

Jen was slowly taking over my duties at McGloughlin construction in preparation for the tour. I didn't want to be some bollocks who broke things off with the girlfriend who loved him because our sex wasn't off the charts. Especially when my girlfriend's brother was my bandmate and best friend.

Besides, Jen was a good woman. Loyal. Beautiful. Kind. Everything I wanted and more. I needed her. She supported me. Kept me sane in the midst of intense family drama.

And I'd had a lot of it.

Da was only four months' sober, after all.

Things with Da came to a head, finally. A few weeks prior, I'd been too exhausted to search for my father during the wee morning hours. A good night's sleep had been costly. Ten-thousand dollars went missing from the company bank account. Money that was earmarked for bills and to pay one of our subcontractors.

He'd gambled it all away in a poker game.

This time, I'd had enough.

I did what I should have done years before. I moved all the money out of the company account and opened a new one. Later that afternoon, Jen and I met with Ma. Together we showed her the financials, the projects that we were working on and the money that was coming in.

Around two in the afternoon, Da woke up and shuffled into the living room. His mostly gray hair was disheveled. Booze seeped out of his pores and he smelled like a trash can.

When he saw us glaring at him, he narrowed his weepy, yellow eyes at me and wiped his bulbous, red nose on his sleeve. "Whattya doin' at home, ya useless cunt?"

It gave me an excuse. Grasping him by the shoulders, I slammed him down on the couch. He cowered but sneered at me. "That's all ye got, boy?"

Ignoring his taunt, I listed each and every transgression he'd committed over the past years, unloading everything and anything I could think of. "You're a disgrace. A disgrace of a man. A disgrace of a role model. A disgrace of a father. I used to look up to you. Now I just want to get away from you. You better clean up your act because I'm done being tied to a life I didn't ask for just to watch you to piss it all away."

He didn't react. Not even a little bit. He just stared through me. Almost like he didn't hear a word I'd said.

I realized that nothing I could ever say or do would make him change his behavior.

But I could change mine.

Standing up to him for the first time felt good.

My family had been held hostage for too long.

I had been held hostage for too long.

Ma took it a step further. With ice running through her veins, she threatened to go back to Ireland with my brothers if he didn't get sober. It was an all-or-nothing ultimatum.

Miracle upon miracles, he quit both the alcohol and gambling cold turkey.

Now, with my departure on the horizon, there was no choice but to let Da come back at work. He couldn't do any physical labor so I continued on as foreman on the job sites and delegated things I hated. Meeting with new clients. Writing up bids. Sourcing new subcontractors. Jen now handled all the books and accounting and would continue after I left.

I hoped she and Da didn't kill each other.

Consequently, I didn't want to do anything to upset the apple cart. Like break up with her. Not when I wanted to go on tour without worrying about the business imploding. I'd only be gone for six months. When I returned, Jen and I could sort out our relationship. Hopefully absence would make the heart grow fonder and all that.

Besides, Jen and I had something much better than passion. We had trust.

I'd never do anything to destroy it.

Neither would she.

So here I was, embarking upon my new journey with LTZ. It was the most excited I'd ever felt in my life. I didn't care that we were sleeping in bunks on a second-rate tour bus. I didn't mind showering at the venues. Fast food was fine by me. Privacy was overrated. After years of putting my own ambitions aside, it was finally time for me to pursue my own dream.

I just prayed Da would keep his shit together.

Because if he didn't?

I would never forgive him.

RONNI

CHAPTER 9
PRESENT DAY

My second attempt to seduce him failed too.

Things were worse than I thought.

He'd stormed off and locked himself in the bedroom. Extreme emotional outbursts were unusual for Connor, so I knew his patience with me had ended. He probably wanted to cool down by himself so he didn't say something he couldn't take back. He was courteous like that.

Me? Not so much. I desperately pounded on the door. "Connor, let me in."

Nothing.

Tears leaked out of the corners of my eyes as I sank down to the floor. Wrapping my arms around my knees, I leaned back against the wall and let my feelings wash over me. I wanted to tell him what happened to me. Why I was at the poker game. Why last night was supposed to be the end of my torment and the true beginning of our marriage.

He was the one person I trusted aside from Kris.

But it was so hard to say the words.

How could he trust me if I couldn't let him fully in?

The door clicked open. Connor took my hands, pulled me up to standing and enfolded me into his body. One hand cupped my head and held it against his chest. The other wrapped around my waist. I clung to him, gripping his shirt in my fists. His heart thumped against my ear.

"Mae, didn't we agree that life is too short to be in perpetual limbo?"

God. I'd put us here. All of this weird dynamic between us was on me. Except, last night was critical, and he's ruined it. If Connor hadn't been there, I would have had everything I needed to put an end to the personal hell that had haunted me since I was fifteen years old. It would have been an end to the tyranny and abuse of so many women.

And finally, I'd be able to go all-in with Connor.

Freely, without anything hanging over my head.

But his interference put me back to square one. Destroyed my element of surprise. Maybe even destroyed any future opportunity I'd ever have to set things right for myself. In an instant, the trajectory of my life had been taken out of my hands.

Again.

"I was so close," I wept.

"Close to what? Why you were there?" Connor stroked my hair soothingly. "Just tell me. I can't help when you shut me out."

"I didn't need your help." I pulled away to look at him. He needed to see my eyes when I said what I had to say. "I *love* you. You're my protector. My best friend. My great love. And you need to trust me when I say that this was something I *had* to do by myself. It predates us. It was very important to me."

"So we're back to that shite again." Connor released me and scrubbed his beard. "*I* need to trust *you*. Except when you keep secrets from me, love, it's clear *you* don't trust *me*. So, while it's nice to hear that I'm all of those things to you, I have a hard time believing it. It feels like you're playing some game. A game I don't like one bit."

I whispered, "But we started as a game."

"Nice," Connor growled, shaking his head in disgust. "One point, Ronni."

I hung my head. "I'm sorry, that was an awful thing for me to say." The last thing I wanted to do was antagonize the man who had been unwaveringly patient with me.

Connor reached up to massage his temples. Moving his hands away, I took over. He loved me to pet his head, and I needed to soothe him after my harsh comment. Combing my fingers through his hair, I stroked his scalp, his forehead, his face.

God, we needed a complete re-do.

After only a few minutes, Connor pulled away abruptly. Almost as though my touch revolted him. "Ya know, Ronni? I'll say it one more time. When you keep things from me, it puts our relationship in perspective—"

"Just say it," I challenged.

He didn't answer. Instead, he strode back into the living area to the window and looked out at the city.

"Connor, I've never lied to you," I pleaded as I followed him.

"Withholding an entire piece of yourself was a lie," Connor's voice boomed. "And now you lied about something as stupid as coming with me to the premiere. What else are you not telling me, huh? Mae?"

It felt like a slap in the face.

Except, he was right.

"Look, I don't want to fight." He sighed. "I don't have it in me to be mad at you right now. Last night scared the shite out of me." He tucked me under his thick, strong arm and we both stared out at the bustling city below us. "You know how I feel about lying. *To me*. This feels like déjà vu."

"I have never cheated on you." I thumped his chest with my palm. "I would *never* cheat on you."

"No, I didn't mean that," Connor clarified. "I'll spell it out for you. You're keeping something from me. Mae, I *do not* want to live separate lives anymore. If you don't feel the same way, you need to let me know so I can move on. I can't keep going like this."

"No. No. No," I protested. "Don't say that, Connor."

He kissed the top of my head but wouldn't answer.

"Are you saying my time's run out?"

"Love, if being a hundred percent real with me means your time has run out, well—"

I pressed my mouth against his to shut him up. He had to know that everything I was doing was for us. My past was an albatross. It held me back.

Connor was my future, my everything.

Our mouths were fused together when he grasped my ass and lifted me like I weighed nothing. I locked my legs around his hips and clung to his shoulders while he ground his cock into my core. His tongue traced a line along my neck. Goosebumps erupted over my arms and neck when he rocked me up and down against his hard length, while suckling the sensitive place under my ear.

Turning my head, I resumed kissing him. Rather, I sipped from him. Savoring his full, pillowy lips as they crashed against mine. Our tongues began a ritualistic mating dance that intensified quickly. We devoured each other. Connor nipped my lip. I roughly gripped his hair at the nape and nuzzled his face. Snarling, he strode toward the bedroom with me firmly in his grasp.

Flinging me onto the bed, he covered me with his entire body. Supporting himself on his knees, with his elbows on either side of my head, he pressed his forehead to mine. "I'm making love to you right feckin' now, Veronica Mae Miller. It seems you need to remember who we are and *what* we are once and for all."

My words came out like a prayer. "Yes! God, yes!"

Connor yanked off his tank and shorts. Now fully naked, every defined muscle in his body made me salivate. I shimmied out of my jeans, with an assist by Connor tugging them off and throwing them to the ground.

Clutching the neck of my camisole in both hands, he shredded it down the middle. When he roughly yanked the cups of my delicate blue lace La Perla bra to the side, my nipples immediately puckered into taut peaks. He cupped my breasts in each hand, stroking the buds with his thumbs. Then his lips were right there, suctioning hard. His tongue swirling in circles. Moaning his name, I clutched the sheets on either side of me.

"Oh, Con," I keened when he nipped and then licked and swirled around each nipple, one after the other. Back and forth. Relentlessly. His hands snaked down my body and I lifted my hips so he could pull my panties down, while he continued his worship of my breasts. Instead, he tore my lace thong off and flung it across the room.

His talented bassist fingers tapped and massaged my clit, then stroked along my seam before plunging into my soaking channel. He withdrew and traced my wetness against my lips. I stared into his amber-gold eyes, which looked like molten fire, and sucked his digits into my mouth. His other hand massaged my pubis, pressing it deliciously against my clit. He pulled his fingers from my mouth and sank them back inside me, this time curling against my G-spot and stroking back and forth. The combined manipulations made me lose control.

I thrust against Connor, who was now holding my legs open with his knees. Kissing down my stomach, he licked my clit and wiggled his tongue against it. Then sucked. All while rubbing my sweet spot inside me. Over and over, he drove me to the brink then stopped, just as I was about to fall over the edge.

My husband was claiming me. Showing me that I was his.

And he was mine.

When I was on the cusp of madness—and Connor always seemed to know when that was—his motions grew faster. His lips sucked harder. Within seconds my clit zinged with pleasure while my inner walls clenched through the most exquisite release deep inside my core.

"Connor! Oh Connor. Connorrrrr," I moaned.

He looked up from between my legs, his lips and beard soaked with my wetness. He kissed my inner thighs, smoothing his hands over my hips. Gripping my sides, he drew me up to sitting. He issued a stern command, "Ride me, Mae."

Oh, yes!

Connor helped me onto his lap to straddle him. Our faces pressed together; our lips skimmed each other's cheeks. He wrapped his arms around my waist to pull me flush against him. I wound my arms around his neck.

We breathed.

In. Out. In. Out.

His cock pulsed and twitched between our stomachs. I reached down with one hand and gripped his hard length. Stroking. My breath quickened. Our lips barely touched. He leaned back against the headboard, shifting me with him. I canted my hips so I could rub my drenched slit up and down against his cock. To give him the visual he craved.

Connor groaned, "Babe, I'm going to explode."

I guided him inside me, reveling in how full he made me feel. Ready to finish what we had started this morning. Circling my hips against him, I moaned when he cupped my breasts and thumbed my nipples. Our lips mashed together and I couldn't help but furiously rock against him while he pounded up into me. As our pace built, Connor held fast to my waist and bounced me on his cock faster and harder.

I arched back to take him deeper. Connor's sneaky finger flicked and rubbed my clit. All the stimulation caused my mind to empty. My soul filled with the overwhelming sensation of completion. Blending together with the love of my life in a way that had no beginning and no end.

I was making love to my husband.

Fucking him.

Whatever you wanted to call it? This was where I belonged.

Connor swelled inside me, his hips gyrating, drilling into my core. He cupped my entire pussy with his hand, using his palm to once again press my mound, this time against his cock still lodged inside me. "Come, Mae. Come all over my dick."

I did as I was told, detonating with an agonized cry. Connor roared my name as he spurted inside me for what seemed like forever. Clinging to each other, we crested on waves of astonishing pleasure.

When we coasted to shore, our breath labored from the exertion, he rested his chin on my neck and kissed my cheek. I didn't want to ever move. He had accomplished his goal. Reminded me that he was the most important thing in my life. I inhaled his fresh, clean scent tinged with our lovemaking. Felt his thumbs circle my belly button. Relished the way his muscular legs felt against my thighs.

He was my nirvana.

His lips pressed against mine when I whispered, "I love you, Con."

Connor was quiet, his arms tightened around me until our breathing regulated. Although he remained semi-erect and I hoped for round two, he shifted his hips and pulled out of me. I reached between our legs and stroked his cock very gently, but his hand covered mine and he moved it away. He rolled out from under me and flopped face-up on the bed.

His hair draped across his chest when he turned to look at me. Seeing his expression, a wave of panic washed over me. His gorgeous face was contorted with the struggle he was having. Despair. Concern. Adoration.

Disappointment.

I was an idiot. Making love wasn't going to fix anything. Fix us. I wasn't being fair to him. He had opened himself up to me. Trusted me with his family secrets. Told me things he'd never told anyone. Shared his life with me. All of it. There was never any doubt where I stood.

I was his everything.

I was the one playing games with him, even if I didn't mean to. It wasn't right. He deserved to feel like he was my everything.

Which he was.

Why was this so hard?

"Mae." Connor tilted my chin up with his fingers so I couldn't avoid him. His eyes fixed me with a silent plea.

I gulped. But I was relieved just the same. "Okay."

His eyes bored into me. "I mean it. We can't go on like this."

"Okay. I'm exhausted. Can we get some sleep first?" I stroked his hair away from his face with both my hands. His eyes closed and he seemed to relax. Just a little. I kissed his eyelids and playfully asked, "Are you my honey?"

His lips curled up slightly at the phrase we always repeated to each other. "Aye."

I tugged on his hand, urging him to crawl under the covers with me. He obliged, spooning me from behind. His arm banded around my stomach possessively. Yet, he wouldn't repeat our special term of endearment.

"Aren't you going to ask it back?"

He didn't answer right away and for a minute, I thought he was already asleep. Then I heard a faint, "No, I don't think so."

"Why?" My voice caught.

More silence. I held my breath, not sure what to feel. What to think.

"Because I'll always be yours," Connor finally answered, burying his face in my neck. "I just can't say it until you're finally mine."

His breathing slowed and his body slackened. Connor was such a deep sleeper, I knew he wouldn't wake up when I slipped out of his embrace and out of bed. Grabbing the hotel robe, I quietly made my way into the living room and looked out at the city that was still bustling with activity in the wee hours of the morning. After staring out the window for a few minutes, I knew that giving Connor the information he deserved meant my life was about to spin out of control.

Into a vortex of pain.

I'd be reliving my shame.

Exposing the deepest, darkest corners of my life.

If Connor wanted all of me, I would try to give it to him. I just hoped I didn't destroy myself in the process.

RONNI

CHAPTER 10
SIX YEARS PRIOR (AGE 27)

What a difference a decade made.

A hit television show. Financial freedom. Happiness. I had it all.

My show, *She's All That*, was a remake of the seventies show *Three's Company.* Centered around my character, Lola Lake, each week followed the antics of me and my two gorgeous, single roommates who vied for my character's affection. Because Lola was clueless about their intentions, hilarity always ensued.

An award-winning formula. I had Emmys to prove it.

In addition to the jaw-dropping money I was earning, I enjoyed a ton of other perks befitting a star of a top-rated network television show. Hair, makeup, nails, massages, personal trainer and a Pilates instructor were all covered. I had my very own driver. A personal assistant. A full-time house manager.

My life finally felt perfect, it sucked that I kept waiting for the other shoe to drop. Waiting for someone to realize I hadn't earned my success. Don't get me wrong, my insecurities were slowly dissipating. Therapy and all that helped. I chalked it up to Kris creating such a supportive, inclusive set. So different from *Hawaiian High*. Every single day was a joy. Working in a safe environment didn't hurt either. Some days I had to pinch myself at being so lucky.

The cherry on top?

I was also in love for the first time ever.

Kip Badal, a stunningly handsome Indian actor from London, started out as one of my costars. With luscious, shoulder-length black hair, soulful brown eyes and sexy British accent, Kip's mere presence gave me butterflies. Shortly after the show started filming, we hooked up. He was my first real lover. Then my first real boyfriend. Then my first live-in lover.

Kip was charming. Funny. Courteous. Talented. He was my everything. We were inseparable. Hollywood's "it" couple. We even had a moniker, "Kronni."

Did I mention I was in love?

Until it all fell apart when Kip's family came to visit from London.

I was putting away some clothes Hannah, my stylist, brought over when Kip joined me in my massive closet to crush my spirit. "I'm wondering if you wouldn't mind staying at your mom's while my parents are in town."

Baffled, I didn't even answer. I just stared at him.

He coughed and toed the ground. "Um, well. I'm sorry I didn't tell you this, but my parents don't believe in pre-marital sex. It's cultural. They actually don't know we're even dating, let alone live together."

"What are you talking about?" I dropped the shirt I was gripping.

"You moved in here over a year ago. How wouldn't they know? They have your address. Plus, gossip sites are always up in our grill."

Kip didn't have the balls to look at me, instead he continued talking to the floor, mumbling. "Actually, they think this is my house."

Now I was stunned. "Wait a second. What?"

"It's no big deal, Ronni." Kip narrowed his eyes. "Don't make it something more than it is. I just don't want any drama with them."

"How am I drama?" I fumed. "You're the one lying to them."

"Can't you just follow my lead?" he begged. "It's only for a few days."

And so I stupidly went along with it.

While I slept at my mother's house, Kip was out and about with his parents. Without me. Deliberately. He scheduled their on-set visit on my day off and introduced them to the entire cast and crew. He ignored me for five days. I never even got an opportunity to meet my longtime boyfriend's family.

I was so confused. Hurt. Clearly, something wasn't right. After his folks returned to London, I confronted Kip. Rather than apologize, he dropped another bomb. His parents had prearranged his marriage to a suitable Indian girl in London. He'd known for a year. There was even a wedding date. In two months, he'd be married to someone else.

Talk about a sucker punch.

Deep breath

Suck it up.

Be fearless.

I learned a valuable lesson: people believe what they want to believe. I was living proof. No way, no how would I let myself be gamed again. By anyone.

I booted Kip out, which meant our breakup and his upcoming

marriage became social media fodder. This time it was a little different for me. Now I was a sad-sack Jennifer Anistonesque sit-com actress loser in love. Not too far from the truth. Unfortunately for Kip, my fans turned on him with a fierceness I didn't expect.

He deserved it.

He tried to play the martyr. When begging for forgiveness didn't work, he tried petulant entitlement instead. Which made filming with the asshole unbearable. I stayed strong though. Even though my heart was broken, I would never let him see me weak.

Couldn't let him see me as weak, more like it.

On the last day of shooting for the season, Kris called me into her office.

"So." She leaned back in her chair and chewed on a pencil. "It really sucks having your first broken heart in such a public setting."

She knew me so well. My throat had a lump the size of a grapefruit. I just nodded.

"You may not want to hear this, but he clearly wasn't the right man for you." Kris stood and hugged me tightly. "Next time, pick someone with a backbone. Someone who will be worthy."

Yeah, right. After Kip, I had no plans to put myself out there ever again.

How could I trust myself?

Kris released me and moved to her sofa and patted the seat next to her. Dutifully, I joined her. "Kip asked to be let out of his contract today, and I said yes."

"Okay," was all I could sputter. I was so relieved.

"Ronni, you were so professional working with that asshat for these last few weeks. I think you should take a nice, long vacation this hiatus."

"I can't. My agent found me a role in an independent film—"

"Oh, I know all about it. Did she tell you that Don Kircher is directing it?"

Holy crap.

"Oh, God no," I choked out.

She studied me before speaking. "Veronica, you are *not* doing that film."

I sank back into the cushions and shook my head. Disappointment washed over me because it was a really great part. Not great enough to take the role. I'd never work with that man again. Someone on my team slipped up. I'd made it clear I'd never work with that pervert. I needed to get to the bottom of it.

We sat in silence for a few minutes while I processed. Then Kris did what she always did. Guided me to a path forward. "I'd love it if you were focused on producing your own movies. Remember when I cast you? We discussed elevating female voices. Creating wealth. Taking control?"

"Of course, I'd love to do that." I recalled our conversation. "I'm just not sure how."

"Why don't you take the summer off? Give yourself a mental break to put Kip in your rear-view mirror. You'll come up with a plan, and I'll help you." Kris squeezed my hand. "Maybe you should go to Europe with your mom."

"Wow. Really?" Excitement coursed through my body. "We've never had a real vacation."

"Then go. Do it. I can have the studio travel agent help you plan your trip," Kris offered. "Have a think about your next steps and we'll hit the ground running in a couple of months."

I threw myself in her arms. She smelled like gardenias, which had become one of my favorite scents. "I'm going to shut off my social media, not check email and really turn off my mind."

Kris laughed. "Sweetheart, it will be the best medicine to get you back on track. I think with some perspective, you'll realize that you have a lot of living to do before you settle down. Have a fling! Just take a couple of NDAs with you."

"What?" I had no idea what she was talking about.

"You're famous now, my dear. And single. Don't let someone use you ever again." Kris winked at me. "You have the power, always remember that."

And that's how Mom and I came to spend my entire break traveling around Europe. We decided to focus our travels on Italy, Spain, and France, visiting iconic cities and quaint towns. In eight weeks, we strolled through museums, wine tasted, hiked, lounged by the sea, took cooking classes and enjoyed a long stretch of time together without any schedule.

As heavenly as the downtime was, plotting my master life plan occupied my thoughts. Kris's words had a profound effect on me. She believed in me to make a difference, and by God I was going to take the opportunity and run with it. I came up with my own three-step road to success:

First, avoid relationships to focus on raising my profile and gaining wealth.

Second, avenge Wynn's death.

Third, make Don Kircher regret the day he ever met me.

Happy to have a plan, on my last night in Europe I decided to attend a festival where my new favorite band, Less Than Zero, was playing. Mom had plans to attend a gallery opening, so she didn't want to go. Kris arranged a VIP backstage pass for me and upped the ante by betting

I couldn't get someone in the band to kiss me. I still hadn't used any of my NDAs and I figured that a fling with a rock star on my last night in Europe was the perfect way to end my vacation.

Challenge accepted.

Clicking through some photos of the band online, I swooned. Every one of them was gorgeous. At first, I was drawn to the lead singer, probably because he looked the most like Kip. The blond drummer was dreamy. The guitar player a solid ten. But there was something about the broody, tall bass player that took my breath away.

He was the one I wanted.

Now it was up to me to make it happen.

CHAPTER 11
SIX YEARS PRIOR

I was first able to breathe—really and truly breathe—when my band's first album became a worldwide hit. After so many years of my homelife misery, LTZ's success was beyond anything I'd ever imagined. Our first tour of the US was initially scheduled for six months. More dates were added, then extended into Europe.

In other words? Life was grand.

G-R-A-N-D.

Touring was like a vacation for me. Truth be told? I never wanted it to end. For the first time in many years, my mind was free of all worries. My band kicked ass. Our musicianship was tight and getting tighter with every show. There was literally no better feeling than to play to thousands of fans who knew the words to our songs.

Well, except for sex. And for me, it had been a long damn time.

When LTZ's tour was extended for the third time, Jen started showing signs of impatience. Scratch that. She was downright pissed. We hadn't seen each other in over a year, and it was a lot to expect of her to continue holding down the fort for me at home. The thing is? I was selfish. No way would I abandon my LTZ brothers. Not for anything. Not even for her.

Because I never, ever wanted to return to my old life.

When the tour was extended for a fourth time, I knew something was going to give. Jen sounded dead inside when we had our daily check-in. "Look, I don't want you to give up LTZ, but your dad is slipping into old habits. Connor, this is not *my* family business. I didn't sign up for two years of this. I can't be responsible for what is happening. It isn't fair."

I knew that I was acting like every other prick rock star who ever became famous. But I couldn't go back. *Wouldn't go back.* I tried to appease. "You have no idea how much I appreciate what you're doing, babe."

When she started to cry, my heart seized. Jen never cried. The situation was officially dire. Jay-sus. Mary. Joseph. Her tears tore me apart. "Don't cry, Jen. Just tell me what you need."

"I need you to let me off the hook. I have another job offer. I want to take it. It's more money, less hours. I can't stand the stress anymore."

Bollocks.

My mouth was suddenly as dry as sawdust. "When?"

She took a deep breath and pushed it back out. "Connor. This isn't to punish you. I understand now, more than ever, why you had to go. The band is killing it and you are where you need to be. It is your decision on what to do with the company. Let your dad run it into the ground? Sell it? Come back and run it? Whatever you decide, I'll support you. But my decision to leave is final."

"Can't you hang in there? Just until I get back?" I pleaded.

"I can't."

Double bollocks.

"Okay. I understand."

What the feck was I going to do? We were halfway around the world in Barcelona. I'd hoped to spend my days off with my bandmates eating tapas and drinking Cava. Instead, I feigned illness and holed up in my hotel room, trying to salvage an unsalvageable situation.

Calling home proved it.

"You've had yer fun, it's time ta come back to yer family," Da slurred into the phone. It was noon in Seattle. On a weekday.

I pinched my nose to avoid yelling at the old drunk. "I'm not leaving the band, Da."

"Useless cunt."

His insults had little impact on me anymore. "Projecting much?"

The phone clicked. He'd hung up on me.

My next call was to my mother. "Ma, what's going on, all hell seems to be breaking loose."

"Your father's drinking again. After Seamus graduates from high school, I'm moving back to Ireland. I mean it this time. I'm done."

Triple bollocks.

All this nonsense infuriated me. When the rug had been ripped out from under us, I'd killed myself for seven solid years to keep my family afloat. If Da was still intent on pissing it all away? My sacrifice was for feckin' nothing. It was all I could do not to raise my voice. "What about the business? Who's going to run it? What about the house?"

But Ma was absolutely defeated, she had nothing left. "I've had enough. *Gabh mo leithscéal.*"

Accept my excuse.

The Gaelic phrase that Da used every time he got poleaxed. Every time he lost money. Every time he disappointed the family again. The space between my eyes began pulsing. It became hard for me to regulate my breathing because I was so furious. If both my parents were truly giving up, what the feck was I stressing about?

Why was it on me?

If I went back to Seattle in the middle of our tour, I'd be out of the band. They'd find another bass player. That option was a big fat nope. LTZ was the best thing that had ever happened to me. Especially because I knew. I *knew* if I went back home to a job and life I hated, Da would piss all my efforts away on booze and poker anyway.

I decided to let the chips fall where they may.

No pun intended.

Besides, I wasn't the only one with problems. All my bandmates were having a rough time for various reasons. Combine that with close quarters. Exhaustion. Homesickness.

We were on edge.

Ironically, in direct contrast to the personal shite we were all dealing with, the band was on a rocket ship to the stratosphere. The crowds seemed to multiply exponentially in each city. Fans recognized us everywhere. Our music was playing on every radio station, in every shopping mall, and our song *Rise* was used as a home-team motivator for sporting events all over the world. Little wonder management was pressuring us to capitalize on our success. They wanted another album immediately.

A few months of making music in the studio sounded like heaven.

To be fair, there was a huge positive development. It was a doozy. I was officially a millionaire. A feckin' millionaire. We all were.

My newfound financial status solved my biggest source of stress. One wire transfer later, the mortgage on my folks' house was paid in full. What money didn't solve was my relationship with Jen. After her departure from McGloughlin Construction, our reason for daily calls evaporated.

She surprised me in Munich to break up with me in person. She'd been having an affair. With her best friend, who happened to be a woman. I didn't have it in me to truly be mad. In many ways it was a relief. I hadn't been a free agent in years. It was surprisingly easy for me to accept that our time together had run its course.

It didn't mean I wasn't mad at her.

She'd betrayed my trust. Lied to me. Cheated on me.

It hurt.

The thing is, I'd been unwaveringly faithful to her despite all the temptation. And let me tell you, there was a lot of enticement. It cemented something in my mind. I wasn't going to allow anyone into my heart for a long time. Maybe ever. I'd given everything to my family. For nothing. I'd been true to my girlfriend, who didn't love me the way I loved her.

At least now, I could focus fully on the three guys who were my new family. My band.

Plus, now that I was single, my dick had come to its own realization. More than anything, it wanted to fuck. And fuck and fuck and fuck. It was feckin' time for me to enjoy my freedom.

I was so sex-starved, within four weeks I'd shagged twenty different women. In all the ways Jen would never let me. Which was eye opening, because I had no idea how bland our sex life really was.

Blowjobs. Phenomenal.

Three-ways. Four-ways. A lot of work. Not my bag.

Anal. Interesting, but I preferred a wetter heat.

Spanking. Restraints. Blindfolds. On me? Nope. Otherwise, fun.

Public places. Bathroom stalls. Stairwells. Tour bus. Backstage. Yes. Yes and yes. I loved the element of danger.

Honestly, I had a lot to make up for.

On our last night of the tour, I decided to make a short appearance at our VIP party to find someone to shag. No reason to sugar coat it, I wanted to find a beautiful girl to get the job done all night in my hotel room. There were new positions I wanted to try. I'd done a bit of research.

Once inside the tent, I immediately spotted a stunner with long, reddish-brown hair, legs for days, and sumptuous tits straining against a tight, black tank dress with some killer heels. She was talking to Ty and Jace in a secluded seating area. Her face grew dreamy whenever Ty said anything. She was clearly smitten with our singer.

Then again, who wasn't?

I was fine with his sloppy seconds, they were usually tens. Just like this gorgeous girl.

Ty, per usual, was on the edge of panic. It was always that way when a woman got too close. He spotted me watching them and motioned me over. We'd developed a routine over the past year. He needed an out. I gladly intervened. The only difference since my breakup? Now, I had free license to partake in his rejects.

My gaze locked on the beauty during my casual stroll over. In that instant, all of the party noise around me dissipated. Her green eyes held all the secrets of the universe. She sucked her succulent plump lower lip into her mouth and looked down at my chest before glancing back up from under her eyelashes.

What a flirt.

It was on.

Before the night was over, those pink, pouty lips would be wrapped around my cock.

Ty's deep voice interrupted my thought. "Connor, this is Ronni Miller."

She stuck out her hand, almost shyly. "Oh, I know who you are. I love LTZ."

Jace chuckled and excused himself. Ty didn't bother, he was like a ninja and slipped away without saying a word. No complaints from me. Now alone, I was left sitting next to the beautiful woman with her hand enveloped in mine. I flicked my thumb over her knuckles. She smelled delicious, like a lemon-meringue pie. I wanted to eat her up.

Snapping out of our eye lock, she looked around and realized we'd been ditched. "Where'd they go?"

"Ty made his patented escape."

"Oh." Her nose scrunched up adorably. Clearly, this lass wasn't used to being rejected.

"So, Ronni? Fancy a drink, love?" I turned up my brogue to eleven. In situations like this, I double-downed on my accent. Chicks dug it. It worked like a charm. I was learning that firsthand with all of the tail I'd been pulling since Jen dumped me.

"Um. Well. Sure." She fiddled with the strap of her dress distractedly before looking up at me. She blinked once. Then twice. "I think I just lost a bet."

Damn.

"Oh yeah? I've been known to gamble. What's the wager?"

She shook her head, almost embarrassed. "A friend bet me that I couldn't get a kiss."

"From Ty?" I laughed heartily. Oh Lord, if she only knew.

She began to giggle. Her cheeks turned pink. "Well, technically the bet was getting a kiss from *someone* in LTZ."

"How much?"

Her eyes widened in surprise. "What?"

"How much was the wager?"

She gathered her hair and twisted it up into a messy knot. "Does it matter?"

97

Good God how I wanted to grip a fistful of that hair and hold it tightly while I rammed into her from behind. "It does."

She threw her hands up. "Fine. But you need context."

"Hit me."

"It's going to sound so dumb. I just got out of a serious relationship and my friend is determined to get me back in the saddle, so to speak."

Ahh. Well, well, well. We were in the same boat. With that little piece of information, how could I resist? Without hesitating another second, I bent down and licked the seam of her lips before pressing my mouth fully against hers. Her pliant lips opened. Our kiss deepened.

Ho-ly shite.

My palms threaded through her luxurious mane and caressed the base of her skull to tilt her head gently. My tongue sought hers and swirled around in a slow dance before I sucked on it. Her eyes opened in surprise at the intimacy, but she relaxed against me. Clutched my shirt in her fists.

My hands roamed downward, skimming her sides. Thumbing the underswell of her breasts before reaching around and grabbing her ass. Squeezing. Pulling her toward me so she could feel my hard cock pressing against her. Her hips gyrated against my erection, making me groan.

Before I knew it, we were going at it like we were starved. Grinding against each other. Tasting. Groping. Forgetting where we were.

More like not caring.

I could have gone on for hours because this Ronni girl tasted delicious. Like some sort of exotic fruit cocktail with a tinge of cool mint.

As much as I wanted to keep kissing her, I had a plan.

When she was well and thoroughly snogged, I released her. Held her away from my body, but lightly gripped her upper arms. She looked down at my prick, which was a clearly outlined ridge in my jeans. She turned her gaze back up to me. Expectantly.

Oh, but what good would it be if she didn't have to work for it?

I was going all in.

Abruptly, I released her and walked away.

Turning, only to say, "You've got your LTZ kiss, beautiful, hope that your wager was a big one."

If I was a betting man, and I was, she'd follow me in— three... two... one...

Except she didn't.

And I went bust.

CHAPTER 12

ONE YEAR LATER

"You're going, she'd have wanted you to honor her wishes, Ronni." Kris, who had become not only my mentor but my best friend, pulled the curtains back from my bedroom window. "It's time to get yourself out of bed."

Sunlight streamed into my room. Shielding my eyes from the onslaught of brightness, I hissed like a vampire, "Please make it stop."

"No can do."

As my swollen eyes adjusted, I saw Kris's backside disappear into my massive walk-in closet, her dramatic black-and-white duster swooshing behind her. Since my mom died two weeks ago, the crushing weight of my emotions was suffocating. I knew Kris meant well, but she hadn't lost someone who had been with her every day for twenty-seven years. I doubted she comprehended the magnitude of my loss.

Kris emerged with a matching bra and panty set. "Let's get you in the shower, sweetheart."

"You don't understand, Kris." My eyes welled up with tears that seemed to be endless. "I need more time."

She sat on the edge of my lush, cream, Egyptian cotton duvet and studied me. Wetness coated my blotched, puffy face. I didn't even bother to wipe the tears away anymore. I laid against the pillows and shut my eyes, hoping for some relief from the unbearable pain. There was talk about antidepressants and Valium after my hysterics at the funeral, but I refused to take anything. I didn't want to diminish any one of my feelings for my sweet mother. She deserved more than a drugged-up daughter.

On the other hand, I really couldn't fathom going on without her.

Only five months ago, my world fell completely apart when the fabulous Mable Miller was diagnosed with stage-four pancreatic cancer. It took her life in a shockingly fast progression. I knew this was something I'd never get over.

I'd never be able to process it.

Her diagnosis came not long after we returned from our idyllic two-month European vacation. By the time we'd returned, my ex, Kip, was gone and Kris retooled the show's concept to focus solely on me. Each week followed another one of my crazy dating mishaps in a quest to find true love.

It resonated. In all the right demographics. Ratings went through the roof. Sponsors loved the good, clean fun. Officially, I was on the A-list.

Mom and I often laughed about how fortunate we had been to explore Europe together relatively undetected. I doubted I'd ever be able to travel like that again, but she started making plans to visit Australia. VIP style. I didn't want to burst her bubble, but I had revenge on my mind. Plans I was putting in motion. There would be no time for a trip. Not for a while.

Still, my mind often wandered to the brooding LTZ bass player who kissed the bejeezus out of me at the festival only to leave me hanging. My panties still got wet thinking about the most intense sexual encounter I'd ever had. And it was only a kiss.

Too bad the guy was an arrogant asshole rock star. At least that's what everyone said about him on LTZ's incredible social media feeds.

Not that I stalked him.

Much.

Just like every other straight man in my life, Connor McGloughlin was a colossal disappointment.

On the positive side, his behavior gave me one more reason to give up on men and focus on my career and my take-down plans. I'd learned a little something after being in the public eye for over a decade. For me, the easiest way to "date" was to beard for hot, closeted gay actors. Win-win all the way. I had gorgeous men to escort me to red carpet events and other public obligations. They got to play boyfriend to the most popular actress on television, which kept them in the public eye. Fun times. No attachments. No heartbreak.

Perfect.

It played right into my persona.

And I was *very* strategic about the actors I bearded for.

Fans always had a hard time separating my real life from my television life. The wacky dating scenarios of my sit-com seeped into people's perception of me as a real person. As such, I'd morphed into America's lovelorn sweetheart. Jennifer Aniston 2.0. My dating life was subject to incredible scrutiny. Online. Tabloids. Social media. Everyone had an opinion about my love life. If you believed what you read in the tabloids or online click-bait stories, any or all of the following was true about me:

I couldn't keep a man.

I dated too much.

I was secretly pregnant.

I hated kids.

I'd become a sad, heartbroken spinster.

I had a secret husband.

I was a lesbian.

I was a virgin.

I think fans genuinely wanted me to have a happy ending, especially after Kip. The thing is, any guy who dared to be in a real relationship with me would be scrutinized. Analyzed. Torn apart. Bearding relationships solved that problem. A closeted gay actor who dated me was, after all, just doing another acting job.

I'd learned long ago to ignore all the crap. The chatter didn't really bother me, it was actually kind of amusing. I'd developed a pretty thick skin. I knew the drill and I used it to my own advantage. My love life sold magazines. Drove traffic. Increased clicks.

So what if everyone thought they knew me and what I wanted?

They were wrong.

I honestly didn't want a relationship of any kind. All romance had ever done for me was interfere with my career. My good-girl image wasn't entirely cultivated. I didn't drink, do drugs, go to clubs or swear. I was nice to everyone, whether they were famous or extras. I'd been through a lot to get where I was.

It was time to cement my future. Focus on anything but love. Earn a crap-ton of money. Increase my power in Hollywood.

Because wealth meant control.

Control meant power.

Power meant leverage.

Of course, it's funny how things are seemingly going your way and then *boom*. You're knocked completely off your axis.

Mom and I were getting fitted for our Emmy dresses. When we were changing, I noticed Marvelous Mable had lost a shocking amount of weight. Her arms were like toothpicks. Her ribs jutted out. I didn't say anything at first, but when my favorite designer, Christian Siriano's seamstress was taking our measurements, she'd gone down three whole sizes.

"Losing weight is never a bad thing in Hollywood." She waved me off, dismissing my concerns.

It didn't work, I was officially worried.

Worry turned to panic a few weeks later when Mom could barely stay awake on set. She complained constantly about how badly her belly hurt. When I managed to get her to eat something, she couldn't hold it down. Convinced she had a secret eating disorder, I enlisted Kris and we tricked her into seeing a doctor, claiming the show's insurance required it for all staff and crew.

The bottom fell when we got the diagnosis. Stage four. Terminal. Cancer had spread to her liver, her lungs, and adrenal glands. The disease was too advanced to qualify for clinical trials and a lot of the newer alternative treatments. All there was to do was to get her meds dialed in to make her as comfortable as possible.

Being unable to help my own mother, with all of the resources I had at my disposal, was devastating.

We'd never go on another trip together.

Never snorkel the Great Barrier Reef.

Never visit the Outback.

Never marvel at the Sydney Opera House.

My sense of control had been only an illusion.

A tragic, fucked-up mess.

Kris, to her credit, did everything she could to make things easier for me. We couldn't shut down production entirely, so she fast-tracked the last ten episodes. We managed to cram twelve weeks of work into four. The entire *She's All That* family rallied around me. It was unbelievable to have that level of support. Not a word leaked to the media. In my industry, it was really unprecedented. Everyone loved and respected my mom. It was impossible not to.

I moved in with Mable during her final weeks. Even after several surgeries, which were supposed to bring her some relief, she could barely get out of bed. We had the best of everything. Specialists. Nurses. Mobility devices. 24/7 caregivers. The cast and crew came by on a rotation to help keep her spirits up. Unlike me, Mable accepted her fate the way she'd tackled everything in life.

Grace.

Determination.

Resignation.

Knowing that Mom was really dying broke me. At first, I refused to accept what was happening and rarely left her side. My neediness surely smothered her, but she more than tolerated it. She never chastised me and my stubborn need to research alternative cures. We slept together at night. I helped her shower. I held her hand when the pain was unbearable.

Watching her decline was a brutal experience. Revenge didn't matter anymore. It wouldn't taste sweet without my mom there by my side.

Right before she slipped away, she stroked my hair and said, "Baby girl, you have been the true love of my life. All I want for you is to find someone who loves you with everything he has in him and for you to love him back. You should travel more. Relax. Have children. As much as you love your Hollywood lifestyle, it isn't who you are. Promise me you'll honor yourself. You're worth it."

"You haven't moved," Kris interrupted my thoughts. "We need to leave in a half hour to catch the plane."

Knowing that I'd never win with my mentor, I dragged myself out of bed, trudged into the bathroom and took a shower. Leave it to Kris to have the softest black Chanel sweatsuit folded neatly on my bed waiting for me. The perfect comfortable travel outfit. It wouldn't be enough for a week away. "I need to throw some stuff in a suitcase."

Kris assured me, "Already done and in the car. Anything we forgot we can get in Sydney."

Maybe refocusing on my mission would help with my grief.

"I've got all the details worked out." She scooted me out the door. "Oh, and I've arranged for us to hitch a ride on a PJ with a rock band. You're welcome."

The drive from my house in Malibu to the air strip wasn't long. Two black Escalades were parked next to our ride, a fancy VVIP Boeing 787 Dreamliner. The crew were loading baggage and what looked like musical equipment into the underbelly. Kris pulled in behind the cars and two valets rushed to open our doors and grab our bags.

The sunlight blinded me for the second time that day. I reached out to shield my face from the brightness. Kris handed me a pair of oversized Tom Ford sunglasses, which I gladly put on. It suddenly occurred to me that we wouldn't be alone on this flight. I dreaded making small talk with a bunch of musicians. I wondered if it would be rude for me to just sleep through the flight.

"Ah, there's Carter." Kris waved at a good-looking older guy with long, dark curls with a few gray streaks. He trotted over and gave her a warm hug.

The aging rocker held out his hand to me. "Carter Pope."

"I'm Veronica Miller."

"Thank you for letting us hitch a ride." Kris smoothed her hair. "Ronni wasn't sure if she would have to cancel. This makes it a lot easier."

"Ah, it's no trouble," Carter tutted. "The guys are already on board. I actually just came by to see my son for a few minutes. I have a meeting in Denver."

After polite goodbyes, he jumped in one of the Escalades and was off. I followed Kris up the stairs leading to the cabin, which were covered by a red carpet. "Who was that?"

Kris wrinkled her brow. "You've never heard of Carter Pope?"

"Um?"

"He's the guitar player for Limelight?" Her statement was more of a question.

"Oh, yeah." I pretended to know more than I actually did. "I've heard of them."

She laughed. "Ohmygod, Ronni. Your distinct lack of pop culture astounds me, considering you are such a huge part of it."

"What do you mean?"

"Carter's son is Zane Rocks, the guitar player for Less Than Zero." Kris stopped in her tracks. "They're who we're flying with."

Wait, what?

"Wait." I grabbed her arm. "You set this up. The dare last summer? The asshole guy I told you I kissed in the middle of the VIP area at that rock festival in Europe? It was the bass player from LTZ. Please tell me he won't be on this plane."

"Oh, I remember. Connor McGloughlin." Kris winked at me before she started back up the steps. "I, for one, am counting on it."

CHAPTER 13

Zane and Ty were arguing about the chorus of one of the newer songs we were working on. Jace was already strapped into his seat and passed out, a mask over his eyes and headphones over his ears. My plan had also been to sleep for the entire sixteen-hour trip until Carter dropped the bomb that Ronni feckin' Miller and another woman were flying to Australia with us.

Now I was wide awake.

It had been at least a year since I'd kissed the lips clean off her. I thought she'd follow me when I walked away. Maybe even beg for more. Most women did. That had been my foolproof plan.

Clearly, I'd overestimated my appeal to the famous actress.

Our chemistry wasn't imagined. Not by a long shot.

I'd just vastly underestimated her.

Television hadn't been a part of my life for years, so I had no idea who she was that day. I figured she was just another stunning actress-wannabe trying to have a fling with a rocker. Scratch that, the most stunning woman I'd ever laid eyes on.

Truth.

Once I found out she'd been famous for over a decade, I suddenly saw Ronni Miller everywhere. In magazines. Cosmetic ads. Billboards. Television. Award shows. There was no escape. Her gorgeous, creamy skin. Thick, luscious hair. Plump lips. Naturally fleshy tits. Her heart-shaped ass. I developed a bit of a secret obsession, which was completely out of character for me. I wanked to the memory of our make-out sesh at least once per week. Or three.

Okay, fine. Five days was my limit. I wasn't a complete feckin' creeper.

The memory of the fair Ms. Miller didn't prevent me from fucking as many women as I could over the past year. I still had a lot of catching up to do after my two-year sex draught. When I wasn't making up for lost time, LTZ recorded our new album, *Z*. We created something incredible. A heartbreak and redemption opus about Ty's lost love Zoey. It would be released in a few weeks, and the pre-buzz was incredible.

Meanwhile, we had to play some shows in Australia and Asia to complete the last touring cycle.

For feck's sake, we were co-headlining stadium shows now. It wasn't that long ago when the sold-out show at our local Seattle club, The Mission, had been our crowning achievement. Every day I gave thanks that I'd taken the leap of faith and stuck with the band. Without LTZ, I'd probably be a slobbering, loser drunk. Just like my Da.

Jay-sus. Where was she?

My heart was beating out of control in anticipation of Ronni's arrival. I couldn't remember ever feeling this jittery. I didn't like it one bit. Over the past year, I'd made a career out of being indifferent to women. It wasn't hard because I usually didn't give two shites about them. Why were my palms sweating over this one? A woman who'd shown absolutely no interest in me.

Bollocks.

At least we were traveling in style. Zane's dad Carter arranged for the jet as a present for completing our amazing album. Who was I to argue with this over-the-top reward? The PJ was brilliant. Each of the plush, black leather seats in the back cabin turned into a flat bed, with sliding door partitions for privacy. The front of the plane featured two full-size bathrooms, complete with a bathtub and shower. In the middle, the kitchen and dining area was set up like a fine-dining restaurant. White linen tablecloths. Curved booths in black suede. A full walnut bar.

Reclining in my seat in an attempt to appear more at ease, I shut my eyes. A few minutes later, a light, lemony-vanilla scent wafted into the cabin. Shite, I'd forgotten how good she smelled. I couldn't help but open my eyes to have a look.

"Hey, everyone, thanks for letting us tag along." A tall woman with red glasses waved to us. "I'm Kris Blakely, the showrunner for *She's All That*. This is Ronni Miller."

Ronni's makeup-free face turned three shades of pink under her absurdly huge sunglasses.

She was even more unbelievable in person than I remembered. Feck. Especially without all the glamour. Seeing her tight, fit body in person made my cock swell. But the first thing I noticed was she was not the bubbly beauty I met in the VIP area a year ago. Her shoulders were hunched, her arms crossed around her body. Something was off. No question.

"Ronni!" Zane-the-oblivious sprung up and hugged her. "I remember you! Carter told me you were coming, I'm sorry about your mom."

"Thanks." She shrank away from his embrace, her voice barely a whisper.

She took off her sunglasses and carefully put them in her case. That's when I got a good look at her. Her skin was glowing but there were dark circles under her eyes. Her cheekbones were much more pronounced. Her jawline sharp, as though she'd lost a little too much weight. When my eyes caught hers, it did me in. The depths of sorrow reflected in her green orbs was devastating.

Every fiber of my being wanted to protect this woman.

Kris took her elbow and led her past Zane and the rest of us. Ronni kept her head down, averting her eyes. Craning my neck, I watched as they settled into two seats in the very back. Ronni folded her legs up under her and curled into a ball. Tucking herself under the large blanket, she resembled a caterpillar in a big, blue cashmere cocoon.

Clearly, it wasn't the time or place for me to reconnect my lips to hers. From the look of things, our backstage encounter was the last thing on her mind. If she even remembered it, that is. Sighing, I unlocked my tablet to try to read. Every so often, I glanced back to check on her. She remained motionless for easily two hours. My senses were on high alert when she rose and walked past me toward the restrooms.

With everyone sound asleep but us, this gave me the perfect opportunity to "grab a snack." She gasped when I was standing in the galley waiting for her when she came out of the loo. "Fancy seeing you, love."

Her face pinkened once more. "Um. Hey."

"Are you doing okay?"

She looked up at me from under her lashes. It was the same look that hooked me that first time, the vixen. Not that she probably remembered. "No, but I'll survive."

"Drink?"

She took the bottle. "Thanks."

"At your service." Jay-sus, I sounded like such a tool.

"Yeah, well a bottle of water doesn't change the fact that you're an asshole."

Whoa, feisty! But yes! She remembered me.

I stifled my laugh with my fist. "Ah, darlin' you were supposed to follow me, not leave me hangin'"

Her eyes bugged out. "What?"

"Ah, it's not important. Are you really okay?" I traced her hairline with the tip of my finger, I couldn't help it. "I heard that you just lost your mother, love."

She gaped at me, then sadly nodded and squeezed her eyes shut. Tears spilled down her cheeks. She furiously wiped them, like they pissed her off. Every fiber of her being seemed to be focused on not allowing herself to completely fall apart. Her body shook from the effort.

"Oh, darlin.'" I wrapped my arms around her. Cupping her head against my chest. Her arms were like noodles at her side, but I held her tightly. "It's such bad luck to lose your ma so young. I'm sure it's the hardest thing to bear."

Her body was wracked with sobs. "Ahhh." I stroked her hair, her body still pressed against mine. "Do you feel like talking about it?"

She didn't answer.

I released her and gestured to the booth. "Tea or whiskey?"

A short guffaw escaped her perfect lips. "Tea, please."

I could feel her eyes boring into me as I brewed it. No matter how much Irish blood ran through my veins, I'd never developed a taste for tea. Nevertheless, I had plenty of practice in my household to make a perfect cup. Complete with a splash of milk and two teaspoons of sugar.

Setting the drink in front of her, I took the opposite seat. It blew my mind at how much I was drawn to her. Almost like her soul was singing a secret song that only mine could hear.

Or some shite.

"She died two weeks ago." Ronni traced the rim of her cup with a perfectly manicured finger, which was painted shiny red. "We were inseparable. I'm so lost without her."

"Tell me what happened."

Despite her heartbreak, Ronni was a gifted storyteller. She opened her heart about her mom's illness and how hard they'd fought. About the treatments they'd endured. She shared stories of their European adventure, which culminated in our, erm, meeting. It was clear how close she was to her mother. I envied her in some ways and was grateful I wasn't her in others.

A parent's utter and complete devotion was something that was only a distant memory for me. Knowing that Ronni's life had been filled with such a special love— My heart broke in a million pieces for her.

A couple hours later, Ronni's eye's widened. "Oh, gosh. Connor? You're not an asshole at all. I'm so sorry for saying that. I've been talking your ear off for too long about the most depressing things. We should get some sleep."

"I'm happy to listen, love." I grasped her hand from across the table and squeezed gently and then released her. "You are so lucky to have had someone like her in your life."

Ronni shut her eyes and sighed. A trace of a smile graced her lips. "Thank you for letting me talk about her. It helps to let it out."

"Anytime. You can tell me anything." I couldn't help but smile. I meant it. I could listen to her recite the phone book and never get bored.

"You have a beautiful smile, Connor."

"Ha Ha. May I ask why you're on your way to Oz?" I desperately wanted to hold her soft hand again. But there was no need to play all my cards right now. Not when she seemed to need a friend. "I'm sure it's not to see us in concert."

Ronni's eyes squeezed shut, a wave of what only could be described as agony passed over her face. "She wanted us to take a trip to Australia. I kept putting it off because my schedule is so packed. I'm going to spread some of her ashes in the places we planned to visit. I'm hoping it will help me cope because it's the only way we can be there together now."

Holy shite.

We were silent for a while. Then I had an idea.

"May I share an old Irish blessing for your ma?" I spoke quietly.

She rested her chin on her hands, which were folded on the table. "Oh, I'd really love that."

I amped up my brogue, shut my eyes and recited:

> *May the road rise up to meet you.*
> *May the wind be always at your back.*
> *May the sun shine warm upon your face.*
> *The rains fall soft upon your fields.*
> *And until we meet again,*
> *May God hold you in the palm of His hand."*

Tears spilled down her cheeks anew. "That is the most beautiful thing I've ever heard."

"Aye."

"Thank you, Connor." Ronni reached over and squeezed my hand. "Really."

Without thinking, I flashed her another smile. Little did she know it was a rarity. "Not. At. All. You're grand, love."

We sat sipping lukewarm tea, staring at each other. It was peaceful.

She seemed more settled and the tears had stopped. Our quiet reverie was interrupted when Ty loped into the room and started rummaging through the cupboards. Remembering Ronni's infatuation with him the last time I saw her, I observed carefully. She glanced at him briefly then looked back at me. Smiled and looked down, almost shyly.

Well, well, well…

One of the flight attendants emerged to ask if we were hungry. We all nodded, and Ty scooted in next to me. The three of us made polite small talk while enjoying a platter of Aussie meat pies, which were magically produced. Scratch that. Ronni picked at hers. We devoured the rest.

She and I kept glancing at each other. Shooting secret looks. As clueless as ever, Ty didn't pick up on our flirtatious vibe. Lost in his own creative head, he wrote in his notebook. Yammering on and on about some lyrics he was trying to perfect. Finally, after it went on too long, Ronni yawned. Tried to cover it with the back of her hand.

"You tired, love?" I interrupted our singer's mutterings.

"Oh, shit." Ty lurched out of the booth. "I'm having a hard time sleeping. I didn't mean to keep you both up."

"You guys are so sweet." Ronni scooted up from the other side of the table. "I have a lot to do when we get in, so I do need to lie down for a while. Thanks for cheering me up a little."

She bit her lip and walked past Ty and me and then through the cabin. We both watched her curl up and bury herself under the blanket. Grief or not, something had sparked between me and her. No question. If it weren't for Ty's interruption, I would have gladly hung out with her for the entire flight.

I decided then and there, this woman might just be worth my effort.

"She seems nice." Ty glanced at me. "Most actresses are so full of themselves."

A rare feeling of jealousy reared its ugly head. "You're interested?"

Ty looked at me like I was crazy. "What?"

"I know you're not going to spend another three years pining for your high school girl." I shook my head. "Maybe you're thinking about finally getting your dick wet."

Ty squinted at my crassness.

"Well?"

"You think I want Ronni Miller?" He scrunched his nose up. "I mean, I don't even *know* her."

"So you aren't interested in her?"

"Christ. I'm not sure why you and everyone else seems to be so invested in my sex life." Ty crossed his arms and scowled. "Why do you care who I fuck?"

I threw my hands in the air. "I don't. But you don't *have* a sex life, Tyson. It's not healthy for a man of your age to be hung up so long on a girl. You don't seem to realize that you could have any woman you wanted. It's not like you need to fall in love or anything."

"So you're saying I should fuck Ronni?" Ty shook his head. "Jesus, Connor. What do you take me for?"

"I didn't say you should, I asked if you wanted to." My head was swimming, this wasn't how I wanted the conversation to go. "I mean, no one would blame you if you decided to live a little."

I mentally admonished myself. I didn't want to push him toward Ronni. I'd wanted to find out where his head was at. For months. He'd been a moody recluse for so long, I was sick of walking on eggshells around him. Ronni was just a catalyst, but this flight wasn't the time to have the conversation. "Look, I'm the oldest in my family and the oldest in this band. So, I notice things. It sucks to watch you suffer. Because at the end of the day, it's self-inflicted."

Ty studied me for a few long seconds. "I'm good, Con. I don't want to date Ronni."

Maybe he wasn't so clueless after all.

"Okay."

Ty slumped into a dining chair. "Look. I know you're right. At some point, I need to get over Zoey. I just can't even imagine being with anyone. My dick isn't interested."

"I don't mean to pressure you. Or shame you, ye' bollocks." I fixed him with my best big brother look. "It's just that after Jen dumped me, I can honestly say that getting back in the game has helped mend my heart. All I want is for you to find some peace. Happiness."

Ty squinched his eyes together. "Connor, can I confess something to you?"

"Aye."

He buried his face in his hands. "I want to explode, and I can't hold it back for too much longer."

"What do you mean?"

"I *am* tired of being sad." Ty looked back up at me. "I *want* to party with you guys and have fun again. It scares me so much because I just worry that I won't be able to stop."

I clapped my hand on his shoulder. "I get that. My da is a world-class drunk. He gambles. He has nearly pissed our family business away more than once. I'm still able to have a few beers. I just keep it under control. So can you. Trust yourself."

Ty nodded, saying nothing. I could tell confession time was over and said good night. During the time we were in the galley, our regular seats had been flattened into beds and made up with fancy linens. Flicking my eyes back to where Ronni was, I could tell she was sound asleep. With eleven hours still to go on the long flight, I figured I'd catch a few winks

118

and try to resume our conversation when I woke up.

The next thing I knew Jace was shaking me awake. Disoriented, I sat up and looked around. The entire plane was empty. "Where is everyone?"

Jace laughed and clapped me on the back. "Ty, Zane, Ronni, and Kris took a limo to the hotel. You were out for the count. Snoring like a bastard. I drew the short stick to wake you up."

Bollocks.

"C'mon. Let's go, sleeping beauty, we have a long day ahead of us." Jace busied himself in his phone, which seemed to be surgically attached to his hand.

Wait. A. Minute. "Jace, tell me you did not film me sleeping."

"And waste your symphony of snorts, wheezes, and sleep-talking?" Jace tapped the iPhone with his index finger. "Gold, pure gold. I may even create a new Insta for—"

My hand covered his mouth. "Give me the phone."

"Fhugh ywguou," he mumbled and shoved his phone down his pants.

No way was I copping a feel of our drummer. I released him. "Feck it."

Grabbing my bag from the overhead, I slung it over my shoulder and lumbered off the plane. Jace was close behind me, laughing so hard he could barely walk. As we approached the waiting Town Car, I shoved him and he stumbled. When he recovered, he tried to place me in a headlock. With easily fifty pounds on him, I deflected and wrapped him in a bear hug. Lifting him. Struggling against my tight hold, he kicked his feet uselessly as he tried to break free. By now I was rolling with laughter too. My stomach actually hurt.

The driver, who was leaning against the car with his arms crossed, glowered at us. I'm sure he had less than zero respect for a couple of rocker Huns like us. I set Jace down and flipped him off before he got into the car. I jumped in the other side. We managed to stop screwing around and enjoy the drive to the hotel. Australia was beautiful, the spectacular Sydney bridge and Opera House dominated the skyline as we approached the city.

My mind began to drift back to the beautiful Ronni. There was something special about her, which had nothing to do with her fame. I was the furthest thing away from being a fan-boy. It's just that I'd never felt such a strong connection to a woman. Even Jen. This was different. My mind drifted to a favorite memory—the scorching kiss from the festival. Just thinking about it made my jeans feel tight.

"So, sir smirk-a-lot, you got the hots for the actress?" Jace elbowed me.

I raised an eyebrow. "What makes you say that?"

"My brother. Please." Jace rolled his eyes. "I haven't seen that look on your face since you first started going out with my sister."

"It's not like that," I lied. "Her mom died, she was crying so I sat up and talked to her."

"Ah." Jace nodded. "Then you'll be happy to know Ty gave Kris and her passes to the concert."

It took every ounce of self-control I possessed not to react when I really wanted to whoop with joy. "Why would I give a shite?"

"Well, I speak on behalf of all of us when I say that it's high fucking time Tyson had a little happiness. That's for sure. But he wouldn't piss on your territory." Jace side-eyed me. "So, you probably need to let someone know if she's off-limits."

I kept my expression neutral. Jace hadn't been there for my conversation with Ty. "He should do what he wants."

As long as it was anyone but Ronni.

Whoa. What the feck was up with my sudden possessiveness of a woman I didn't really know? After seeing her again, I couldn't deny that my desire for her was visceral. Consuming.

After grilling him, I didn't *think* Ty had the hots for Ronni. Then again, I also hadn't staked my own claim. Maybe he'd changed his mind. I had no idea if she was interested in me, but I did know one thing.

If I had my say?

Ty and Ronni together would be over my dead body.

RONNI

CHAPTER 14

W hen I found out we were flying to Sydney with LTZ, Kris nearly had to physically drag me on the plane. Mainly, I was mortified to see Connor again. After the big ginger kissed me and ran, he was firmly on my "dead-to-me" list. Still reeling from my breakup with Kai, I found his abrupt departure did a real number on my confidence. It ignited every single one of my insecurities.

My hackles had gone up when he joined me in the galley of the plane. Then he'd floored me by admitting he wanted me to follow him the night we'd met. His warm, comforting embrace settled me for the first time since Mom died. I'd misjudged him completely. He sat for hours listening to me talk about Mom's illness. Without interruption.

Who was this man?

His recitation of the beautiful, haunting poem? In his slight Irish lilt? It touched me so deeply that in that moment I tumbled into full-blown, heart-fluttering infatuation.

When Ty joined us for a snack, I only had eyes for Connor. He only had eyes for me. It was like an invisible string connected us together. I was so drawn to him it actually frightened me. So enamored that I took myself to bed. The feelings were too overwhelming to process in my grief-stricken state.

This man was too much.

I had to put up some walls.

Connor was still sleeping when we disembarked the plane. I was partly disappointed but mostly relieved. When Ty and Zane offered us a ride to the hotel and all-access passes to their show, it didn't take much for Kris to convince me we should go. It was almost like I couldn't stay away. For the first time since mom got sick, I got dressed up. Had a few drinks. Let loose.

Kris and I had an absolute blast. We danced. We sang along. I'd never been on stage during a live rock show before. Who knew how completely awesome it would be? Not me. Now I was absolutely hooked.

It didn't hurt that Connor was positioned right in front of me the whole night. Being so close allowed me to study the big bass player without fear of being noticed. Boy, oh boy, I was smitten. This man was so unconventionally handsome yet understated. He wore shredded, skinny black jeans, a black tank, black boots. His tall, lean frame was perfection. Broad, defined shoulders. Biceps as big as my thigh. Actually, every one of his muscles were sculpted. Not from the gym, from hard work. He was absolutely luscious.

God, his face. His reddish-brown curls flowed long and loose across his strong forehead, revealing his piercing, light-brown eyes. His full lips were obscured a bit by his neatly trimmed beard. Cheekbones like blades sloping into a defined jawline.

Yes, all the guys in LTZ were prime male specimens, but I couldn't take my eyes off Connor.

The man oozed stability. Strength. Confidence. He wasn't aloof, he smiled occasionally and connected with the audience. Music flowed through him, but he wasn't showy. All substance. No hype. I was fascinated by how he silently communicated with Jace. Together, they controlled LTZ's pace.

Over the past twenty-four hours, all my preconceived notions of him had been squashed.

"It's your turn, Ronni!" Zane clapped his hands in front of my face, snapping me out of my daydream. "Truth or dare?"

I wasn't sure what I'd done to deserve having four overgrown LTZ band puppies holed up in my penthouse suite after the show, but here they were. I was loving every minute of it. "Truth."

A chorus of boos taunted me until Zane shushed them. "It's all good, don't listen to them."

Connor stifled a grin. His amber eyes sparkled when they caught mine. Which happened a lot.

"What did you think of our show? The new songs." Zane crossed his muscular arms over his chest. "Be honest."

Kris took a sip of her gin and tonic and winked at me. "Yes, be honest, Ronni."

I shot her a look and faced the LTZ guys. "Let me preface this by saying that I'm a little tipsy and I don't get out much."

Groans all around.

"Why do I feel like I'm not going to like this?" Ty shook out his gorgeous mane of dark-brown hair before reaching for another beer. "For the record, I felt off all night."

"I wonder why," Jace slurred. He was effortlessly sexy even though he was fall-down-wasted drunk. It was the first thing he'd said since they all invaded my room at two a.m. He'd spent most of the night furiously texting with someone and drinking really strong cocktails.

Connor held up a hand. "Lads, let her answer."

I took a deep breath. "You guys deserve all of the success you're having. The new songs are going to change your life. Ty, your voice—"

"Sucked tonight," he interrupted, swallowing a mouthful of beer. "Having Alex here threw me off my game."

Jace made himself another Jack and Coke. His fist pounded the counter before he toasted the room and slammed the entire drink down in one go. "She's fucking engaged."

Connor got up and joined Jace at the mini-bar and palmed his shoulder. The drummer shot him a weak smile, shook out his hands like he was shaking off his mood and fixed another drink. "Ronni, I didn't mean to interrupt. Finish what you were saying. For the record, Ty never thinks he has a good show."

"Okay. So—I say this as a performer myself, but it felt like you're still working the new songs into the set list. The crowd loved you, and truthfully? I loved the show. *Loved* it. You'll get it where you want it after a few gigs."

"You are a keeper." Zane put his arm around me. He was darling. Dark curls cascaded around his shoulders. His smile lit up the room. As gorgeous as the swarthy guitar player was, he was more like a little brother that I wanted to put in my pocket and take home with me than someone to kiss. "Your turn to choose."

I sproinged one of his curls and watched it bounce back in place. "Of course I choose you, Zane. Truth or dare?"

"She loves me," he mouthed to the others before bending his head toward my ear and loud whispering so everyone could hear. "Dare of course!"

Connor groaned, "Oh Jay-sus, Ronni. What have you done?"

"My dare is a hybrid." I laughed. "Zane, I need you to tell me a secret about each of your bandmates. Something that no one else knows you know."

"Done!" Zane rubbed his hands together gleefully. "Here's your scoop: The new album is about the girl who broke Ty's heart before we left on our first tour. That part everyone knows. The secret I know is he carried Zoey's engagement ring around with him for three years. Yesterday he threw it into Sydney Harbor. I think he's finally ready to move on."

Ty looked stricken. His knuckles turned white and I thought he'd crush his bottle of beer. Connor smiled at his bandmate. "Ah, Ty, my brother. It's a good thing to move on. At least you didn't get dumped for a lady."

"What?" I did a spit-take with the swallow of beer I'd just sipped.

Jace moved to the other side of Ty and draped his arm over his shoulder. "Yes, it's true. Connor dated my sister for a million years. Everyone thought they were the perfect couple until she showed up in Munich to tell him in person, she'd fallen for her best friend Becca."

Connor waggled his eyebrows at me and then at Ty, whose demeanor had softened. He even smiled a bit. Zane joined his band brothers and clinked his bottle to theirs. "In case you were wondering why our fine drummer—who usually holds his alcohol better than he's doing tonight by the way— is so wasted, Alex is Zoey's best friend. She and Jace secretly hook up sometimes even though it's not really a secret. Tonight, she showed up backstage with a Crocodile Dundee fiancé. Bailed mid-show."

Kris started laughing. Well, not just laughing. Hysterically laughing. It was catching. Soon I snickered and began giggling before succumbing to a full chortle. Jace fell next. Then Zane. Connor and Ty brought up the rear. All of us were rolling so hard we couldn't stop. When one of us recovered, we'd have a moment of peace. Invariably, someone would snort or snuffle, instigating a whole new round of belly-straining whinnies.

In the middle of our fit, I managed to spurt out, "Zane, what about you? What's your sad sack love story?"

Zane jumped onto the coffee table, whirled toward me with his arms held skyward and bellowed, "The woman I've been in love with since I was six years old is having a baby with the biggest douchebag on the planet!" He took a deep bow, jumped off the table and grabbed another beer.

"Fiona's pregnant?" Ty stopped mid laugh, his eyes wide. "Which douchebag?"

"Corey Johnson." Zane flung himself onto the sofa. "That dickhead from high school."

Ty scratched his stubble. "Whoa. Didn't see that one coming."

"Yeah." Zane sipped his beer and looked off into the distance before perking back up again. "Kris and Ronni haven't shared their shitty love stories. You know our secrets, tell us yours!"

I nervously glanced around the room. Aside from joining us in the laughing fit, Connor remained largely silent. Not aloof, he was definitely participating. More like he was a quiet, calming presence. The glue that held everything into place for this group. He nodded to me as if encouraging me to spill my beans. I opened my mouth to speak...

"I'm getting divorced." Kris held up her gin and tonic and toasted the room. "No drama. We're best friends. I just work too much and he wants to be with someone who isn't focused on her career."

"Oh, Kris!" In my inebriated state, I flung my arms around her, nearly knocking her over and spilling her drink all over her in the process.

"You've never said anything. I'm taking too much of your time! You should fly back and try to fix it!"

She clung to me tightly. "No, darling. It's been a long time coming. I'm at peace with it." Kris got up and wiped herself off and fixed another drink.

"God, love sucks." I finished my beer and slammed it down on the table. "Why does anyone ever want to fall in love, it's pointless!"

"Your story can't be that bad." Connor chuckled. "I mean, seriously. Did you hear all of our stories?"

"At least your humiliation wasn't on the cover of every tabloid." I looked directly at Connor when I told my tale of woe. "I thought I was living with the love of my life and planning a future together. Little did I know he'd committed to an arranged marriage and told his family that we were a fake couple used to generate publicity to promote the show."

Connor's eyes sparked but he didn't say anything.

"Even I didn't see that one coming." Kris tapped her pink-manicured finger against her glass. "Cowardly little bitch, that one."

Ty blinked at me. "Harsh."

"She's right." I crossed my arms over my deep v-cut dress. "That's why I have a foolproof plan to avoid getting my heart broken ever again by someone who isn't worthy."

"God, please tell me." Ty shook his head and laughed. "I need it."

"I'm a beard."

"What the hell's a beard?" Jace raised an eyebrow.

"Ronni likes to go to events with gay actors who are still in the closet." Kris rolled her eyes. "Somehow she thinks this is her solution. The guys don't get passed over for manly, heterosexual roles. She has fabulous-looking dates on the red carpet with no pressure."

Connor, who hadn't taken his eyes off me, raised his eyebrow quizzically.

"Shots!" Jace saved me by passing out tequila shooters. "Ty, I didn't make you one, obvi."

Ty swirled his finger in the air. "You know what? I'll do a shot. It's high time I let loose. Tonight has been one of the funnest nights I've had in a really long time."

"Fine by me." Jace poured another one and the six of us all clinked our glasses together and downed them.

Ty tapped his finger on his chin. "Hmm. This beard thing, does it work for dudes? Are there any beautiful lesbians that need a date?"

"Tyson, no way. You've got to rip the bandage off. Once you get naked with someone other than Zoey, you'll be fine." Zane gathered the glasses up and began to refill them. "I've banged so many people that I'm actually bored."

"People?" Kris stumbled. She was as drunk as me.

"Nothing wrong with exploring your sexuality." Zane handed out the shots. "I have no shame in my game."

"I miss sex," I sighed and downed my shot.

Connor, still mainly observing, waved off Zane's offered shot. His sexy, bowed lips tilted up into a grin at my comment.

"Me too." Ty slammed his tequila down. "I'm gonna do it."

Jace guffawed, "You're going to do 'the sex?' With who? Ronni?"

Ty flipped him off. My eyes must have been filled with panic because he strode over, plopped down next to me and took my hand. "Relax. You're a nice girl. There's no way I'm going to ever fuck anyone I like again. From now on, I'm all about the hate fuck."

As they'd done all night, my eyes flicked over to Connor. He was looking at the two of us, his jaw set. Still silent, but I saw him glance in disdain at my hand enclosed in Ty's. I stood to move away but my body wasn't cooperating. The last shot did me in.

Before I crashed in a heap to the ground, Connor scooped me up and whispered into my ear, "You're killing me, you know that, right?"

Whoa.

"Connor, can you be a honey and tuck her in?" Kris slurred. "I haven't been this drunk since college. You rock boys are a bad influence on me."

"I'll walk you to your room." Ty tucked her hand under his arm and grinned. "I promise I won't try anything."

Kris licked her lips. "If I wasn't still married…"

"I'm too heavy, put me down." I halfheartedly batted at Connor's arms, which were wrapped tightly around me.

"Light as a feather." Connor strode toward the bedroom. "Lads, straighten up before you go, yeah?"

My eyes felt super heavy. Connor's neck felt like the perfect place to burrow my head. "Wanna do the sex with me?" I licked his neck. He was so yummy.

"I'm not going to answer you right now. Fair warning, I won't be able to control myself if you do that again, love." Connor kicked open the bedroom door.

"Mmmm." I stroked Connor's soft hair. Looked up at him with my best seductive pout. "I *so* want to make you lose control."

The last thing I remember was Connor kissing my forehead and saying, "Ronni, you already do."

CHAPTER 15

She licked my neck.

She asked if I wanted to have sex with her.

She wanted me to lose control.

My dick was harder than it ever had been in my life. I could hear Jace and Zane cleaning up in the living room. Meanwhile, I sat stroking Ronni's hair, contemplating whether it would be creepy to slip into her bathroom and rub one out.

Yes, I decided. It would definitely be creepy.

Something about this woman undid me. God help me, she and Kris watched the show from stage right, which meant they were literally ten feet from me the entire time. I tried not to pay attention to them. I failed miserably. Ronni wore some sort of shimmery, black low-cut dress that showcased her fantastically voluptuous tits. Her curvy booty was also perfectly on display in the tight little number. High wedge sandals made her sleek legs look a mile long. Thick, red-brown hair cascaded around her shoulders in waves.

She was transcendent.

Kris insisted we come up to their suite after the VIP party. Ordinarily, if we had a stopover in a city, Ty would ditch us and hole up in his room. Jace, Zane, and I would probably find chicks to hook up with. This night was so different. Low-key and fun. Stress-free. We hadn't done something like that as a band in a long time. It was nice not to have to be "on" with people we didn't know.

Yeah. Hanging out with these two women was a welcome change.

Crossing to the other side of the bed, I pulled back the duvet and fluffed up the pillows. Returning to where Ronni lay sleeping, I carefully picked her up and tucked her under the covers, taking a minute to stroke her soft hair. Bending down, I breathed her in. Delicious. Lemons. Vanilla.

I wanted to lick her too, but I refrained.

I would never take advantage of her when she wasn't conscious. Besides, it didn't take a genius to figure out she was really vulnerable. She didn't come off like a broken bird. Not by a long shot. Ronni exuded self-confidence. Her wry sense of self-depreciating humor and blatant flirtatiousness was charming. Engaging. I could tell she was used to being famous, and also deft in the art of becoming invisible when she didn't want attention.

The thing is, a stunning young woman like Ronni didn't give up on falling in love because of one wanker. Something ran deep with her, but she held it close to her vest. Every part of me felt vehemently, fiercely protective of this woman whom I'd barely spoken to. Except, somehow it felt like I'd known her my whole life.

God, she was wicked smart. I'd overheard Ronni and Kris talk about their plans for a new production company. They were investing their own money to develop projects written and directed by women. Something about creating institutional wealth, whatever that meant. They had a very special relationship, that much was obvious. It gave me comfort knowing that Ronni had Kris to help her cope with the death of her mother.

There I went again in my head. Almost as though Ronni was mine to take care of. Scratch that, not even "almost." I *felt* like she was mine.

Now I had a dilemma.

Jay-sus. Ronni Miller was under my skin something fierce. I was leaving in a little more than twenty-four hours for a short tour in Asia before our new album was released. Followed by the usual shit-ton of press and publicity. We'd be on the road again for at least a year. More, if the album sold well. Projections indicated that it would.

I'd already lost one girlfriend because of the distance. It wouldn't be fair to start something up with someone new. Especially someone as well-known as Ronni. We'd be fodder for the press and trolls. Which would put even more pressure on us.

And that was if she meant it when she said she wanted me.

Shite. I was overthinking it.

I had to get a grip on myself.

The next day I slept in, taking advantage of a break in our schedule when I had the chance. Determined not to spend the day pining over the beautiful actress, I tried to convince Jace to join me in the gym. He declined with a resounding "fuck no." Undeterred, I threw on my workout gear and hit the free weights. Hard. I loved working out in hotels, the equipment was top notch and no one ever used it.

When I'd finished up two hours of reps, I indulged in a lengthy yoga and stretching routine. It was so rare for me to have an entire afternoon free—let alone by myself—I wanted to drag it out as long as possible. When the door clicked opened, I was annoyed. Set up in an L-shape, the gym's mat area was around the corner from the front door, so it was impossible for me to see who came in.

I could hear the treadmill start up and someone running. Peering around the corner, I saw a woman with her hair piled up on her head in some sort of messy bun. She wore skintight black workout pants with a pink stripe and a matching sports bra. Her tight, toned body was flying at a punishing pace. Impressive.

When the universe presents you with a golden opportunity, you take it. At least that's what I told myself when I strode out and smiled up at Ronni. So lost in her run, she didn't notice me at first. Then her eyes opened slowly. As though she felt my presence. The look on her face when she saw me?

Surprise.

Not that I was standing there. More like I was a wish come true.

Ronni punched the controls to stop the treadmill and popped out her earphones. "Connor, you scared me!"

"You're grand." I handed her a fresh bottle of water. "How do you feel, love? Did you remember to hydrate?"

She took it, blushing. "I'm sorry about—well. I was drunk last night."

"We all were. That was yesterday. I have only one question for you today."

She stared at me, mouth slightly open. Unsure of what to say.

"Didja mean it?"

Her blush deepened. "Mean what?"

I just winked.

She hopped off the treadmill, grabbed a towel and mopped her forehead. Swigged a bit of water. Warred with herself at what to say. Finally, she sucked in a deep breath. "Yes."

I stepped toward her. She gulped. Her green eyes bored into mine, questioning. Begging, maybe. I smoothed my palm against her cheek. Ronni leaned into my hand, wrapping her arms around herself as if she didn't trust herself not to touch me. My thumb found its way toward her plump lips. Traced them.

Every woman before Ronni evaporated in that instant.

There was only her. Had only ever been her.

I just hadn't known it.

Until now.

Caressing her bare arms, I unwound them and took both her hands in mine. Interlacing our fingers. Squeezing gently. Our eyes locked with each other. Conveying a myriad of the emotions running between us. Lust. Confusion. Respect. Fear. Hope.

"Connor..."

I pressed my lips to hers. Pulled her toward me by our clasped hands. Her little surprised squeak made me smile, especially when her lips opened for me. Our tongues touched and teased. Our lips nuzzled and explored. Kissing Ronni was a revelation. Our last time, although I remembered it fondly, was a dare. Aggressive and passionate. The promise of an amazing fuck. No depth.

This kiss?

A promise.

Of what life was meant to be.

RONNI

CHAPTER 16

The only word I could formulate after the greatest kiss in the history of all kisses, now or in the future, forever more, was, "whoa." Our lips reluctantly parted. My eyes were still squeezed closed. I gripped his hands tightly, nearly white-knuckled, to keep me upright. Our bodies were just close enough to feel each other's heat, but only our fused hands were touching.

"Open your eyes, love." Connor's lilt snapped me out of my trance. I obeyed. Slowly fluttering them open. Taking in the giant Celtic God across from me, raking his eyes across my face. "Now that was class."

"Class?"

Connor laughed. "It means amazing. Stupendous. The best. Class."

My heart fluttered. What had just passed between us was monumental. Once in a lifetime. Equally uncomfortable and intrigued, I couldn't look away from his penetrating gaze. Connor's intensity was magnetizing.

"Spend the rest of the day with me." Connor brought our clinched hands to his chest and rubbed my inner wrists with his thumbs. "Just us."

My heart sank. "I'm meeting Kris in an hour; we're supposed to explore the city."

"Let's send her out with Zane, she'll have a blast." Connor remained focused on us, keeping our connection.

"But—"

Connor brought my knuckles up to his lips and kissed each one. "Please, love. Take a chance."

An hour later, I was dressed in a casual Zara denim halter maxi dress and a pair of gold, sparkly Fit Flop thongs. My favorite comfortable low-rent outfit chosen from a sea of designer clothes Kris packed for me. Sure, I loved playing dress-up and all the glam that accompanied my profession. Today I was off the clock. The girl who came from simple roots. I didn't want Connor to think I was trying too hard.

Holy moly, every single neuron in my body was tingling and on high alert. Never in my life had I been so simultaneously excited and scared to death about spending time with someone. This felt big.

So big.

When Connor suggested that Zane would hang out with Kris, it didn't occur to me how he was going to pull it off. I mean, Zane was a few years younger than Connor, possibly even young enough to be Kris's kid. What the heck were they going to do? What was the band going to think about Connor and me spending time alone together? Had I gotten so used to being in fake relationships that when something real came along I'd forgotten how to act normally?

Skittish, I couldn't help but peek through the peephole to see when Connor would arrive. The third time I looked, Connor's big frame moved into view. He was about to knock on the door when I opened it before he had the chance. "Hey!" I quickly stepped outside of the room into the hallway. "Kris is still inside, so we should hurry."

"What? Why?" Connor put one hand on my shoulder to stop my momentum, the other kept the door from closing all the way.

Flustered, I dropped my card key. "I thought we were having a secret squirrel kind of day."

"No feckin' way." Connor spun me around and gestured to go back inside. "Ronni, I'm not the kind of man who hides in the shadows. Let's go and talk to Kris."

Almost on autopilot, I turned and reentered my suite. Connor was right behind me, his hand guiding me on my lower back. Once we crossed into the living area, which thankfully had been cleaned after last night's impromptu party, I didn't really know what to do. So, I stood there doing nothing.

Connor soothingly rubbed my back. "Is Kris here?"

I nodded. Realizing I was acting a little nuts, I found her in her room zipping up her boots. "Connor wants to take me out today."

"Oh, honey! That's fantastic." Kris smoothed her hair. "I think it's just what the doctor ordered."

"He's in the living room."

Kris was up and out the door in seconds with me following close behind. "Well hello, Connor. I hear you're stealing our girl away?"

"If you don't mind, Kris." Connor took my hand. "We leave for Japan tomorrow. I'll confess I'm a bit smitten with miss Ronni, so I couldn't let this opportunity pass me by."

Kris fluttered her hand by her heart. "My oh my, Veronica. The big guy is a keeper."

I was completely flummoxed. No one had ever really claimed me. Kip surely didn't. Everyone else I "dated" was a pure business transaction.

It kept me safe. My heart. And my body. My "loser in love, America's sweetheart" persona had been carefully curated. It worked for me. Allowed me to focus on acting. And hopefully, producing. In an instant, my flight instinct kicked in. "If you have other things to do with the band, Connor, I totally understand."

"Not at all, love." Connor squeezed my hand. "There's nothing I'd rather do than spend the day with you."

Swoon.

"You should go." Kris shooed us with both hands and winked. "In fact, don't come back until late. Really late. Better yet, tomorrow!"

"Are you sure?" She so eerily could read my mind. "I mean tomorrow we're going to do Mom's ceremony."

Kris wrapped our hands, which were still clasped together, in both of hers. "I'm not only sure, I insist. It's a promise I made to your mother. Remember what she said to you before she died. Don't wait to embrace all of the wonderful experiences that come into your life. Have a great time."

Connor's hint of a smile erased all my doubt. Today was a once-in-a-lifetime chance. I'd look back on this moment and regret it if I didn't take a leap of faith.

Connor's phone pinged with a text. "Zane. He's at the front door. Can I let him in?"

A few seconds later, Zane bounced in. Wearing a plain white t-shirt and jeans with his hair tucked up in a baseball hat, he bowed in front of Kris. "Milady, I request the pleasure of your company this fine day as we have both been ditched by our loved ones."

All of us laughed at the guitar player's silliness.

A few minutes later, Connor and I were strolling hand-in-hand toward Circular Quay like it was the most natural thing in the world. He'd tied his long hair into a ponytail. Black jeans. Black boots. Black T-shirt. I was beginning to see a pattern to his fashion choices. I loved it. While we were in line to board the ferry, he stood behind me and wrapped his arms around my waist, pulling me back against his chest. Like we were a couple. A real couple.

That, I didn't know what to do with.

"You're tense, am I being too forward with you?" Connor nuzzled the top of my head. He was easily six or seven inches taller than me. For the first time in my life, I felt small.

I looked up at him, his face was serious. Concerned. "I'm just not used to this."

He loosened his grip. "Used to what?"

I didn't answer because the line began moving and we boarded the ferry. We took a seat outside in the warm sun. The slight breeze blew my hair into my eyes. Connor smoothed it away, cupping my face. Looking at me like I was more interesting than the gorgeous scenery around us. "Used to what?" he repeated.

"I've never had this." I gestured between us. "Not like this."

His eyebrows furrowed then softened. He kissed my forehead. "Me either."

Connor draped his muscular arm around me and I nestled into his side. He rested his chin on the top of my head. It wasn't long before we were pulling into Darling Harbour on the other side of the city.

"I thought we could grab something to eat. You don't get this figure easily." He patted his hard, flat stomach and held out his hand.

Placing my hand in his felt like the most natural thing in the world. "Sure."

A few minutes later, we were seated outside at Adobe Bistro. Connor ordered a burger with extra fries and a salad. I stuck with just the salad. I felt awkward. I realized I'd really never actually gone out to eat without some event attached to it. Of course, I'd been out to meals with my fake boyfriends. Kip and I had been out at a ton of events, some of which included dining out. How was it so that until this very moment, I'd never actually been sitting across from someone on a date having to make conversation?

I'd lived a weird life, that's why.

Connor seemed perfectly at ease. Like this was old hat. I wondered about the women in his life. Whom he'd loved. Who had loved him. It made me feel crazy because the thought of this man with anyone else was agonizing. I wanted him to be mine. Only mine. Which was incredibly stupid. He was leaving for a long tour with his band in the morning.

"I loved hearing about your mom on the plane." Connor leaned back in his chair. "You had such a special bond."

Ah, Mable. Surprisingly, I didn't get a pang in my heart when he brought her up. Talking about my mother with Connor was, well— Natural. "She was one in a million."

"Tell me more about your special plan to honor her."

"Oh. Well. Kris and I have come up with our own little ceremony. Tomorrow, we are going to bring her with us to all of Sydney's sights and take pictures. Then we'll do the same in Melbourne and again at the Great Barrier Reef. Kris obtained permission from a few of the local councils to scatter a bit of Mom in all of the locations. We'll play her favorite music, watch her favorite films, and celebrate everything about her."

Connor took my hand across the table. "That sounds lovely, so it does."

Every now and then, I'd hear a bit of Irish lilt in his voice. It made my female parts tingle. A lot.

When the food arrived, Connor wolfed his meal down in moments.

I was so used to my daily calorie intake limitation, I only picked at my salad. The beers and cocktails from the night before had blown up my diet. I'd put on two pounds in two days.

Connor glanced at his empty plate and then at my full salad bowl. "Good God, what am I like? Can you tell I've been around guys all of my life? Eating is like survival of the fittest. Do you not like your salad? Do you want something else?"

"No, I'm just not super hungry," I lied.

Connor raised an eyebrow.

"I mean, I'm on camera for a living. I'm a big girl with a bad metabolism, so I always need to watch my weight." I heard myself babbling. "It's the nature of my job."

Connor's intense gaze penetrated my soul. "You're magnificent. About as far away from a big girl as there is."

"That's because I literally watch everything I eat." It slipped out before I could stop it.

He just nodded. Accepted what I said without judgment. Filed it away somewhere. "I'll get the bill and we can take a walk?"

For the next few hours, we strolled through Sydney. Talked. Laughed. He told me about his big family and his dad's construction company. I shared some funny stories about filming *She's All That*. Being with Connor was easy. Effortless. He kept things light. Fun. No matter what we were doing, he touched me. Held my hand. Put his arm around me. Brushed errant hair out of my face. I felt comfortable. Relaxed.

Also? Horny as hell.

His effortless masculinity was intoxicating.

"I've never met anyone like you." I played with his fingers as we sat on a bench overlooking the Sydney Opera House. "I feel like everyone thinks they know me. Or has some preconceived notion of me. Today's the first time I can remember just being me in a long, long time."

"Ronni, I'm not going to lie." Connor pulled me onto his lap and wrapped his arms around me. "I'm feeling something for you that is pretty overwhelming. I'm not quite sure what to do, because I want you desperately. The truth is, I'm leaving on tour again. Our new album is supposed to blow up and there's no telling what that means for my band."

My heart sank. This is where he became like every other man. Priming me for disappointment. Ugh.

"When we went on the road the first time, I was in what I thought was a permanent relationship." Connor stroked my hair. "I was with Jace's sister for many years. She helped with the family business when I left."

"Is this the girlfriend that left you for another woman?"

"Aye."

"Is this when you tell me you think I'm great but…"

Connor pressed his finger to my lips. "Shh. This is where I tell you I'm full-blown over the feckin' moon for you. This is where I tell you that I want to be inside you right now more than anything in this entire world. What is happening between us is unlike anything I ever have felt before."

I could feel my heart pounding like a drum. Knowing that what he was saying wasn't a line. Knowing that this man was the real deal. I reached up and cupped his face. He leaned into my hand, much like I'd done earlier in the day. "I've never met anyone like you, Connor McGloughlin. I'm in way over my head."

"We both are, love."

"So, what do we do?" I nuzzled his neck.

Connor tightened his arms around me. I could feel his hard length pressing against my thigh. "Will you let me make love to you tonight?"

I didn't want to be just one more notch in his belt. The odds were already against us developing anything meaningful. I was halfway in love with him after only forty-eight hours. Intellectually, I knew I was in a vulnerable state. I'd just lost my mom. If we had sex and he disappeared from my life it would devastate me.

"What if I told you I wasn't ready?" I whispered.

Connor didn't say anything, just kissed my temple. He never spoke a word he didn't think about first. That he didn't mean. "I'd tell you that I'm not ready either. Once I have you, Veronica Mae Miller, and make no mistake—I will have you, that will be it. For damn sure I will never let you go."

CHAPTER 17
SIX MONTHS LATER

For six months I'd had second, third, fourth, and fifth thoughts about leaving Australia without getting naked with Ronni. Mainly because since then it was all I thought about day in and day out. Wondering if her nipples were rosy pink. Or cocoa brown. Did she shave or wax. Landing strip or bare. Or, holy mother of god, was she au natural.

Jay-sus. My dick was hard all the time imagining everything about her. Even when on stage, my mind wandered to her dancing to the side of me in that low-cut dress. During downtime I clung to memories about our date. How the corners of her eyes crinkled when she laughed. The way her lush lips felt against mine. The phantom feeling of her perfect body pressed against me. A waft of lemon. Or vanilla. Any one of these memories meant an instant boner that threatened to drill its way out of my jeans.

Let me tell you, Veronica Mae Miller had ahold of me in a way I'd never experienced in my life. It didn't help when the source of my sexual frustration was on the cover of every magazine with a wanker named Kendall Phillips.

I mean, c'mon. What kind of name is Kendall for a dude?

Obsession aside, it wasn't like we'd made any promises in Sydney. The reality was we wouldn't be in the same city for a while. And then, only for a day or two. On my side, LTZ commitments were exploding because our album was not only at number one, the song *Down* was turning into a breakout smash. Ronni, on the other hand, had a grueling filming schedule for *She's All That* in Los Angeles.

It was time for me to face reality. There was no doubt we'd had a tremendous time together in Australia. Since then, the time difference had been a serious buzzkill of the high I'd felt after our date. Sure, we'd texted often, FaceTimed every now and then and even sent each other a few pictures. None of which meant we had anything true. Or meaningful. Well, a friendship, maybe.

The thing is, I'd been there, done that with Jen, and look where that got me.

Except with Ronni, I ached to hear her voice. To see her face.

It was the type of longing that lingered and wove its way through every organ in my body.

I had a few days to think about it at home in Seattle. We had a short break before our gargantuan new tour kicked off in Los Angeles. I pinged Ronni when we landed, hoping she'd give me reason to fly down early. I was in a car on my way to my folks' house when my phone buzzed. Delighted, I punched the button to accept her video call.

I wasn't prepared to see her rumpled hair against a mountain of pillows. She peeked out from under an expensive-looking cream comforter. Still in bed. Jay-sus. She was magnificent. Sexy. Her green eyes blinked at me through the screen. "You're back," she said with a giggle.

My duplicitous cock engorged painfully at the sound of her sweet voice. "That I am, love. You look so beautiful." My sentiment might have seemed trite. Uninspired, even. Yet, it was the simple truth.

Ronni rolled her eyes. "Filming went until midnight last night. I just woke up; there's not one chance in hell that I'm beautiful right now."

She was so very wrong. I couldn't take my eyes off her. "I'd be a lucky man to wake up to you like that every day."

"Connor McGloughlin, if you're going to feed me cheesy line after cheesy line, then I'm going to hang up right now." Ronni wagged her finger at me.

I chuckled at my little ball-buster. "Fine, no cheesiness, love."

Ronni held the phone higher and gave me a pout. "Oh, Con. It's been over a week since we've talked. I've missed you."

"If you're serious about missing me, I can pop down early to see you." I relaxed back against the soft, black leather seats of the Town Car. "I just have a few things to take care of in Seattle before the US leg of the tour."

"So mysterious. What do you have to take care of?" Ronni shifted so she was on her side, her shiny reddish-brown hair cascaded over her bare shoulder.

"Ah, nothing that interesting. Just a few things with my family's construction company."

"Okay. Vague much?" Ronni teased.

In deflecting, my tone came out evasive. "Mae, it's not a big deal. I don't want to get into it right now."

She winced for a split second before flashing a practiced smile, which didn't quite reach her eyes. "Um, okay. Closed topic."

Shite. What did I have to hide, anyway? "Ah, love. Don't take it that way. I'm tired from the flight and it's... Well, it's a sore subject for me. It has nothing to do with you."

Ronni glanced away from the screen and looked out her bedroom window then back at me. "Okay. Sure, I get it."

Suddenly, the tension through the phone was palpable. I'd fucked up. I wasn't trying to be a dick. It's just that we were a world apart. On a video call. Not ideal to have heartfelt and intimate conversations. I squinted into the screen. Debating how much to tell her. Being raised Irish instilled a distinct code of privacy. Keeping family business in the family and all.

That being said, if I wanted a chance with this woman, I had to suck it up. It was up to me to gain her trust. "It's hard for me to talk about it, Mae. A lot of shite went down in my family after my da was hurt in a car accident years ago."

Her face softened. "Con, I really wasn't trying to pry into your personal life. You can tell me anything. Or nothing. It's up to you."

I swallowed. Didn't know what to say or how to say it. I prided myself on being a strong man. An honest man. This woman had me tongue tied. The last thing I wanted to do was scare her away.

"I know!" Ronni's smile lit up the screen. "Let's skip all of the boring family drama and get to the good stuff. Am I getting a VIP pass to your show at the Staples Center? It sold out. My agent can't even get a ticket."

My blood pressure immediately regulated. Relieved at the reprieve, this was a topic that was much easier. "You can come to any show you want in any city in the world as my special guest, love."

"Kris too?"

"Of course." I beamed into the phone. "But not that bollocks, Kennedy Phillips."

Ronni stuck out her tongue. "It's Kendall. You know that. And you know he's gay."

"Doesn't mean I like it."

She threw back her head and laughed. "Oh, is the big, strong manly man Connor McGloughlin *jealous* of my gay boyfriend?"

I fixed her with my most menacing glare, one that worked on every rat bastard in the poker halls I'd had to drag my father out of. "I. Don't. Like. It."

"Connor, we're not a couple. You don't get to judge me." Ronni narrowed her eyes. "I've been fighting to have a career on my own terms since I was fifteen years old. Trust me. When I tell you I know what I'm doing? I know what I'm doing. If we're going to be anything to each other, you better respect that."

Whoa. Feisty girl. I wasn't going to win this argument, at least not at this stage. She was pointing out the obvious. I'd overstepped. *Remember, Connor. She's not your girlfriend.* "Okay. Fair enough."

"Okay?" Ronni sounded surprised that I'd acquiesced.

"Look, I'll lay my cards on the table. I haven't been with anyone since our date in Sydney. That's because I'm interested in you, Veronica Mae Miller." No matter what shite life threw at me, even after watching my father's downfall, I knew who I wanted to be as a person. Until I either got the green-light or the heave-ho, there was no way I'd fuck someone else after our date in Sydney. Ronni was too special. A unicorn among women. I couldn't risk losing my chance, however slim it was, with her.

In other words, I ruled my dick, my dick didn't rule me.

"Oh. Wow." Ronni stared at me with wide aqua-green eyes. "I didn't realize. I guess I just thought..."

"You thought wrong." I winked at her. "Now, love. My car is about two minutes away from the house. I need a few days to finish up my business here. Do you want me to come down early, or no?"

"Yes!" Ronni kissed into the camera. "You can stay at my house."

"Your bed?"

"Hold your horses, studly." She wagged her finger at the camera. "I haven't made up my mind yet."

The car pulled up to my folks' Capitol Hill home. I flipped the phone to show her the three-story, sage-green craftsman before turning it back to me. "I'm here."

"What a gorgeous house," Ronni gushed. "Is that where you live?"

"Aye."

"Ping me later?"

"Aye."

Coming back to Seattle was always bittersweet. When I was away, it was easier to avoid some of the lingering problems my folks were still having. On the other hand, while I was at home it was never long enough to fix what had been broken for a decade. Taking a deep breath, I used my key and opened up the front door.

"Hey!" My youngest brother Seamus looked up from the book he was reading from his vantage point on the grand staircase.

Throwing my bags down, I sat next to him and hugged him tightly. "You're almost as big as me. Jay-sus."

Seamus shrugged. Like me he was a man of few words. "Aye."

We both stood, he gestured for me to follow him. The house looked stunning. In the dining room, all the hundred-year-old, built-in cabinetry had been completely refurbished. The mahogany inlay hardwood floors gleamed. I could smell something delicious cooking. I followed Seamus through the dining room into the kitchen where Brennan stood slicing a loaf of fresh soda bread. My ma was stirring something on the stove.

"Connor." Ma rushed to me, tears in her eyes. "You're a sight for sore eyes. I'm making your favorite Irish stew."

"Ah, Ma. You didn't need to go to the trouble." She looked frail. Her hair was now fully gray and tied back in a bun. I hugged her tightly.

Taking my cheeks in her hands, she looked up at me. "Not. At. All."

"There you are, ye cunt ye." My brother Liam bear-hugged me from behind. His twin Padraig stood to the side, his blue eyes glinting. God, had it really been three years since my brothers and I had been in the same house? I'd been so anxious to get out of Seattle and away from McGloughlin Construction that I rarely came home. And then only to check on the business. Visiting my family wasn't high on my priority list anymore.

Somehow the energy was different. It felt right to be here. The four of us joined Seamus and Cillian in the living room. We commenced talking all at once about everything and nothing at all, falling right back into a routine that I missed. Because of the utter hell I'd lived through, I'd truly forgotten there were good times with my brothers. And now Cillian was old enough to help Da. Seamus and Brennan were on the college track. The twins were attempting to follow in my footsteps and pursue music. "Guys, the demos are feckin' brilliant, so they are. I'll send them to management and see if your band can open for us when the tour hits Seattle."

"No shite?" Padraig shook his head. "That would be amazing."

Out of the corner of my eye, I saw da leaning against the archway between the kitchen and the dining room watching us. His hair was neatly combed. He looked fit. Healthy. More importantly, sober.

"Da."

"Connor."

We hadn't spoken in a year. Our last interaction nearly ended our relationship, at least as far as I was concerned. I wanted him to take the business back over but couldn't let it happen because he'd started drinking again. A year ago, I gave him an ultimatum. Rehab or I was selling the company.

He chose rehab.

Meanwhile, Cillian graduated from high school and offered to step in. At first, just to keep an eye on things. Except, my brother absolutely loved the business and put his whole heart and soul into it. Now, Da who had been sober for a year, ran the company with his middle son. It was flourishing once again.

It was time. Before I left for Los Angeles, Da would have McGloughlin Construction back. He and Cillian could sort it out from there.

"You look well." I nodded to him.

He moved toward me and held out his hand. I stood and took it. He pulled me to him and we awkwardly hugged. "Welcome home, son. I'm so proud of you."

My brothers all looked at the two of us expectantly. Seamus jumped up and patted my arm. "Da hasn't slipped all year. Business is good. He's been fixing up the house."

I looked around, noticing more of the work that had been done. "It looks grand, so it does."

Da beamed at me. A lump formed in my throat. I hadn't seen his eyes clear for ten years. Unexpectedly, my mind wandered to Ronni. I felt awful she would never have another opportunity to have dinner with her mom. Grateful that Da was seemingly healthy, I realized that time healed all wounds.

"Hawks?" Brennan clicked on the television just in time to see the kickoff for the Seahawks game. Ma brought us each steaming bowls of Irish stew and a basket of the freshly sliced soda bread. I had a wonderful evening with my family eating delicious food watching Russell Wilson and the Legion of Boom crush the 49ers.

Looking around the room at the McGloughlins cheering on our

football team, I felt happy. Despite the fact I'd soon be back out on tour for God knows how long, I had my family back. Something I'd never take for granted again.

CHAPTER 18

I was beginning to panic.

How in the hell had I built up some fantasy that Connor McGloughlin— the bass player for friggin' LTZ— and I were soul mates?

Did I really believe the second we laid eyes on each other birds would flutter around our heads? Hearts would pop out of our eyes?

We didn't *really* know each other. Sure, when our lips touched it was like electric ice cream. The zappiest zing and the creamiest deliciousness. As bazonga as he made me feel, we weren't a couple. We were basically nothing and I was acting like a snoopy girlfriend. Even though I had no desire to have a real boyfriend, I'd been thinking of him literally every single second since he'd left me in Sydney. It didn't mean he had the same obsession.

I'd be loath to forget that Connor McGloughlin was a six-foot-six, mammoth hunk of a silver-tongued devil rock star. He likely had women like me in every major city around the world.

Except, he told me he didn't.

Should I believe him?

And, not to toot my own horn or anything, wasn't I his equal? It's not like I was some groupie. My fan base was probably as big as his was.

So, could it be possible that he was as nervous as I? Argh! I didn't know what to do with these huge feelings. I'd been trying to play it so cool over these past months of long-distance communications.

In reality, I was a goner.

As much as I tried to deny it, after Australia, my heart already belonged to him.

Now, I was just another lovesick girl counting down the days until the guy I had a crush on found time to see me. For two or three days.

Then he'd be gone for who knows how long. Months. Years?

Arrrrgh.

Good God. I was late. The studio car was scheduled to pick me up in fifteen minutes. Dragging myself out of bed, I shuffled to my closet and pulled out my black Chanel track suit. I'd shower and get glammed up on the set. Minutes later, I heard the car service honking at my front gate, so I hustled out the door and settled in for the ride to the studio.

I took out my phone to check email and download any last-minute changes to the script. When I saw my inbox, all my breath whooshed from my lungs. At the top was an email from Connor. My heart tried to claw its way out of my throat. It took me easily five minutes to get the courage to open it.

1:55 a.m.
To: vmm@vmm.com

From: connorm@ltz.com
Subject: I'm sorry.

Mae,

I'm sorry I was so evasive on our call earlier. I'm also sorry I didn't call you back right away. It's about 1 a.m., I just had a tremendous night with my brothers watching the Seahawks and eating a gorgeous meal cooked by my ma.

It was the first time I'd spent with my folks and my brothers in nearly a decade without any tension or stress. Tonight, when I looked around at my family, I thought of you and your mom. I'm truly sorry that you lost her at such a young age. I hope that I expressed that to you properly in Oz.

So about earlier, I'm not comfortable with long, drawn out conversations about myself. I'm usually of the mindset that what's done is done. Life is for living, and all that. Why dwell on the past?

Mae, something about you makes me want to let you in. I'm not even sure why. I just know that there is something between us. Something that matters. I decided that it would be easier if I just wrote you and trust you won't run screaming. I'll dive in.

In Australia, I told you about my folks and how they immigrated to Seattle from Northern Ireland. I bored you with stories about Da's construction business. You know about my load of brothers.

I told you a bit about Da and me butting heads about his plans for me to take over the business and how I ran it when he had his accident.

Except, what I haven't gotten into is my complicated relationship with my da, and how I've stayed away from my family for the past three years because of it. When you and I spent the day together in Sydney, I kept thinking about how you won't get to have time with your mother ever again. Ever since that day, I've been trying to figure out how to fit into my family again.

It's so hard to talk about. So hard to put a voice to how I feel. I'm not a songwriter like Ty or Zane. For me, the words get jumbled up in my head and it's sometimes easier to just ignore.

So you see, Mae, coming back home to Seattle brings up a lot of emotions. I'm still angry at my Da, but I love him and feel bad that he was dealt a shite hand in the prime of his life.

I downplayed what happened after my Da's accident. In reality, I dropped out of high school and got my GED in order to take over the business. Da was out of commission, and we didn't know how long his recovery would be. Despite our differences, it was an easy decision. Family is everything. I wanted my brothers to finish school and have a normal life. I didn't mind at first, truly. For all of our head-butting, it was a no-brainer.

Da struggled, though. Drowned himself in whiskey. Gambled the company money away. For eight years, I tried to keep things running—and I managed barely—but it wore away at me. My days were spent running jobs and bidding on new ones, my nights were spent driving around Seattle and pulling Da out of bars. When it escalated into back-alley poker games, I learned poker to win the money he lost back.

Eventually, I had to keep everything in my name to protect my family from his descent into destruction.

Joining LTZ saved me. Saved my sanity. It allowed me to stop being codependent with my alcoholic father. Never in my wildest dreams did I imagine how successful the band was going to become. I left on our first tour thinking I'd be gone for six months, but didn't come home for two years.

As I mentioned, I've avoided interacting with my family. I felt resentful for so long. I didn't want to fight. Or apologize. I just needed space.

So right when you called, I was mentally preparing myself for more of the same-old, same-old. Truthfully, I didn't know what I was walking into. This time, I'm happy to report, spending time with my family has been really nice. Da is doing well. So is my mother. My brothers are all bollockses but I love them.

Anyway, I don't mean to ramble, but I wanted to apologize. And let you know what was up.

My gorgeous girl, it's nearly 2 a.m. and I'm knackered.

I still want to come down a couple days early to see you, if that's okay. It will give us a couple of weeks to spend together before we leave. Call me tomorrow.

xo C

I read and reread his email at least twenty times. Picturing a young Connor facing such a tragedy. At roughly the same age as when I started filming my first series. We had a shocking amount in common. He wasn't some pampered rock star. No wonder he seemed so stable. Grounded.

He'd grown up too soon.

Like me.

Adrenaline coursed through my veins.

This man was under my skin. Flowing through my blood.

He'd taken the first baby step into relationship territory. For all my earlier grump-a-lumps, was I really willing to open up to him, though? I had secrets that would make his skin crawl. Secrets that no one on this earth knew about.

I had a choice.

Be brave enough to meet him halfway?

Or run screaming in the opposite direction.

CHAPTER 19

I spent a good part of the next morning jamming with the twins. So many years had gone by and it felt feckin' amazing. Their band, Fireball, was starting to gain a real following and I was determined to try to help them anyway I could. After we were done, I made a few calls.

The rest of my day consisted of various errands with my wee brother Seamus. By the time we made it back home, it was mid-afternoon and still no word from Ronni.

Bollocks. I probably scared her off unloading my shite on her.

Determined to take my mind off of her, I began sorting through my stuff up in my room. It was time to get rid of a ton of old crap I'd accumulated. Not that I was moving or anything. I mean, at some point, I'd purchase my own house. All the other guys had already bought something. For me, it was hard to commit to Seattle. Sure, it was my hometown and all, but I wasn't sure if it was where I wanted to settle down permanently when we were off the road.

At least that's what I was telling myself.

My phone buzzed in my pocket while I was in the middle of packing up boxes with old clothes I'd never wear again. Figuring it was one of my bandmates, I let it go to voicemail. I wanted one entire day off from them.

Just one.

When I checked my messages an hour later, my heart raced. The call I'd missed was from Ronni.

Immediately, I FaceTimed her and couldn't keep the ear-splitting grin contained when her sweet face filled my screen. "Mae! I missed your call, love."

Her mega-watt smile was breathtaking. "Oh, Connor. Thank you for your email. It meant so much that you shared a bit of yourself with me. I don't talk about my life much either. I don't have many friends, except for Kris. I've been burned. By costars. Bosses. This business. So I keep my circle tight. Call it self-preservation or whatever."

"Ah, I hate to hear that. I get it though. More now that the band is getting well-known. There's a lot of fake-ass shite." I leaned back on my childhood bed to relax into our video chat.

"Is that a picture of you?" Ronni held her finger up to the phone.

I turned my head and grimaced. "Jay-sus. Aye. It's me in my football uniform."

"You're adorable."

I laughed. "You're calling a six-foot-six man adorable?"

"I call it like I see it. You're my adorably gentle giant, Con." Ronni batted her eyelashes dramatically. "But, seriously, thank you for that note. I've said it before, but I'll say it again. That night when you guys came back to my suite after your show, I had one of the best nights of my life. It was the first time I'd let loose in forever. And our date was the most normal I've felt since I was fifteen."

I got lost in the conversation because it was effortless. Over the course of an hour I learned why she got into acting (Lizzie McGuire obsession), about her dad (killed in Iraq, she never knew him or his family) and how her mother scrimped and saved for Ronni's acting, dancing and singing lessons.

She had dozens of questions about the band, which I answered. It was fun to share stories of our first tour, where we were crammed into a tour bus with our entire road crew. After living out of a bunk for going on four years, it was easy to forget how weird the bus rituals were until you explained.

"So, you weren't allowed to poop on the bus?" Ronni's eyes were wide. "Where did you go?"

"Rest stops. The restrooms at the venue." I couldn't help but laugh. "With ten stinky men crammed together, believe me, it's a good rule."

Ronni cocked her head, "I guess it's similar to being on set except the opposite. You only poop in your own trailer."

"Are we still talking about shite?" I made a stink face.

"Connor." Ronni's face grew serious. "Don't you know? All roads lead to poo."

She got me good. I couldn't stop laughing. In fact, I couldn't remember laughing so hard with someone in my life. I had an idea and hoisted myself off the bed to head into the twins' room. "I've got something to show you, Mae."

"Please don't say the toilet."

"Well, it is a *lovely* toilet."

"Connor!"

I opened the door to the bedroom where a sexy surfing poster of Ronni from *Hawaiian High* was still affixed to the wall. Gleefully, I reversed the screen on my phone so she could see it. "So, I totally forgot about the fact that my younger brother still has this poster up. Imagine my surprise to connect the dots when I got home."

When I flipped the phone back around, something in Ronni's expression chilled me to the bone. She recovered quickly and smiled and laughed, but there was a sadness behind her eyes. "Ah, Mae. I was just teasing you about the poster."

"It's fine, that particular set doesn't have too many fond memories."

"Oh?"

"Yeah." Her smile was forced. "It was a very toxic environment. I was body-shamed every day. The people in power were horrible. My costar committed suicide. The whole experience nearly made me quit acting. So—"

Bollocks.

"I didn't know any of that," I sighed and retreated from my brother's room. "I'm sorry I brought it up. I don't want to do anything that will stir up bad memories. I want to make you feel good. Happy."

She waved me off. "Oh, I've had tons of therapy. I'm fine now. Great, really. Kris rediscovered me, and as you know she's been like the big sister I never had. My current show is a very welcoming and healthy place to be."

"I'm glad." I smiled, unsure of what to say to her. I had an inkling there was more to the story, which would be better discussed in person.

"You are a good man. Such a good man." Ronni made a kissy-face into the phone. "Thank you for caring."

"I do care, Mae."

We stared into the phone at each other. Her beautiful hair cascaded across her shoulders. Her green eyes shone. We were having a moment. Something was passing between us. Like we understood each other on some level that neither of us had experienced before. My feelings for Veronica Mae Miller were overwhelming. I wanted to run away from her as much as I wanted to run to her.

Ronni broke the spell. "I care too, Connor. I'm really looking forward to our visit."

"Well, you're in luck then, love." I returned to my room and resumed lounging on my childhood bed. "Alaska Air Flight 1202 on Saturday. I get in about 2:30."

"Wow, it's official. This is really happening." Ronni blushed.

"Aye."

She playfully pulled back the phone and fanned herself and began talking in a perfect Southern Charm accent. "My, my, Connor McGloughlin. You know how to make a girl swoon. I'm soooo glad you booked your flight. My heart is pitter pattering at the thought of seeing you."

"Your accent is flawless, I'm impressed."

"Well, it is my job." Ronni flipped the screen around revealing a large, expansive patio right on the edge of the Pacific Ocean and then flipped it back. "Hopefully that gives you even more incentive."

"Holy bejeezus, that's some view."

"I know, I love living on the water." She was on the move; her face was moving in and out of camera.

"Ah, Mae. I've got to go. Ma's calling us down for dinner."

She stopped to peer into the screen, her hair was blowing around her face. "I really am excited to see you. And nervous."

"Don't be. We'll be grand."

We said our goodbyes and I headed down to the living room, settling back on the new sage-green Restoration Hardware custom couch in my folks' living room. I couldn't help but feel moony about Ronni. Every time we spoke, that girl burrowed her way even deeper into my heart. Getting to know each other long-distance was unconventional. But real. This wasn't about being a rock star and famous actress. It was about Connor and Veronica.

Who we were.

How we came to be here.

"Connor, we're eating in the dining room," Ma called from the kitchen, interrupting my train of thought.

As I joined them, I reflected on the past couple of days. It felt wonderful to be reconnected with my family. Like it used to be before Da and I started fighting in high school about me joining the family business. Hopefully, Da would stay on the straight and narrow.

Ma made a Christmas-size feast for my last night at home. Turkey, ham, roasties, green beans, fresh bread. The whole she-bang.

"Ma, this is amazing. Thank you for cooking for me." I kissed her cheek and sat down. "It's been ages since I've had proper, home-cooked meals."

Brennan sat next to me. "I won't be able to make the show in LA after all. I've got a research project due."

"Ah, you're grand." I handed the bowl of colcannon to Padraig. "By the way, looks like my request for Fireball to open for us when we play Key Arena is going to be granted."

Liam socked Padraig in the arm. "No shite! That's feckin' amazin'."

"Not. At. All." I couldn't help but smile.

"I've got something to say, now that my sons are all home for the first time in ages." Da looked around the table and regarded each of us with watery eyes. "I'm proud of all of you, I don't say it enough. I'm sorry for all of the trouble I've put this family through, so I am."

His sentiment choked me up a bit. Da hadn't ever been loose with apologies. Or overly expressive with his emotions. Well, other than drunken rage. It felt good. "Ah, Da."

"Maureen, will ye bring me that envelope?" Da gestured to Ma. She smiled and reached behind her where a large manila envelope rested on the banquet. Da took it from her and handed it to me.

"What's this?" I took it and opened it. Inside was a deed. "Seriously, Da?"

"It's proper order. You put your life on hold for us for nearly a decade." Ma's eyes welled up with tears. "Without your support, we'd have lost everything, Connor. We can't ever repay you, but we wanted to do something for each of our boys. With Jen's help, we built eight townhomes on Beacon Hill. One for each of our boys. We're selling the other two and retiring. Cillian is taking over the company, so when we do the paperwork tomorrow, I'll have you transfer it to him."

I looked around the table. All my brothers were waiting for my reaction. I didn't need the real estate. Or the money. What I did need to do was graciously accept the gift. "Thank you, Ma. Da."

Life with my family had come full circle. I had closure. At nearly twenty-eight years of age, I felt ready to focus on just myself for the first time in my entire adult life.

First thing on my list was to convince Veronica Mae Miller that we belonged together.

Once she was officially mine, the entire world was going to know about it.

RONNI

CHAPTER 20

It was hard to concentrate on set knowing Connor was en route to Los Angeles. I could barely contain my excitement and had to physically restrain myself from gushing about him to everyone.

He was my own special secret.

Nearly every day since Australia, I'd chastised myself for passing up the opportunity to be with Connor. And tonight, I'd finally be in his arms again. My thighs were clenching together just from *thinking* about seeing him naked. When it actually happened? I might spontaneously combust. My sex drive was revived and on overload. It had been nearly two years since Kip, after all.

Aside from wanting to climb him like a tree, this man made me feel safe. Protected. Even though we'd been continents apart for the past few months, I felt like I really knew him. At least I hoped I did. One thing was for sure, Connor knew more about the real me than anyone.

He didn't know everything, of course.

I wouldn't want him to think less of me.

Some secrets were meant to be taken to the grave. Mine fell into that category. Part of me felt guilty. He'd opened up to me in a way I hadn't expected. Learning about his past with his family and what he'd done for them made me respect the hell out of him. The other part of me was happy to keep the past in the past. Why screw things up with Connor?

His pursuit of me was too delicious.

And overwhelming.

It was like he was staking his claim.

The thing is? As excited as I was to see him, I was worried about measuring up. Over the past few months, we'd talked a lot about our past long-term relationships. He knew that despite being with Kip for so long, I wasn't very experienced sexually. There were things Kip wouldn't do to me and wouldn't let me do to him. As for Connor, after Jen, he'd gone a little nuts living the rock star life. He told me their relationship was more platonic than romantic, which made sense because she was with a woman now. I liked that we were very open in our communication about sex, so I wasn't sure why I felt nervous.

Okay, that was a lie.

He claimed he'd been celibate since Australia.

Since our date.

That's why.

I mean, until Connor kissed me. First in Europe then in Sydney. I honestly didn't think I'd ever want to have sex again. Our date changed my mind about relationships. I wanted Connor. He was a real man. Clearly, a very sexual man. So far out of my league. At least I knew with him, I'd finally figure out what all the fuss was about.

Glancing at some movement across the room, I spotted Kris walking on set to talk to the studio audience. My scene was starting soon. I had to get myself together. Thinking about sex with Connor was too distracting. Repeating my daily mantra, I visualized the blocking. The lines. My performance. It made me feel grounded.

I had the power to control my own life. There was no need for me to worry about living up to Connor's expectations. Because there was a more important question at stake:

Would Connor live up to mine?

Until I knew that for sure, I wasn't about to fall in love with him. Not when he was going to be on tour for God knows how long. Surely, he wouldn't—couldn't— remain faithful to me over the long-haul.

God. I had to stop getting ahead of myself. My mind was spinning in circles. We'd been on *one* date. A few phone calls. My hard, cold reality was Connor was coming down early for an extended booty call, pure and simple. I'd be wise if I treated this visit for what it was. Like every other twenty-something woman on the planet. I'd enjoy our time together, but it would be stupid to jump head-first into a serious relationship with a rock musician. No matter how much he made my girlie parts tingle.

Don't get me wrong, I wasn't going to deny myself a little Connor booty call for the next two weeks. But, it had to be under my terms.

The love thing? Commitment?

Off the table.

I had more important things on my mind. It was high time for me to do something to stop some of the terrible things that were happening in our industry. I had power. Clout. And a foolproof strategy. Mom's illness and death put things on hiatus. My plans had been set in motion, though. Nothing was going to deter me from my goals.

Not even Connor.

Hannah was waiting for me in my trailer when I got done on set.

Hanging in my wardrobe was the most gorgeous soft-pink Prada sleeveless dress with tiny little lace details along the bodice. Her knowing smirk made me laugh when she handed me a bag from Sara's Lingerie, a store I'd never been to, but Hannah swore by. "You're going to need to put these on under that dress."

I reached into the bag and brought out the softest, most beautiful Empreinte black lace bra and matching panty set. "Hannah, these are stunning! Why haven't I worn something like this before?"

"Um, why would you need to? You date gay guys." She guided me to my vanity and pressed on my shoulders so I'd sit. "The hot bass player is the perfect excuse to introduce you to luxury lingerie."

Looking at Hannah through the mirror, I envied her quirky sense of personal style. She was the one good thing to come from my *Hawaiian High* audition. Her startling-blue eyes blinked at me through her pink, polka-dot glasses. She wore a huge, boxy shirt dress that barely skimmed her knees with pink combat boots and thigh-high cable-knit socks. No one should pull this look off, but she looked like she was fresh off the runway. "You should be a fashion designer instead of wasting time with me."

She rolled her eyes. "I like being a stylist, now stop stalling and let's get this stuff on your body so Connor can take it all off."

"Hannah." Kris had entered the trailer. "If you can push her in the right direction, I'll give you a raise."

Hannah whipped open my makeup drawer, grabbed my spritzer and touched up my makeup. "I'm going to do my best."

"Ronni, you're smitten with the man, I'm daring you to do something about it." Kris moved in front of me and smoothed my hair out of my face. "There's no reason on earth not to."

I stood and grabbed all my bounty and stepped into my changing room. "You both suck."

Once I had the gorgeous underwear on, I looked in the mirror and ran my hands along my sides, my stomach. Turning to see how I looked sideways in the mirror. From behind. I'd never felt so beautiful. And nervous. Was I really doing this? It all felt so surreal. Slipping the dress over my head, I loved how it skimmed my body like a dream. I stepped out to model for Hannah and Kris.

"Just beautiful, truly." Kris took my hands. "You'll knock his socks off."

"I'm not trying to do anything but keep things real," I protested. "He's leaving on tour in a couple of days, this isn't going to go anywhere."

Ignoring me, Hannah handed me a pair of nude Valentino Rock Stud kitten slides. "You'll want to look sexy but be able to kick these puppies off."

"Thank you both, I've gotta go. Connor just texted me. He's heading to my place right soon and I need to get home before he gets there." My heart thundered in my chest. "Wish me luck."

At my urging, my driver flew through backroads to get me home in forty minutes, a record.

For all of my inner and outer grumblings, my heart was so full at the thought of being with Connor. He was worming his way into my heart. It scared the life out of me because I wasn't a big believer in fairy tales. I've never seen one in real life.

Truthfully, I didn't know what I was getting into.

I was about to find out.

CHAPTER 21

O f course when the band heard I wanted to go to LA early, they all decided to come too. With our new album, *Z,* blowing up management wanted extra rehearsal time for us to get ready for the tour. It was going to be our biggest ever, and probably the most important.

Luckily, we were flying private. Ty decided to have a party for one at his new house in West Seattle. Which meant all of us were running a couple of hours late.

To say I was annoyed was an understatement. Over the past six months, LTZ's dynamic had shifted fairly dramatically. Almost in a self-fulfilling prophecy, Ty plunged head-first into the rock and roll lifestyle. Unlike me, the man had literally no self-control. Drinking and drugging enough for all four of us. So far, he'd created embarrassing scenes. Had sex in the VIP tent with a groupie in front of everyone. Was prone to disappearing acts.

Don't get me started on the belligerence.

Ty, the man who'd avoided parties and social interaction for three years, was taking things to new levels. It worried the living shite out of me. I'd left home to get away from babysitting a substance-abusing grown man. The hell if I was going to start all over again.

Not when the rest of us were growing up. Zane had all but stopped drinking. He still shagged anything that moved. Otherwise, he was pretty tame, mostly spending his downtime learning new instruments. I was blown away by his capacity to pick something up and master it. In the past year, he'd conquered the violin and electric piano.

Jace had also slowed way down, mainly out of necessity. His social media duties were beginning to overwhelm him. Plus, he'd largely taken over the fan and VIP events. Management was trying to convince him to give it up. Concentrate on his drumming. He wouldn't give in, saying he preferred to keep busy.

As always, I was the steady one. I'd never been one to get poleaxed. Not after Da. My worst vice was good beer and junk food. Since my date with Ronni, shagging random women had lost its appeal. Who could compare? The woman was in my mind at all times.

And in my heart, so she was.

As much as I was looking forward to spending time with her, the perils of starting a relationship before I was going out on tour weighed on me. Something huge was happening between us. I knew she was special.

But I'd been in this position before. If it couldn't work with Jen, how would it work with a famous actress who bearded for gay men to avoid dating?

Odds were not in our favor.

Once we landed, Ty and Zane did a few interviews while I met with Fender to talk about upping my endorsement. Finally, after all the meetings were over, our tour manager checked us and the crew into the London Hotel for the week. Not that I'd be staying there. After riding up the elevator with the lads, I slipped back down to the lobby. I was waiting for my Uber and thought I'd shoot Ronni a quick text.

Connor: I'm finally done, love. On my way

Mae: Perfect timing, I'm almost home from set

Connor: Remember, no pressure Mae. I just want to see you.

Mae: I hope you want to do more than see me…

Connor: you're killin' me love

Jace waved his hand in front of my eyes. "My brother, I've been trying to get your attention."

"Aye. Sorry."

"Do you want to head up to the Roxy? There's a couple of good bands playing tonight." Jace gestured toward Sunset. "Maybe grab a beer at the Rainbow."

Hanging out on the Sunset Strip was the last place I wanted to be. "Nah, I've got plans."

"Oh, really?" Jace elbowed me. "With whom?"

"I've got a date."

Jace's face was priceless. It was almost as if he had never heard the word "date" before. "With whom?"

I shrugged. "Mae Miller."

"Who?"

I didn't say anything.

Jace rubbed his chin. "I've never known you to go on a date, even when you were with my sister."

"Well, I guess there's no time like the present."

My phone buzzed, indicating the Uber was there. With a wave to

Jace, I headed out the door to my ride. Once I was in the car, my heart began beating so fast I was having a hard time catching my breath. Forty minutes later—Sunset traffic was always such a bitch— I was calmer. Some might say Fonzie by the time we pulled up to her stunning beach house.

My fist was raised to knock on the door, when it flew open.

"Connor!" Ronni flung herself at me. "God, I'm so happy to see you."

Being cool was out the window. Ronni crushed against my body while I inhaled her lemony deliciousness. All bets were off. Self-control be damned. I moved slightly away with my hands on her upper arms and looked directly into her green eyes. "Ah, Mae. Love."

Our lips crashed together in the kind of passion that I'd heard about but never experienced. I lifted her and she straddled my body, arms winding around my neck to hold on. We devoured each other like we were starving as I carried her inside. Ronni locked her legs across my back when I pressed her against the wall. Grinding into her core, my cock was like a homing missile.

I belonged inside her.

Every day.

Every hour.

Every minute.

Her lips were the softest. Her skin was the smoothest. Every part of Ronni was made especially for me. She moaned when I thrust up against her, arching her back to get closer. Our kisses grew sloppy, reckless. Ronni ripped at my shirt. I gripped her ass to drive her against me harder and faster. At some point, I remembered where I was and took things down a notch. Feathering kisses across her face. Nuzzling her neck. Stroking her sides soothingly.

Our breathing was still heated and needy, but I wanted to show her what she meant to me. That she wasn't and could never be just a quick fuck. In the moment, all of my previous thoughts about our rotten odds of being together evaporated.

Because the truth of the matter?

Veronica Mae Miller already had my heart and soul.

Now it was up to me to capture hers.

RONNI

CHAPTER 22

When Connor texted he was on his way, I calculated that I had about five minutes to spare. I bombed through my front door, managed to put on a fresh coat of lipstick and smooth my dress before the jitters got to me again. Anxiously, I looked through the peephole only to see my burly man raise his fist to knock. Unable to resist, I flung the door open. So much for being subtle.

"Connor!" In an instant, I took in his chiseled, bearded jaw, hair softly cascading around his shoulders in waves, light-brown eyes boring into mine. I couldn't help it. I launched myself at him. "God, I'm so happy to see you."

He smelled so manly, like the forest after rain. Connor's strong arms crushed me against him. He felt like home. I wanted to burrow into him and never leave. He gently gripped my bare arms and looked at me like I was a chocolate sundae. "Ah, Mae. Love," he purred in his Irish-tinged lilt, causing me to nearly melt into a puddle on the floor.

Like magnets, our mouths found each other. Exploring, gnashing, finding our rhythm. Connor easily lifted me. I clutched at him wildly, wrapping my arms around his neck and hooking my legs around his waist. When he pressed me against the wall and ground against my core, my new underwear became drenched. I'd never, ever, ever, ever felt like this. Aroused beyond all reason. Every part of me throbbed with desire for Connor. Only Connor.

I couldn't help but moan when he thrust against me, like his cock knew it was meant to be inside me. To reside there perpetually. The thought of that possibility made me feral. I ripped at his shirt. Needed him closer. He lifted me like I weighed nothing, squeezing and gripping my ass cheeks while we ravaged each other's mouths. I was a wild animal, finally uncaged. Uninhibited. I'd never felt so safe and so out of control at the same time.

Connor took charge, slowing things down dramatically. Kissing my entire face softly, slowly, reverentially. His lips grazed my chin and suckled on my neck, while his big hands roamed all over. Calming me. Bringing me to the present. As my mind quieted, I was able to *feel* everything that was happening to my body. Slowly, my eyes opened to find Connor watching me. Checking in. His consideration of my feelings evident. We sipped from each other's lips, like savoring the finest Barolo. I nipped his lower lip before pulling away and burying my face in his neck.

Hoping he felt the same magnetic pull.

Gently, Connor set me back down but held me tight against him and we rocked together with our arms around each other. His hard length pressed between us. Connor's hand spanned the back of my head as he held me to him. "Connor, what are you doing to me?" I murmured into his chest.

He just hummed, his lips pressed to my temple. We continued to rock side to side, almost like we needed to take a minute but couldn't bear to not have every part of ourselves touching. Wordlessly, I pulled away, took his hand and led him through the open-plan living room down into my master suite. No man had ever been here, and I wanted it to be Connor who imprinted himself into my home. Into my heart.

"Mae, are you sure?" Connor stopped me. Caressed my hair. Cupped my cheek. "I want you so much, but I don't want…"

Without saying another word, I smashed my mouth against his to stop him from having any second thoughts. From treating me as fragile. I wanted him more than I'd wanted anything in my life. Frantically, I tugged at his T-shirt to untuck it from his jeans. Connor grabbed the hem of my dress and pulled it up and over my head, revealing my awesome new underwear. I stood nearly naked in front of him, thrilled that his eyes nearly bugged out of his head.

"Did you wear this for me?" he rasped.

My face must have turned a million shades of red, I looked down at my feet. Connor's finger traced up my arm, along my neck and to my chin, where he tilted my face up, so I was looking directly into his eyes. "Please, Mae. I asked if you wore this for me?"

"Yes," I whispered.

The flames behind his eyes nearly scorched me. "Sweet, gorgeous girl, I— I… I'm overwhelmed." His hands wove through my hair and he bent to kiss me. Our lips touched, and he murmured against my mouth, "You're the most exquisite woman I've ever laid eyes on, love."

Desire unlike I'd ever felt, by a mile, sent shivers through my body. This man was the real deal. I took Connor's hands in mine and brought them to my breasts, never breaking eye contact. He cupped them, thumbing my nipples, which puckered at his touch. I reached behind my back to unclasp my bra. Connor groaned when it came off in his hands, leaving me naked on top when the lingerie floated to the ground.

"Roses," he sighed. "Dark-red roses."

I looked at him quizzically.

"Your nipples are like roses. I've wondered about them so often." Connor bent to suck a taut peak between his lips, lightly grazing it with his teeth. Sucking, swirling his tongue around my nipple. Moving to the other side, he mumbled, "Delicious."

Overwhelmed by the sensation of Connor worshiping my breasts, I nearly stumbled. His strong arms held my hips steady, but he didn't stop licking and sucking my nipples in his mouth, one after the other. His thumbs stroked the top of my panties then dipped underneath the fabric to my heat. Circling closer and closer to my center. I couldn't help but look down and watch what this man was doing to me. Connor was driving me out of my head with his persistent exploration.

When his lips and tongue left my breasts and kissed down my ribs to my stomach, I couldn't help but grab handfuls of his wavy hair and cling to him. His amber eyes flicked up to check in with me. I nodded, and in an instant, my panties were around my ankles. Connor nuzzled my folds, then using the width of his tongue, licked my seam.

"Ohmygod, Connor." I tried to pull him away from me by his hair, the sensation too much. Instead, he gripped my hips tighter and kneeled in front of me. Lapping at me, wriggling his tongue through my folds. Exploring every inch of my pussy as though he was memorizing each curve. Each crevice. My head lolled back. Nothing had ever felt as good as this.

Nothing.

Connor's knees nudged my legs apart slightly so he could get better access. I was mesmerized watching him devour my pussy, suckling my lips and then my clit into his mouth, pulsing it against his tongue. My stomach muscles clenched as a fuse deep inside my womb ignited and zapped through my body to the sensitive nub Connor was nibbling on and exploded, taking me to Venus. Mars. Anyway, to another galaxy.

Somewhere formerly unknown to me.

I was so happy that he was the first to ever taste me this way.

The only one.

"Ohgodohgodohgodohgod," I couldn't help but chant while my hips thrust hard against Connor's face. His grip on my sides remained firm until an orgasm for the ages ripped through my body. When he released me, I sagged to my knees in front of him, where he cradled me against his chest. Looking up at his trimmed, reddish beard, which was slick with my juices, I saw him smile. Pure light.

"Ah, Mae. You taste so sweet." He stroked my hair so gently. Kissed my temple. His other hand rested at the curve of my back. It was only then I realized that while I was completely naked, he was still fully clothed. I wanted to see him. Feel him. Taste him. I cupped the bulge in his jeans and stroked up and down. His cock, which was already hard as a pole, jumped at my touch and grew harder. Connor laughed. "He's very eager to meet you."

I reached for his buckle and undid it. "Then, why are you still dressed?"

"No reason at all." He grinned.

Connor finally, *finally* yanked off his T-shirt. Holy mother of Jesus, was my man ripped. An intricate kaleidoscope tattoo wound around his left arm. A Celtic knot circled his right bicep. Every single muscle was sculpted to perfection. My mouth watered. I wanted to lick every inch of his body.

Instead, I traced the outline of his abs with my finger down to his open belt. His hands rested gently on my waist as he watched me unbutton and unzip his black jeans, revealing black Calvin Klein boxer briefs. Not to mention a bulge the size of a plantain straining against the fabric. Using my thumbs, I pulled his underwear down to release his cock.

I looked up at him wide-eyed. "Holy moly, Connor. He's not going to fit inside me."

"Oh, I'm sure he will." Connor laughed as he took my hand and brought it down to his length. I gripped his shaft with his hand over mine. A pearl of liquid seeped out of the tip, I bent to tentatively lick it like a lollipop before becoming more brave and suctioning the tip between my lips. "Fucking hell, Mae." Connor palmed the back of my head so he could thrust into my mouth. "Ah, Jay-sus."

He knew how little experience I had in this department, so I felt empowered at his reaction. I wanted him to feel as good as he made me feel. Enthusiastically, I doubled down on the suction and reached between his legs to cup and caress his smooth ball sac. Almost inadvertently, his hips jackknifed, causing me to gag when his penis hit the back of my throat. Tears poured out of my eyes.

"Whoops, love. I'm sorry." Connor stroked my cheeks with his thumbs. "Let's go a little slower." Fast. Slow. I didn't care how we got there. Tasting him made my pussy gush. I loved sucking Connor's dick. I wanted him to come in my mouth.

Who knew?

Connor pulled out, however, and stood to kick off his shoes and jeans and take his underwear off. I didn't move, hypnotized by watching him get naked in front of me for the first time. He held out his hand, which I grasped, and he tugged me up and into his arms.

"We need to get a couple of things out of the way. I'm clean. I was celibate for a couple of years, as you know, and afterward I always used condoms. I've also been honest with you. I haven't been with anyone since before Australia, Ronni. I'm not a cheater." Connor guided me toward my big wrought-iron custom bed where we sat side by side, my hand enclosed in his. "If you don't want to do this tonight, love, it's fine. Tonight. This week. Forever. It's all about what you feel comfortable with."

I raised my eyebrows. He thought that being with someone else would be cheating on me? That was a conversation for later, though. I needed him to know that I wanted all of him. Now. "Oh, I'm ready for this. So ready. Does it *seem* like I'm not into it?"

He glanced down at my hard nipples and back up to me, raising one eyebrow. "Oh, I think that you are. Aye."

"Well, I *know* you're into it." I resumed stroking him, flicking my thumb over his weeping head. "Do you want me to finish blowing you?"

"Good God, Mae. I'm going to come all over you if you say the word 'blow' again." Connor moved my hand away. "I'm not gonna lie, being inside you is all I've thought about for months."

I licked my lips and looked him directly in the eye. "Blow."

"You're out of control." He shook his head, laughing.

"In all seriousness, I'm clean, Connor. I haven't been with anyone other than Kip. I've been on the pill since I was a teenager. Oh, and in case you aren't clear, this is happening." I stroked his hair, his arms, his body. "I want you. You are absolutely the most handsome, studly man I've ever seen. You being inside *me* is all I've thought about too."

"Did you say studly?"

I nodded.

He smiled.

I smiled back.

We stared at each other. Breathing in. Breathing out. Just for a few seconds. I was pretty sure I could hear both of our heartbeats. Knowing he was waiting for me to take the lead, I took his hands in mine and kissed his knuckles. One at a time, with a little tongue swirl as a bonus. Connor let my hands go and pulled me onto his lap, so I was straddling his hips. He held me fast at the small of my back with one hand. He gripped his cock, which was bobbing between us, with the other. Stroking the head against my clit. Back and forth. Dipping it inside my pussy occasionally to slick it up.

Fascinated, I watched Connor slowly feed his cock inside me. I adjusted my position, which meant I smashed my breasts against his lips. He caught a nipple in his mouth and sucked hard. Instantly, my arousal gushed around our joining bodies and I was able to take all of him. Our satisfied moans and the smell of our arousal permeated the room when we were fully connected. Connor laid back on the bed, his ab muscles contracting. "Ride me, Mae. Show me how you like it."

I'd never done it in this position and the sensation of being filled up by a man as big as Connor was intense. I braced myself on his strong chest and swiveled my hips side to side. Up and down. In circles. Figuring out what I liked. Connor watched me, fascinated. "You're concentrating so hard; how do you feel?"

"So full of you. You're hitting me so deep, I'm chasing something—" My eyes squinched shut in ecstasy when his cock rubbed against an insane spot inside me. Grinding my pelvis against his, I rubbed my clit against his pubic bone. Gasping, I looked up at him. It felt as though I'd discovered a secret treasure.

Connor's palm snaked to my lower back and he pressed me against him. "Take it, Mae. Take what you need."

I was already there. Stimulation zinged through my body. "Connor, God." My body heaved with a full-body release so intense I collapsed on his chest. He kissed my forehead and rolled us over, still joined. His palms pressed my thighs apart and held them there. His hips rolled and then pistoned. His little grunts of pleasure peppered with, "Aye. Aye," drove me wild. I thrust up to meet him, gripping his wrists.

His entire face contorted when he emptied inside me, gasping out, "Mae, love. Aye!" before collapsing on top of me. I rubbed his back and stroked his hair as he twitched inside me.

"Connor, are you alive?" I kissed his eyelids, which were fused shut.

"Arghblkt," he mumbled, rolling off but cradling me against him. His entire body heaved. His penis was wet with our combined release. "Holy bejeezus."

My head rested against his chest and we lay there for what seemed like hours. Content. Sated. Happy. He ran his fingers through my hair. "I feel transformed," I whispered.

"Oh yeah?" He chuckled, kissing down my face before taking my lips in a sweet kiss. "How so?"

"I never knew it could be like that." I gazed at him, this man who turned my world upside down. "You have a magic penis."

The skin around his eyes crinkled and he broke out into the biggest smile I'd ever seen. "Magic penis, eh?"

I nodded, reaching down to stroke said penis.

"I think the magic is the two of us. I never knew it could be like that either." He looked down at his erection as it sprang back to life. "Maybe you have magic fingers, I've never recovered that fast."

"We are magic, that's what I think. And I don't ever want to get off this magic carpet ride, Connor."

"Me either, sweet girl."

And for the next forty-eight hours, we didn't.

CONNOR

CHAPTER 23
TWO WEEKS LATER

Soaking in Ronni's extra-large jetted tub with my arms wrapped around her was the type of utter bliss I'd never known. Growing up on construction sites with my brothers didn't lend itself to bubble baths. Taking one with the woman that I'd been naked with for two weeks? Priceless.

Or whatever that credit card commercial used to say.

"Can we stay in this bath forever?" Ronni looked up at me, lemony bubbles clinging to her hair. "Every one of my muscles is so sore."

Yeah, that was all me.

Cupping her breasts, I squeezed gently. "I'll give you a boob massage, will that make it better?"

She wiggled her butt against my cock. "Only if I can give you a wiener massage."

"You just called my penis a wiener?" I laughed, rolling her nipples between my fingers. "Are you twelve?"

Ronni splashed me and giggled. "I suppose you want me to call it your cock."

"You can call my penis anything you want, love. As long as it gets to visit your pussy every day." I leaned down to suckle behind her ear.

In all seriousness, my time with Ronni had been life changing. Not just the sex, which was the best of my life. I mean, I'd never had an opportunity to spend a weekend naked in bed with a girlfriend before (highly recommended). Equally awesome was having such a long stretch of time to get to know Ronni. We spent every night together. Eating dinner. Telling each other about our day. It gave us plenty of time to learn about all of the little things. Her favorite flowers (sunflowers). Phobias (spiders, duh) and what she was like as a child (feisty, just like now).

As for me, I shared stories of my brothers and our shenanigans growing up. I'm pretty sure I impressed (bored) her with my vast construction knowledge. She was opening up. So was I.

For the most part.

For all of the great stories about *She's All That*, Ronni deftly evaded my questions about her days on *Hawaiian High*. It was more in how she avoided talking about it that confused me. She'd change the subject so often, I sensed she was keeping a big part of her life from me. Call it instinctive, or whatever. I just knew it was too early in our relationship to push her. Not when everything else about our time together was, so far, outstanding.

By now, all of the guys knew I had a girlfriend named Mae who lived here in LA. Yes, girlfriend. I don't think they'd caught on that Mae was actually Ronni, which amused me greatly. I wasn't about to give anything away if they couldn't put two and two together. The lads slagged me something fierce when they discovered I'd given up my room at the

London to stay with Mae. As for Ronni and my "coming out party," so to speak? I figured why not our Staples Center opening show? Ronni and Kris would be there as our guests. Seemed like the perfect time.

As we neared the show date, my band obligations began to ramp up. Especially with our album, *Z*, climbing the charts and Ty's angry breakup song about Zoey called *Down* taking off like a rocket ship. My bass line drove the entire melody, which made its success all the better.

In any case, we were in high demand. Every radio station seemed to be playing *Down* a million times a day. Management actually wanted us to make an old-school video, so we squeezed it in during rehearsals. We also had interviews. Management meetings. Tour meetings. Photo shoots. It was a lot.

The petulant part of me wanted to play hooky. Stay with Ronni. Make love to her over and over again. Of course, my professional side won out. I'd wanted this opportunity my whole life. All of us in LTZ had. Now it was here. We were about to launch our first headlining tour in arenas all over the US and Canada. I certainly wasn't going to do anything to blow it. Luckily, Ronni was busy filming her show and working long hours too.

Which made the moments we had together in the evenings so sweet.

I thought I'd known love with Jen, so I did.

I knew nothing.

Ronni? All-encompassing, mind-blowing, heart-exploding, soul-searing, life-changing love. This woman's happiness meant more than my own. Making her every wish come true? On my to-do list. Showing her how precious she was? Every. Single. Day. What I learned about Veronica Mae Miller in our compressed time together?

My girlfriend was the most compassionate, hard-working, intelligent, funny, loving woman on the planet. The guys were going to lose their minds when they found out Mae was Ronni. I couldn't wait to see the looks on their faces.

"You're lost in thought." Ronni craned her neck to kiss the side of my mouth. I angled down to capture her lips fully. Our soft kisses turned more passionate, so of course my dick hardened against her pert ass.

"Let's get out of the tub, love." I nudged her. "The water's a bit cool, don't you think?"

"If we get out, then we're one day closer to reality." Ronni shifted up and turned to face me. The lemony bubbles wafted around us. "I don't want this to end."

"Why would it end? We're a couple."

Ronni placed her hands over mine, which were resting on the edge of the tub. "We can't be a couple out in public right now. You know that, right?"

My face contorted into a scowl. I just stared at her.

"Oh, Connor. Let's dry off. We need to have a talk." Ronni stood, the water and bubbles sluiced off her slim frame. She plucked the oversized, white towel from a hook and wrapped it around herself. My face must have reflected how unhappy I was because she clutched my forearms when I stood to dry myself off. "Hear me out, I don't want you to be mad, but I have something important that I'm working on that affects our relationship."

Silently, we dried off. I was none too happy about this turn of events, but I pulled on a pair of track pants and a black T-shirt. Ronni wore a pink tank top and a pair of yoga pants. She tried to catch my eye, but I averted my gaze. I couldn't let her see how torn up I was.

"Okay, Ronni. Let's go talk."

I followed her through the wide hallway into the fancy marble kitchen. She grabbed a couple of beers from the fridge. She gazed up at me with tears in her eyes. "Let's go sit on the patio by the pool, we can listen to the ocean and I'll tell you a story."

Confused, I followed her through the floor-to-ceiling accordion doors. Ronni's patio featured a huge infinity pool overlooking the ocean. Two-person lounge pods were scattered around the edge. We had our favorite pod, the one closest to the sand. Over the past two weeks, we'd spent a lot of time cuddled up here watching the waves. Shagging. Talking.

I was really hoping this discussion wouldn't ruin the entire experience.

Once we were situated, I couldn't help but wrap my arms around her. "Tell me what's on your mind."

"You've asked, and I've been avoiding it, but I haven't really told you anything about my time on *Hawaiian High*." Ronni's voice was barely audible over the waves.

"It's okay, love." I petted her head, rubbed her shoulder. She was clearly broken up about something from that time in her life. I wanted her to feel safe talking about anything with me. It was necessary to build trust if we were going to have anything real. "You know you can tell me anything, right?"

"I hope so, this one is hard." Ronni tensed; her voice broke. "My time on the show ended badly, and when Wynn killed himself, I just couldn't cope."

"Sweetheart, relax." I turned us so we were spooning, clasping her tightly to me with one arm, cradling her head with my other. "It will be okay, I promise. Just tell me."

"Okay," she sighed, visibly uncomfortable. "The show had two producers, Merv and Jared. As I've told you, my costar Wynn and I were very close. What the general public doesn't know is that he was gay."

"Whoa." It shocked me. "He kept up a good front."

"Yeah. Well, you have no idea how true that is. So, whenever Merv was around I began to notice things were off. Wynn became withdrawn and melancholy. At first, I chalked it up to nerves. Merv took it upon himself to give all of us notes on our acting. He got off on criticizing us and belittling the cast's acting skills. Especially in front of other cast members."

"What a feckin' wanker!" I thought the music industry was bad.

"Yeah, he really was. Except with Wynn, it was different. He insisted on private meetings. Just him and Wynn alone in Wynn's trailer." She took a deep breath and composed herself. "One night, Wynn and I were waiting in his trailer for a night scene we were filming. By this point, we were close, so I had the courage to ask him about the meetings with Merv. That's when he confessed he'd been cast in *Hawaiian High* after attending one of Merv's pool parties in Hollywood. Apparently, there's an entire ring of Hollywood bigwigs who covet an invitation to one of Merv's events. Directors. Actors. Producers. Many of them are married with families. The pool boys are the draw. They are treated almost like chattel. Used with promises of roles in movies. Or television shows. It all depends on how far they are willing to go."

A tear seeped from her eye. I wiped it away and kissed her temple. "Shite, Mae. That's a feckin' disgrace."

"I know. It makes me sick to think about it. Wynn thought I was naive, because half the cast on *Hawaiian High* got their roles at similar functions. He was right about me being naïve and thank God I was. Anyway, Merv liked boys. The other producer, Jared, liked the girls. In any case, Wynn believed he was indebted to Merv because he was told he'd be fired or worse if he ever said anything."

Even with the questions I had whirling around in my mind, I stayed silent. I didn't want Ronni to clam up.

"God, to think of the auditions I went on and didn't get callbacks for. I never knew what evil I was up against. And once you know something like that, you can't unknow it." Ronni's green eyes peered up at me. Searching mine.

"My sweet girl." I squeezed her reassuringly. "Fame has such a dark side. I'm learning that every day."

Ronni burrowed into me. We sat clinging to each other for a few minutes. Without saying anything, I knew this was hard for her to talk about.

After taking a deep breath she continued, "It does have a real dark side. And I started to pay attention. Noticed a lot of very sketchy behavior. For instance, the showrunner followed one of my female costars into her trailer and the next day her part was significantly beefed up.

"Jay-sus. "Did she report him?"

"No, not when she benefitted from it." Ronni looked off into the distance. "But a different time, he revised a scene so another actress would be topless and fired her when she refused. He actually called her 'unprofessional' and a 'troublemaker.' There was a lot of gossip about his demands and expectations, and I believed all of it. It never touched me because my mom was always on set with me. Gratefully, she kept me safe.

"I'm grateful too." I stroked her hair softly. "Thank God."

"Everything comes with a price. In all likelihood, Mom's daily presence on the set gave them an excuse to write me out of the show. I was protected from abuse, which made me dispensable. When I was fired, I was relieved to be let out of my contract. On the other hand, Wynn was devastated."

"Why?"

"Wynn stormed out of the table read to his trailer when it became clear my character was written off the show. Merv, who was on set that day, followed close behind him. Now that I knew about those parties and the ongoing expectations, my heart sank. I couldn't believe how selfish I'd been, wanting to escape. Then I felt guilty because I'd be free. But Wynn? He'd be on his own, living his own personal nightmare. My best friend had endured abuse in silence for so long. The *Hawaiian High* environment allowed it."

"Sounds like they embraced it," I growled. My fierce protective instincts were kicking in. I couldn't believe my ears. The kind of shite Ronni and her costars put up with.

"According to my therapist, it's called normalizing it," Ronni explained. "At the time, neither my mom nor I knew that though. So, I took off after Wynn with her close behind me. The entire cast and crew just stared at me when I pounded on the door. I was literally screaming at him to open it. I looked and sounded crazy. And no one moved an inch. No one intervened. They just stood there watching my meltdown. And everyone knew what was happening."

I couldn't bear to hear much more, but I needed to be there for her. To find out what made her the person she was. "So, Wynn never opened the door?"

"No. The crowd dissipated, but Mom and I waited. It was agonizing. After about a half hour, Merv left the trailer, tucking himself into his pants as he descended the three stairs to the ground. Mom and I rushed inside to check on Wynn, not sure what we'd find." Ronni took a deep breath. Her eyes filled with tears. "He was sitting in his underwear on a stool smoking a cigarette. My mom put her arm around him to try and comfort him, but his eyes were hollow and disassociated."

Ronni started crying. I held her. I thought I'd had a fucked-up early adulthood. This took the cake. "Wow. Mae. I don't know what to say, love. I have a hard time wrapping my head around what you must have felt in that moment. I'd probably have murdered the bastard."

"Well, I asked him what he was going to do about what happened. Like, if he would report it. I told him we'd back him up." Ronni shut her eyes and shook her head. "He told me that he couldn't do anything because he needed the money and he didn't want to be blackballed in the industry. Nothing I could say or do would convince him. It was and still is the most heartbreaking thing that has ever happened to me. To watch someone that I cared for admit that he had no one. That he had no choice. No power. No will to change his lot in life."

"It sounds like you did everything in your power to help him." I assured her.

"I didn't. After that day, he ignored me and cut me out of his life the second Mom and I moved to Los Feliz. A month later, Wynn took his life. The thought of him with those predators haunts me to this day." Ronni was sobbing by the time she finished. My entire body enveloped her, my arms banded around her middle to keep her tight against me. I didn't want to say anything. Just let her know that I'd be here for her no matter what.

"I think about Wynn's death every single day, Connor."

"Of course." I kissed her temple and forehead. "I completely understand."

"No, you probably don't. The reason I'm telling you all this is because I've made a vow to myself on behalf of Wynn that I intend on keeping." Ronni wound her fingers with mine. "There's a method to my madness in dating gay men."

I was wondering where all this was leading. "Well this I'm dying to hear."

Ronni squeezed my fingers with hers. "I don't care about publicity or the spotlight. I'm bound and determined to use my celebrity status to make a change. You see, dating me gives a partner a certain level of credibility in the publicity game. What it means for the men I fake date is

203

they become more visible. Which translates to being coveted. The guys move to the front of the line at castings. They have no need to go to those parties and get exploited or worse. One date with me and they'll get ten or twenty thousand IG followers a day. These days, a social media following is more important to casting agents than sex."

"Really? I had no idea." I could kind of see where this was going. I didn't pay too close attention to what Jace did with our band's social media, but I knew LTZ had millions of followers and it been crucial to us moving the needle on our popularity.

"My plan is, if enough of these guys can get some success in their own right, together we can expose the people in the industry who are exploiting people." Ronni turned in my arms so I could see her face. "That's one of my goals; to stop it from happening. I can't do it alone, the guys are helping me and helping themselves and others."

I stroked her hair and used my thumbs to wipe the remnants of her tears. "You're magnificent."

"Do you really think so?"

"I do." I was genuinely touched at how selfless she was being. "Only, I'm not the kind of man who wants to share his woman with anyone else. Not by a long shot. Make no mistake, Mae, you're mine."

"I *need* to bring Merv down, Connor." Ronni took my face in her hands. "It doesn't mean I'm not falling for you. I am. Deep. Fast. Hard. It scares me to no end. But, if we're going to be together, I need to see this through. My plans have been in motion since before my mom got sick. When Kris gave me my break, I promised her I'd make a difference. This is what I'm doing. Please. Do you understand?"

"What's your end game?" I scrubbed my beard, feeling helpless but, frankly, really feckin' impressed. I just needed to know how I fit in. *If* I fit in.

"You know I'm fake dating Kendall right now for another couple of months. He's up for a movie role, and I think he'll get it. That will be a reason for our breakup. Separation made us grow apart, blah, blah, blah." Her eyes danced and she gestured wildly with her hands as she explained the madness. "I have a calendar set for the next couple of years. Every six months or so I'll have a new fauxmance."

My mind whirled. "Two feckin' years?"

"Tell me this, Connor." Ronni shook her head sadly. "What else would I be doing when you're on the road for God knows how long? Your first tour was extended time and time again. LTZ's new album is even bigger than the last, and now you're going out to support it for who knows how long. When are you coming home this time? Would we *really* be together?"

I didn't know how to answer that. "Um. Well—"

"Look at it from my perspective. If you and I become a public couple right now, you're going to be the one under scrutiny. Every fan you hug. Every girl who flashes her boobs at you. Every groupie that comes on to you. All will be evidence that you're cheating on Ronni Miller."

"I don't cheat. I'm not a cheater," I growled.

Ronni ran her hand through my hair. "Of course you aren't. That's the issue of being with me. As important as my plans are to me, making sure you don't get caught up in the whirlwind of my celebrity is just as important."

She touched her forehead to mine. "Do you see? I don't think it's going to work to be public right now.

We looked at each other sadly. Feckin' hell. What could I say to her? Everything she said was absolutely true. She articulated everything I'd been worried about in the first place and added a whole pile of shite on top of it. She didn't deserve to wait around for me and put her own life on hold. I'd asked that of Jen. I surely wouldn't do it to Ronni. I didn't care what anyone said about me. Ronni had a mission. A purpose. And a damn good one at that.

"I'll go." I kissed her gently on the lips and scooted over to get up off the lounger. "I totally get it, love. You're right. I'm being a selfish bastard. Why would you want to start something with me now?"

"Connor." Ronni stood. "That's not what I meant."

"What did you mean then?"

"Us. I'd like there to be an 'us.'" Ronni shrugged and looked down at the patio. "It's just going to have to be on the down-low. I'd like to see where this goes. For you to trust me."

Trust was one thing. But as long as she was with other men—sexual relationship or not—there was no "us." My heart plummeted. All fantasies about Ronni dissipated into the ether.

So, I did the only thing I could manage without losing my cool.

Without breaking down.

I headed to the house to collect my things.

RONNI

CHAPTER 24

My heart felt like it was being ripped out of my ribcage. I couldn't move. Nearly paralyzed watching Connor walk away from me. Probably for good. I'd pushed him too far. Our relationship was too new to sustain this strange situation we found ourselves in.

God! What was I supposed to do?

How had I fallen in love with him so deeply?

So fast?

Yet, what I said about him leaving on tour wasn't wrong. What I said about being involved with me wasn't wrong either. They were simple facts. I was a realist. Experience taught me that it was the only way. Why should I have to stop what I'd put in motion to appease his fragile male ego? I'd poured my heart out to him. Explained why what I was doing was important. Not just to me, but to many. My role in all this would actually help stop abhorrent behavior by some of Hollywood's most deviant power players.

Or maybe, he thought I was finding excuses to push him away?

Either way, I cared too much about him to let him leave like this.

Dashing back to the house, I found Connor stuffing his clothes into his duffle bag. He looked up at me and back down quickly. I swear I saw mist in his eyes. I ran to him and flung myself into his arms. "Connor, my honey."

"Mae," he choked, trying to step back from my assault. "I can't…"

"We can." I hooked my arms around his neck and threaded my fingers at his nape. "We can."

Connor rested his hands on my waist and touched his forehead to mine. "No, we can't. You're right about me leaving on tour. It killed my last relationship, Mae. I don't want to do that to you. I don't want to interfere in your plans either."

"No, you are misunderstanding me. This isn't the same thing." I led him to my bed and we sat, clinging to each other's hands. "You being on tour didn't kill your relationship with Jen. She embraced who she was. Her own sexuality. It would have ended no matter what. Either way, our past relationships don't matter. I want us to be a couple, and I don't want it to be a secret. Except, right now for me, there is a greater good at stake. And for you too. All I was trying to explain to you was we *both* have commitments. For a couple years or so."

"I don't know what you want from me." My gentle giant looked so vulnerable it took me by surprise to see him broken up. "This is so complicated. Maybe too complicated."

"I know. And I don't have the right to ask this of you." I rubbed my thumbs over the tops of his hands. "But you're such a special man, Connor McGloughlin. I want you in my life."

"Aye. I want that too."

"So let's be together. We will find a way to see each other whenever possible," I vowed. "My show's on hiatus in three months, I'll get your schedule and when you have a break I'll come to you."

Connor's eyes lit up. "Brilliant. And when you're working and I get a break in between legs of the tour, I'll fly back here to LA to be with you."

I clapped my hands excitedly. "Absolutely! And we'll FaceTime every day, no matter if it's just for a second to check in. We'll text. Call. Whatever it takes. Just to be together however possible."

"So it's official." Connor took both my hands in his again. "You're my girlfriend. We're exclusive. There's no one else."

"One hundred percent. You're *my* man."

"Mae, I *do* trust you. You know that, right?" Connor studied me; his eyebrows furrowed slightly. "I can't lie, I'll hate every second seeing you out in public with other men. Even if it's fake. Just the fact that I have to say this out loud is surreal, you realize that, right?"

"I know. Hollyweird. You have no idea how often it happens though. Professional athletes. Even musicians."

"Until I met you, love, I had no feckin' clue."

"Look, I totally understand because I'll murder a bitch if she puts her hands on you." I pursed my lips. "But I trust you too."

"And you were right. Fans put their hands on us all the time. At meet-and-greets. Out in public. We're always getting manhandled. Or female-handled as the case might be." Connor took a deep breath. "The point is, I can't promise I won't be jealous. Or overreact sometimes."

"It sounds like we're in the same boat there."

Connor dragged his knuckle along my cheekbone. "Promise me if you ever have questions, you'll talk to me. Let me know how you're feeling."

"Same."

"Okay."

"Okay."

"I'd at least like to tell the guys that we're together, Mae. And my family." Connor studied me. "I don't want to lie to them. Lying is my limit. It was the reason I was most upset about the Jen situation. It hurt that she couldn't tell me what was going on with her. I was really looking forward to telling the guys who 'Mae' was tomorrow. My plan was to snog the life out of you in front of them and freak them the fuck out."

As much as that idea appealed to me on literally every level, I shut my eyes and shook my head. Knowing what I was going to ask of him was unfair. A horrible way to begin our relationship. "There's nothing I want more, but until I'm done with this project can we keep things between us?"

"Oh." A look of uncertainty crossed his face. He considered it. A myriad of emotions flickered in his eyes before he sighed. Nodded. "Aye. I guess."

"I'm just worried there will be a leak. An inadvertent slipup." I explained. "It would make it seem like I'm cheating on Kendall and all the publicity efforts would be lost. Not just lost, actually, annihilated. My own reputation as a good girl is at stake, and my cash cow is that image."

"Ronni, you're an honest, hardworking, beautiful woman. Why not just be authentic?" Connor's deep voice rasped. "Aren't you overcomplicating things?"

My heart squeezed. I couldn't explain my true personal stake in this. I wasn't ready. As much as Connor valued honesty, I knew I might never be ready to disclose my entire truth to him. For now, until I was more sure of him and us, it was better to take his acquiescence as a small victory. "I hear where you're coming from, but *please*. Can you just trust that I know what I'm doing? I've been at this media game for a long time, as crappy as it is."

Connor rested his palms on my knees and squeezed. "I'll try. You keep mentioning some plan for dating these guys. I need to know *something* Ronni. Otherwise, this isn't going to work for me. Put yourself in my shoes."

He was right.

"Sure. That's fair. The first thing you need to know is there is a rhyme and reason to how and why I hand select each of my boyfriends." I air-quoted the word boyfriends so he was sure about my intentions for the reference. "I'm starting to produce my own scripted content projects with Kris. The guys are first vetted because they are perfect for a role on either my current show or in an upcoming project. Ordinarily producers and financiers have full approval over who is cast. With Kris and I wearing producer hats, we now have full control."

He nodded, urging me to continue.

"So, that doesn't mean we aren't savvy. We cast people with at least some sort of following so it doesn't look weird. Talent on the cusp of success. Hungry, but need a little push over the edge to get there. Kind of like me when Kris gave me my break."

"Okay. And you're the push. With you pushing your followers to them, they become more coveted?" Connor relaxed a bit. It made my heart swell that he was really listening to me.

"Exactly. But it goes even deeper. A while ago, an actor who had a bit part on *She's All That* became a good friend after I found out he knew Wynn. It turned out they went through the Merv pool party circuit at the same time. I came up with a plan to bring Merv down, and he's is helping me."

Connor studied me. His face gave nothing away. I was beginning to realize that he had the most extraordinary poker face. He'd learned well from his days bailing his dad out. I thought I'd developed a pretty good ability to read people, but I couldn't read him right now. "Go on." He motioned with his finger.

"Sure. Okay. So, now my friend's on the front line. He vets my fauxmances to make sure they have acting chops, ambition, and are genuinely nice and deserving people."

"How?" Connor's face remained impassive.

I sighed. The final criteria was dark, but necessary. "Well, they are all men who have been subjected to or witnessed firsthand Merv's or his friends' demands. Preferably with evidence. Oh, and they must be willing to help me expose the situation. This narrows down the playing field significantly.

Connor raised his eyebrows. The first indication he was surprised at where this was going. "Why the feck would they do that?"

"It's a win-win situation." I crossed my arms defensively. "Giving these guys a jump-start on their career is my 'payment' to them. In exchange, they agree to speak on camera. I might make it into a documentary or something. It's not just about Merv, although he will likely be prominently featured. His comeuppance will be icing on the cake. My bigger-picture issue is stopping the blatant exploitation of *men* trying to make it in Hollywood. The dude casting couch is alive and well, and just as bad as the #metoo movement. Maybe worse. But men don't talk about it. There's an even worse stigma."

He looked up and away and nodded to himself. He'd paid close attention to everything I said with minimal comment. More points for the big guy for not jumping in to mansplain why what I was doing was stupid. I gave him time to process my brain dump. After a few minutes he focused back on me. "Where will you show this documentary?"

"It doesn't matter. I'll probably leak word of it somehow. Maybe I get picked up by Netflix or it goes traditional distribution. That part I haven't figured out; it all depends on what footage I get. My first filming session isn't for another month, so I'll know more then. Bottom line, my end game is taking down Merv and his asshole cronies. Once this is out, they'll never work in Hollywood again."

"Kris knows about this?"

"Not exactly. She obviously knows about my bearding. She thinks it's mainly to avoid having a real relationship after Kip and Mom."

"I wouldn't be too sure, Mae. She knows about me." Connor sighed. "So does Hannah. Zane covered for me on our date in Australia. Jace knows I'm spending time with a woman named Mae. It wouldn't be that hard to figure all of this out."

Connor was one sharp cookie. The thought that Kris knew more than I'd told her crossed my mind on more than one occasion. "True. Look… If they do, we'll deal with it. I'm not some duplicitous person. I don't like lying any more than you do. This isn't meant to be a secret forever. I'm gathering the information I need. As soon as I have enough footage, I'll let Kris in on everything. I'm just asking you to help me keep up the ruse in public until then."

"Huh."

"Just think about it," I implored. "It doesn't hurt us. Keeping to ourselves protects us from having to be in the public eye at such a critical stage in our relationship and in both of our careers."

Connor pinched his nose between his fingers. "Except it's still complicated by the fact that I have to lie to the people closest to me. That's the part I'm not on board with."

"I said down-low, not lie. It's not for long. Like I said, I'm getting Kendall's story on film next month. My other guys are already lined up. All with crazy and compelling stories, complete with evidence."

"You're so far down the path, Mae." Connor seemed resigned. "Feck. It'd be a dick move on my part to give you some stupid, worthless ultimatum."

"Connor, no one in the world knows more about this than you do right now. I'm telling you because I trust you. I want you to trust me. Our circumstances are keeping us apart anyway. I'm asking too much of you, I know that. Please. Would you be willing to play along for a few months until I know what's what?"

Connor said nothing, just looked at me.

"Connor, we know what's real, don't we?" I gestured between us. "This is real. The past couple of weeks have been the best of my life. Being with you is everything. I want to give us a chance. I just—"

Connor crushed his lips to mine, parting my mouth to suckle on my tongue. His hand spanned my back and he dragged me onto his lap. Enclosed in his strong arms, I hooked my legs around his waist. We buried our head in each other's necks and clung to each other, squeezing so tightly that it felt like our souls merged in that instant.

Connor nudged my chin with his and claimed my lips again. "Veronica Mae Miller, I love you. I feckin' love you with all of my heart."

Hearts exploded out of the top of my head. My dreams had come true. "Oh, God. Connor Riley McGloughlin. I love you so much."

Our lips smashed together. Hands ravaged each other. Our clothes went flying across the room as we undressed in record time. This man was *everything*. He was mine, and I was never letting him go. My unicorn. My love. My super honey, Connor McGloughlin.

"I want to make love to *you* tonight." I threaded my fingers through his auburn tresses. Stroked the soft hair of his beard. Using my knuckles, I softly dragged my hand down his neck, down his pecs, and across his heaving stomach to his cock, which was flush against his belly button. "I want to take care of you. You are always taking care of me and everyone else. Let me."

Gripping his hard length in my hand, I took him in my mouth and sucked on his crown. He breathed out, "Aye. God. Mae."

Swirling my tongue around his tip, I gently cupped his scrotum and pulsed. Looking up at him, I found him gazing at me with a look so reverential it made me want to give him the greatest pleasure he'd ever known. Over the past two weeks he'd showed me what he liked. How he liked it. I wanted to give it to him. Always.

"You really have no idea how deeply I've fallen in love with you, Mae." He stroked my hair while I kissed down his shaft and sucked his balls into my mouth. "Jesus, feck. I'm not just saying this because you're driving me out of my mind."

Moving my way back up, I took his cock in my mouth as deeply as possible and hollowed my cheeks to create suction while I circled my tongue along the sensitive ridge under his tip. My saliva pooled when I tasted his sweet essence. I kept up my pace for a while, delighting in hearing Connor's affirmative grunts and sighs as I worked him over. His hips bucked up against me, his hand wound around my hair. I hummed and resumed pulsing my fingers on his scrotum. He came down my throat with a loud roar.

I drank down every sweet drop and swallowed, licking him clean afterward.

"You are so delicious, my honey." I kissed up his ripped abs and hovered my mouth over his. "Let me give you a taste." With this man I'd found the courage to take control of my sexuality. My desires. Fantasies. Connor made it easy for me because sex with him was off-the-charts.

Connor scanned my face, his body still heaving with the aftermath of his explosive orgasm. I pressed my lips to his and he opened for me.

Savoring him, I explored the depths of his mouth with mine. He sucked on my tongue. Our kisses were sweet, exploratory. Loving.

"I don't taste that bad." Connor laughed. "I'd only do that for you, Mae."

"Why *do* you taste so good?" Cradled in his arms, I traced his lips with my finger. "Not that I have anyone but Kip to compare…"

Connor covered my mouth with his hand. "Don't you say it, Mae. As far as I'm concerned, you're mine and I'm yours. We both have romantic pasts, but there is no reason for us to bring them up when we are making love. It's you that I'm with. You are in my heart. You *are* my heart."

"Oh, Con." His sentiment zinged straight through me. Then I poked his chest. "You didn't answer me, though. About why you taste so yummy."

"Shite. To tell you, I have to break my own new rule." Connor shook his head and held up a finger. "Jen would never go down on me. Ever. It makes sense now, of course. She didn't like dick. I thought making my spunk taste nicer might help. I avoided dairy and made sure to eat plenty of cinnamon, peppermint, and fruit like pineapple and berries. Voila!"

"Presumptuous." I couldn't help but giggle. "Are you saying you ate pineapple for me?"

"Feck yeah!" Connor booped my nose. "And I'll eat ten pineapples a day if you'll suck me off like that, love."

"Consider it done."

"Mae, in all honesty, I've never felt like this before. I really had no idea until you." Connor stroked my back as he stared into my eyes. "There is *no one* but you. I want this to work between us."

"We'll make it work." I smoothed his hair from his face. "I promise. Just have faith."

Connor didn't answer, instead he pulled me on top of him and grabbed my ass, scooting me up so my pussy hovered over his face. "Enough sappy shite, it's your turn," he growled and thrust his tongue through my folds. He kept a strong grip on my hips and guided me back and forth as he nibbled, sucked and licked me into a frenzy. Gripping the top of my headboard, I let him maneuver me so expertly every inch of my core was sampled by Connor's mouth. Just when the stimulation became almost more than I could bear, he wiggled his tongue on my clit.

Stars. Fireworks. Explosions. All of the cliches. All true. My man rocked my world. I rode his face like a wanton cowgirl hussy, because I had zero control over myself around him.

Once he licked me clean, Connor rolled us over so he was on top of me and caged my head with his hands. "Taste yourself and me together, sweet girl."

He plunged his tongue into my mouth at the same time he plunged his cock into my pussy Gyrating so his pubic bone hit my clit, Connor drove into me as we savored each other. It didn't take long, declarations of love and excellent foreplay had me primed and ready. I went over first, Connor followed with a groan.

Afterward, we laid together holding hands. Staring into each other's eyes. I knew I was asking too much of him and that he didn't know the whole story, but I'd do anything to make it work between us. In the grand scheme of things only one thing mattered.

He was my honey.

And I was his right back.

CHAPTER 25
SIX MONTHS LATER

I was keeping it together, but our arrangement was a lot better in theory than in practice. No one was any wiser about the extent of our relationship, but I wasn't about to go out of my way to hide it either. We'd managed to see each other about once a month when Ronni could make it work. Usually for just a night. After shagging like rabbits in my hotel room, we'd order room service and she'd fly back.

Not ideal, but it was what we had to work with.

Sure, we were constantly in contact. Virtually, that is. Texting, talking on the phone, and video chatting.

Our career ambitions made it impossible for us to have a normal relationship. All in all, everything was moving along, considering we were a continent apart most of the time.

I wanted more.

Bottom line? I loved Ronni with all of my heart, but it was hard to be someone's secret. It didn't work for me. Not even a little bit.

Maybe it was because in six months, my life had drastically changed. If I thought we were well-known before *Z* came out, I truly had no idea what popularity really was. The album exploded LTZ into the stratosphere beyond all predictions. We'd been nominated for multiple Grammys for feck's sake. It felt like every single person on the planet knew me and all my bandmates.

I was used to Ty and Zane taking the brunt of public recognition. Now that I was part of the mix, it made me appreciate what they'd shouldered for the first few years of our success. Fans lost their minds when one of us were around. Right now there was no way for me to run to the store or just take a walk without a crowd gathering.

After a few scary incidents, all of us now had an assigned security detail. There were new safety protocols. How we arrived and departed the stadiums. Hotels. Layers and layers of people were put between us and our fans. Everything was orchestrated to a science. At first it seemed like overkill. Unfortunately, it was the only way for us to get through the day on schedule.

Touring at this level was no joke. Concert days were packed from morning to night with interviews and radio appearances, sound checks, our shows and VIP commitments. We still had to eat, shit, and shower. Often it didn't feel like we had time to do even that.

What a feckin' high, though. Seriously. We'd sold out the US tour in minutes. Shows were added in most of the major cities. We played our first Coachella, headlining the festival. Last night and tonight we were in New York at Madison Square Garden. Two shows. Both sold out.

Never in my wildest imagination did I dare believe I'd be here.

Our incredible success meant significant perks and comforts. For instance, we were no longer crammed in one bus. Our crew had two buses to themselves and we now had three trucks full of equipment to create our arena tour experience.

LTZ traveled in a pimped-out customized rig. We had a huge lounge area with reclining media chairs, a seventy-five-inch television and access to every paid streaming service available. We'd converted the back master bedroom into a recording studio/practice area, which helped us while away the hours in between shows. The kitchen was nearly full sized, with stainless steel appliances and a u-shaped booth. Our bathroom had a full shower, cupboards for all our toiletries and a separate crapper.

Because, as I told Ronni, no one was allowed to shit on the bus, except in the case of a dire emergency. Road etiquette 101.

Rules were rules.

The best part was each of us had our own space. We'd converted the bunks into private bedrooms with doors that locked. Each was outfitted with our own media center, a small closet, and dresser drawers. Best of all? Soundproofed.

All the better to block out the incredible amount of fucking that was going on during this leg of the tour. Jace. Ty. Zane. All of them were out of control, but they honored our sex rules. Yes, we had those too. First, no one was allowed on the bus without at least one of us there. Second, when the bus was moving, it was only the four of us and our driver. Simple.

Tonight's New York gig was the last in the states before LTZ jetted off to Europe for a few festival shows. Then South America. Back to Asia and Australia. If the album was still charting by the end of the year, we'd be touring on and off all next year too. It wasn't finalized yet, but more US and Canada shows were being added and then a full European festival circuit.

So, my life was scheduled for a very long time.

But tonight? I was feckin' over the moon. Ronni was in NYC. She and

Kris flew in and would be at our show. I couldn't relax, that's how excited I was to see her. After the show? We had three entire days together before she had to go back to work. I planned to make the most of them.

I also planned on convincing her to take our relationship public. It was time. I wanted to marry this girl.

She would be here shortly. In the meantime I had another feckin' photo shoot. The entire Delta Sky360 Club had been transformed into the branding for *Z* because management was hosting an exclusive VIP after-party for celebrities, politicians, and our friends and family. With only three hours before showtime, the stadium annoyingly scheduled photo ops with the MSG bigwigs. As always, I was the first one to arrive.

"Connor, my brother." Zane flew through the sliding door, his vintage Les Paul slung behind his back. He never let the guitar out of his sight. "Jace is on his way, have you seen Ty?"

I rolled my eyes. Ty's drug and alcohol use was still so very out of control. He was like a kid in a candy store. It was a miracle he pulled it together so professionally on stage. My patience was razor thin. "No, try looking in his dressing room, he's probably fucking some PA."

Zane huffed out a breath. "Don't be so judgmental, Connor."

Jace wandered in the room to save the day, tapping on his phone as usual. "Did you meet those publicists? Andrew and Sienna? Katherine likes them. She wants me to step down and hand everything over."

"I haven't, but it sounds like a good move," I encouraged.

"Jace, have you seen Ty?" Zane asked. Always the one-track mind, that one.

"Yeah, Sienna wanted to talk to him about some stuff for Europe."

A few minutes later Ty strode in, surprisingly sober. "Hey, my dudes."

Zane threw an arm around his best friend, then stared at his buzzing phone. "Carter just texted. He's here with Ronni Miller and Kris from

Australia."

"Now?" I asked too fast. So not Fonzie.

"Yeah, security is bringing them up here."

A moment later, the sliding doors opened and my heart skipped a beat. It was only the photographers. They got to work setting up lighting and whatever else it was they needed to do. The rest of us sat around, buried in our phones. Well, I pretended to be buried in my phone. I really had one eye on the door.

Seconds later, Carter burst through, tugging Kris behind him. Ronni followed, wearing a short, fluttery pink dress. Her eyes bored into mine then looked away. Everyone hugged and milled about, having various innocuous, animated conversations. Ronni and I smiled and nodded, stealing glances amid the chaos.

When the photographers finally got set up, we were wrangled into various positions for what seemed like a million pictures. Kris, Ronni, and Carter heckled us from the peanut gallery. Finally, it was over, they packed up and left.

"I've got to go warm up." Ty stalked off. Say what you will about his descent into destruction, the man never missed his vocal warm-ups.

Jace was on his phone, probably posting some shite on social. He followed Ty out the door shortly after.

"Kris, do you want to come with me and Dad to grab a snack?" Zane had one arm around Kris and the other around Carter. He looked me in the eye and winked. "Maybe Connor can give Ronni a tour of the Garden."

Ronni's eyes widened, but she didn't say anything. Kris laughed. "I think that's a fine idea. Connor, you don't mind, do you? Giving Ronni a tour? Of the Garden, that is?"

My girl's face turned a million shades of red. Feckin hell, she was magnificent.

After they left, I popped my head out of the door to make sure they were really gone. By the time I turned around, Ronni was right in front of me. I grabbed her hand and practically dragged her to the elevator down to where our dressing rooms were. Once inside, our lips crashed together and she climbed me like a tree. My dick was its usual homing-missile self, angling for her pussy through my jeans.

We needed no words.

I guided her to the black leather sofa, unbuckled my belt and knelt between her legs. Gripping her hips, I pulled her to the edge of the couch. Guiding myself into her wet heat, I became mesmerized, watching myself penetrating and withdrawing from her beautiful, pink pussy. Rubbing her clit furiously with my finger. Ronni gripped both sides of my face and strung her fingers through my hair, caressing my cheeks with her thumbs. Urging me on. Whispering how much she missed me. Loved me. Adored me. In no time, I was lost and spurted inside her as her walls squeezed my cock through her own release.

With all energy expended, I collapsed on top of her. My mouth sought hers. She ran her fingers through my hair and caressed my head the way I liked. We made out slowly. Kissing. Nuzzling.

"I love you so much," Ronni murmured into my neck. I stroked her back. "I needed that. I miss you. I miss your body."

I cupped her face and kissed her, taking great pleasure staring into my woman's green eyes. In person. "Aye."

She climbed off me, adjusted her panties and smoothed her skirt. "You made a mess, sir. I need to clean myself up."

Jumping off the couch, I raced to the bathroom and returned with a warm washcloth. "Sorry, love. I was in a bit of a sex haze. Let me."

After I tenderly wiped her and readjusted our clothes, we lay curled up together on the sofa where we'd just made love. Ronni massaged each of my fingers. "So, I guess Zane knows we still have a thing."

"He always knew." I kissed her forehead. We had to talk about our future, but not now before the show. "Jace probably has an inkling, but he's never too chuffed about other people's business. Ty, as always, is in his own head. Stop worrying, my honey. You're safe."

"I'm not worried, Connor." Ronni's lips found mine. "I'm just happy to spend the next few days together."

"FIFTEEN MINUTES!" One of the crew bleated through a bullhorn.

Reluctantly, we got up. Ronni ducked into the bathroom for a last-minute touch-up. When she emerged, I handed her two All-Access laminates. "Here you go, my love. I know you want to skedaddle out of here to find Kris. I'm late to meet the guys."

Ronni grabbed my T-shirt and dragged me in for another kiss. "I'll be watching you."

Half an hour later, Ronni and Kris were dancing on stage next to me. New York was always special. Tonight, with Ronni here? It was even better. When I say that each show was more incredible than the other, it wasn't a lie. After hundreds of shows under our belt, the connection I felt on stage with my band-brothers was dynamic. Intuitive. Jace and I were the heart. Zane and Ty were the soul. Together, we were magic. The entire stadium sang each and every word to our songs.

In the VIP area after the show, Ronni and Kris mingled with the elite of New York while Jace, Zane, and I hobnobbed with all the industry folks. Ty was sitting on a sofa in the corner with a bottle of Jack Daniels and a beautiful Victoria's Secret model dry humping him.

Lovely.

"Well, Ty's certainly lost all of his inhibitions." Ronni's sweet voice interrupted my voyeurism. "He's literally falling down drunk with some girl's bare tits in his face."

"Aye." Unable to resist touching my woman, I pulled her into a hug. "Welcome to the new normal."

A tall woman in a cheetah jumpsuit with her jet-black hair pulled back in a severe ponytail approached. "Ronni Miller! I didn't know you knew LTZ."

Ronni turned and squealed, grabbing the woman's red-taloned hands. "Sienna! Yes! I've been friends with all of these rock star hunks since we were in Australia a year ago!"

Cheetah-pants stuck out her hand. "Sienna King, your new publicist."

"Sienna's my publicist too!" Ronni gushed. "She's so much fun, you guys are going to love her."

Something about her raised my hackles, but my interaction with publicity was minimal, at best, so I decided to ignore it. I took her hand. "Welcome to the LTZ madness."

"My plans are already in motion." She nodded toward Ty and the model who were now practically having sex in the middle of the room. "Time for that gorgeous specimen to up his publicity game. No need for him to bang groupies when he can pull the cream of the crop."

"Be nice to him, Sienna." Ronni took her arm. "He's sweet. A little tortured."

This conversation was not my cup of tea. "If you'll excuse me, ladies. I've got to do my part and chat with a few people. Enjoy the craic."

When I walked away, I caught Ronni's eye and nodded to the door slightly. A few minutes later, we slipped out and my security guard, Adam, whisked us on a golf cart to a waiting car. No one at the party—which was at maximum capacity—was the wiser. The driver let us off in the loading area of our hotel, where a VIP concierge was waiting to escort us up the service elevator to our room. One thing that was great about superstardom? Discretion, if you played your cards right.

Once we were safely inside my room, Ronni and I held each other. Soaking up our closeness. We were free for a glorious three days. A luxury for us. I wasn't going to waste a minute.

"Let's get naked and stay that way, Mae." I held my hand out to her.

"I thought you'd never ask." Ronni one-upped me by yanking her dress over her head and throwing it at me before running toward the bedroom in only her panties.

This woman.

She was my heart.

My soul.

She was my everything.

It was time for everyone to know it.

RONNI

CHAPTER 26

NINE MONTHS LATER

I'd been sobbing for three solid hours.

My face was a puffy, bleary mess. My lungs hurt. Every muscle ached. I was curled up in a ball in my media room rewinding and rewatching the footage. It was heartbreaking. More than I ever imagined. My heart seized knowing what Wynn had endured. This project was taking everything out of me. At least we only had one more day of filming my series, and then I'd be free for four months. Aside from a small part in an indie film I was shooting outside of Dublin.

I know, I know.

But, I took the part so I'd be closer to Connor when he was on the European festival circuit over the summer. We hadn't been able to see each other for months because he was halfway around the world and I was filming. Suffice it to say, FaceTime sex wasn't cutting it for me anymore.

And I *knew* it wasn't cutting it for him.

He told me so in New York. Nearly a year ago. If it wasn't for LTZ's incredible success and his travel schedule, there was no doubt in my mind. Connor would have been long gone. No self-respecting man would agree to stay in the sidelines and watch the woman he loved pretend to be with another man. Let alone the four men I'd been public with since we'd become a couple. It wore on me too. It took a lot out of me to pretend to love anyone but Connor. Bottom line, I needed my man to be *my* man. I just needed a little more time.

As if I'd conjured him up, my phone buzzed next to me.

I connected to the video to see his grinning face peering at me through the screen. "Ah, there she is."

"Hi, babe." I sniffed.

Connor squinted, his face contorted with concern. "Mae, have you been crying? What's wrong, love?"

"The footage." I tilted the phone so he could see where I was sitting. "I almost have what I need. Only two more interviews to go. I'm putting it on hold until after I get back from Europe. I'll finish it early next year."

He didn't say anything. He didn't have to. Not being together was a big sore spot in our otherwise beautiful, if unconventional, relationship. "Next year."

"Well, yeah. I can't finish it because I wanted to be in Europe. So we could be together for a stretch."

Connor looked up and away. After logging hundreds of hours of video chats, I was beginning to learn his mannerisms. The look-away was one of his tells when he was upset and wanted to avoid saying something he didn't mean. He looked back at me. "When do you get to Dublin?"

"Day after tomorrow."

"Have you made a decision about the Belfast show?" Connor's amber eyes bored into mine through the phone. "I'd like to bring you to the house."

A couple of months ago, Connor bought an estate overlooking the sea in Belfast as a vacation home for him and his family. The day after their show at the SSE Arena, he was meeting with one of his aunts, who would oversee the renovations. "Of course, my honey. I'm going to spend every minute I can with you. Why would you think otherwise?"

"I'm just tired, so I am." Connor scrubbed his beard with his big hand. "I miss you. We haven't spent enough time together lately. Jay-sus I sound like a whiny eejit."

"You don't. I miss you too. So much." I brought my lips to the screen for a kiss. "Don't forget you were with me for a week here in Malibu. We had three days in Charlotte. I popped up to Portland. We even had ten days in Petit St. Vincent over New Years. You're just as busy as me. I think we're doing the best we can."

"Aye." Connor's lips curled up in a smile. "The private beach villa was a nice touch."

"You can't take away the memories of being naked for five solid days." I pulled my top over to flash my pink bra. "If you play your cards right, I'll show you a nipple."

"You're a wicked one, Veronica."

I laughed, grateful to have shaken off my malaise and maybe his. "Oooh. I know you're serious when you call me Veronica."

"I love you, babe." Connor smiled. "I'm sorry I'm being a bollocks. As much as I love my job, it's exhausting being on the road like this. I'm ready for a break and I won't have one for another few months. I want us to be together."

"I love you so much, Connor. I want that too." I worried about my big guy. He put everyone's needs ahead of his own. Including mine. I knew I wasn't pulling my weight with him and wanted to get some good quality time in. "We'll be together in two days. We'll stay at your new house. I'll try to cook. All summer you can come to Dublin when you have a day off, it's only a two-hour flight from anywhere in Europe. Maybe we can even steal away for a little vacation after your tour before you have to go back to Seattle."

I could hear someone shouting for Connor in the background. "That sounds nice. Except for the cooking part. Ah, feck. They're calling for me, Mae. I gotta go."

"Love you!"

But he was gone.

Clicking the screen off, I thought about the project I'd spent so much time on. It had spiraled out of control. My show was demanding in the best of times, and I'd been working too much to meet my self-imposed schedule on my bring-down-Merv campaign. I'd run into numerous roadblocks. Kendall backed out at the last minute when he was cast in a superhero movie. Three guys backed out of our bearding arrangements. All these delays were putting a strain on us. Connor was doing his best to be understanding.

At least today we didn't fight.

But it was definitely becoming a point of contention.

How could I stop now, though? At least there was a finish line.

For part one. I just hoped part two went quicker.

Even if it meant delaying completion of the Merv exposure, taking four months off to do the film was my effort to put things right between us. To give us some time together. Not that it was a hard decision to make. Spending quality time with Connor would be worth the delay. He was my everything. As unconventional as our relationship was, the big guy meant everything to me.

It was working.

Right?

But for how much longer?

My phone buzzed in my hand. Byron.

"I can't believe you're really leaving," he whined as soon as I accepted the call.

I pinched the bridge of my nose with my fingers. He meant well, but sometimes he was too much. I shouldn't have answered. "I know you're disappointed, but this is a role I couldn't pass up."

"I'm putting my career on hold for this, Ronni. At some point I'll need to get the Ronni girlfriend special to get myself back on track."

My head started to throb. Why had I put myself in this position? When I started, it all seemed so simple. That was before I'd met Connor. Before we'd fallen in love. My enthusiasm for bearding was nonexistent these days. My thirtieth birthday was just around the corner, and I was playing games with my love life. With the love of my life.

"Ronni?" Byron snapped me out of my thoughts.

"Sure, B," I agreed halfheartedly. "After all of this is done. Look, I've got to get packed. I'll be in touch."

Two days later, I landed in Dublin. Kris's office arranged for a private concierge at the airport to handle all my arrival tasks. From my first-class seat, I was whisked in a golf cart to a private lounge where I was able to shower and change into a sleeveless, black Prada dress while the VIP team handled customs and my luggage. By the time I was finished, my chauffeur, who was on call during my stay here, had arrived. Which was probably the best news for the good citizens of Ireland, considering I was a terrible driver.

While in Dublin, I was staying a little outside the city center in Howth. My house was lovely, in a gated community with all the modern amenities, an open-plan kitchen and living area, a game room and a cinema room.

The views of Howth village and the Irish sea were stunning from every room, and I was delighted to discover a private rooftop garden. I couldn't wait to get Connor here and christen the place.

"How long do you need, miss?" My driver Tom was politely standing by the door while I checked out my temporary home. "We need to get going if you want to be in Belfast by eight."

Thank God I'd pre-packed a suitcase so I didn't have to sort through my things. I gestured to the right bag, Tom grabbed it and we were off so I could see my gorgeous man.

It took a while to get out of the city, but once we were on the M1, I was able to take in a lot of the scenery. The lush, green hills and gorgeous little cottages that dotted the landscape were so charming. My giddiness at being in Connor's native land was palpable. Maybe it was the excitement at finally seeing my *real* boyfriend in person after a few months.

My All-Access pass was waiting for me at the private entrance to the stadium. Connor made sure one of the crew escorted me backstage. Winding through the bowels of the large arena, I was shown where the dressing rooms were. Each of the guys had his own space and there was also a common area for friends and family.

So far, not too many people recognized me, which was a relief. It wasn't often that I could mingle with a bunch of people I didn't know without hearing their opinions about my sad love life both in real life and on the show. One of the things I wanted to talk to Kris about when I got back was having an end date for *She's All That*.

I was ready to move on.

Mainly because it was time for me to spread my wings. I wanted more control over my schedule. Kris and I had dozens of projects we wanted to work on, but she was so busy with my show and the four other shows she had on air, I barely saw her anymore. It didn't mean I couldn't give developing things on my own a try. My documentary was living proof.

Equally as important? I wanted to finally be with my boyfriend. I wanted to get married and have his babies. To walk with him proudly on the red carpet. For me and the kids to travel with him when LTZ was on tour and just be a family. Was that such a bad dream?

Pure heaven. When I got back home from the movie shoot, my number-one priority would be to get my list accomplished by the end of the year. Put an end to the madness. I'd surprise Connor on New Years and we would be free.

"Ronni Miller!" Zane burst out of his dressing room and swooped me up in his arms. "What the hell are you doing here?"

I hugged Zane hard. He was the best. "Surprise! I'm here to see the show. I'm filming a movie in Dublin and saw that you guys were kicking off your European tour in Belfast!"

Ty and Jace followed him and I got hugs from the two rockers. Connor stood back, his fists resting on his hips. His gaze was animalistic with a hint of mischief. Ty ducked back into his dressing room to do his vocal warm-ups. Zane winked at me and tugged Jace's sleeve. "Dude, let's go check out the opener for a sec."

Connor held his hand out to me after they left. I rushed to him and he pulled me into his private dressing room and locked the door. As it always was between us when we'd been apart, we devoured each other. Mauled each other. Tried to climb into each other's skin.

"God, I love you so much." I was straddling him, grinding on his steely bulge and nibbling on his ear." "I need you, Connor."

Connor's hands spanned my back, he was rocking me back and forth against him. "I wasn't going to fuck you until later, but I can't wait."

I unbuckled his belt, unbuttoned his jeans and reached in to pull out his steely hard cock. Connor hoisted up my dress to my waist to find I wasn't wearing panties. "Fuuuuck," he growled. Grinning from ear to ear, I positioned him at my entrance and sank down on top of him.

Home. I was home.

"Feckin' hell, Mae." Connor's head lolled back, his face in a pleasurable grimace. His grip on my hips tightened as he pounded up into me. I wound my arms around his neck as we chased a speedy climax. "Jay-sus, I'm sorry. It's been so long, I'm coming."

His callused finger rubbed my clit when he flooded me with his release. I was right there with him. My entire body trembled with aftershocks. I collapsed on top of him, my face buried in his wavy auburn hair. "Ohhh, I missed you," I mumbled into his neck.

He stroked my hair and kissed my head. "I'm so happy you're here, my love."

I realized we hadn't even kissed yet, so I remedied the situation by sucking on his pillowy lips and winding my tongue together with his. A sharp rap on the door startled both of us. "You're on in half an hour." We heard the same message being delivered to the rest of the guys by the crew member as he made his rounds.

After cleaning ourselves up, Connor headed out with the rest of LTZ to start the show. I stayed back until they were into their third song, then took what I now considered "my place" on the side of the stage next to Connor. The show was incredible, with all sorts of new pyrotechnic effects. The back-up singers were new. The production had been taken up a big notch, which was understandable. LTZ was the biggest band in the world right now.

The after-party was at the Titanic Experience. Connor had to make an appearance, so I had my driver take me separately. While LTZ was on their private tour, I looked around the exhibit and tried to enjoy the experience. Unfortunately, jet lag had set in and I was nearly falling asleep on my feet. Not wanting to be a wet blanket, I found an area where some big, cushiony armchairs were set up and took a seat.

The next thing I remembered was Connor gently shaking me awake. "Mae, love. Wake up."

Horrified that I'd fallen asleep in the middle of a party, my first thought was that my picture would be plastered on every British tabloid with the headline:

"GOODY TWO SHOES ACTRESS DRINKS HERSELF INTO OBLIVION AT AN LTZ CONCERT."

Connor assured me that there were no photographers so there was no reason to worry. I let it go.

Connor led me toward the door. On the way out I spotted Zane onstage playing with an Irish band, Jace was talking to a stunning girl with long, black hair and Ty was making out with a red-haired girl whose bare boobs were flopping about. Classy. "Let's get you out of here, my gorgeous girl."

"I love you, Connor." I yawned. "Sorry I'm so jet-lagged. I really can't wait to spend the summer with you."

Connor kissed my temple and guided me out to the car. Tom, my driver, stood waiting and opened the door so we could get in. "Aye. Let's get you to my house so we can wake up together. my honey."

"I want to wake up to you *every* day, my honey." I snuggled into his strong, muscular arms. "Do you want that too?"

"You have no idea, Mae." Connor tightened his grip around my body.

"Let's make it happen," I mumbled as I drifted off to sleep.

"I'm trying, Mae," he whispered. "But we need to discuss exactly how and when we're going to get there. Because I'm beginning to give up hope that our relationship is ever going to be a priority for you."

CHAPTER 27

As I looked out the bedroom window at my new house, I had a rare, quiet moment to contemplate my life. Undoubtedly, one of my favorite parts about LTZ's success was financial freedom. Thinking back to the agonizing decision to leave my family's business, I thanked God every day that I'd trusted my gut. If I'd stayed, I'd probably have followed my Da's path into a life of drinking and gambling. Instead, for the most part, I was living my dream now.

I didn't have to worry about my family much anymore. Da had been sober for years. Now that he'd retired and Cillian was running the business, he and Ma bought a Caravan and were spending a lot of time traveling around the US. My twin brothers signed with our management company and were making a run at a music career too. My other brothers were finishing up their graduate degrees. The McGloughlins had turned the corner. All of us.

The situation with Ronni wasn't working for me. I wasn't proud of myself for feeling the way I did. It felt like she was allowing her fauxmance situation to go on endlessly. She wouldn't tell me what the end game was. For a year and a half, all I kept hearing was, "trust me."

I trusted her not to cheat on me. I trusted that she loved me. I for sure trusted that she wanted me, because having sex with her was transcendent every time. For both of us. Our bodies were made just for each other.

Call it instinct. Call it whatever you want. I *knew* she wasn't being completely honest with me.

And I didn't know why.

I had to talk to her, but I was conflicted. Mainly because my own travel schedule for LTZ loomed for months into the future. After our European tour ended, we were shooting a documentary in Seattle for a month. Then off to South America. When we returned, she and I would have a few months together while we recorded the next album, but I'd be off again on tour.

In other words, I didn't want to be a hypocrite.

I didn't want to be the guy who didn't take responsibility for my own role in our separation.

We both had very busy schedules, and hers kept her in Los Angeles while I would probably always be touring somewhere. Be away for long stretches of time. As much as I loved LTZ, I had to ask myself some hard questions too.

Did I want to live this way forever?

Or should I make it easier on Ronni and find a way to be with her permanently even if it meant leaving all that I'd worked for behind? As much as I loved being in LTZ, I was exhausted. I didn't want to go at this pace anymore.

I wondered if my band brothers were as weary as I was.

Gazing out at Belfast Lough from my master suite, I couldn't believe I owned this gorgeous estate. I'd bought it sight unseen because I wanted my family to have a place to call home when they visited our extended family here in Northern Ireland.

Close to Belfast and located right on the shorefront, my new house had a gated, private entrance and was surrounded by spectacular, dramatic landscape. Designed to maximize the stunning views, it had a reception area, a living room with a wood-burning stove, a huge master suite with his-and-her closets and four en suite bedrooms. To the rear of the property was a spacious open-plan kitchen/dining area with custom cabinetry, a utility room and study. The entire house featured incredible custom herringbone oak hardwood flooring. Outside, I had a detached triple-car garage with a huge loft.

Yeah, as a builder, I noticed the details in a place.

Truthfully, it was my ideal home. I couldn't have designed it better myself. It had great bones and tons of modern, custom features. Aside from some minor renovations of the decor, it was perfect. I could see raising kids here. Converting the loft into a creative workspace to write music. Or maybe it could be a playroom.

But I was getting ahead of myself.

"Connor?" Ronni's sleepy voice called out. I looked over at my beauty snuggled under the new down comforter my aunt bought when she set up the house. "The bed's awfully cold without you."

My dick sprang awake under the towel I had wrapped around my waist. I padded back to the bed and sat on the edge next to my girl. I smoothed her hair away from her face. "Good morning, sleepy head."

She smiled and stretched her arms over her head, causing the sheets to shift. A rosy-red nipple popped into view. Unable to resist, I reached over and wiggled my finger on the tip, causing it to tighten. "I need a shower."

She swatted my hand away. "Then I'm all yours."

I followed her to the pristine, white-tiled, walk-in shower and turned on all the body jets and the rain shower. My aunt had stocked the house well. A few different shampoos and body washes lined the built-in shelf, including Ronni's Oribe brand and her Lemon Summer Vanilla body wash from Bath and Body works.

"Connor, you are so sweet!" Ronni held up the shampoo bottle. "This is my favorite stuff. You didn't need to go to that much trouble."

"Aye. Of course I did." I stepped in next to her and cupped her cheeks in my palms. "I want you to feel at home here."

At my words, Ronni's entire body relaxed. I squirted some of her lemon body wash on a bath puff, wet it and began to gently cleanse her perfect peaches-and-cream skin. Her forehead rested against my chest, her hands clasped my waist while I soaped up her back. Next, I washed and conditioned her hair. Throughout it all, my hard dick bobbed in between us.

Reaching down, Ronni stroked me from length to tip before squatting and taking me into her mouth. She gripped my ass with one hand for balance, the other held my cock firmly in her fist. My palm splayed on the tiled wall while I watched myself disappear in and out of her pink lips. Her green eyes were fixed on mine as she worked me over.

Unable to control myself if she continued, I gripped her upper arms and pulled her up off me, causing my dick to spring free of her warm mouth. Reaching in between her legs, I slipped my arms under her hamstrings and lifted her to straddle me. Then turned and backed her against the tiled wall of the shower, impaling her with my throbbing cock.

I needed her hard and fast before I could take my time with her. Aside from some FaceTime diddling and the quickie in the dressing room, we hadn't made love in nearly four months. I was pent-up something fierce.

Driving into her relentlessly, I winced with a pleasurable pain when Ronni's nails scored my back. She whispered into my ear, "Yes, Connor, give it to me as hard as you can."

Spurred on by her encouragement, I fastened my lips to the soft skin under her ear and nibbled and licked her erogenous zone. Ronni's legs hooked around my waist and she used her heels to push me into her faster and faster. Her breaths grew short and the darling little mewls she made right before an orgasm grew louder. I hoisted her ass up to change my angle in order to see her beautiful face when she came all over my cock. I went over with a grunt right after.

With our arms wrapped around each other, I pulled out and helped her regain her footing. Our kisses were leisurely, reverential. I felt somewhat relieved. Sex with her always helped us reconnect in mind, body, and soul. I never wanted to let her go.

After we dressed, I gave Ronni a tour of the house while we waited for my aunt to arrive. When we'd seen the whole place, I hoped she liked it. "So, Mae? What do you think of my new home?"

"I love it!" Ronni danced around the room above the garage with her arms spread wide. "It's so peaceful here. So beautiful. I love Ireland. This house is the bomb."

I smiled. It was the reaction I hoped for.

Mostly.

"Connor, are you planning on moving here?" Ronni's excitement morphed into discomfort. I couldn't tell if she was sad I might be leaving or if she was worried that I'd ask her to move here with me. "It's a very extravagant home to have as a vacation property."

I walked over to the window and looked out at the sea. "I've always dreamed of having my family home close to where my parents grew up. But, in answer to your question, I guess it all depends."

"On me?" Ronni stood beside me, her hand rested on my biceps. "Is that why you wanted me to see the house?"

I tucked her under my arm. "Maybe."

"Tell me the truth. Are you upset that my project isn't done yet?"

I kissed the top of her head. "It's part of it. Except the other part of me knows I have no right to be upset with you. I'm more upset at our situation. We got our itinerary before the tour, and I'm booked up for a long time with LTZ shite."

Ronni's arms were wrapped around my waist. She squeezed. Then sighed.

"Mae, you have your choice of any man in the world. I can't expect you to stay in a relationship like this. It's not what you deserve." I kept my gaze fixed out the window. "I'm supposedly living my dream, and all I really want to do is plan my future with you."

"Oh, Connor." Ronni stroked my cheek and dragged her nails through my beard. "We *are* planning our future, there are a few minor obstacles in our way, but it won't be forever."

"Would you ever want to live here with me? Maybe not full-time, but part-time? I'd love to convert this space into a recording studio. Or, better yet, a playroom." My voice was soft. We'd never talked about kids. Or marriage, for that matter.

"I'm so in love with you." Ronni tilted her head up and kissed my lips. "I would love to live here with you someday. Part-time or full-time."

"I know now's not the right time, but you do know where this is heading in my mind, don't you?" I searched her eyes. I needed some sort of confirmation that our hearts were on the same path. "I want us to be married. Have kids. Build our lives together in the same place. Or places. The hows and wheres don't matter to me, Mae."

Ronni's eyes moistened. She threaded her fingers through my hair,

God how I loved when she did that. "We're on the same page, my honey. I promise."

A loud, piercing voice interrupted our heart-to-heart. "Connor?"

I shouted, "Auntie Saoirse, we're up here."

Clomping footsteps followed and my aunt burst through the doors wearing a thick wool coat, jeans, and rain boots. "Ah, Jay-sus, let me get a look at ye."

"Please meet my girlfriend, Mae Miller." I tucked a hair under Ronni's ear. "She flew in from the states to see the show last night."

"Well, that's just grand, so it is." Saoirse clasped Ronni's hand in hers. "You're the spittin' image of that American actress, so you are."

Ronni blushed and peered up at me. "Yeah, that's funny. I get that a lot."

After we visited with my aunt over tea and biscuits, I thanked her profusely for getting the house set up. We walked through the property and Saoirse made a list of the improvements I wanted completed. We declined her invite to dinner, and she left us with a knowing smirk.

We settled into a routine and after a few days I just couldn't bring myself to voice my concerns of our long-term prospects to Ronni. When we were together, it didn't feel like the things I worried about mattered. Or were even relevant.

It felt like we were on solid ground.

We planned out the next few months and how we'd find time to be together. I'll give it to her, as peeved as I initially was that the movie was postponing her project—and thus us—into next year, having her stationed in Dublin while I was touring Europe was a stroke of genius. Not only did it give her an excuse to come to our shows, her filming schedule was fairly easy to navigate around. As part of an ensemble, she had a couple weeks of intense shooting. Otherwise it was two or three days on and four or five days off.

Idyllic. That's the only way possible to describe the summer.

I was lulled into a sense of comfort for a while.

Ronni popped over to London for our shows at Wembley Stadium. That's where I put two and two together that Jace had a bit of a covert romance going on. At our second show, Ronni saw him kissing a tall girl in an Austin Powers getup. Talk about paper-thin walls, Ronni and I were in hysterics listening to their extremely loud shagging.

Always ready to slag my bandmates, anytime Jace asked me a question that required an affirmative response? I called out as loud as possible, "Yeah, baby!" Ty, who was in the suite on the other side of Jace's room, joyously joined me. It drove Jace batty. I liked to think of it as payback for his years of embarrassing social media posts.

Headlining festivals throughout Europe was trippy. The red carpet was rolled out in every venue. Whatever indulgence and luxury we could imagine was at our beck and call. I'd never taken advantage of rock star amenities until this tour which, I had to admit, came in handy to romance the woman of your dreams.

On my days off, if I wasn't at her lovely Dublin rental, she was with me in gorgeous five-star hotels all over Europe. Manchester. Dubrovnik. Lisbon. Amsterdam. Prague. Oslo. Berlin. Barcelona. Vienna. All in all, it was the most quality time we'd ever spent together in one stretch.

Each minute we were together, we fell more deeply in love.

At least I did.

We were so compatible. On all levels. Not just sexually, although our desire for each other was off the charts. We talked a lot more about marriage, babies, and our families. Ronni shared more stories of her life and filming. She spent time with LTZ at our shows and became a good friend to all of us.

When I was frustrated with Ty, whose behavior was growing more and more destructive, she talked me down. "He's your friend, you should be there for him when he needs you. Even though you're worried, it's his journey." She was right, he wasn't my dad after all. Still, he was on management's radar and I tried to look out for him as best I could.

Similarly, when she lost a bearding engagement, even though I wanted her to say she was through with all of it, I encouraged her. "Mae, you'll get what you need after you go home. I'll be cheering you on." I was trying really hard to be at peace with her arrangement now. The time we were spending together made me feel better about things. Like there was a light at the end of the tunnel, and I was getting a preview of our lives together. Someday.

Which is probably why, when we were separated for a few days, I didn't miss her on a deep, guttural level. There was no more gnawing worry that a kiss we shared might be the last one.

I knew one thing for sure.

I'd never get enough of her.

LTZ had a rare four days off after our sold-out show at *Stade de Paris*. I booked Ronni and I into *Baumaniere*, a five-star luxury hotel in Provence for a romantic getaway. During the day, we explored little towns throughout Provence. In the evenings we dined on the terrace of the three-Michelin-starred restaurant called *Cabro d'Or*.

Surprisingly, neither Ronni nor I had ever indulged in a chef-tasting menu up until that night. She was constantly watching her weight and fine dining had just never occurred to me. Needless to say, in that one phenomenal romantic experience, we became foodies. And winos.

When the tour wound down in Rome, Ronni couldn't make the show because of her shooting schedule. I flew out the next morning to spend a week with her in Dublin before she was due back in LA to begin shooting the new season of *She's All That*. I'd be in Seattle to film our documentary and then off to Latin America for a four-month tour.

When that leg was over, we were officially on the home stretch of supporting *Z*. While I was thrilled to learn our new album would be recorded in LA, which meant Ronni and I would have uninterrupted time together, it was somewhat of an illusion. Once the new material was completed, we'd only have a couple weeks off before heading out on the road again.

First, a New Year's' Eve headlining gig in Times Square, then four months in Asia and Australia for the final leg of the *Z* tour. Home for a few weeks to do publicity for the new album release. Aaaand... The entire cycle would begin again.

As our time together in Europe came to an end, the truth hit me over the head. LTZ's success was and always had been the real barrier to any hope of a long-term relationship with Mae.

Our separation was my fault. Not hers.

I didn't want to believe we were doomed.

But holding out false hope?

That wasn't fair to either of us.

RONNI

CHAPTER 28
FOUR MONTHS LATER

66 **H**oney, I'm home!" I shouted when I walked through the front door.

No one answered.

Connor had been living at my house for a few weeks while LTZ was on a short break. I hadn't seen him for a couple of days. The rest of the band was in town and the guys were working on new music. I knew I had to get used to an empty house. After the New Year's show in NYC, Connor would be gone for four months to write the rest of the songs they needed for the album. In the spring, he'd stay with me when they recorded the new record. Then he'd be out on the road again.

Loving a musician meant long periods of time apart.

From the time we'd been back from Ireland, he'd been distracted. I tried not to read too much into it because in between their live performance obligations, they were on a short timeline to finish up their follow up to *Z*.

Instead, I focused on the things I could control. My new bearding boyfriend was Sam Ababio, a gorgeous black actor from Ghana. He wasn't gay, but he'd attended one of Merv's parties when he first got to town and was roofied. Of all the guys that I'd recorded, his story was going to bring the whole operation down. I just knew it.

The only challenge? Connor was pissed. He'd gone along with my project for the past couple of years because my fake boyfriends had been gay and therefore, in his mind, not a threat. Sam wasn't either, but Connor didn't like that he was a straight. It pushed him over the edge. He flat-out told me that I'd broken our arrangement during an argument. Bottom line? Connor was over my bearding life. Truthfully, so was I. After my contract with Sam was up? I was done. It would be almost time for Connor and me to "come out" as a couple.

Finally.

Glancing at the clock, I knew I had to get some sleep. My car was picking me up at 6:00 a.m. for our final day of filming before the holiday break. There was only one problem. I was wide awake. Instinctively, I felt like something was off. My scalp was prickling, and the last time that happened my mom was diagnosed with terminal cancer.

I decided to try one of my tried-and-true methods of falling asleep. A couple of melatonin usually did the trick. After I washed the pills down with a glass of water, I crawled into bed and texted Connor.

Mae: Where's my honey?
Connor: ...
Connor:...
Connor: in the studio, we're writing
Mae: ok, I've got an early call, just took melatonin gonna crash
Connor: ok, I dunno if I'll be back before you leave

Mae: I miss u
Connor: u2
Mae: I love u
Connor: u2 gotta go xoxo
Mae: xoxo

I hated that I was feeling so needy. I didn't want to interfere with the things he needed to do, but I missed him. He was pulling away. There was no doubt about it. Sam gave him a good excuse, after all.

Connor was such a strong, proud man. He'd been patient beyond belief. Always willing to take control in our relationship. He planned everything. Made sure he accommodated my schedule. Now that LTZ and all the guys were more famous that any celebrities in the world, it was probably time for me to step up and show him how important he was to me.

Instead, I changed the rules.

Without even talking to him about it first.

I must have fallen asleep because the next thing I knew, my entire body was cocooned against a wall of muscle. Connor's hair cascaded over my cheek. His massive biceps were wrapped around my stomach. "Did I wake you?" he whispered in my ear.

Turning in his arms, I pulled him closer to me. Seeking out his lips with mine, I sucked on his bottom lip. He returned my kiss. Our tongues tangled lazily. I nestled into his chest and hooked my leg over his hip.

"I want you, Mae," Connor rasped.

Grasping both my hands in his, he entered me inch by inch. Watching me. Studying me. His hair fell in a curtain on either side of my face as he lowered his lips to mine. He brought our hands up above my head and rolled his hips like a wave. Driving into me. Deeper and deeper.

The intensity of our lovemaking nearly made me look away.

It felt different.

Like he was memorizing me.

Like it was the last time.

The prickly scalp thing was back in full force. I knew I was being paranoid. He'd already promised me forever. I needed to focus on the fact that the love of my life was worshiping my body right now. Making love to me like I was a goddess. That's what I should be thinking about. How good he made me feel.

How good he always made me feel.

"I love you so much, Connor." I tried to stare into his soul as I said the words. Tears seeped from the corners of my eyes as our bodies rocked together.

Connor released my hands and reached underneath us to cup my bottom. Gripping both cheeks, he took control of my movements—rocking me up to match his thrusts, which were becoming faster and harder. Still, he kept eye contact. Punctuating each motion with the words, "I. Feckin'. Love. Fucking. You. Veronica. Mae. Miller."

Not exactly the sentiment I was after, so I tried to screw the words I wanted out of him. Hooking both arms around his neck, I crushed my mouth to his. We ground our pelvises together almost violently, causing his pubic bone to press against my clit while his cock stroked my G-spot. Connor's face contorted into pleasure-filled grimace when he came inside me with a roar. It was like he pulled my zip line skydiving. A fast descent into unmeasurable ecstasy followed by a floating parachute sensation as I came down from the intensity of it all.

Connor flopped over on his back and cradled me to his body with one burly arm. His hand spanned my hip across my stomach. I laid across his chest, my hand resting on his hard pecs. We didn't say anything. Just breathed.

My alarm ringtone went off, *Rise*, LTZ's hit single off their first album. It seemed like the appropriate wake up song a few months before I met the guys, and I'd never changed it. Connor kissed my forehead. "It cracks me up every time."

I leaned up on my elbow to look at him. Traced the lines of the tattoo that snaked around his arm. I had to assuage my prickly feeling. "You didn't say you loved me, Connor. You said you loved fucking me. I've got to ask. Are we okay?"

Connor blinked a couple of times. He didn't answer.

"Connor?"

Sighing, shook his head. "I can't lie to you about how I feel. And no. I don't think we are, Mae."

My scalp prickled again. I could feel my heart rate escalate. "Why?"

"Do you really want to have this conversation right now?" Connor squeezed his eyes shut and sighed heavily.

I grabbed my phone and punched in a text to Kris. In nine years of making *She's All That*, I'd never been late once. I was cashing in on my good will. "I just let Kris know I'm running behind. So, the answer is yes. I think we need to have this conversation now."

Connor got up and pulled on his boxer briefs and sat on the edge of the bed. "Why did you think to ask me that question?"

"Because I feel like you're pulling away. I'm all-in with you and now I'm terrified that you want to break up." I grabbed his LTZ T-shirt and slipped it over my head. It was so big I must have looked like I was drowning in it.

"I'm tired, love. Now's not the time"

I cupped his face with my hands. "Make love to me. Again."

Connor pulled away. "Don't try to fuck me as a way to distract me."

Crap. I didn't realize he knew. "Wow, you really think a lot of me," I spat.

He raised an eyebrow and just shook his head.

My heart began to race. This was it. This is how we were going to end.

"Maybe we should take some time apart. You can take another two years to finish up your project and maybe we can try again when you're ready to be with me. For good." Connor was resting his elbows on his knees, his face was buried in his hands. "I'm knackered, Mae. It's not helping matters that we're not moving forward in our relationship."

His comment wasn't unexpected, but it made me defensive. "Connor, I don't want to break up. I'm at the finish line. Really. Truly."

He scowled. "Good for you. Truly. The thing is? I'm so feckin' sick of being your dirty little secret. Of trusting that this is going to end someday. I don't know what you're up to, what you're end game is. It sucks. I think I'm done."

His words pierced my soul. I remembered feeling exactly the same way when Kip left me to get married to someone else. I'd been devastated when I'd been *his* dirty secret.

Had I really done that to Connor?

"Ah, Mae." Connor looked up at me, his voice a whisper.

I couldn't bear to look at him.

"Just tell me everything. Please. I know you're keeping secrets and it kills me that you don't trust me fully. After all this time. I'd never do anything to hurt you, don't you know that by now?" His words were emotional, but his voice was measured. "The only conclusion I keep coming to is you don't want this. You're not all-in with me. This thing with Sam proves it."

Ohmygod. No!

I raised my head. He deserved that much. "Do you really think that?"

"Look, Ronni. Maybe you'd be better off with someone like Sam. A sensitive artist type or some shite. I'm not trying to spout off some macho crap, but I've been really feckin' patient with you." Connor's eyes danced with suppressed anger. "I've been willing to sit on the sidelines for two years while the world sees you in fake relationship after fake feckin' relationship. It's weird. I've *always* thought it's weird, but I *have* trusted you."

"You *can* trust me."

Connor squinted at me. "Then tell me everything. Now. And I mean, right now."

I couldn't answer him. Nothing would come out.

"Okay. God dammit. I know where I stand. I didn't want to believe it, but I know." Connor's eyes revealed a deep devastation that I never believed I would cause. "Now, I've got to draw a line for myself. For my self-respect as a man. You've made a decision to publicly date Sam without even once talking to me about it. Asking how I felt. Now, I think I need to make mine. I'm not okay with you and Sam. Not even a little."

My eyes must have been as round as saucers. This wasn't happening. I knew I was going to be pushing the envelope. I knew my bearding career was strange, even by Hollywood standards. But the greater good was at stake. "I told you why Sam is so important to the project. It's critical—"

"I get it," he interrupted. "And I'm not telling you what you're doing is not important. I'm very proud of you for putting yourself on the line like you're doing, when you may never get anything out of it. But it's *your* choice, Ronni. Somewhere along the line, I've lost my ability to make a choice."

"That's not true," I protested.

His face softened. "Ah, but it is."

"I'll call it off." I reached for his hand. "I'm not willing to lose you

255

over this. *You're* more important."

Connor took my hand, dwarfing it in his big palm. "I shouldn't be. We're not going to see each other for months when I leave for the Asian tour. When I get back, the cycle will start up again. The bottom line is, even before the Sam situation, the reason I knew I had no right to tell you how to live your life is because I've known that being with me isn't fair to you. The truth is right in our faces, Mae. As much as we love each other, we can't sustain this anymore."

"Please, Connor. Don't do this." Tears spilled down my cheeks.

"God, Mae. Don't feckin' cry." Connor pulled me to his chest. "I can't stand it."

"Then stop talking this way," I sputtered.

Connor grasped my shoulders and held me away from him, boring his amber eyes into mine. "Fine, I'll stop talking that way if you come up to Seattle with me for Christmas and spend it with my family. I'll introduce you as my girlfriend of two years and finally be able to come clean to the guys, even though they all know anyway."

My face crumpled. That, I couldn't do. No matter how much I wanted it. My loud, wracking sobs shook the bed.

"That's what I thought." Connor released his grip and stood. "I'm just going to go back to the studio."

"I don't want this to end," I sobbed. "Please reconsider. Take some time and reconsider. I love you. I love you so much."

Connor wrapped his arms around me. "I know, Mae. I love you too. But, we're at an impasse."

Tears streamed down my face as I watched him gather up his things. He took his time to neatly fold his clothes and put his toiletries together. Stoically, he shoved everything into his oversized duffle bag. When he was packed, he reached into his pocket and handed me his FOB to my house.

"I'm not taking it back, it's yours," I rasped.

"Not anymore." Connor sat next to me and took my hand. "This is for the best. For you. For me."

"I don't understand what's happening. You were just inside my body. You just told me you loved me."

He kissed my temple. "I do love you, Mae. There will never be anyone else. My heart is broken. As I said many times before, you're it for me. I need some time apart from you to make sure this is the right relationship for me."

"That sounds so lame. So cliche," I spat.

"Aye, so it does." He released his grip on me. "But it's the truth. My truth. The way I see it, you'd still rather have fake relationship after fake relationship with dudes who won't make you feel anything instead of a real relationship with the man who wants to make you feel everything."

To which I should have reassured him. I should have pleaded my case. I should have called it all off with Sam and begged for forgiveness.

But I did none of those things.

After he left, I pulled myself together and made it to the studio. It took my glamour team an extra half hour to fix my puffy, red eyes. As the consummate professional, I managed to get through the day without crying. I was saving that for when I got home. To my empty house.

When I stepped out of my trailer, I nearly collided with Kris, who was on her way to check on me. Taking one look at my face, she wrapped her arms around me. "Oh, Ronni. What happened with Connor?"

Into the wee hours of the night, I filled her in on all of it. Everything. Including the full scope of my project, the first part which was nearing completion. In fact, I confided to Kris all that I should have confided to the love of my life. Before it was too late. When I'd gotten it all out, Kris was overwhelmed but her eyes shone. "My God, Ronni. You are a badass bitch!"

"What?"

"Let me get this straight. You've managed to get footage of men confessing in great detail all of the horrific crap that that rat-bastard Sofer has been pulling for all of these years. Now, you have a straight man who is willing to share his story, which as you know, will bring down the entire house of cards." Kris tapped her finger to her chin. "No one has any clue about it? When I told you to make a difference, you really decided to be an overachiever, my dear."

"Connor's been so patient, Kris. And now, I've lost him because of it. It's hardly worth it."

Kris regarded me seriously. "I doubt that is true, I've seen the way he looks at you. But even if it is, you owe it to yourself to see this through. When you're done, go get your man."

My eyes filled with tears. "What if it's too late by then?"

"Then he wasn't ever worth it, sweetheart."

I appreciated my mentor's words of encouragement. I did.

But I also knew that we had the truest love and I was stupid enough to let it slip away.

It was me who wasn't worthy of Connor.

CHAPTER 29
FOUR MONTHS LATER

1:42 a.m.
To: connorm@ltz.com
From: vmm@vmm.com
Subject: An end of an era

Dearest Connor,

I know you'll be back in town to record your album soon, if you're not here already. I hope you're not bothered by all of the emails I've sent you over the past few months. Maybe you're not even reading them. I suppose that's a huge possibility.

Ah, well. I'm taking a chance.

I have some news. I told you that Kris and I decided that next season was going to be our last. Although I was sad, honestly? I'm excited. The show has given me everything. Professional opportunities. Money.

Recognition. A lifelong friend and mentor. Relationships that will carry my career wherever I want to take it (and I have some really cool plans!).

It also brought me to you.

So yes, a bittersweet day to be sure.

Tomorrow, if you think about it, read the LA Times. *Another project finally came to an end this week too. A great relief. Sam's story put the nail in Merv's proverbial coffin. Kris and I decided not to attach my name to it. I'm fine with it. Although his comeuppance came with great personal sacrifice, it's enough for me to know that an entire ring of predators will never hurt anyone again.*

By the way, I'm hearing good things about the new music. Carter had dinner with Kris the other night, he raved about it.

To say that I miss you would be a lie. How do you miss your limb when it's been ripped from your body? You don't. You endure. I'm not trying to lay any guilt on you, my love.

I'll just keep wishing on a star.

I love you.

Mae

I nearly jumped out of my skin when I felt a palm on the back of my neck. "Jay-sus, Da. You scared the life outta me."

"I thought I'd find ye up here, so I did." Da gazed out at Belfast Lough from the loft. "This is quite the spot you've got here."

"Aye."

I was glad my folks were here with me at my Belfast house for a couple of weeks before I had to do PR for our album. They were staying on for a few months to catch up with family after I left. Da's hair was fully gray now. He looked frail. Too frail for only being fifty-one years old. "How are you gettin' on, Da? Really?"

"I'm al'rite, son." He squeezed his fingers on my neck. "I have my good days and bad."

"Aye. I guess we all do. Surely."

"This is a mighty big house to keep up."

I'd been having the same thoughts. My not-so-distant memories of Ronni and I christening every room in this house were hard to put out of my mind. Her heartfelt emails made it difficult for me to keep her at a distance. Every time I got a new one, it was all I could do not to fly into LA and whisk her to off to Vegas. Marry her. Lock her down.

But that wasn't the best thing for her. Or for me. Especially not when she'd wrapped up the project she'd been obsessed with for years. And now that her show ended? Without her crazy schedule, my absence in her day-to-day life would be intolerable. I'd be gone for God knows how long when the next tour started. It's not like she could come out on the road with me, after all.

Truth be told, I regretted how I'd ended things. It was too harsh. Too abrupt. It seemed necessary at the time because I was devastated when I found out about Sam. I'd tried to hide it. At the same time, while I was willing to play second fiddle to Mae's convoluted bearding schemes when the dudes weren't a threat, I just couldn't stand it once Sam entered the picture.

Jealous as feck.

Rather than risk being dumped for someone else, I'd done the dumping this time.

"Penny for your thoughts." Da nudged me.

"Not worth a penny."

Da peered out at the sea and scrubbed his beard with his hand. "I gave up any right to give you advice a long time ago. But the only reason a man is as despondent as ye? A good woman. Does yer mood have somethin'

261

ta do with the actress?"

I looked into his amber eyes, which were exactly like mine. "How'd ye get on with Ma after—"

"She believed in me, so she did," Da cut me off. "I gave her no reason to for many years. She prob'ly should have left. During the bad years, I'd like to think that she focused on all of the good ones and hoped we'd get back to 'em."

I nodded. Looked back out the window. "Ronni's been writing me for the past few months."

"You love her?"

"Aye."

"Connor, I've not been a good da to you for many years. After me accident, I was broken. I'd been workin' me bollocks off and bein' incapacitated made me feel like a lesser man. I took it out on me family. On yer girl Jen. I lashed out. Was a right arsehole."

I couldn't help but smile a bit. "Aye."

"It took a long time to right the ship." Da crossed his arms. "Me point is, don't create problems where they don't exist. Problems will come. Ye deal with them. The love of a good woman is the end game. Not the houses. Not the gold records. Not the ambition. If ye love this gal, make it right with her. Don't let her go."

"Aye. Good advice." I surprised him with a hug. "For the record, you've been a great da for most of my life. I'm proud of all you've overcome. I'm proud to be your son."

Da's eyes watered. He nodded and clapped my back and left me staring out at the sea.

I opened my tablet and clicked on the *Los Angeles Times* link.

"BOYS TOWN SEX FOR ROLES SCANDAL ROCKS

HOLLYWOOD"

"#metoomen Movement Spreads Like Wildfire"

It took nearly thirty minutes to read through the article. When I finished, tears streamed down my face. I couldn't even comprehend what Mae had endured to break this story. With absolutely no credit. She never made this about her, Ronni Miller's name was nowhere near the byline. A reporter from the *LA Times* was getting all the credit for breaking this story, which went far beyond the #MeToo movement.

The article featured dozens of horrific stories about Merv Sofer, which made Harvey Weinstein look like a choirboy. From casting couches to drugged-up pool parties to paid escorts to out-and-out blackmail, Sofer had used an extensive web of power to groom unassuming young men trying to make it in Hollywood and create a code of silence. There were even allegations of murder.

Today, around the time the article dropped, the twenty men who were featured simultaneously filed complaints of extreme sexual misconduct against directors, actors, casting agents, publicists, and financiers. According the article, more were expected to come forward.

Then it hit me.

My God, Mae had taken down an entire sex ring.

The entire time we'd been together, I'd never known the extent of the project. She'd been tight-lipped about why she needed to keep the details secret. Why she couldn't tell me everything. Now it made sense. It was clear why she'd been a steel trap and insisted on honoring her bearding confidentiality agreements.

She hadn't been trying to keep me out of her life. She was doing the honorable thing. Trying to protect the lives of these men she considered friends. Men who were putting themselves in danger to expose such powerful people.

I felt like a right arsehole. I'd been fortunate to have this fearless woman in my life and I'd been getting my panties in a snit over stupid, stupid shite. She'd pleaded with me to trust her. She agonized when things didn't go according to her plan. Still, she never gave up single-handedly pursuing justice for her friend.

What did I do?

When I felt left out, I was impatient.

When she dressed up to attend a red carpet event with a fauxmance, I sulked.

When she needed more time after facing roadblocks, I used ultimatums and tried to impose timelines.

When Sam came into the picture, instead of supporting and trusting her, I dumped her.

Sam's story *was* her ace in the hole. This was an innocent man, who was married with a small baby, trying to pursue the Hollywood dream. He met Merv at a casting call, was thrilled to be invited to a "networking" party, only to wake up and realize he'd been drugged and raped. When he confessed what happened to his wife, she used all their savings to leave him and move back to Ghana with their child. He was offered a speaking part in a blockbuster superhero movie but turned it down. He said it wasn't worth his mind, body, and spirit.

Ronni was a revelation. In this moment, reading about her incredible work, I was crestfallen. Time and time again, when all she had asked of me was patience? I'd let her down. I'd actually believed she was stringing me along. That our relationship would end, just like it had with Jen. Despite all my baggage, she never made me feel anything but wanted.

She. Wanted. To. Be. With. Me.

And she still did.

I flew down the stairs to the main house where my ma was pulling out a shepherd's pie from the oven. "Connor, dinner will be ready in five minutes."

"Aye." I kissed her on the cheek and hurried to the guest room where I was staying. Grabbing my wallet, I logged onto the British Airways website and booked a first-class flight to Los Angeles for the next day.

My folks and I had a delicious meal. Da was going to take care of a few maintenance projects while they were staying at the house, so after dinner the three of us walked the grounds and made lists.

"Leave it to me, son." Da slapped me on the back. "We're happy to stay as long as it takes to get the place ready."

Hands on her hips, Ma surveyed the garden. "I'm going to find a gardener, Rory. Connor needs someone to keep these up on a regular basis. Before you know it, the place will be overgrown."

"Have you guys ever considered moving back here?" I gazed out toward the sea. The view never got old. I felt so at home here, like my legs were rooted to the soil.

My parents looked at each other, then at me. Ma spoke, "Connor, this is the type of home you should raise a family in. When you settle down."

"Hopefully sooner rather than later, you're not getting any younger," Da added helpfully.

After dinner, I packed and got to bed, my mind on the most beautiful, sweet girl in the universe. I thought about how I could be worthy of her taking me back. Despite her sweet email, I knew there was no clear path. All the good intentions in the world didn't change the fact that our jobs kept us apart. The best I could hope for was spending a couple of quality months with Ronni while we recorded. To worship her the way she deserved.

And beg for forgiveness.

The next morning, my car picked me up at four a.m. and drove me to Dublin airport, where the concierge whisked me through security and onto the plane. After a six-hour layover in London, I touched down in LA just before seven p.m.

I gave the driver Ronni's address.

It was time to reclaim my girl.

If she'd have me.

RONNI

CHAPTER30

7:14 a.m.
To: vmm@vmm.com
From: connorm@ltz.com
Subject: You are EVERYTHING

Mae,
Let me start this off by apologizing.
I'm a thick-headed, stubborn, Irish-tempered arse.
I don't deserve you.
It doesn't mean I don't want you, because I do.
What you did is nothing short of amazing. I hope you know how incredibly proud I am. Humbled. Honored that you still care about me.
Forgive the short email, my plane's about to leave. I'll arrive in LA tonight around seven.

I'm coming for you, my love.
I hope you'll have me.
You're my honey.
I love you.
I really, really love you.
You're my everything.
Let's reattach the limb.

Xoxo
Your honey (hopefully), Connor

My phone crashed to the floor. I'd been reading the email from Connor while walking through the back tunnels of JFK. One of my security detail picked it up for me and showed me the screen. It was smashed to bits, little shards were missing. Completely and totally ruined.

I nearly burst into tears.

"Ms. Miller, I'll get this replaced," Kim, my handler promised. "We'll get you to the meeting and by the time you're done, I'll have it sorted out."

I gave her a hug. "Thanks, Kim. I appreciate it."

At least I'd been able to read his sweet email once. I felt like running down the corridor and shouting at the top of my lungs, "Connor loves me!"

But he was in Los Angeles

I was in New York.

Our planes probably passed each other over LAX and now I couldn't even text him.

In the car ride to Manhattan, I freshened up my lipstick and powdered my nose. Normally, I wouldn't take the red-eye, but Sienna and Andrew had presented me with a lucrative endorsement opportunity from Cover Girl. We were meeting today to go over the details. I'd not lent my name to many products over the years, but it was time to spread my wings and start my life outside of *She's All That*.

I was beginning to think this trip was a bad idea when my heel caught and broke in the grate outside the midtown skyscraper. Kim was on the phone with a private concierge at Bergdorf, organizing a replacement pair of shoes within seconds. In the meantime, I hobbled the thirty steps from the sidewalk to the lobby and took off both shoes once I was inside.

Kim already had my name badge waiting, we bypassed the long line at security and were whisked up to the fifty-first floor. The lobby was ultra-modern, decorated in slate gray with pops of orange and pink. The reception table was pure white with pink neon LED lights. The whole effect felt very nightclubby.

God, I didn't want to be here. I wanted to turn around and get on a plane and get back to Connor.

Andrew, wearing gray slacks and a black sweater was waiting for me. After kiss-kiss greetings, he led me through a corridor with more gray walls and pink art to a conference room overlooking Times Square. Sienna was already in the room, her hair pulled back in a severe ponytail. Always the fashionista, she wore a simple, flowy black Chloe shirt dress that skimmed mid-thigh and sky-high Louboutin snake-print platform sandals.

My Diesel skinny jeans and an oversized black Zara sweater seemed a little out of place next to Sienna.

"Ronni, where the hell are your shoes?" Sienna laughed. "Only you would show up here for a meeting with Cover Girl barefoot."

Gritting my teeth at the snark, I just shrugged. "My heel broke, Kim's grabbing a new pair of shoes for me."

After our successful meeting with the cosmetics company, my publicists had a few other things to discuss with me. Andrew powered on the SmartScreen and gestured for me to sit. "Before we finalize the details on the Covergirl endorsement, we have a few other points of business."

"That's fine, after we're done I'd like to catch the next flight back to LA, something's come up." I sat in a vivid-orange conference chair and looked at the screen.

"We're supposed to have dinner with—"

I was adamant. "Somethings come up."

"Way to be professional." Sienna rolled her eyes, stood and took the clicker from Andrew. "Now, Ronni, I think it's high time you win your second Emmy. I know you've resisted our efforts in the past, but you have to admit your work on this last season of *She's All That* is deserving. You will have to play the game a bit, though."

"What do you mean?"

"Since your mom passed…" Sienna made the sign of the cross over her chest, even though I knew damn well a woman as shrewd as she had never stepped foot in church. "…well, your PR efforts have been lacking. I know you've never paid attention to these things, but to get an Emmy nom we need to start like yesterday to get your name in the trades."

I sighed. "Guys, let's just go meet with them. I can't miss a flight just to talk about the Emmys."

"Of course not, honey." Andrew wagged his finger. "We have some inside information for you about that book you're looking to option."

"I'll cut to the chase. We just signed Finnegan O'Roarke." Sienna cocked her hip and bobbed her head. "We can get you the rights."

Connor often told me about his parents and how they grew up in Northern Ireland during the Troubles. O'Roarke published the most haunting memoir of a young family torn apart in 1972 and followed the characters through the end of the modern Troubles. It won every major literary award and almost every director worth his or her salt wanted to do this story.

"Why didn't you say so??" I squealed. "That's amazing!"

"Not so fast." Sienna tapped her long, red nail on her lip. "Just because he's our client, doesn't mean O'Roarke is going to give a sit-com actress with a new production company a shot without a point in the right direction."

I squinted at the shrewd woman. "You think an Emmy win will get me closer?"

"Of course. Plus, I'm happy to nudge him in the right direction, but I need a little something in return."

Here we go

"What?"

Andrew walked over to the console where a copy of the *LA Times* was open to the expose. He pointed to the article. "Nice work."

"Yes, I read it. Crazy stuff." I tried to keep my face neutral. A poker player, I was not.

"You've been working on this for years, Ronni. Don't try to deny it." Sienna sat across from me and stared me down. "It wasn't hard for me to figure it out. *Hawaiian High.* Wynn. Merv was a producer. Don't forget, I arranged all of your beards. For the first time in my entire history of setting this stuff up, my client picked out the guys. You obviously had a reason."

I guess I could have tried to deny it, but my heart was beating so fast I did the next best thing. I shut up. My publicists were trying to get me to buy their silence about my involvement with Sofer's comeuppance.

Great. Just great.

"All we need you to do is two small favors, which will be beneficial to all of us." Andrew leaned against the SmartScreen. "Get yourself in the Emmy race. And we need you to beard for Tyson Rainier."

My mouth dropped. "Excuse me?"

"Andrew and I don't have any Emmy PR wins. We need that on our CV," Sienna explained. "Less Than Zero has been our client for a while now. Ty was our cash cow for years, he'd party and fuck random women. The coverage was epic. *I'm* the one who helped propel that album to the top by making him a bad boy. Now that he's on the straight and narrow, he's boring. B-O-R-I-N-G. He won't get wild anymore. He barely even shows up to interviews. We need to get him back out in the spotlight."

"Why me?"

"Oh, Ronni. You really are so adorably clueless. So is Ty. You're perfect together." Andrew laughed. "We need to dirty up your image a little to convince O'Roarke you can handle the subject matter. He's gritty. Real. You're known as a comedic actress. And the 'woe is me no one will date me' PR routine worked for a while. Now it's tired. I'm over it. The public is over it. It's time for a shake-up. You need to be seen with a hot, raunchy, famous guy like Ty. If the world thinks you're with him, you'll gain instant street credibility."

"Not to mention, O'Roarke's favorite band is LTZ," Sienna added helpfully.

"I'm friends with all of the guys in LTZ." I shook my head. "I can't beard for Ty. It would be weird."

"Would it be the worst thing in the world to be seen with the most gorgeous man in the entire world, Ronni?" Sienna licked her lips. "I can tell you from first-hand experience, that man's cock is a fine, fine specimen."

First, eeeewwww I don't want to see Ty's cock.

Second, um, not as gorgeous as Connor's…

"No." I shook my head harder and punctuated it with a wave of my hand. "Impossible. I'm done with bearding altogether. I'm happy to do the Emmy thing—"

Andrew cut me off. "Ty's going to be your date at the Emmy's. We are going to give O'Roarke the most epic experience. No one else vying for his blessing will think to do that. He'll be putty in your hands because you'll have him to yourself for the entire night."

"You won't have to worry about Tyson really liking you, he's still hung up on some bitch from Seattle that inspired *Z*," Sienna snarled.

"Look, I appreciate that all of this seems like a great opportunity. It's just not for me." I stood, grabbed my purse and decided to get myself out of this craziness. What I told them was true. I was done bearding. Connor loved me. It was our time now, we'd waited for far too long.

"What if I sweetened the pot even more?"

I stopped at the door and looked over my shoulder. "Make it quick."

"Have you heard about Don Kircher's poker games?" Andrew smiled. "Highly illegal. Big stakes. And all of that is well and good, but the after-parties? Think Sofer on steroids."

My entire stomach seized. I felt dizzy. The next thing I knew, my face was barreling toward the floor.

"Ronni!" Andrew rushed to my side. "Are you okay?"

"Just let me breathe." My voice sounded like my windpipe had burst. I sat on the floor with Andrew and Sienna looking at me like I were an alien. God damn panic attack. Closing my eyes and taking deep breaths helped me calm down. I felt my heartbeat regulate. Finally, I was able to speak. "What do you mean?"

Sienna's voice was soft. "Don't you want to take him down too, now that you got Sofer?"

My third and final vow was to take out Kircher too.

For myself.

When the story came out, of course Kircher was in the back of my mind. I wanted to bring him down, but I didn't have any idea how to get to him. The difference between Kircher and Sofer was visibility. Don's ascent from television showrunner to blockbuster film director was quick, but effective. He was the most sought-after director in the world. Every actor worth his or her salt wanted a part in his new film, *Phantom Rising*.

Except for me, of course. I'd never work with him again. I'd made sure of it after the near debacle a couple of years ago. Not that he didn't stop trying. He tried to cast me in every movie he made. Always by audition. The thought of what he'd expect of me as an adult made me want to vomit.

So this offer? To take him down? I couldn't refuse.

Could I?

Connor's gorgeous face flashed in my mind.

Glancing at the clock, I knew I had to wrap things up to catch the next flight out. He was the most important thing right now. Everything else would have to wait.

"Look, guys, I appreciate you setting up these meetings. We have a lot to think about. As far as Tyson's concerned, I need to give it some thought. It's a big decision." I hugged both my publicists. "Give me a couple of weeks."

"I'll give you one week." Sienna crossed her arms. "Otherwise we won't have enough time on the Emmys thing."

"Fine."

I turned to leave and Sienna put her hand on my shoulder and pierced me with a glare. "I'd really hate for anyone to learn that you were behind that story."

Point taken.

When I returned to the lobby, Kim was waiting for me with my phone and a pair of Alexander McQueen metal-bar knee-high boots and some soft socks. Gratefully, I put them on. "I'm going back to LA, we need to get to JFK."

"I've checked you into the Four Seasons."

"I'll pay for the room, I need to get home." I got into the Town Car and fired up my phone. No texts. I read my email from Connor again. Swooned. Then I sank back into the seat and thought about my day for a minute. Cover Girl was going to be awesome. Working with O'Roarke would put me on the map behind the camera, a role that had great appeal to me. The rest was batshit. Bearding for Ty was the craziest thing I'd ever heard. Connor would never understand. The Emmys? Meh. I could take it or leave it. I would have been happy to help my publicists out on that account. Until the not-so-veiled threat. They could fuck themselves for all I cared. Except, the Don Kircher thing threw a real wrench into things. It could be my only chance. I just needed to digest it all.

Because I'd like nothing more in the world than to bring that disgusting animal down.

Well, there was one thing I wanted more.

And that was Connor.

Before I made any decisions, I had to find out where we stood.

CHAPTER 31

To: connorm@ltz.com
From: vmm@vmm.com
Subject: Re: You are EVERYTHING

Connor,

I was on a plane to NYC! I missed you.

You don't know what it meant to see your email. I've been on cloud nine all day. I tried calling, but your phone went right to VM. Now I'm on a plane back to you.

Go to my house, Connor. I'm on my way. I've let security know to let you in.

I really, really love you.

I'll ping you the second I get in.

Xoxo
Your honey, Mae

I was so relieved to see that Ronni finally replied to my email. After I stopped by her house right from the airport to find she wasn't there, I was gutted. I certainly couldn't blame her for getting on with things. Or ignoring me. She'd sent me dozens of emails I didn't bother my arse answering.

Because I'm a stubborn Irish idiot.

In LA, without Ronni and the guys, there was little that interested me. Still jetlagged, I checked into the Sunset Marquis, put in my earphones and immediately fell asleep. I woke up at half past three, starving. Rather than ordering up room service, I had another idea.

Connor: do you have dinner plans
Kris: ???
Connor: it's Connor
Kris: I know that, did you mean to ask me to dinner?
Connor: Y
Kris: I could do an early dinner, have meetings later
Connor: Perfect, meet me at Osteria Mozza?
Kris: Impressive
Connor: if you say so, the concierge made a reservation for me

When I arrived, I saw Kris sitting in the back against a black-lacquered half wall underneath a window into the kitchen. After exchanging a quick Hollywood hug, I took a seat across from her in a black-leather cafe chair.

"I have a bone to pick with you." Kris peered at me through red-rimmed reading glasses behind her menu. "When Ronni's unhappy, so am I."

I crossed my arms over my chest. "I'll be waiting for her when her plane touches down in two hours."

Kris regarded me and went back to reading the menu, not acknowledging my comment. "So much for me staying off carbs."

"She never told me everything, you know. I'm an ass, there is no doubt about it. I didn't have all of the information, though." I tried to explain. "I lost it when she told me she was bearding for a straight man. It wasn't what we agreed to. I was jealous and overreacted."

"I'm surprised you let it go as long as you did." Kris closed the menu. "Why would you let her get away with all of that?"

Not sure if it was a test, I just looked at Ronni's mentor. Not answering.

Kris stared right back, not backing down.

"I love her. I adore her. I wanted to support her even when I didn't understand it. It got to be too much for me."

"Putting her needs ahead of yours?"

"Aye."

"Why?"

"It wasn't like I didn't *trust* trust her. I knew she wouldn't cheat on me. It just felt wrong after how close we became that she couldn't open up to me." I rested my head in my hand. "I didn't have room to talk. I'm always on the road. It's such a disaster, all of this."

"She's been through a lot, Connor. Therapy's helped, but a lot more went on when she was in Hawaii. It's not all about Wynn. *Hawaiian High* was probably the most toxic set I've ever heard of. She didn't escape, but it's not my story to tell."

Wait, what?

What she said caused a pang to my heart. If someone hurt her like Wynn had been hurt, I'd kill them. No bother. No remorse. I steadied my breathing so I didn't erupt in front of Kris in the middle of a popular restaurant. "Look. My plan is to be her support system. I love her. Unconditionally. At the end of the day, I invited you to dinner because you're her family. I felt like I needed to man up and make it right with you."

She stared me in the eye and tapped her finger to her lip. "Ronni's a headstrong woman. Underneath her sweet persona, she's ruthless. When she sets her mind to something, she goes for it."

"I love that about her."

"Are you in this for the long-haul, Connor?"

"Aye. I am."

"Good, then let me see if I can help you get your girl back." Kris waved the waiter over to take our order.

Before dinner was finished, I'd gotten an earful. She gave me insight. Direction. A few surprises. We devised a plan of our own to help her get closure. After talking with Kris, I felt relieved. It cemented in my mind that my girl was worth every sacrifice I could ever make for her. She was my priority in life. Above all else.

Forever.

On my way back to Ronni's, I stopped by my hotel and checked out. I had a few days before the rest of the guys arrived. My plan was to get reacquainted with Mae in each and every room of her Malibu mansion. All day. All night.

After I convinced her to marry me.

After all, we were finally free.

Considering it was such a beautiful, warm evening, I decided to wait outside on her deck in our pod. The perfect place to watch the sunset over the Pacific Ocean until she got home. She'd texted me from the airport, so I expected her within the hour.

It was rare for me to have nothing to do.

It was nice.

Relaxing.

The waves lapping against the shore were meditative. Soothing. The sky had turned almost violet with shards of orange and yellow gradually exploding into breathtaking pinks and purples. My mind cleared and I felt at peace. This was where I belonged.

"My honey, you're here." Ronni caressed my shoulder.

Reaching up, my hand covered hers. Turned my head to see Ronni's green eyes shine with un-spilled tears. "Ah, Mae. Come to me."

She moved to face me and held out her hands so I could take them, which I did to pull her down on my lap. She straddled me and I wrapped my arms around her. She buried her beautiful face into my shoulder. My dick was so hard against her heat, all I wanted to do was be inside her. Words could come later. Now, I needed my girl.

"I have so much to say to you—" She pressed her lips to mine. "Not now."

My voice caught. "Mae, love. I want you. So much. There's no way to be gentle. I don't have it in me."

She answered by sucking on my earlobe. "I don't want gentle. I want to feel every inch of you."

For a long moment I just held her gaze. Questioning. Making sure she was on board. When Ronni nodded her response I groaned and fused my mouth to hers. It wasn't a kiss. It was an invasion. Wild. Stroking. Mindless. She pulled my T-shirt up over my head and threw it to the ground. In turn, I divested her of her sweater and got to work on the button of her jeans.

"My boots—" Ronni said between kisses and I noticed her knee-high boots zipped over her pants.

"Feck 'em," I growled. "No time."

I sat up with Ronni in my lap, moved out from under her and swiveled our positions so she was pressed against the edge of the pod. Positioning myself behind her, I roughly yanked down her jeans, exposing her tiny pink panties. She wiggled her luscious heart-shaped ass, leaving me with no option but to run my finger down her spine, along her anus and down to her slit, finding her soaked.

With little grace, I yanked down my zipper and took out my needy cock. Wordlessly I pressed my hips against Ronni, molding myself to her body. She reached around with one hand and hooked her arm over my neck, pressing her ass against my engorged shaft, baring her graceful, silky neck to me. With no patience left, I hooked my fingers on each side of her panties and ripped them down, suckling on her nape all the while. Her skin felt like it was burning in contrast to the cool air around us now that the sun had disappeared over the horizon.

Reaching around her body, I slid one hand up her taut stomach to cup her breast through her sheer, lace bra. When my thumb brushed against her puckered nipple, what was left of my self-control evaporated. I moaned low in my throat, positioned and thrust into my love to the hilt. Dragging my mouth along her neck and chin, I slammed into her, feeling drugged with desire. Ronni turned her head to capture my lips. My arms wrapped around her to hold her tight against me so I could devour her while remaining deep inside her.

Feck, I needed this woman.

More than anything else in this world.

I bent over her, causing her to fall forward. She caught herself and gripped the edge of the lounger so she could hang on while my hips canted into her. Hard. Staccato. Thrusts. My hands spanned her hips, my fingers dug in as I unleashed my inner beast. Pounding and pounding into her. With abandon. Unable to control my most banal urges.

"Ahhhhh, Connor," she screamed, bucking back against me.

"Come for me, love." I reached around to rub her clit, only to find her own hand swirling around her sweet spot. That was all she wrote. Unable to control myself an instant longer, I howled and spurted deep into her body.

Four months of pent-up desire exploding in one phenomenal release.

To prevent myself from collapsing on top of her, I clutched the pod on either side of her. My hips were still pumping with abandon, my cock still hard as a pole. Ronni's little mewls nearly undid me, she circled her hips against me. When I felt coherent enough, I pulled out and watched my come seep out of her opening.

My woman.

My seed.

Spilling out of her.

Feral caveman instincts overtook my self-control.

Reaching to the side, I grabbed her ankle and unzipped her boot and repeated the process on the other side. I stood to kick off my shoes and peel off my jeans. Ronni slipped out of her boots and I tugged her jeans the rest of the way down.

She laid against the lounger, stretched out fully. Her creamy skin beautifully shimmered against the cushions. Her knees splayed open just enough so I could still see our combined release glistening between her legs. Her rosebud nipples pointed at me, beckoning. "I want you to be buried inside of me for at least a week, can you handle that?"

Holy shite. This woman. I wanted to devour every single solitary inch of her.

"Aye, my love."

There was no doubt Ronni knew she was a stunning woman. Everyone said so. She'd been deemed the most beautiful woman in the world many times in many publications. One of the many reasons I loved her was she never acted uppity or more important than anyone else. She all but ignored it.

Still, I couldn't stop myself from telling her. "You. Are. So feckin' gorgeous, Mae. You're mine. I feckin' love you."

"Show me, Connor McGloughlin. Show me that you're all mine." She extended her hand. Taking it, I knelt between her legs and leaned over her. Ronni snaked her arms around my neck and pulled me in for a kiss. The second her full lips touched mine, I was lost again. Anytime this woman welcomed me into her glorious body was nothing less than a miracle. I slid her hips closer to my still rock-hard dick. Her pussy was still wet and swollen, the fragrance from our sex wafted around us.

Ronni's head fell back. She gripped the sides of my face and arched her body, pulling me to her distended nipples. "Suck on them, Connor, please."

I flicked the tip with my tongue, she sucked in a tight breath. "Ohhh…" Her hips undulated against my cock, which rested against her belly. I could feel her plump and needy pussy against my balls. Wee Connor wanted to get inside her tight body again. Make her come over and over and over again, until she couldn't take it anymore.

"Feckin', hell, baby. I'll never get enough of you," I murmured against the underswell of her breasts, laving them with my tongue and sucking her rosy nipples hard into my mouth one after the other.

Her hands skimmed over my shoulders, down the contours of my biceps. "You'll never have to, my love."

She threaded her fingers through my hair while I continued to worship her world-class tits. With one hand, I reached down between us and rubbed the crown of my cock back and forth against her clit, savoring her little breathy moans as she circled against me. I sat back on my heels but canted my hips to tease her entrance with my tip. Ronni shuddered and clung to me. "God, I'm so wet, I want you inside me again. So much."

In all my years, I'd never seen anything so hot as the sight of my dick in between Ronni's bare, glistening pussy lips. Spread open for me, while the last remaining embers of daylight flickered out around us.

Tonight was a religious experience.

"Connor." Her voice was ragged. She looked at me through hooded eyes. Clutching my cock, I tapped my crown on her clit, watching it pulse with need. Ronni wiggled her hips, trying to get closer.

Our hands roamed each other's bodies, mapping each other's every angle. Every crevice. Every dip. Every hard plane. Her ample breasts heaved. At some point, our hands clasped together and she spread her legs wider so I could position my cock against her opening and push inside.

My breath was ripped from my lungs when I looked into her eyes. Our souls merged in that instant. Became one. My cock stretched her soft, tight tissues. Her slick pussy enveloped me, as tight as a fist. Ronni's eyes fluttered shut. Helplessly, she uttered an agonized, "ahhhhhhh" as I thrust deeper and deeper.

I'll love you forever.

I released her hands and palmed her breasts, rolling her pert nipples between my fingers. Pinching. Stroking down her body, I gripped under her ass and looked down at the thick base of my cock stretching her wide. Disappearing inside her. My entire body shuddered. Her long, shapely legs were spread over my thighs. Her arms were flung over her head.

I'll love you forever.

Ronni rolled her hips against me. "Oh, Connor," she groaned. Needing her flush against my body, I supported her weight and pulled her up. She was impaled on my lap, her knees on either side of me, giving her more control. My woman lifted and ground against me, I pulled her down and thrust up against her.

Push and pull.

Yin and yang.

Perfect together.

"You are so feckin' hot, love." My voice was husky. Strained. "Fuck me. God. Fuck me hard. I'm yours, Mae. I'm always yours. I've always *been* yours."

"Oh, baby," she cried. Biting my earlobe and winding her arms around my neck she rode and rocked, chasing her nirvana. Out of my mind with lust, I managed to slip my hand between us to finger her clit. Her body greedily bucked and bucked and bucked against it, causing an inferno of release to build at the base of my spine.

I'll love you forever.

Fire pooled in my balls. Biting my cheek, I rubbed her sweet spot in quick circles. She sobbed and cried out, gripping my wrist where I touched her. "Faster," she pleaded. "I'm gonna come so hard, babeeeeee…"

She threw herself back against me, her body milking me, exploding in heaving spasms. The intensity of her orgasm left me no choice but to join her. My orgasm pulsed deep and hot inside her.

Twisting around, I rolled her on top of me, snuggling her trembling body until we eventually settled. The warm California air caressed our bodies, a salty ocean breeze danced around us. Caressing her hair and her back, I kissed her over and over.

Neither of us spoke. We didn't need to.

Eventually we both fell asleep.

My last thought before drifting off…

I'll love you forever.

RONNI

CHAPTER 32

"Do you want a glass of wine?" I pointed to a bottle of pinot grigio in my fridge.

"No thank you, I'm not drinking anymore." Tyson was staring out at the ocean through my big picture window in the living room. "I'll take sparkling water if you have it."

I located the bottle of Pellegrino. "Lime? Lemon?"

Ty turned toward me, his eyes were the exact color of the water he was admiring. "Both, thank you."

Carrying the drinks over to the coffee table, I tamped down my nervousness. I'd agreed to go through with another bearding ruse with Ty. Tonight was my first one-on-one with the singer to go over expectations. Details.

"Thanks for doing this. I think." Ty sat and took the sparkling water. "I've got to tell you, this is a very weird situation for me."

I smiled at the handsome singer. His long, brown hair gleamed in the sunlight. His face was covered in signature stubble. He wore a white t-shirt and threadbare jeans with black boots. "Don't sweat it, Ty. We're friends. It's a mutually beneficial arrangement."

Ty regarded me thoughtfully when I sat next to him, our knees barely touching. "I like you, Ronni. I'm thinking it's time for me to move on with my life. I've been hung up on my ex-girlfriend for so many years, I don't really know who I am anymore."

Not exactly the conversation I thought we'd be having. Although, Connor told me he didn't think Ty knew the extent of our relationship. After Australia, he'd been either fucked up or in his own world whenever I'd been around the band. "It's good you've made such positive changes, Ty. I was worried about you. I think everyone was."

Ty leaned back too, turning toward me. His sweet, earnest face broke hearts all over the world. When he wasn't wasted, the man was quite possibly the most considerate, polite guy I'd ever met. His vulnerability brought out my nurturing instinct. Combined with his masculine, sexual energy? Potent. Magnetic. I could totally see why every woman on earth—but not me of course—fell in love with him.

"That's a cool tattoo." Ty pointed to my relatively new ink located on my upper inner arm. I'd had it done after the Sofer story came out. It was script of part of a letter my mom left for me after she died. Connor and I had gone to his favorite tattoo parlor on the Sunset strip. He got a new Celtic band around his right arm while I suffered through the worst pain I'd ever felt. But it *was* cool. I loved it. I loved that we'd been tatted together even more.

"Be fearless in the pursuit of what sets your soul on fire"

I was so lost in my thoughts about my mom and getting tattoos with Connor that it took me completely by surprise when Ty leaned over and kissed me.

"Whoa!" I pushed him away. "It's not going to be like that with us, Ty."

His eyes grew wide, his face turned beet red. "Oh, shit. Ronni. I thought I was supposed to actually take a stab at a relationship with you. I'm sorry if I offended you."

"Jay-sus Feckin' Christ, Rainier." Connor boomed through the kitchen into the living room. "Catch a feckin' grip on yerself."

"Connor?" Ty was clearly shocked. "What are you doing here?"

I couldn't help but giggle at the comedy of it all. "Oh, Ty. You don't know I'm with Connor?"

"What???" Ty's face contorted cartoon-style.

Connor nudged his way in between us and gathered me to his side. He pointed at Ty. "Ronni and I have been together for years, you're trying to make the move on my woman, you bollocks!"

Ty's eyebrows raised so high I thought they might fly off the top of his head. "I thought your girlfriend's name was May, what happened to her?"

Connor's voice boomed, "Veronica *Mae* Miller, you eejit!"

I couldn't help it, it was too funny. I burst out laughing. The look of possessiveness on Connor's face when he whipped around to see what was so funny only fueled the humor of the entire situation. He fixed me with an annoyed glare. Which made me lose it even more. The corner of his lip quivered, then turned up, and soon my giant was laughing uncontrollably too. It was catching, Ty joined us. For ten solid minutes, the three of us laughed until we cried. Tears streaming down all of our faces.

"Stop! Stop!" I yelped, "My stomach can't take it anymore."

Connor wiped the tears out of the corner of his eyes and, still guffawing, in a swift move put Ty in a headlock. "Don't you ever make a move on my woman again, pretty boy."

Ty threw his hands up in the air, his smile wide. "Not a problem. Ronni, I think you'll agree that the kiss didn't do any more for you than it did for me."

Which set us all of into another fit of laughter.

When we all regained our composure, Connor got up to head back toward the bedroom and put his gruff face back on. "I'll leave you two to hash out the details. But, Rainier, know that I'm not thrilled with this arrangement. Not one bit. I'm going along with it for Ronni's sake."

We watched Connor stalk away and I turned back to Ty and shrugged. "I guess now you know."

Ty slouched against the cushions, looking over at me. "I'm sorry for trying to kiss you. I had no idea you were with Connor. Or really what this whole arrangement is supposed to be."

"We're rehabbing your slutty image and dirtying up mine." I patted his knee. "All we have to do is milk this PR ride for all its worth. I'll guide you through."

"What's in it for you, anyway?" Ty's eyebrows knitted together. "Why would Connor agree to this?"

"Connor knows I'm doing Sienna a favor in exchange for some help with a project I'm hoping to produce. He's staying here with me while you guys record your album." Of all people, Ty didn't need to know my business. Or the real reason why I'd agreed to this stupid arrangement.

"I don't get any of this. Sienna's always wanting me to be something I'm not which I thought was fine if it helps the band. I can't pretend to understand anything about PR. I just want to make music. Play shows…"

"You're fine." I socked him lightly in the arm. "It's no big deal, Ty. You'll be my date at the Emmys. We'll go to a couple of red carpet events. Maybe dinner at Nobu. Stuff like that. We'll have a few articles written about us. In a few months, we'll be a distant memory in people's minds."

Truthfully, I regretted agreeing to this arrangement. Sienna didn't have any connections I couldn't make on my own. Her threats of blackmail revealed what a snake she really was. Risking my relationship with Connor didn't seem worth any of this. He and I discussed it rationally, though. Connor was surprisingly supportive. He knew that getting connected to Finnegan O'Roarke would be a game changer for me.

Except that wasn't my real reason for doing it.

I hadn't told Connor that Sienna promised to feed me information about Kircher's illicit poker games. She was going to feed me the details over the course of my "relationship" with Ty. By the time our contract was over, I'd have enough ammo to take him down. I didn't feel good about keeping it from Connor, but I also didn't want to rock the boat when we only just got back in it.

I just couldn't pass up the chance at a final act of redemption to set me completely free.

There was no need to tell anyone the real reason why I agreed to beard for Ty. Not yet. Because maybe no one would ever have to know about what happened.

Not even Connor.

So here I was, bearding again. For the next few months, Ty would be my public boyfriend. LTZ was in Los Angeles working on their next album, so it was easy to coordinate our schedules to attend a few different events together. Connor's only stipulation was easy to agree to: before every event, he wanted to shag the bejeezus out of me. "To remind you who you belong to when you're holding his hand," he said.

Considering my heart *did* belong to him, it was a pretty awesome compromise.

Ty and I did a great job of convincing people. Despite the fact that we were in public for a grand total of ten times, the world believed that

Ty and I were deeply in love. I taught him how to navigate the press and paparazzi like a champ and to become invisible when he didn't want attention. Hannah dressed him for the red carpet at the Emmys, and for the first time in his life, Ty took an interest in fashion. His green-plaid suit put him on multiple best-dressed lists. Fashion brands began coveting him.

So it was kind of fun.

Until it wasn't.

Our coupledom popularity exploded. I hadn't counted on the world thinking we were the second coming of Brangelina. Sienna and Andrew were overjoyed about the extraordinary interest "Tonni" was generating in the entertainment world.

Me? Connor? Not so much.

Because it changed the narrative.

Even though he and I were very much together, LTZ fans were going batshit crazy at the thought of me and Ty as a couple. The scrutiny was exponentially more than what I'd experienced with Kip or any other faux relationship. So, I got one thing out of it. My good-girl image was officially smudged, paving the way for the Finnegan O'Roarke collaboration.

It wasn't worth it. Ty and I became the most coveted couple in years. Our images were everywhere. Photoshopped, mostly. Paparazzi followed us everywhere, but they never got their "money" shot. That's because we only were in public at prearranged outings. With little "real" information about us, rumors of weddings, babies, and cheating followed us everywhere.

At least Ty was becoming a good friend. He spent a lot of time with Connor and me at my house. We learned of his plans for a foundation to help underserved kids like him learn music and the arts. He talked about Zoey. The songs on *Z* made so much sense now that I had more inside information. I encouraged him to reconnect with her, because it seemed to me that for Ty, there would never be any other woman.

I found it crazily romantic that this coveted specimen of a man had been brought to his knees by true love.

I mean, I felt the same way about Connor, after all.

Unfortunately, the more popular he and I became as a couple, the bigger the problem we had. I'd never in a million years imagined how ingrained we were becoming in pop culture. Connor and I realized that when the time came, our own *real* relationship was going to look nefarious. Like we'd cheated on Ty. His own bandmate.

Needless to say, Connor was furious.

He hated games. He hated lies.

Rightfully so.

He wasn't a cheater.

If we went public, he'd be the other man.

I'd put our relationship in a secondary position.

Again.

What was wrong with me?

I couldn't help but wonder how much he'd be willing to put up with before he'd end it for good.

I soon found out.

On Valentine's Day, LTZ happened to be playing a special hometown show in Seattle to raise money for Zane's friend Fiona's nightclub. Ordinarily, in Seattle, the guys really didn't get bothered much. There were no paparazzi. We thought it would be a low-key night. It was my opportunity to meet Connor's family after the show.

Instead, Ty and I were ambushed. Sienna showed up with a full team from *People* magazine. She'd arranged a behind-the-scenes article with a bunch of staged photographs of Ty and me as a loving couple in his hometown.

I still tried to stick to the original plan as much as possible. After sound check, per our sexy agreement, Connor and I had just finished christening his dressing room. Like a shark, Sienna was waiting to strike when I left to get ready for the photo shoot.

"You're breaking the agreement." Her tall, lithe frame clad in zebra-print jeans, sky-high Prada boots, and a black-fringed halter, was waiting for me outside his door.

Ignoring her, I turned and walked toward Ty's dressing room.

She easily caught up.

"Don't think I haven't known about you and Connor all of this time, babe." She tapped into her phone as she walked alongside me. "You're playing a dangerous game. If you mess up in this thing with Ty, I'm canceling the meeting with O'Roarke."

Her increasingly distasteful antics left me furious. She was a stone-cold opportunist. Luckily, I was able to hide my disgust for the woman who'd been handling my PR for years. A woman I'd recommended to LTZ. I knew how to play the game, and no one was more street smart than me at this point.

I stopped to face her. "What exactly do you need from me, Sienna?"

"Six more months."

My mouth must have hit the floor before I recovered. "Not a chance."

"Fine. I'm canceling the meeting."

"The fuck you are." Connor walked up behind us. "A deal's a deal."

Sienna scowled. "Oh look, Mr. Grumpy has a voice."

He stared her down. She knew from the look on his face not to fuck with him.

But I didn't need Connor fighting my battles. I was fully capable. "You best not threaten me, Sienna. I am not extending with Ty. Neither of us want that."

"You're nuts, Ronni." Sienna scowled. "Your relationship with Ty has made you the most famous woman on the planet."

Connor growled.

"You care about that, I don't. I never have. So you can forget about the *People* magazine feature tonight if you say one more word." I got right up in her face to stop her when her mouth opened like a fish. "Seriously, one more word and I'm not doing it. We're overexposed enough, it's already going to be a challenge for Connor and me to ever be a public couple after this without some backlash."

Connor lightly placed his palm on my lower back. I appreciated his silent thank-you for standing up to her. I appreciated that he held his tongue. I hoped my words showed him that our relationship meant everything to me, even though the situation I put us in was the opposite. I couldn't wait to put "Tonni" in the rear-view mirror.

And replace it with "Ronner."

"You and Connor can never be a public couple after Ty and you break up." Sienna crossed her arms, her eyes glinted with ire. "How would you possibly manage that with LTZ's fans?"

Connor's reaction was visceral. "The fuck we can't. We can and we will."

I reached for Connor's hand in a show of solidarity. "I agree with Connor."

"You're both idiots." Sienna rolled her eyes condescendingly. "Connor will be annihilated as a home wrecker. '*Ty's bandmate breaks up the perfect couple.*' Ronni will be the slut that fucked two members of LTZ."

Holy shit, she'd planned this.

If steam actually could come out of someone's ears, it would most certainly have been coming out of Connor's at that moment. His face reddened. The red deepened to purple. I could tell it was taking every ounce of his energy not to lose his cool.

Because she'd hit the mark.

Mission accomplished, Sienna smirked at him in triumph and flounced off, flipping us both the bird as she walked away.

"I need a new publicist." I chewed on my thumbnail, looking under my hair at Connor. Thanking God she didn't bring up Kircher. "She's crazypants."

Connor didn't say anything. I could see the gerbils spinning on the wheel in his head. From around the corner, I could hear the rest of LTZ approaching. The next thing I knew, Zane had his arms wrapped around me. Ty and Jace stood close to Connor, grinning at the zaniest band member snuggling me. They were all clearly excited about the hometown show.

Connor, on the other hand, was quiet. Too quiet. I could tell he was livid.

Ty glanced from me to Connor, picking up on the weird energy. "Everything okay? Ronni, we're supposed to go to the VIP lounge for the *People* interview."

Jace glanced between me, Ty, and Connor. "I tried to tell you all this was a colossally stupid idea. Sienna is on a power trip. It's time to knock her down a peg or two. Remember, she works for us. And you, of course, Ronni."

Connor leaned close to my ear and pointed to the VIP lounge. "Can you please go get it the feck over with."

So we did.

And I knew, I was so done.

After the photo shoot was over, Ty hugged me tight. "Let's end this,

Ronni. It's not worth it. I'll take the fall for you so Connor can play the hero."

"It's probably not necessary. I do agree though. This has gone on long enough. Let's think about how." I hugged him back. Tightly. I knew my voice sounded weary. "I'm sorry this has turned into such a mess."

"It's not a problem. All I can think about is if Zoey and I were still together and I had to see her pretend to be in love with one of my best friends, I couldn't handle it." He stroked my hair. "I don't blame Connor for being pissed. This fake publicity thing isn't right. I don't want to do it anymore. I'm not a liar. Neither are you."

His blue eyes were so sincere. I gave him another squeeze. "Ty, you're a good man. It's kind of you to say, but with respect to my public relationships, I've been a liar for many years. I thought there was a good reason, but now I'm not so sure. This is hurting Connor. He's a strong, proud man who puts everyone's needs first. Always ahead of his own. I love him so much, and I just can't hurt him for one more minute."

"It's settled then. I'll walk you to his dressing room so Sienna doesn't freak the fuck out." He held out his arm to escort me down the hall. "She's my biggest nightmare, truth be told."

I was beginning to think she was mine too.

Ty rapped lightly on Connor's dressing room door. A grizzled older man who looked like an older version of Connor opened and let us both in.

"Where's Connor?" Ty asked.

"Right feckin' here." Connor emerged from the restroom. "Is your photo shoot over?"

His entire family looked at both of us with hardened eyes.

I wanted to disappear through the floor.

Connor crossed the room to my side and put his arm around me.

"This is Veronica Mae Miller, my girlfriend. As I've explained, she's Ty's fake girlfriend right now for PR purposes. And yes, we know it's stupid. Ronni, meet my ma and da, Maureen and Rory McGloughlin. These gits are my brothers, Seamus, Cillian, Brennan, Liam, and Padraig."

"I'm pleased to meet all of you." My voice cracked. "I'm sorry it's under such weird circumstances. When Ty, Connor, and I agreed to go along with this, we had no idea—"

A sharp rap on the door interrupted me, it was time for the show. Ty excused himself to do vocal warm-ups, leaving me with Connor and his family. We made small talk, but I was feeling very awkward and ashamed to make any type of positive impression.

I mean, how could I?

Despite our personal drama, the guys put on an amazing hometown show, raising over three hundred thousand dollars for The Mission, a club where LTZ got its start. I wish I could have enjoyed it more. Standing in my usual spot, on Connor's side of the stage with his family, I certainly had higher hopes for my first parental meeting than how it had panned out.

All the guys were making appearances at the VIP party. Sienna all but forced me to attend with Ty and take a few more pictures for *People*.

I wanted to disappear into a hole.

Connor, to his credit, was never far from my side. Neither was Ty. Between the two of them, they kept me fairly insulated from all the looky-loos wanting autographs. Or selfies. I just wasn't up for it.

The night wasn't all bad, I spent some time hanging out with Zane, Carter, and Fiona Reynolds, the owner of The Mission, and her stunning daughter. Jace introduced me to his folks and sisters—including Jen and her girlfriend Becca. When Connor and Jen excused themselves and sat in a corner talking, the pang of jealousy I felt was debilitating.

Through my bearding relationships, I'd put Connor through this for years.

The entirety of what I'd done crashed down upon me. I couldn't have been more blue.

"Cheer up." Becca put her arm around me. "I'm so glad those two are talking, it's been a shame that they lost touch."

"Yeah."

"I'm confused." Becca studied me. "Jen told me you're dating Connor. What is all of this business with Ty?"

"It's a long story."

A long night.

Rather than staying at his townhouse, Connor booked us a room at the Four Seasons in downtown Seattle. In the car on the way to the hotel, we sat on opposite sides. Looking out opposite windows.

"Ty and I decided this has got to end." I broke the silence. "It should have never happened in the first place."

Connor didn't look over at me. "If you want me to talk you out of it, you've got the wrong guy."

"I had no idea it would go this way, Connor."

"None of us did."

I took his giant hand in mine. "Do you still love me?"

"Aye."

"I know you're upset, talk to me."

"I'm upset, but not for the reason you think." Connor squeezed my hand in his. "I just wish you'd talk to me, Mae. When I left it was because I thought you didn't trust me. Or maybe because I thought you *couldn't* trust me. Then I learn you had legitimate reasons and feel like a right arsehole for the feelings I was having. But we work it out. Because I love you. Really love you. And now there's Ty. *Feckin'* Ty. I hated it. I hated this absolute *farce*. But I did it for you. Against every single one of my instincts. I didn't want to be some wanker that doesn't support his woman—"

"Connor." I interrupted. "None of this has ever been about you. Or us."

"Ah, but it is. This Ty thing is an absolute shiteshow. I'm doing my best not to be reactive here." Connor looked away, some of his hair catching on his beard. He brushed it away like it annoyed him. "Look. If you promise me that this is the end of all of this, I'll drop it. Play the game. But, sweetheart in my *gut* I *know* there's something else."

I swallowed. *What did he know?*

"Just. Don't. Lie. To. Me." Connor punctuated each word by punching his fist into his palm.

What did he know?

No.

He couldn't know.

The thought of telling Connor—or anyone—the truth about Kircher filled my body with anxiety. He'd think differently of me and the choices I'd made. Sofer was one thing. Kircher. No. Off the table. As much as I wanted to trust him with my secret, I was scared.

Too scared.

I didn't want to lose him.

How did a girl like me get into this mess?

Three weeks later, when Connor and the rest of LTZ were in the studio, I was sitting in the production office waiting for Kris to go over the Finnegan O'Roarke offer when my phone pinged inside my purse with an incoming text. Hoping it was Connor, I grabbed it only to be disappointed to see it was from Sienna.

Sienna: u'll thank me, look at your cover

I clicked on the link to see the preview of the *People* article. As expected, the front cover was a close up of our faces, me looking up at Ty laughing. He looked down at me with a huge smile on his face. Two people couldn't have looked more in love. The headline read, *HOW RONNI MILLER FOUND TRUE LOVE WITH A REFORMED BAD-BOY.*

Thumbing through the article, it was a whole lot of fluff and crap and lies. Pictures of us looking more than cozy. Like we were in love. My acting was on point. Too on point.

I felt sick.

"What's wrong?" I hadn't even heard Kris come in.

I handed my phone to her. She scanned the article. Her eyebrows raised as she read. "Well, then. Has Connor seen this?"

"Not yet."

"Ronni, my dear. When are you going to pull your head out of your ass?" Kris took a seat across from me. "You're going to lose that man."

"I'm screwing up so badly right now." I squeezed my eyes shut. Shame had been my constant companion for weeks. "I don't see a way out."

Kris scowled. "What's really going on here?"

I sighed. Didn't say anything.

"Tell me, Veronica."

It took me a couple hours to fill Kris in about Kircher and the poker games. Sienna had actually done me a solid and came through with a crazy amount of information. Armed with enough ammunition to take on the man who had nearly ruined my life, the victory seemed hollow.

"*Everyone* knows about the poker games, babe. He thinks he's untouchable. Which makes him vulnerable." Kris's eyes bored into mine. "He'll get caught. Trust me. You need to stop. Let. It. Go."

"I can't." I shook my head sadly. "He's hurt a lot of people."

"You don't need to save the world. This is not Sofer. Don Kircher is the most powerful man in Hollywood right now, Ronni. Neither of us like it. I just want you to consider that we are at a tipping point here. You're not just an actress. You're my producing partner. We have a series starting to shoot in Vancouver this summer. You'll be working on the movie next year. I need you to be smart."

Well crap.

Kris needed me to be smart.

Poor woman, clearly she'd bet on the wrong girl.

CHAPTER 33

FIVE MONTHS LATER

Before I met the guys in the studio, I'd had a very important meeting. Who would have thought that Sienna King could actually be useful? Sure, I knew what her ulterior motive was. It couldn't have been more transparent. She didn't like me and wanted me out of the way.

The thing about narcissists? They always thought they were smarter, faster, better.

Which made them easy to deal with.

And easier to fool.

By the time I made it to the studio, Jace was gone. Our headlining gig at Coachella wasn't for a couple of days, but he wanted to catch the entire festival, so he'd left for Palm Desert on his own. Zane was nowhere to be found, but Ty was sitting at a small table with one of his notebooks, looking frazzled.

"Yo." I saluted him as I pushed through the door.

Ty looked at me warily. Since the Seattle benefit show, he'd kept his distance. Probably for good measure. For the past couple of months, the anger I'd felt at this Ronni-Ty fauxmance situation caught up with me. It was bound to happen. Unfortunately, since I wasn't going to direct my anger at Ronni, Ty had been on the receiving end of my bad mood. More than once.

Unfairly.

It had been building, but something inside me was triggered when Ty announced he was buying a house in Hollywood. I'd poked at him. Mocked him. I'd even yelled at him about the pictures. Made some shitty comments under my breath about them. Insinuated some things I shouldn't have.

He was understandably confused. I tried to be friendly. "How's the song coming along?"

Ty's hair was tied up in a man bun, a style I'd never wear no matter how much you paid me, but to each his own. "I'm just not very inspired."

"I know the feeling. Let's get out of here. Wanna take a drive?"

Twenty minutes later, the two of us were on our way to Ronni's house in Malibu in her black Audi R8, which I usually drove when I was in LA since her driver took her to and from set. Thirty minutes later, we were lounging in a pod overlooking the ocean with two ice-cold root beers.

"When do you close on your house?" I clinked my root beer bottle to Ty's.

Ty frowned at the sore subject matter. "Um. Probably next month. Look, I know…"

"I'm sorry for being such a bollocks." I gazed out at the sea. "It's been a struggle for me to keep up this ruse, you know? There's a reason Ronni was willing to do it. What I don't understand is what's in it for you?"

"Look, Ronni's become a good friend to me, but you're the one she loves. And you're the one that's more important to me, my brother." Ty leaned back against his hands, which were clasped behind his head. "What is baffling to me is how a low-key rock band from Seattle has gone down the rabbit hole with all of this PR bullshit. There's not a goddamn thing in this for me. Sienna and Andrew seem to be the only beneficiaries."

"I'm glad you said that." I took a sip from my drink and looked at Ty. "If I let you in on something, will you help me?"

Ty nodded. "Of course."

"We'll give these PR hacks a little taste of their own medicine."

By the time Ronni got home from the studio, Ty had made dinner and I was setting the table. She walked into a domestic scene with her real boyfriend and her fake one, clearly taken by surprise. "What's all this?"

"Ty and I had a little meeting today, love." I wrapped my arms around her and kissed her temple. "We've figured out a potential solution to our problem."

"Look, I appreciate…"

"Wait, Ronni." Ty placed a huge, chopped salad on the table and gestured for us to sit. "We talked about this in Seattle, and I want out of this. Now. This entire thing is too contrived and complicated. It's not who I am, and I don't think it's who you are."

Ronni nodded sadly. "I've regretted agreeing to this from the first day. It has nothing to do with you, Ty."

"My love, we're already in a situation where it will be impossible for us to be together without a ton of backlash." I held her hand and rubbed her wrist with my thumb. "Tomorrow night we have figured out a way for you and Ty to end it and clear the way for us. Of course, only if you're on board."

The three of us hatched what we thought was a foolproof way to end the Ty and Ronni fauxmance for good. Immediately after we finished eating, Ronni called Kris to get her blessing. Next, Kris and Ronni fired Sienna and Andrew. No fanfare, she was just done.

Why keep someone poisonous in your inner circle?

Ty and I both felt the same way about LTZ. Sienna had to go. When we saw Jace and our manager at Coachella, we planned to convince them to fire Sienna too.

As for Ronni and me? The sense of relief she and I both felt was palpable. Our sex life had been as strained as our relationship for the past few weeks. The second Ty left, we shagged like rabbits throughout the night into the morning. We both had a new lease on life.

A path to our own future.

The next evening, Ty and Ronni went out to dinner at Mr. Chow in Beverly Hills, a very popular celebrity-sighting location, which guaranteed there would be paparazzi around. For good measure, Kris tipped off a couple of higher-ups in the news media. Considering the insanity of the coverage over the past few months, it was mind-blowing that my girlfriend and Ty had really only been seen together a few times.

The trap was set.

As for myself? I waited at Ronni's house on our pod. Drinking a Guinness. Watching the waves ebb and flow. My thoughts were filled with plans of our future together. It had taken some time for me to work through everything, but my meetings with Kris had helped in so many ways. I was going to do whatever it took to defend my woman.

The woman I planned to make my wife had lived most of her life on television sets in a bubble. The *Hawaiian High* experience was traumatic. *She's All That* had been a joy, save for the bollocks she dated. Through it all, Ronni was a well-adjusted, loving dynamo whose heart was as big as the sun.

Her one fault? She was determined to take on the world. Alone.

She didn't ask for help, ever.

It was her way of keeping control.

Even with Kris, she never called in favors. Never asked for special treatment. Not once made demands or threw diva fits. She was kind to everyone around her and treated the entire crew the same as the actors. Kris told me she'd seen something special in Ronni and had never once regretted her decision to give her the role that made her uber-famous. Now she'd made Ronni her official producing partner.

With a new chapter of our lives approaching, it was tempting to step in and fix everything. But, I loved Veronica Mae Miller with all my heart. Part of loving her was letting her figure out things for herself. As far as leaning on me? Or asking for help from me? She needed to get there on her own. The reason I knew all of this?

I had been the same way.

When I learned to rely on someone—Jen—my life infinitely improved. Thrown into running McGloughlin Construction, I'd been a lot like Ronni, determined to do everything myself. Not trusting anyone, including my own family to help had nearly broken me. All that changed when Jen stepped in and, without preaching, supported me. LTZ was the same, we had each other's backs.

For now, I'd have Ronni's back. I would support and protect her. I'd be patient. Ronni would get there with me. I wasn't on a timeline. I wasn't going to push her. I'd be waiting.

She was worth it.

My only line in the sand?

After tonight? Fauxmances were a thing of the past.

For feck's sake.

Her lemony-vanilla scent hit my nose a couple of minutes before

Ronni snuggled up to me in the pod. We lay together in the dark, listening to the ocean. Enfolding her into my body, I waited for her to tell me how the evening went down.

She had other plans.

Her fingers deftly reached inside my lounge pants and pulled out my cock, which was already semi-erect. Firmly gripping me with one hand, she bent to take me in her mouth. Stroking. Sucking. Licking. I watched Ronni's lips and mouth work me to near insanity before I flipped us both over and knelt between her legs.

Staring down at her, I took both her hands in mine and clasped our fingers together. "Is it done?"

"Yes."

"Good. I'm going to fuck you, Mae. Then I want to hear all about it."

By the time I'd made her come for the third time, she was a noodle. I carried her into the bedroom and tucked her in. She fell asleep immediately. There was plenty of time to talk in the morning, so I showered and joined her in bed, spooning her tightly to my body.

For the first time in ages, everything felt calm. Right.

We had an early start, a helicopter was taking me, Ty, and Zane to the Indio grounds of Coachella. Ronni was still sleeping when I went into the kitchen in just my boxer briefs to make some toast and coffee. She padded in a few minutes later, yawning. Her hair disheveled. Wearing nothing but a pair of panties and a tank top that did little to hide her rosy, erect nipples.

"Ah, Mae. You're a treat." I waggled my eyes and handed her a cup of coffee. Admiring the view as she shimmied onto one of the counter stools. "You fell asleep before you could tell me what happened."

With both hands, she held the steaming cup to her nose and breathed. Then sipped. She looked up at me and smiled. "So, we ended up staging a fight. It was kinda awesome. Although Ty's not an actor, so he's probably going to get some backlash."

"What did he say?"

"I was trying to keep the fight pretty mundane. I yelled 'I can't believe you.' And 'You're impossible.'" Ronni took out her phone and pulled up *TMZ*. "He yelled, 'How do you expect me to be faithful to you when we're apart most of the year."

I shook my head. "He went there?"

"Yes, I called him on the way home to yell at him for real. He told me he did it on purpose. That the world thinks badly of him anyway, so might as well preserve my reputation."

"A martyr, Jay-sus."

Ronni sipped her coffee and handed me her phone. "He's a good guy, Connor. I'd like to help him reconnect with Zoey. I don't think he'll be truly happy unless he tries."

"I think we should mind our own business." I set the phone down without looking at it and moved around the kitchen island to where she was sitting. Standing behind her, I palmed her breasts and thumbed her nipples. Leaned in for a delicious coffee kiss. Ronni turned and slid her hands across my hips before moving around to cup my ass and tug me closer in between her legs.

My tongue invaded her lips and sought hers. My cock filled and nestled into the juncture between her legs. "Ohh," Ronni breathed, hooking her legs around my thighs.

"I. Don't. Have. Time," I said between kisses, although wee Connor definitely had other ideas. So did Ronni, she yanked Calvin Klein's down, releasing my engorged cock.

"Make time." Ronni kissed along my chin, reached down and moved her panties to the side.

"Jay-sus, woman." I shoved myself in, to the hilt. "You'll be the death of me."

Hurriedly, we chased a quick but explosive release and jumped in the shower together where we went at it again. By the time I'd thrown on a pair of jeans, my driver was frantically texting me, wondering where I was. With a quick kiss, I ran out the door. Ronni was skipping the concert, for obvious reasons.

Luckily, thanks to the helicopter ride, we made it to Indio with plenty of time to spare. Me, Ty, and Zane wound our way through the maze of production. We had a quick soundcheck, but there was no sign of Jace. He wasn't answering his texts, which was highly unusual. We took our places on stage without him. At the last minute our drummer dashed up, looking like the cat that got the cream.

"Nice of you to show up, J." Ty purposefully spoke into the mic.

"Must have been a pretty good night," I replied.

Ignoring all of us, Jace started tapping out a beat. We finished soundcheck in about ten minutes, then headed to our dressing room to grab some food before the first round of press started. I'd shown Ty and Zane the press coverage on the helicopter ride over, so it was surprising when our marketing guru didn't say a word.

"Jace, where have you been? You haven't blown a gasket, so I guess you haven't heard the news," Zane blurted out to our drummer.

"Stop making it such a big deal." Ty shook his head.

"What happened?" Jace asked.

"Ty and Ronni broke up," I answered. "It was quite the spectacle."

"You all know we staged the whole relationship, she's in love with someone else." Ty pointed at me. "The three of us were sick of the lies."

"Jesus, I leave you alone for a minute." Jace donned his reading glasses and started tapping on his phone. He stopped to scroll through whatever was on his screen. He glared at Ty. "For fuck's sake. You're determined to ruin your own life."

"No, I'm trying to take control back. I'm not a liar." Ty was defiant. "It was wrong of you and the PR team to make me have a fake girlfriend."

"Well, you certainly managed to get yourself in the press again." Jace turned his phone. On the screen was a graphic picture of Ty getting his cock sucked on by some chick. "Nice work."

"God damn it!" Ty stalked toward the dressing room. "I'm not doing any interviews. We should have waited until tomorrow."

Jace yelled after him, "You sure as fuck are." Then he buried himself in his phone, his brow furrowed in frustration.

I palmed his shoulder. "How bad is it?"

He showed me his feed filled with headlines about Ty. What a fuck-up he was and how poor Ronni's heart had been broken again. It literally dominated every news feed. I puffed out a breath. "Such shite."

"I warned him. I warned you." Jace shook his head. "Now I've got to call Sienna. Kill me now."

Even though Ronni and Ty's breakup was all anyone wanted to talk to us about, we managed to put on a phenomenal show. I hitched a ride back to LA with Ty in the chopper. Ronni had been texting me all day. All of Ty's old booze and sex paparazzi pictures were out in full force. My girl felt awful.

"Tell her it's fine." Ty flicked through his tablet. "At this point, we have no choice but to let it play out. It's crazy how easy it is to manipulate the media. I'm just sorry that we let it go this far."

On a personal level, I was happy it was over. On a band level, the entire situation was fucked up. We weren't some old seventies band where all the members fucked each other's girlfriends. Now, somehow, this bizarre story would take root as part of LTZ's history.

The entire situation spurred some pretty serious discussions. Jace called a band meeting to request we slow things down. It was music to my ears. And to Ty's. The three of us were ready to create a better balance between our lives outside of LTZ and the band commitments. Zane was the only one who wanted to keep up our crazy pace, but he was overruled three to one.

Our new album would be out soon. We decided to scale way back on live shows for the next year. Now that LTZ was an established and successful band, we didn't need to play every single show we were offered. All of us had other things we wanted to explore outside of the band constraints.

For me, that meant Ronni.

Her life was moving forward too. Although production had stopped a couple of months earlier, the series finale of *She's All That* aired a couple of weeks after Coachella. The network gave the show a proper send-off, complete with interviews, behind-the-scenes footage, and parties.

My girl didn't ever rest, though. Kris and Ronni were producing a gritty Netflix series that was filming in Vancouver BC over the summer. Early next year, they were producing a movie based on Finnegan O'Roarke's book. In Ireland.

Me? I was going to enjoy my new relaxed schedule with my band.

After this next album cycle?

We were taking a year off.

At least.

I planned to spend each and every day of it with Mae.

And thereafter, for the rest of my life.

RONNI

CHAPTER 34
THREE MONTHS LATER

My "breakup" with Ty took a huge weight off my shoulders. Connor and I were back on track. Our lives had easily clicked together for the first time in our entire three-plus-year-long relationship. Who would have thought that giving up fauxmances would have a positive effect on my real one?

LOL.

Boy, did it ever.

Connor's new, more relaxed schedule with the band took off so much pressure. He was away for a month or two at a time. Then off for a couple of weeks. On breaks, he spent time in Seattle with his family and with me up in Vancouver BC, where I was filming *Stalked*, a limited six-episode series Kris and I were producing. Originally, I planned to take on an acting role, but I recast it. My learning curve on the production side was too steep, and I wanted to get it right.

It also gave me more time with my man.

Connor and I spent most of our time together in solitude. We weren't actively hiding our relationship. Our day-to-day lives were so overstimulated, we needed a break. Each of our careers required us to be around people constantly. As highly recognizable celebrities, public outings created situations to navigate. Fans were awesome. Mostly they wanted an autograph. A selfie. To tell you how much they loved you. All wonderful sentiments.

Right now, it was too much.

We just didn't want the pressure for a while. Or the scrutiny. Because when it was just the two of us? Magic. We relaxed. Made dinner. Watched shows. Listened to music. He tried to teach me to play guitar. I read lines with him. Sometimes we just sat in the same room and read.

A good portion of our time was spent in bed.

Well, not always in bed.

Making love with Connor just got better and better. We knew each other's bodies as well as our own. He was so in tune with me. I felt like I could almost read his mind. I knew what he needed and wanted to give it to him. Our connection was unreal. Neither of us had any inhibitions with each other. Sex with Connor was beautiful. Precious. Hot. Dirty.

Transcendent.

God, I loved this man with every fiber of my being.

I'd never felt so settled in my life.

Connor and I didn't specifically talk about the future, but I knew where our relationship was heading. We belonged together.

And together we would be.

For the moment, we had a year's worth of preexisting commitments to get through. I didn't have a lot of time off because our filming schedule for *Stalked* was on a fast-track. Mainly, I wanted to finish principal photography a few days before Connor departed for his longest tour stretch this time out, four months in Asia.

I met him at the Fairmont Chateau Whistler for a long weekend, where I arranged for us to have the Gold Penthouse suite. The mountains were gorgeous, the fall foliage was the perfect backdrop for romance. Not to mention, there were few better VIP concierge experiences. Gondola ride with a picnic at the top of Blackcomb? Check. Private dining by a Michelin-star chef flown in just for us? Check. Couples massage? Check.

Naked sexytimes? Check. Check. Check.

We spent Christmas and New Years apart, but now that LTZ was producing a few songs to be included on a blockbuster soundtrack, Connor and the guys were on their way to LA where they'd be residing throughout the spring. He'd just texted me, so I was waiting in our pod to share my own exciting news with my man.

"Well, well, lassy." Connor approached carrying a giant bouquet of red roses and raked his eyes up my bikini-clad body. "If that's not the way to greet a man."

I leapt up to throw myself in his arms. He easily caught me and I wrapped my legs around his waist. "Oh, babe. I've missed you so much!" Our mouths fused together. We were lost in our reunion until our lips were nearly chapped. All worth it. "Come up to the house, Connor. I'll put these in water."

He eased me down. Arm in arm we smooched our way inside. "You're a sight for sore eyes, Mae."

"Are you hungry? There's some prepared meals in the fridge, we just need to heat them up." My eyes flashed as I put the roses in water.

Connor picked me up and slung me over his shoulder, carrying me through the kitchen to my bedroom. "I'm hungry for you," he growled, slapping me on the ass before depositing me on the bed and ravaging me for the next hour.

Sated and pressed against Connor's hard chest, I relaxed as he ran his fingers lazily through my hair. However much I loved snuggling with my honey, I couldn't wait any longer. "What do you think about going to Ireland with me this summer?"

"What? When?"

"Kris and I are going to do some scouting and meeting with local production crews in Dublin and in Belfast. Now that *Game of Thrones* has wrapped production, we want to snap them up before they take other jobs." I sat up, gesturing wildly. I couldn't help it, I was so excited at producing my first movie. One that surely would be an Oscar contender. "Our plan is to film next year."

Connor's face beamed with pride. "Mae, that's brilliant. Our schedule is finally winding down. When we're done recording the soundtrack, it would be great to get back to the house. I haven't been there in a while."

"Maybe we can invite your folks. I'd like to get to know them better, especially after…"

Connor lightly gripped my face with both of his hands. His eyes shone with adoration. "Wait, really?"

I leaned in and kissed his sweet lips. "Of course, Connor. We're together."

"Aye, I'd love that." Connor pulled me on top of him. "I love you, Mae."

"I love you too." Something about how he said it made me feel a bit sad. We hadn't talked about it in a long time, mostly because we were just living our lives within the parameters of our own career obligations. "There's nothing keeping us a secret anymore, unless you think we need to deal with it from an LTZ PR perspective."

Connor said nothing. He cupped my breasts and pinched my nipples.

His cock grew harder between us. "I don't give two shites about PR. You know that Mae."

Looking into his eyes, which seemed to hold a million questions, I decided not to push him. If something was bothering him, he'd let me know. We were on solid ground now. Tonight was for reconnecting. I grasped his beautiful, engorged cock and fed it inside me. Slowly so he could watch our bodies join. We were off to the races again.

With all the guys of LTZ in town recording, it gave me a great opportunity to invite the entire band and Kris over for Easter. I hadn't seen the rest of the guys in months. Probably since Ty and I had "broken" things off. He couldn't stop talking about his new foundation and how Zoey—*the* Zoey—was a lawyer now and helping him put it all together.

"I told you! You're meant to be." I nudged Ty with my butt. "Don't waste this opportunity."

In all the years I'd known LTZ, I'd never seen Ty smile so big. Connor came up behind him to put the singer in a headlock. "It's been a month and he *still* hasn't made a move on her. Rainier's game is still lacking."

"Trust me, I've got it." Ty maneuvered away. "She's coming to the launch party."

"I'm sorry I can't make it, Ty." I tucked myself under Connor's arm. "I'll be in Ireland."

"Next time." Ty glanced at Connor and me. Connor squeezed me to his side.

Jace, as usual, was buried in his phone and oblivious to all of us. Zane stood behind him, craning his neck to read his texts. "Poppy?" he taunted.

Jace didn't look up from his phone, just slugged Zane in the arm.

"Ow!" He rubbed his increasingly bulging bicep. "If you expect me to be a genius in the studio, you shouldn't damage the goods."

Jace rolled his eyes.

"How's the recording going?" Kris brought in a tray of charcuterie, which the guys descended upon like wild cheetahs.

"Kircher stopped by today," Zane said with a mouthful of cheese and crackers. "He made us an offer to write the title theme song. It's official."

Hearing the name sent my heart plummeting to my toes. I felt faint. My legs crumpled. Connor held me up but was a bit panicked. "Mae, are you okay? Honey?" He helped me to the sofa.

Kris rushed to my side and took my hand. I shot her a look when she opened her mouth.

She shut up.

"I'm fine, just give me a minute." I shook Connor off and took some deep breaths.

The rest of the night was a blur. I tried to engage, but the idea that LTZ was working with Kircher made me physically ill. I wanted to throw up. Mostly, I just listened as the guys rambled on about this chord and that lyric. Smiled. Nodded.

"My brothers, can we call it a night? Ronni's exhausted." Connor had kept a close eye on me all evening. Watching me. I was grateful when he ushered his bandmates out the door.

Half an hour later, thank God, we were getting ready for bed. Connor caught my eye in the bathroom mirror while we brushed our teeth. "Are you okay, Mae? Really?"

"Of course." My voice came out too bright. Fake. "You were right, I'm just very tired."

I couldn't read his expression, but I knew he didn't believe me.

"You know you can tell me anything. Right?"

I did know that. Except, for some reason, I couldn't. There was never a way for me to get the words out about Kircher. Maybe because it had been so long ago. Sixteen or seventeen years now. It really bothered me that my life was still defined by my time on *Hawaiian High*. I felt defective. Bringing the bastard down would repair me. I knew it. Until then, there was no need to worry the love of my life unnecessarily. It's not like I was in danger.

Anymore.

I realized that Connor had been talking to me and I hadn't heard a word he said.

"Mae?"

I blinked at him through the mirror. "Oh, sorry. I'm just surprised that you guys were doing a Don Kircher film."

He just stared at me. Willing me to say something?

Or I was reading into it.

That's the thing about secrets. A part of you is always worried that you've been found out.

Could he know?

Byron and I had only just resumed discussing the project to take Kircher down. Before that, we'd hit a snag. He was being stubborn about a six-month fauxmance with me. First of all, no woman, even me, could sell a fake romance with Byron. Second and most important, I was retired. Thus, we were still at an impasse.

Still, I'd never really been great at covering my tracks. I scanned my brain, wondering if Connor had found something in the house to tip him off. I never wrote anything down. Mainly because I never wanted there to be one piece of physical evidence. No email. No text. No handwriting.

This was important in the grand scheme of things.

Seemingly accepting my nutty behavior, Connor put his toothbrush away. We climbed into bed. Connor spooned me, firmly holding me against his big body with his arm around my middle. Every single nerve zinged when he whispered into my ear, "Please talk to me. You can trust me, Mae."

"You don't think I do?" I challenged, putting him on the defensive. Nothing like a good dose of gaslighting. God, I was the worst.

And he was the best. Connor wrapped his other arm around my head and stroked my cheek, completely wrapped around me like a security blanket. "Of course, my love."

Rather than answer, I wiggled my ass against his hard cock.

Silencing him with sex.

That always seemed to work.

Case in point?

When he slipped inside me and we started to make love, there were no more questions about Kircher.

CHAPTER 35
THREE MONTHS LATER

Quite frankly, from the time I met with Kris a couple of years ago, I'd once again slipped into old patterns. Mainly, I was frustrated and a little hurt that Ronni didn't trust me enough to tell me she was plotting something new. It had to do with Kircher. According to Kris something went down between them that was traumatizing to her. I didn't fault Ronni's mentor for refusing to tell me. As she made perfectly clear, anything about Ronni's past that she wanted me to know? It was up to Ronni to tell me.

The fact that the woman I loved had been hurt and was keeping it a secret from me?

It festered.

And had been festering for a long time.

Which is probably why the engagement ring I'd bought months ago was hidden in my Seattle townhouse and not on its proper place—Mae's finger.

When we found out about the soundtrack for Kircher's project, *Phantom Rising*, my first inclination was to veto it. We didn't really need to do it. It added a lot of obligations to our plate when we were finalizing our year-long hiatus. All of us needed time away from one another to rejuvenate our creative energy.

My personal reason, of course, had to do with protecting Mae.

This was a pretty unique opportunity, however, and the rest of the guys were excited. They didn't know squat about Kircher and Ronni. Technically, neither did I. Even though I wanted to protect my woman, until she felt safe confiding in me, it would be weird if I made a big deal about it.

Plus, Kris and I found a way to potentially use an old skill of mine to help her. On the down low.

Poker.

During his pitch, Kircher invited all of us to one of his famous underground poker games. It gave me an in. A front-row seat to his sordid world. One I could take full advantage of. The game was an incredible way to gain information. I was an expert, after all. I'd saved the family business using my stealth skills. I'd ferret out all this guy's demons and take him down. For Mae.

All I had to do was show up and shut up. Feign ignorance and glean as much information as possible.

And oh, did he covet me at the games. He loved having one of the biggest rock stars in the world in his orbit. So now I had a standing invitation. It was never my intention to become part of the inner circle. Quite the opposite, and I made it clear that I really had no interest in being there. I always hemmed and hawed about going. Sometimes I just wouldn't show. All by design.

It made me all the more attractive to the eejits. So when I actually made an appearance, it was purposefully. Only when Ronni was out of town. Any money I made sat securely in a bank account set up specifically for the winnings. I figured the information I'd gathered would be helpful in some way.

I wasn't sure how. Yet.

Until Ronni felt comfortable confiding her history with Kircher, it was all kept in the vault of my brain.

On Easter Day, when Ronni had a panic attack after finding out LTZ was working on the soundtrack for Kircher? It chilled me to the bone. Something really bad had happened. I gently tried to get her to open up. To let me in completely. She clammed up and said nothing when I fully expected her to give me an ultimatum.

The soundtrack or her.

That's what I wanted. Some reaction—any reaction—from her to give me a clue how I could help her. How to support her. Instead, she reverted to her old habits. Diverting me with a marathon shag. Which, as always, was fantastic. Unfortunately, afterward? She pretended we didn't even have the conversation.

The entire situation tormented me.

A man had to be able to take care of his woman. It was a fundamental obligation, as far as I was concerned.

Luckily, before I got all caveman on her, I made an appointment with Ronni and Ty's therapist-to-the-stars, Lisa Kinkaid. Mainly to see what I could do as her partner to support her. To allow us to move forward freely. While Lisa, appropriately, didn't share any of the details, she was able to give me good counsel on how to be a stand-up guy.

The most important thing I took away was to simply reassure her I was there for her. Since I didn't know the details of her trauma, I was strongly advised not to push her beyond where she was comfortable. And while I was half-crazed to get the situation closed and behind us, my own timetable should not be the driving factor.

She also reassured me that Ronni's way of handling things wasn't personal. It didn't diminish our relationship or her love for me. Lisa felt confident that Ronni would open up to me about Kircher someday. I had to trust that. Whether it was ten more days or ten more years, I would love her unconditionally. Without judging her.

Once I came to accept this? Everything fell into place in my mind. With a renewed sense of peace.

No more delays. I was ready to make Veronica Mae Miller my wife.

On my way to Dublin, I'd stopped briefly in Seattle to pick up precious cargo. I was coasting up the M1 on the way to my Belfast house where Ronni was waiting. She and Kris had been staying there for a month, scouting locations and meeting with production teams for her feature film with Finnegan O'Roarke.

If I needed any more proof of her commitment to me, Ronni's choice of the story for her debut feature film couldn't have been more deeply personal to my family. O'Roarke's memoir had won a lot of awards, that was true. Somehow I knew that her extraordinary passion for this project was more about showing me, not telling me, that I mattered. My roots mattered. My heart burst with pride and awe.

What a wonderful sight to see Ronni, Kris, and my aunt Saiorse waving at me in the driveway. Ronni jumped in my arms and after a soul-quenching kiss, I hugged the other two women. Throughout dinner, the female energy in the room was like wildfire as they excitedly filled me in on each and every detail of their adventures. I didn't mind. Saiorse, Ronni, and Kris were like three peas in a pod. Seeing Ronni feel so comfortable with my auntie warmed my heart.

Much later that night, in a sex haze of ginormous proportions, Ronni and I lay facing each other in the moonlight. The quiet of the Irish countryside combined with the soft lapping of the waves outside our window was peaceful. Ronni traced my face with her pink-manicured finger. "You're my everything, Connor McGloughlin."

I gulped. Emotion overtook me. This woman never asked me for anything. She accepted me. She never demanded to get married or to prove my love for her. Not once had she ever complained about my schedule with LTZ. Her ability to stay grounded while being so famous was mind-blowing. Her loyalty and dedication to avenging Wynn changed the world. She was also fun. Hardworking. Successful. Incredibly beautiful. Her heart was as deep as the ocean.

It was beyond time.

I rolled out of bed, walked around to her side and pulled her up. Leading her to the giant picture window overlooking the lough, I gestured for her to stay put. I crossed the room to my bag and took out my small package. As I approached my naked girl standing in the glow of the moon, I knew that, although unconventional, this was the exact right way for me to propose.

For us.

Kneeling in front of her, both of us naked as jaybirds, I gently took her left hand. Her eyes widened so big I could see the universe shining in her pupils. "Veronica Mae Miller, you are the absolute love of my life, so you are. I will forever be your protector, you lover, your best friend, and hopefully the father of your children, if you'll have me. Will you—"

"Aye! Aye!" Ronni threw her arms around my neck. "Aye!"

"You haven't even seen it yet!" I laughed in between kisses. "What if it isn't up to your standards, love?"

"Fine, I'll have a look."

I opened the green-velvet box to present her with the rare three-and-a-half carat vivid green diamond ring, set in platinum with seventy white diamonds circling the big gem and making up the entirety of the split band. I'd had it custom made. It was one-of-a-kind.

Just like my Mae.

Ronni sank to her knees looking up at me, her green eyes filled with tears. "Oh, Connor. It's exquisite."

I took her hand and placed the ring on her finger.

She was going to be my wife.

My eyes filled with tears too, I couldn't help it.

Ronni and I clung to each other. She sobbed like a baby, which brought out a deep flood of my own emotions. A six-foot-six, two hundred and fifty pound man was reduced to a sniveling mess. All because we were, after many years, finally and officially each other's future.

We didn't want to wait. We didn't want a big to-do. We were keeping our circle tight. The band would understand.

Seven weeks later, on a beautiful clear day, Ronni and I married on the shores of Belfast Lough in front of my da, ma, my brothers, Kris, and Saoirse. I wore a simple custom-made black suit with my hair loose the way Ronni liked it. My beautiful bride wore a simple satin white dress with shimmering crystals and pearls decorating the edges of a plunging, backless, sexy surprise. Her gorgeous red hair was held up by flowers from the garden Saoirse so diligently tended to.

For our reception, Ma made the cake and a wedding feast. Accompanied by the twins, I serenaded Ronni with *The Voyage*, a beautiful song by a famous Irish folk singer, Christy Moore. It summed up everything I could ever hope to say to my wife:

The Voyage

I am a sailor, you're my first mate
We signed on together, we coupled our fate
Hauled up our anchor, determined not to fail
For the heart's treasure, together we set sail

With no maps to guide us we steered our own course
Rode out the storms when the winds were gale force
Sat out the doldrums in patience and hope
Working together we learned how to cope

Life is an ocean and love is a boat
In troubled waters that keeps us afloat
When we started the voyage, there was just me and you
Now gathered 'round us, we have our own crew

Together we're in this relationship
We've built it with care to last the whole trip
Our true destination's not marked on any charts
We're navigating to the shores of the heart

Life is an ocean and love is a boat
In troubled waters that keeps us afloat
When we started the voyage, there was just me and you
Now gathered 'round us, we have our own crew

Life is an ocean and love is a boat
In troubled waters that keeps us afloat
When we started the voyage, there was just me and you

Now gathered 'round us, we have our own crew

Late into the night, my family ate, sang, danced, and played music on a rare warm summer night in Ireland. It was the most perfect wedding a man could ever hope for.

And now, I had the most perfect wife.

RONNI

CHAPTER 36
PRESENT DAY

Connor found me pacing back and forth across the living area of the suite muttering to myself in the wee hours of the morning. I hadn't even noticed him watching me because so many thoughts were jumbled up in my head.

I'd just sent him an email that I couldn't take back. He hadn't read it yet, of course. He rarely checked email unless we were apart.

"Mae?" Connor grasped my arms, startling me.

"God!" I screeched. "You scared the shit out of me."

He released me and squeezed his eyes shut. "This is out of control, love. *You* are out of control."

"I'm not! I'm just frustrated." I flung myself on the sofa and punched one of the cushions. "I just want you to trust me and you don't. I can't believe we are back here again."

He narrowed his eyes and stared at me.

"I know it looks like I'm acting crazy." I slugged the sofa again for good measure. "There is a method to the madness, though."

"You want me to trust you?" Connor crossed the room to the fridge and grabbed two waters, then paused as if to consider exactly what he wanted to say. Returning to the couch, he sat and handed me one of the bottles. "Just tell me what you were doing there that night. Let's start there."

I clasped my hands in my lap and looked down. Completely aware that dragging my feet about all of this was ridiculous. I'd sent the email. Why couldn't I just tell him to his face? I knew he'd support me however he could. The big guy had come through time and time again. What was keeping me from taking a leap of faith?

Connor's phone buzzed. Despite the late hour, he picked up. "Yeah?"

After grunting a couple of "uh-huh's" and "okays" he hung up. A soft knock on the door followed and Connor let Katherine into the suite. If she was surprised to see me still there, she didn't let on.

Usually impeccable, Katherine was disheveled and looked dead on her feet. She gave us an update about Zoey. Having witnessed Ty's debauched behavior first-hand over the years, I wasn't surprised to learn that psycho-Sienna filmed herself giving him a blowjob when he was wasted. He had no recollection of it happening. The publicist showed the video to Zoey, who ran out of the hotel in hysterics. Sergei saved her life by tackling her before she ran into traffic. After surgery, she'd apparently broken it off with Ty.

Again.

Now Connor was in an emergency band meeting. In the middle of the night. Instead of being mad, I was grateful. It saved me from explaining myself. At least for the time being. Alone time would give me some time to think.

Because something had been niggling at me for the past day.

I'd made an assumption about why Connor had been at Kircher's poker game. Given him the complete benefit of the doubt. The thing is, I'd been knee deep in this mess for so many years, not much slipped by me. So, as soon as Connor left with Katherine, I pulled out my tablet and loaded a blind-item gossip site that all celebrities claimed they didn't know about but actually followed religiously. Scrolling through the last couple of days' entries, I found what I was looking for.

GOSSIP SCHMOSSIP Item 124

The Poker Room: Earlier this month, we told you about the A+ list director whose poker parties are legendary. While the game itself is above the board, what happens afterward is, well...

Never one to pass up a financial opportunity, our director charges up to 100K to play in the game and up to $100K for the "after" party. The after party is no poker game. Sources tell us it can turn into a full-blown orgy. Invites are limited to A-listers. Phones are confiscated at the door. Nothing is in writing.

Our director's favorite pastime is scouring Instagram for "models" who want to make a few extra bucks for certain "favors." He never has problems finding women to participate in these poker soirees.

Why? The promise to further their acting career. Don't believe me? He has a waiting list a year long of "candidates."

Get this, the women even pay an entry fee of up to $250. Is it worth it? Damn straight. Some women who have attended claim they never leave without at least 10K in their pocket. Often more. Depends on what they are willing to do. And with whom.

The director? He pockets the rest. Easily a cool million each game.

Curious whose been to these parties? (a) the television actor on the top-rated rated family drama; (b) the married superhero in a comic-book superhero franchise is a regular; (c) the singing and dancing host of the late-night talk show; (d) a bass player in the biggest band on the planet.

My entire body felt like it was frozen solid. I couldn't breathe. It was so obvious.

Connor.

Jesus.

I had to face what was in front of me. If Connor was the rock star in the blind item, it meant the other night hadn't been his first time at that bastard's poker parties. He'd been there before.

Why?

My heart seized in agony.

I wanted to believe it was some sick joke. Maybe Sienna was playing some sort of game. She'd made threats in New York. Did she plant some bullshit story to get back at me and LTZ for losing two big clients? Still, behind every gossip item was a kernel of truth. There was no denying I saw him at Kircher's New York poker game. Which meant in all likelihood he'd been at his regular games in Hollywood.

Why would Connor keep this from me?

And yes, the irony was not lost.

The one thing that kept me sane was knowing I'd be the one to bring Kircher down. Now that the element of surprise was gone, my chance was over. Gone. Poof. Oh God, he knew about me and Connor now too.

The full impact of the past couple of days hit me like a ton of bricks. Connor had ruined any chance I ever had to bring Kircher down.

Why was he there?

My phone pinged with a Google alert. God, what now? I clicked on it and if I thought I was devastated before, little did I know how far I had to fall.

GOSSIP SCHMOSSIP Item 142

Little Miss Priss: We have it on good authority that a very popular unlucky-in-love comedic actress is behind the very public takedown of a certain big-name producer. Oh, but there's more. Our goody-two-shoes might not be such an angel after all. An audition video for a tropical angsty teen drama has been uncovered, and well— shall we say so is America's sweetheart. Seems that she was no stranger to using her—assets—to get cast in a lead role. A bit hypocritical, we'll just say it...

CHAPTER 37

With nothing resolved with Ronni, I was pissed we were having a band meeting. In the middle of the feckin' night. Her pacing and muttering scared me shiteless. What was she keeping from me?

I knew she needed to work it out on her own, but it took every ounce of self-control I had not to get up to wrap my arms around her and comfort her. Protect her. Keep her safe from what frightened her.

Instead, my Irish temper emerged and I had to go and confront her. Exactly the opposite thing I should have done. We were interrupted when Ty got back from the hospital. He called a band meeting and I had to go. All of us in LTZ, including Katherine, were exhausted. Mentally and physically. To say we did not want to be there was an understatement. On the other hand, Ty was my brother who'd been through a huge trauma.

I *had* to be there.

Against my better judgment, I left my wife alone.

"I need to apologize to all of you and to Katherine." Ty made eye contact with each and every one of us.

"You don't owe us anything, my brother," Zane said quietly.

Katherine was having a hard time keeping her eyes open. "Ty, Jace, and I have been going for nearly two solid days with no sleep, if you want to say something, that's fine, but please make it quick."

I didn't have the energy to say a word.

"Fine. Okay. I know this shit has been going on for eight years," Ty addressed us seriously. "So much of what happened in the last two days has been completely my fault—"

Zane tried to stop him. "Dude—"

Ty wasn't having it. He launched into an epic apology for not taking accountability for himself. His physical and mental demeanor almost changed before our eyes and he let us all off the hook and vowed to take responsibility for himself and for Zoey, who was going to recover fully after some time to heal and physical therapy. The state of their relationship was in flux.

I couldn't help it when I blurted out, "Jay-sus Christ. Here we go…"

Ty narrowed his eyes and gave it to me good. "Connor, I'm not sure what the fuck your problem with me is, but it ends here. While I'm sure you're rightfully annoyed by my latest scandal, rest assured it's the final one. *Finito.* And, for the record? I didn't fuck Ronni. Okay? I never fucked Ronni. She's become one of my best friends, so deal with it…"

For feck's sake.

I didn't hear anything else. What was he at? Ty knew I didn't think he'd fucked Ronni. He was trying to make things "right" with me in front of the band on his Zoey redemption tour. My God the man was so clueless. Everyone in the band already knew what was up. Ty was so lost in his own bubble sometimes. My first thought was how funny Mae would find this. Then I remembered. We weren't in the happiest place.

Because I was an arse.

My phone buzzed. A text from Ronni.

Mae: Check your email.

Mae: I had to go back to LA. Please don't worry about me.

Connor: WTF? Mae? Where are you?

Mae: On the plane.

Connor: Mae, Do Not. Leave. Without. Me.

Connor: You're scaring me, love. Please wait. Let me figure this out with you.

Connor: We can do this together.

Connor: Mae?

"I gotta go." I bolted up and ran to my suite and threw open the door. No sign of Mae. Tore around the place. Nothing. Her suitcase was gone.

Feck!

CHAPTER 38

3:22 a.m.
To: connorm@ltz.com
From: vmm@vmm.com
Subject: It's time you knew the truth about me

I wish I could tell you what I'm about to tell you to your face, my love. I just can't.
I'm sorry I'm not stronger.
All the therapy in the world, and I've been through a lot, doesn't change the truth.
My entire life and career started with a decision I made when I was fifteen. A decision I wasn't equipped to make. It's haunted me. Which is why it has been so important not to be a victim. To take control of this and all the decisions in my life. To right all of the wrongs on my own. I thought

it would heal me, and in many ways it has.

I'm stalling. We've just had such a magical year. When you proposed and we got married, I thought I'd finally just put it behind me. All I wanted is for us to have a normal life. Be your wife. Have kids.

But here we are. At yet another crossroads.

When we first started getting to know each other, do you remember me telling you about the audition for Hawaiian High *in the pink-and-white polka dot bikini? I only gave you a small part of what actually happened. Here's the full truth:*

As you might recall, I was determined to win over the director and the producers because I wanted a better life for my mom and me. Merv Sofer, Jared Graham, and Don Kircher were the three men in that auditorium.

The makeshift dressing room I told you about? It was really a short, sheer curtain. I convinced myself that no one could see through it, but that was a lie. They'd set it up so that the kids who were auditioning would have to change in front of them. Most of them were probably smart and wore their swimsuits under their clothes. Unfortunately, I refused to even bring my bikini, so I had to use this "room" to change. Knowing that these men were about to see me completely naked. There was no other way.

"Of course there was, just leave," you might say. And the thought crossed my mind. But I really wanted this job. I blamed myself for being in the position I was in. I just blocked it from my mind and carried on. Because really? Was it so bad?

I convinced myself it wasn't.

That it was worth it.

I was fine.

Right?

When I was on stage, they looked me up and down. Leered. It was gross. Like I was a dessert in a glass case they were choosing from. One of them even licked his lips.

Still, I ignored the creepy feeling that took root at the base of my neck and spread its way up my scalp. The thing we call intuition. The body's protective mechanism that was telling me something was really off. Fifteen-year-old VMM wasn't great at trusting her intuition.

Swallowing the lump in my throat, I stood there while they picked apart each and every one of my features.

Thick thighs.

Flabby arms.

Good hair.

Pretty good face.

Nice tits? Are they real?

I wonder if they're real?

It would be great if they were real.

My spine prickled some more. I knew what was coming. I knew I should run as fast as I could to get away. I was right. Kircher told me to take off my top. Apparently, it was important for authenticity that they could verify my tits were real.

Without my mom there, I had no one to tell me not to do it. Of course, they'd planned on separating the kids from the parents, that's how predators work. Again, I convinced myself everything was fine. Figuring, at least twenty girls had been here before me and they were fine.

I was fine.

Right?

I also reasoned that this was a professional audition. For a network television show. Actors and actresses had to be ready for anything. It all boiled down to one thing.

How much did I want this part?

Determined not to show my mortification, I untied my bikini top and my boobs popped free in all their teenage glory. Trying not to cry, I overcompensated with sass. They asked me to cup my breasts with my hands and push them together. I did as they asked. I looked each one of them in the eye as I did it. For good measure, I cocked my hip. Trying to show that I was confident.

No way were they going to see how scared I was.

Or how humiliating it was to be topless while they leered at me.

I remember standing there waiting for further direction. Each moment ticked by slowly. Bravado aside, it was off-putting to have grown men openly gawk at my body. Assessing me. Murmuring and pointing. Deciding if I was hot enough. Thin enough. Boobalicious enough. It was all so disgusting. These jerks didn't even bother hiding what they were doing.

Still, I smiled.

Because I was fine.

Right?

Kircher started adjusting the crotch on his pants. I was inexperienced but I knew what that meant. Then he asked me how old I was, and I told him.

Fifteen.

The three of them huddled and whispered. Looking up at me occasionally.

Sofer called me "sweetheart" and asked me to turn around slowly.

So I did. I turned around and faced them again.

I'll never forget the condescending snotty voice of Kircher telling me I didn't turn slow enough. He actually dragged out the word slooooooooowwww to illustrate the cadence he expected. To see if I was camera ready for the beach."

I tamped down the tears. Obeyed. It was the most demeaning experience of my life. I had to hold it together. When I finished my rotation my composure faltered when a red blinking light above their heads caught my eye.

A camera.

I couldn't stop the full-body flinch.

Sofer noticed my reaction and looked over his shoulder. He told me not to worry. That they recorded everyone to keep everything straight. He called it "SOP."

Standard Operating Procedure.

By now, standing there topless, I would have done and said anything to get out of there. So, I pasted on a smile to avoid crying. I smiled at them. I told them it was no problem. It was fine.

I really wanted to vomit.

They all started laughing. I overheard one of them say that my consent was on tape."

Kircher told me to sign the waiver on the way out and they'd be in touch. Made some comments about how hot I was as I tried to tie my top back into place before I left. All I wanted to do was throw up.

I was in survivor mode. I needed to get myself out of there. So when my top was back in place, I backed away, still smiling. I even thanked them for the opportunity.

All of this was on film.

Once I was out of the room, I signed the release and was desperate to go home. Take a shower. Forget what had happened. As I told you before, I pulled my T-shirt over my head and my jeans up over my suit. I burst out of the building in search of my mom.

When she asked how it went, I never told her.

I was fine.

Right?

Except I wasn't. Seeing those men on set? I wanted to quit every day. Wynn and I kept each other sane. When I thought I should tell someone? Like my mom? I remembered the blinking light and knew there was a naked video of me out there. I would die if Mable saw it. Die. Watching me prance and turn topless for these old fucks. As if I liked it?

I felt trapped.

I've been trapped.

That video is out there, Connor.

I've been living in fear of it being posted somewhere for my entire adult life.

I've never told a soul about this. Until you. Until now.

And it gets even worse.

On my eighteenth birthday, the day Don sent my mom home, he didn't ask—he told me—that he was going to meet with me alone in my trailer to go over my performance before I went home.

Officially, I was terrified.

The story I've always told was that I ran to my trailer to grab my purse and found him lounging on the sofa in only a bathrobe. And that when I saw him, I got out of there and went home. Mom figured out a workaround in the contract. Blah Blah Blah.

That's not exactly what happened.

Shocked beyond belief, at first I remained frozen in place. I couldn't move. I remember babbling that people were waiting for me at home. I even slung my bag over my shoulder and started to back up.

Unfortunately, I wasn't able to escape before he opened his robe and exposed himself. I'll never forget it because it was the first time I'd ever seen a man's penis in real life. Let alone one that was fully erect. It didn't look like I thought it would (and now I can confirm that the rumors of his deformity are true), but before I could comprehend what was happening, he started jacking off. Laughing at what had to be my expression of utter horror. He then issued a warning with his hand on his dick, "Ronni, you're an adult now and it's high time we had a real conversation about your future as an actress. And, of course, how you're going to get ahead in this business."

I backed up toward the door, but he stood and moved toward me. Still stroking himself. I was paralyzed in horror. Kircher continued to move toward me. Now pulling faster. And faster. The lecherous look on his face is forever burned in my mind. Then he stopped and, with a loud grunt, ejaculated in an arc that splatted on the floor. Barely missing my stomach.

He let go of his penis, which flopped over like a mushroom against his thick swatch of pubic hair. I couldn't take my eyes off it until he spoke up. He said he beat off to my audition video all the time. That it was one of his all-time favorites. He called me a little minx. He told me I wanted him. He demanded that the next day I should be naked and ready for him at lunch so he could pop my sweet little cherry. As my birthday present.

I didn't speak. Somehow, I found my legs and ran to my car as fast as I could go. I also didn't cry. Couldn't process. Just survived. I barely made it back to the apartment without crashing. Totally forgetting about my party. I burst through the door where Wynn and a couple of the crew were hanging out with my mom waiting. I smiled and hugged everyone.

I was fine.

Right?

Mom noticed something was off with me. She ushered everyone out. When we were alone, I told her that Kircher was in my trailer in the bathrobe. Nothing else. She was enraged and it made me scared to tell her more. You know the rest.

We just couldn't afford to leave.

A year later, I got fired.

And then I had lots of therapy.

I was fine.

Truly. I was fine. I knew it wasn't my fault what happened. I learned my triggers. I survived.

I was a little damaged. Had some baggage.

But I was fine.

Except, after he fired me, Kircher actively tried to kill my career. I think his plan was to make it impossible for me to get work with anyone but him. Kris somehow found out about the video (there were others) and arranged to meet with me. That's when I had a panic attack at the audition, and Kris hired me anyway.

That time I was in New York for the Covergirl meeting? When you and I were figuring out our relationship? Sienna asked me to beard for Ty. In exchange, she offered me information on Kircher. That's when I learned about the poker games. He uses them to fleece industry types and lure unsuspecting girls into his disgusting web.

When Ty and I were a "couple," Kircher reached out to my agent. He wanted to cast me as one of the leads in his new film Phantom Rising, *which I turned down. The next thing I knew, LTZ was asked to do the soundtrack. I couldn't help but wonder if I'd dragged you all into his filthy web. Or if he thought it was a way to get to me.*

In the meantime, my lawyer worked some voodoo magic with Sofer and Graham. Kircher is toast. While I wish he was going to rot for what he did to me, the statute of limitations has passed. But there are plenty of other #metoo moments that will destroy his career. A lot of the cast are coming forward. With Harvey Weinstein rotting in jail, I can't wait for Kircher to join him.

Crazily enough, it's going to be the poker games that wipe him completely out. Actually, a specific poker game. The one in New York. When I first found out about the games, Byron—my friend who has been helping me all of these years— learned how to play from a World Series of Poker winner. Mainly so he could just get in. The authorities have planted players in many of his games over the past year.

What he's doing is illegal, but when he brought the game to New York it opened up a ton of other federal charges. In other words, various law enforcement agencies have built an ironclad case.

He's going down.

Maybe even tomorrow.

You asked why I was in New York. Byron was wired at that game. He got himself kicked out so he could bring me in toward the end of the night. You see, I volunteered to go to confront Kircher, and hopefully give the case a huge boost. Kris told me there was an undercover agent there, so I'd be safe.

And have my own closure. Put an end to this so I could move on with my life. We could be together and move on with our lives.

Connor, all I wanted was to report another Sofer-type victory to you. Everything would finally be fine.

Right?

So I lied.

And there you were.

Why were you there?

I don't want to believe the worst.

But here we are.

I read and reread the email about fifty times. Unable to comprehend the horror of what Ronni went through as a young girl. Holy feckin Jaysus.

I was going to kill Kircher with my bare hands.

But first, I had to get to Ronni.

To make sure she knew I wasn't a monster.

RONNI

CHAPTER 39

Throughout the entire flight home, I felt sick. Nauseous. I actually threw up in the airplane bathroom because of the stress.

I'd finally been able to tell Connor the truth. The coward's way. I mean, who sends an email like that to their husband?

Me.

Of course, I'd sent it before I'd pieced the blind item together with Connor. He didn't know that yet. I wasn't going to apologize for finding redemption on my terms. I didn't need protection from my past. I had to right that ship myself. Glancing at my watch, I realized it was time to pull myself together, we were landing soon. Whenever I flew commercial, paparazzi would be waiting. Splashing water on my face helped. Digging through my purse, I found an old lipstick, which I slicked over my lips and rubbed a bit on the apples of my cheeks so I didn't look too washed out.

My big Prada sunglasses would hide my eyes. The chic black overcoat I always traveled with would cover the clothes I'd been wearing for days. It was as good as it was going to get for someone who hadn't slept in days.

There was no time to lose sight of the bigger picture.

As exhausted as my body was, my mind was a whirling dervish. Sleep? It hadn't been possible. Using some breathing techniques I learned in yoga, I tried to settle myself down and figure out what to do. Didn't work. How could it when the bottom fell out of your life as you knew it?

To calm myself, I repeated my mantra.

Deep breath

Suck it up.

Be fearless.

It helped. Reminding myself that I was a strong, wealthy, competent woman, who had worked hard to get where I was, I began to get my mind straight. Wallowing while I waited to confront Connor? Idiotic. Getting my ducks in a row was smart. I snagged my laptop, methodically went through all my security protocols and accessed the mountains of evidence I'd compiled.

Scanning my documents, I had to be sure that Connor wasn't some predator. I couldn't trust my instincts right now. So, I looked for Connor's name. Obscure references. Nothing. I watched and rewatched footage. Nada. I read and reread the blind items. Scoured the other blinds for any clue. There was only that one mention. If only there were more to go on. I wanted to give him the benefit of the doubt, but I knew what went on at those poker games. The New York game wasn't his first.

It ate at me.

Connor prided himself on his honor. His honesty. His integrity.

So why was he there?

Lack of sleep was causing me to hallucinate. With one final mental push, I fired off an email to Kris and slammed my laptop shut.

Indulging in another moment of self-pity, I let my frustration wash over me. I flung my hands up and let out a loud "arrrrrghhhh" into the ether. I'd been fighting to bring Don Kircher down so I could put my past behind me and finally be with my husband. He'd been exceedingly patient with me. So caring. Never pushing me. He asked questions, but he never pressed me too hard.

Why?

In my exhausted state, I could only think of one explanation. Which meant my heart was officially broken. My future officially in tatters. Because I *knew* it wasn't a coincidence that he'd been invited to those games. No way. It killed me to think that Connor got sucked into Kircher's inner circle.

If he had, our relationship was over. I'd never, ever forgive him.

No way.

Oh, and if I confirmed he was part of *anything* Kircher-related?

I'd bring him down too.

CHAPTER 40

I wasn't sure why she ran.

But I knew it wasn't good.

On my way to the private airstrip, I was forced to call and wake Kris up when I couldn't get hold of Ronni. The rest of LTZ hopped a different plane to Seattle, but I had to get to LA as soon as possible. I wasn't one to ordinarily splurge on stupid shite like PJs. In the wee hours of the morning, I made an exception and chartered a plane.

The one thing I knew? Mae wasn't going to shake me loose, that was for feckin' sure.

Kris was waiting when I touched down in Burbank. "She actually thinks you got sucked in, Connor." Kris handed me a trough of coffee. "It's best we go together."

Jay-sus.

"Aye."

We drove in relative silence to Ronni's house. Not much needed to be said. Truth be told, I had no idea how much about Ronni's past she knew. I assumed all of it. But, now that I knew what she'd been through, I was never going to break my wife's confidence. So I kept my mouth shut.

Kris *did* know why I was at the poker game, which is why I felt the importance of having her with me. At least in the beginning. I think both Kris and I were hoping she'd understand why we did what we did. Why we kept my involvement secret from her.

What a clusterfuck. Neither of us were privy to her plans with that eejit Byron.

We pulled up to Ronni's gate. Kris was going to stay put while I went in to find her. Just in case. I wasn't sure where she'd be, but I decided to check the most obvious place first. Sure enough, my beautiful wife was in our pod, in yoga pants and a T-shirt, dozing in the morning sun. The tide was out, but the gentle breeze blew a salty freshness around us.

Kneeling beside her, I reached out to brush a stray hair off her face. Her eyelids fluttered. She curled herself tighter in a ball and started mumbling in her sleep. Not wanting to scare her, I whispered, "Mae, wake up."

She stirred, but only moaned and batted her hand in front of her face.

"Mae, love. Wake up." I gripped her shoulder lightly.

Her eyes popped open and she bolted upright into a sitting position. "Connor!"

Eyes flashing with a myriad of emotions.

Wariness. Betrayal. Anger. Love. Hope.

My girl, who had been through so much and thrived instead of caved. My girl, who was strong and deceptively unassuming. My girl, who'd carried an incredible burden and used it to make herself stronger. My girl, who had opened herself up to me. Given me that gift.

A gift I'd never, ever take for granted.

"Don't look at me like that." She covered her face with her hand. "I don't want your pity, Connor."

"Mae, I'm looking at you with all the love in my heart. I don't pity you, I'm in awe of you. My wife is an incredible example to both women and men." I took her hands in mine. "I'm looking at you with gratitude. Gratitude that you were able to trust me. Tell me your deepest secrets. I'll never take that for granted, my love."

Ronni yanked her hands away and spat, "You already have, Connor."

Ahh, the poker game. "May I explain?"

"I told him about that psychopath a while ago, Ronni." Kris walked up behind us, interrupting. "Connor came to me after you started bearding for Sam. I told him Kircher had a compromising video of you at that audition. I didn't tell him specifics."

"Has it really been eighteen years…" Ronni stared off into the distance, as though she'd never considered the time frame.

My eyes bored into hers. Pleading. She was my heart. My soul. "Mae. I'd do anything to protect you, my love, but I knew how important for your own healing that you protected yourself. I spoke with Ty's therapist. She told me I had to give you the space to work it out. To learn to let me in."

Ronni buried her face in her hands.

Kris and I exchanged glances. She sat down next to Ronni. "Veronica. You're not alone. We're your family. Before she died, I made a promise to your mother that I'd look after you. You've done a lot of work to heal. To come to terms with what those awful men did to you and other young men and women."

"So all along, you knew." She shook her head sadly, her eyes riddled with hurt as she looked at both Kris and me.

"Ronni, you've never told me what specifically happened." Kris took one of Ronni's hands and rubbed it in between hers. "But I've been in the business a long time. Kircher's tactics are not secret in this industry. So, no. I don't know what he did to you, but I'm not an idiot. No one on that set got away unscathed."

A tear trickled down Ronni's cheek. She wiped it away with her free hand.

My knees were aching from kneeling on the hard tiles. I pulled another one of Ronni's pod loungers close to hers, sitting on the edge. "Mae, when Kris told me about the video, she also believed that something worse likely happened to you on set."

Now that I knew, my belly filled with acid just thinking about what he'd done to her.

"If you knew, I don't understand why you didn't just ask me about it." Ronni leaned her head on Kris's shoulder. Kris put her arm around Ronni.

"As I said earlier, I went to a few therapy sessions with Lisa." I rested my elbows on my knees, holding my face up with my hands. "I didn't know why you couldn't tell me. Some of the decisions you made, I… Well, I…didn't understand them. I'm not going to lie. I've been very hurt that you couldn't talk to me. It's taken every ounce of patience to hold my tongue. I'm not always successful. But, I came to learn that if I pressed you too hard—forced you to share before you felt ready to trust me—it might backfire."

Realization crossed Ronni's face, but all she said was, "Oh."

"Darling, you always deflected when I brought it up. After Sofer was sentenced, I thought it was over. I couldn't figure out why you decided to beard for Ty when I knew you loved Connor. You weren't thinking things through methodically like you'd done for years. Something was clearly amiss." Kris leaned her head against Ronni's. "That's when I brought in Connor to help."

"When the band was asked to do the soundtrack, I was the only one who knew the connection between Kircher and you. Something clicked for me, call it good Irish intuition because I was going to exercise my veto on our participation altogether." I glanced over at Kris, who nodded. "I spoke with Kris about it. She told me about the poker games. You might remember that I spent a fair number of evenings bailing out my da in those back-alley games in Seattle. I figured, how hard would it be—"

"You were trying to help me?" Ronni bolted up, nearly knocking Kris over. "Oh, thank God."

Kris chuckled. "God, Ronni, please don't tell me you thought…"

I stood and took my wife in my arms. "I don't blame you. You weren't thinking straight. I would never do anything to hurt you. I was there because I was working with your lawyer, Ronni."

"All those months I was agonizing over how to get more evidence. To put all of the nails in that psycho's coffin," Ronni murmured. "Byron took poker lessons. He was wired. Your lawyer had another plant in New York—"

I grasped her shoulders. Looked her in the eye. Willed her to figure it out.

After a beat, realization dawned. "You." Her eyes filled with tears.

"I'm a determined man, Veronica Mae Miller." I touched my forehead to hers. "I didn't know the details of what happened to you. I only knew I didn't want us to put our life on hold for that bollocks anymore."

"It doesn't explain why you were so angry at me." Ronni moved out of my embrace and pointed at me. "Obviously, you knew I'd be there…"

"He didn't, Ronni," Kris interjected. "He was there specifically because *you* weren't supposed to be there."

"Aye, I was angry at you because I thought you were putting yourself in danger. A man who'd hurt you. Even if I didn't have all the details,

Mae. I could feel it the second you came in. Your body language scared the bejeezus out of me. I did not want to out you. I tried to remain calm. Quiet. But when he got near you? If you could have seen the look in your eyes…" My fists squeezed and released. Squeezed and released. I was so agitated. "You can't expect a man like me to sit back and not protect his woman. I've been patient, but I was pushed to my limit. Nothing, and I mean *nothing* means more to me than your safety. Your well-being. I couldn't stand by."

Ronni's face softened. "I'm overwhelmed."

"I'm so proud of you." Kris's voice cracked. Tears pooled in the usually self-controlled woman's eyes. "Kircher used that video to try and isolate you and make you feel ashamed. But you took control of your mental health. You've done everything I've ever asked of you and more. You, my dear, are not just a victim and victim's advocate, but a survivor and a survivor's advocate."

I closed the gap between us and cupped my wife's face tenderly. "You're not alone. Thank you for opening up to me. For sharing your story on your own terms. We've had a long journey, but I know everything happens for a reason. I would live the exact same life in the exact same way if it led me to you. You, Veronica Mae Miller, are worth everything. You are my everything. You are *my* honey."

Ronni shook her head. "People know about my audition video. Gossip Schmossip posted a blind item about me."

"It's taken care of." Kris nodded. "Really."

Ronni wrapped her arms around my waist and buried her face in my chest. Squeezing me. Clinging to me. Melting into me. I enveloped her into my body. One arm banded around her waist, the other around her shoulders and head. Kris caught my eye and motioned that she was leaving. We stayed put for who knows how long.

The sun was high in the sky now. Morning was giving way to the noon hour. I led Ronni by the hand up into the house. Through the kitchen. Into our bedroom, not stopping until we were next to the giant walk-in shower. "Let's wash off and get some rest. That is if we're okay."

"We're more than okay." Ronni lifted up my shirt and I helped whisk it off my body. I got to work on my boots and jeans while she stripped out of her lounge clothes. I adjusted all the shower heads to spray us with fountains of warm water. "For a minute…"

I silenced her with a kiss. There was no need for her to voice her doubts about my involvement. The entire situation was bizarre. Confusing. Horrifying. And over. Kircher would never hold anything over Mae's head again. "I feckin' love you."

"I feckin' love you too." Ronni ran her hands down my arms and took my hands in hers. She guided me to sit on the long teak bench and sat on my knee. Nuzzling my cheek. Trailing her lips along my jawbone. Biting my lower lip. Eventually, her lips found mine and we tasted each other sweetly. Tentatively. She smoothed my wet hair from my face and kissed my forehead. My eyelids. My temples.

I supported her back with my arm, which rested on her hip. I hooked my other arm under her legs so she was sprawled over my thighs, then plunged my fingers into her channel. My thumb circled her clit slowly. Deliberately. Increasing the pressure. Our kisses grew deeper, the rhythm matching the tempo of my circles. Despite the warm temperature of the water, her nipples puckered into taut, rosy peaks.

My lips drifted to the space between her neck and ear that drove her mad. Ronni arched and bucked against my plunging fingers, thrusting her breasts up toward my lips. This left me little choice but to suckle and graze my teeth on her nipple. To kiss the space between her breasts and worship her. Lick her collarbone.

Consume her.

My cock pressed against her outer thigh, growing harder with each clench of her pussy around my digits. From her little whimpers, I knew she was getting close. God, I wanted—no needed—to taste her release. Shifting us so she was lying flat on the bench, I hovered over her. Making sure she was comfortable.

Her brown eyes blinked up at me, and I knew in that instant that our pasts were truly behind us. "Connor, I don't ever want to be without you again. I need you. So much."

"Ah, love. I've always been right here." I licked the rivulets of water sluicing down Ronni's breasts. Following their trail down her flat stomach. Splaying my hands on her inner thighs, spreading them wide. I licked the hollows of each her legs at the juncture of her pussy. Blew on her bare sex. Nuzzled her folds with my nose, breathing her in. Delectable.

Ronni moaned when my tongue invaded her opening. I flicked it over her clit while plunging my fingers back inside her. Loving her sweet, musky taste. I knew every single millimeter of my woman's body. Every spot that made her crazy. I'd spent years memorizing her. My fingers sought out and found her sweet spot deep within and I stroked it while nibbling on her throbbing nub.

One of Ronni's legs rested on the floor of the shower, she dug the heel of her other leg into the bench, allowing her to thrust up against my mouth. Rolling my tongue over her clit, I savored her little bud. Her fingers clenched my scalp and held me in the place she wanted. I licked her slowly until her whimpers grew louder, turning into keening moans. Crying out as her orgasm ripped through her body. I tried to soothe her through several aftershocks with my tongue. Then kissed my way up her body, stopping to suckle each nipple on my way back to her mouth.

Ronni reached for my cock and stroked, gently cupping and massaging my scrotum. I needed no foreplay, my cock was harder than I could ever remember on this monumental day. The day where Ronni and I truly became free.

I scooped her up so her legs were draped over my arms. She was spread open for me as I backed her against the shower wall. I watched my cock plunge into her. Disappear into her body. Over and over. Ronni watched too. Both of us mesmerized. Her arms were looped around my neck, but there was no way I'd drop her. Never.

The telltale zing at the base of my spine caused my hips to cant harder. Almost of their own volition. Our eyes locked. I plunged into her over and over, the emotion of our joining overwhelming. Her lips sought mine and our tongues tangled. Never breaking eye contact. My arms tightened under her legs and I shifted my angle, driving into her as I came with a loud roar.

Flooding her.

Marking her.

Forever.

Mine.

RONNI

CHAPTER 41

T he smell of barbecued steak still lingered in the air. Zoey, Alex, and I lounged on chairs around Ty's pool, comparing our food-baby stomachs. The two women were fantastic. It was early days but for the first time in my life I felt like I might have real girlfriends.

Earlier, at Ty's request, I brought my friend Christian Siriano and Hannah over so we'd all look amazing on the red carpet the next day. It had been a fun girl's day of pampering.

Carter, Zane, and Ty were deep in conversation with Zoey's Dad. Likely about Ty's plans to propose to Zoey. Yeah, I was in on the secret. Ty wanted a woman's opinion about the ten-carat rock he'd commissioned. It was stunning. Not as stunning as my own engagement ring, which was safe at home. Its debut would be soon.

As if he had ESP, Connor caught my eye from across the pool where he sat chatting with Zoey's mom. Tonight was the first time I'd come with him to an LTZ event as his date. It was so cute how he checked on me a lot. Not in a creepy way. In the most caring, loving "she's my feckin' wife" kind of way.

I loved it.

God, I loved him.

"Finish the story, Ronni!" Zoey nudged me. "Stop making googly eyes at Connor for just one second."

I so liked Ty's girlfriend. Learning more about her side of their journey, I realized that every couple had their own road to love, however convoluted it might be. You couldn't judge. Take Alex. Connor connected the dots for me. She was the girl Jace had been broken up about in Sydney years before. He warned me that although she and Jace were living together in Seattle, they were going through a rough patch. You couldn't tell from the way they looked at each other. I hoped they'd find their way.

Nevertheless, I decided not to share my truth-or-dare stories from that night.

Yet.

Or ask Alex, a popular influencer in her own right, whether Kircher ever invited her to one of his disgusting poker parties.

Yet.

"Okay, okay. When Ty and I were first discussing our agreement, he didn't really know what bearding meant. It was such a struggle to explain a concept that we would pretend to be in love for the photographers and cameras. I mean, I'd been pretending to date people both on set and off for years, so I didn't think about it twice."

"He has no game." Zoey giggled. "Neither do I, it's a miracle we ever got started. It sure didn't help us get back together."

Alex chimed in, "The night you guys met, listening to the two of you try to flirt was the most painful experience of my life."

I laughed. "Ohmygod! That makes so much sense. When I tried to hold hands with Ty on the red carpet, the look on his face was priceless. Like my fingers were made of fire. I leaned in and whispered for him to give the photographers a show. He was like, 'You want me to sing?' Eventually, he got the hang of it."

Zoey furrowed her brow. "Oh, I saw the footage, I tortured myself watching it."

"Repeat after me: It was fake." Alex sat up and tried to nonchalantly locate Jace, who had gone inside.

"You don't need to worry, Ty always loved you. Always." I gripped her hand. "We spent most of our outings talking about you. And Connor. Or, picking out people who were having conversations we couldn't hear and making up what we thought they were saying. He's hilarious."

"O.M.G. He still loves to do that." Zoey squeezed my hand back. "And I'm not worried, we've always loved each other, that's the truth. It just took us a while to get here. What I can't believe is you and Connor have been together for all of these years. Out of the spotlight! How did you manage to stay under the radar? You're both so famous."

"It's a fine art. Alex knows." Alex nodded her agreement. "You have to play the game. Give them a version of yourself. Learn how to keep the real you for your loved ones."

"When I first started my Insta, it was super fun getting recognized. It was always a means to an end for me. A business." Alex relaxed back down in the chair. "Jace taught me a lot about that part of it, which helped keep me grounded when I started making real money."

We both looked at Zoey, who was listening to us intently. "Yeah. I've had to learn pretty fast. No more dashing out in front of taxis."

"You better not." Ty joined us, placing a scorching smacker on Zoey's lips. "Butterfly, we have an early start and then the show, I'm thinking we should call it a night."

On the drive home, Connor and I snuggled in the backseat. For the past month, we'd rarely left the house. Soaking in the last few days of being incognito. I'd never complain about having an extended period of time with Connor, especially when neither of us was on a strict schedule.

Which basically meant we ate, slept, and shagged. Mostly shagged. All of the feckin' time.

"Did you have fun, love?" Connor kissed my temple. "You seemed to be getting along grand with the ladies."

"I did. They're great." I batted at his chest. "So, were you going to tell me about seeing Zoey's boobs?"

Connor's face reddened. "Which time?"

"What!"

"Oh, aye. Twice I saw the fair Zoey's rack. The first time I walked in on them going at it in the practice space at Carter's house." Connor palmed my breast with his hand and squeezed, pinching my nipple for good measure. "The second time was after our wedding, when Zane and I were working out the bass and guitar melodies for the soundtrack in Ty's pool house. We couldn't help but look when Zoey stood topless in the window."

"You're heathens." I swatted him.

"Ah, love. It's taken this long for you to figure that out?" Connor took my left hand and clasped it in his.

"I guess we're even then. I pretended to kiss her man, and she showed my man her tits." I jokingly pouted.

Connor stroked my naked ring finger with his thumb. "Are you ready to blow everyone's minds?"

"I'm more than ready."

Looking back, I never really believed that Connor had anything to do with Kircher. I think all the stress and lack of sleep in New York messed with my mind. When I flew back to LA, I'd completely forgotten about the interview I'd done for Ty and Zoey, which got bumped back a week while they covered her accident.

Using all my media savvy skills, I'd charmed the reporter with a promise of an exclusive interview about my real long-term relationship. Rather than giving the sound bites that Sienna prepared, I confessed my relationship with Ty was fake and what Sienna's role had been in setting it up. It was delightful to put another nail in her coffin.

On the day of the show, Connor texted me during rehearsal about the special effects Ty had planned for Zoey. We agreed, it was their special night. Complete with a butterfly light extravaganza. LTZ's concert would not be the right place for me to wear my engagement and wedding ring for all to see on the red carpet. Instead, I'd invited everyone over to my place for a sunset clam bake (catered of course!) and our own big reveal.

Low key. The way we both liked it.

Well, maybe not that low key. I would be on the cover of *People* Magazine next week, after all. Connor and I were going to be publicly outed in a preapproved article dedicated to our love story. Complete with pictures from our wedding in Ireland.

It wasn't the main piece, however.

Because the real reason I was a cover-girl?

I'd agreed to be a figurehead of survival in Hollywood.

In a coordinated effort with the *Los Angeles Times*'s new expose on Kircher, who'd been arrested this morning, *People* was running an entire piece about *Hawaiian High*. Featuring interviews from most of the surviving cast and crew members. We were scattered all over the world, but we'd managed to have an emotional Zoom meeting ahead of time. It was healing in so many ways.

As for the article, I held nothing back about what I'd gone through. It was important for me to expose the most toxic television set in history. My fellow survivors felt the same way. Byron, Sam, and all my other fauxmances were cooperating with the article too. There was no doubt about it, I was nervous to share the secrets I'd kept hidden for nearly two decades.

I had to, though. It was for the greater good.

To make sure there would never be a repeat of what happened in Hawaii.

Anywhere.

In the meantime, I was enjoying LTZ's show, which was stunning. Hanging out on the side of the stage with Zoey and her family, Alex, Carter, and Kris was even better. My small inner circle was expanding in a wonderful way. It made me feel like Marvelous Mable was looking out for me.

Surrounding me with love.

I felt lighter somehow.

Fearless.

EPILOGUE

"**C**onnor, I said will you be in town for the opening?" Zane snapped his fingers in front of my face.

I'd been checking the time. Ronni's plane was late. We were due at my folks' house after Ty's big proposal. It looked like she might miss the big event, which I knew would break her heart. She'd become very fond of Zoey since the holiday show and wanted to be here to witness their happy ever after.

"Sorry, my brother. I'm just waiting for Ronni to text me that she's on her way. When is the opening?" Zane and Carter hadn't been able to save The Mission from the land developers tearing it down, but they'd bought an old rundown theater in the Columbia City neighborhood, renovated it and created a new arts compound.

"March 5th."

I shook my head. "Ach, no. We'll be back in Ireland. Ronni's shooting the movie. I'm gonna be an extra, so I am."

"Oh, that sucks." Zane looked sad. "I wanted all of us to be there. I'm not happy about this break."

I put my arm around him. "We all need it, Zane. Even you."

"I guess."

"I bet Fiona's thrilled." I clapped his back. "From what you said, she was pretty broken up about the loss of the building."

Zane's face clouded. "I'm not sure if she is. Nothing I do seems to make a difference with her. I just want her to be happy again."

My phone buzzed loudly in my hand.

"It's okay. Go ahead, Connor." Zane gave me a half smile. "I'll check the tuning on the guitars."

Setting a mental reminder to invite Zane to visit us in Ireland, I looked down at my phone.

Mae: Just touched down. We shouldn't be too long.

Connor: Gotta love PJ's

Mae: play your cards right and you might be getting a different kind of J.

Connor: Jaysus you want me to sport a woody at the big engagement?

Mae: just a little something to think about.

Connor: Gotta go, time for me to play.

Mae: Dang it. Oh well. We'll be there soon. Make sure Alex films it.

Connor: I think you'll have plenty of options

Carter was gesturing to me wildly, so Zane and I took our places in the living room and started playing *And I Love Her* by the Beatles. The room looked beautiful. Full of lit candles, sparkly Christmas lights. Huge sprays of white flowers and red poinsettias.

As we all knew she would, Zoey enthusiastically accepted Ty's proposal. Everyone was milling around congratulating the happy couple. Except for Jace, who was being a right eejit. After he threw a bit of a tantrum and stormed out, Zoey calmed him down. He and Alex were currently in one of the back bedrooms fighting. Talking. Who knew? Jace seemed to be completely on edge lately. Our year-long break was going to come at the perfect time.

Looking around, I felt pretty lucky to be part of such a wonderful extended family, which was now growing. As much as I was enjoying myself, I couldn't wait for Ronni and Kris to get here so the three of us could head over to my folks' house and spend the rest of the holiday with my family. I pulled out my phone to check the time.

Mae: We're walking up to the front door, can you let me in so we don't disrupt everything?

Connor: Y. On my way.

"You're leaving too?" Zane crossed his arms defiantly.

"Relax, Zane. Your dad is here. If you come over tomorrow, *my* da would love to see you," I tried to placate him.

"Okay. Yeah. I'll text you." Zane's attention was already diverted. He was across the room talking to Carter before I could tell him that Ronni was here.

Quickly crossing the room, I opened up the door. Ronni was stunning in a simple green sweater dress and knee-high black boots. Her hair was swept up on one side and held up by a sparkly clip. Kris, as always, looked polished in a white pantsuit that tied at the waist. Taking Ronni's hand, I led them through the foyer into Ty's sunken living room overlooking Seattle.

Everyone squealed with delight at their arrival.

"This is breathtaking, Ty." Ronni hugged both Ty and Zoey and the two women appropriately gushed over their respective rocks. Of course, they held their hands up together. A couple of million dollars of diamonds on our two girls' wee fingers. It was hard to believe how far Ty and I had come. When we met, we could barely make ends meet.

Even though we were also having dinner at my parents' house, Ronni and I didn't want to be rude, so we sat down with the rest of the group. Seconds after we were seated, Ty began to speak, only to be interrupted by Alex and Jace, who felt the need to announce the worst-kept secret in band history. They were together, I mean. Duh.

Eejits.

At least it gave Ronni and me an out.

"We'll leave with you." I got up and stood from the table, holding my hand out to my wife. I claimed her as mine whenever and wherever we were these days. We gave Kris a hug, who was staying here at Ty and Zoey's tonight and would join us for Christmas Day at my folks'.

Once outside, I wrapped myself around Ronni. Even a few hours without her was too long. "I've missed you, love."

"Me too, Connor." She ran her fingers through my hair. "The appointment went well."

"I wanted to be there." I pressed my lips to hers. Ronni's clout in Hollywood had grown to epic proportions. Now that it had been revealed she'd been behind the demise of the most evil men in Hollywood, my wife was a coveted woman. She could write her own ticket. Doors she never knew existed were opening to her. My woman, the international symbol of badass.

Ronni shivered. "There will be plenty other times. Let's get over to your folks before I freeze up here in this Seattle cold."

"I'll keep you warm." I waggled my eyebrows before opening the car door for her.

The family home was across town, giving us a beautiful view of the city all lit up for Christmas. The Great Wheel was done up in red, white, and green, with giant candy canes criss-crossing the center. When we came up over the hill by Volunteer Park, the gorgeous craftsman mansions were all done up with lights.

"If it weren't for the weather, Seattle would be a great place to live," Ronni teased.

"Yeah, yeah, yeah." I winked at her as we parked in front of the house. "Are you ready for the McGloughlin experience? I haven't been home for the holidays in years. Ma's going to go all out."

"I'm ready."

"You're really not going to say anything?" I stared her down. It never worked. Didn't stop me from trying.

"Why? It's so fun to watch you want to ask but refuse to ask because you're so stubborn."

"Feckin' hell." I pressed my palm over her belly. "Tell me."

"You have super sperm. Resistant to all birth control. Looks like you've knocked me up with twins." Ronni covered my hand with hers. "Your boys."

"Aye?" Tears stung my eyes. "Ah, Mae. That's brilliant."

Ronni's eyes also shone with happy tears. "The studio has agreed to push the movie a year to accommodate me."

I couldn't resist kissing the life out of her. My wife. Soon to be the mother of my children. Every dream of mine coming true. "What will we do now? The movie was supposed to take up our entire year."

"Do you know what would make me the most happy?" Ronni clasped my hand in both of hers, bringing it back to her belly, which had just the slightest swell. "You and me. Our Belfast home. Doing nothing but eating healthy, resting, and making sure these little boys are healthy."

"Shagging?"

Ronni's lyrical laugh never failed to enchant me. "Lots and lots of shagging."

It was eerie how in tune we are. "You're okay giving birth there?"

"Of course. It will keep us out of the spotlight. To focus on what's important, which is you and me and our sons." Ronni shifted in her seat to face me. "Connor McGloughlin, I love you. This is everything I've always wanted. *You're* everything I've always wanted. And you're going to be the very best father."

Ah, this woman. She'd reduced me to a blubbering mess. Tears streamed down my face. A father. A feckin' father. "You are my everything, Mae. I'm so proud to be your husband. I already love these little guys so much." I rubbed her belly.

"Alright, big guy, dry your tears." Ronni wiped them away with her thumbs and kissed me softly. "Let's break the news to your folks that they're going to be grandparents."

Hand-in-hand we gave Da and Ma one of the best Christmas gifts they'd ever had.

I knew Ronni's mom was watching over us.

Not only my family had come full circle.

We now had an entire crew.

THE END

If you loved FEARLESS – claim your FREE Prequel Novella NOW by signing up to my mailing list!

If you have a couple of minutes, PLEASE leave an honest review! It really helps self-published authors like me to spread the word!

ABOUT THE AUTHOR

When she was only 15, Kaylene Winter wrote her first rocker romance novel starring a fictionalized version of herself, her friends, and their gorgeous rocker boyfriends. After living her own rock star life as a band manager, music promoter, and mover and shaker in Seattle during the early 1990s, Kaylene became a digital media legal strategist helping bring movies, television, and music online. Throughout her busy career, Kaylene lost herself in romance novels across all genres inspiring her to realize her life-long dream to be a published author. She lives in Seattle with her amazing husband and dog. She loves to travel, throw lavish dinner parties, and support charitable causes supporting arts and animals.

The Less Than Zero Seattle Rocks Series is her debut in the world of Rock star romances. Kaylene hopes you'll love the gorgeous, sexy, flawed rockers and the strong, beautiful women who capture their hearts.

CONNECT WITH KAYLENE

Email: kaylenewinterauthor@gmail.com
Website: www.rockerromance.com
Kaylene: https://www.instagram.com/kaylenewinterauthor/
Reader Groups: https://www.facebook.com/groups/rockromance/
Bookbub: https://www.bookbub.com/profile/2883976651
Goodreads: https://www.goodreads.com/author/show/20367389.
Kaylene_Winter
TikTok: @kaylenewinter
Twitter: @kayleneromance

BEHIND THE SCENES
FEARLESS EDITION

One of my favorite writers is J.A. Huss, she writes twisted crazy stories, and they are amazing. I've never met her but hope I do someday to tell her what an inspiration she is. Anyway, one of the things I love about her books is her free-thinking ramblings about the book she just wrote. I probably won't be as eloquent as her, but I thought this would be a new format for me to try out.

Nothing in this section is edited or proofread, there will probably be typos (especially if I don't have my reading glasses on – don't judge, I just am in denial that I need them). Mainly I'll just word vomit for a couple of pages on the inspiration behind my latest book.

Many of you who have been reading my books know that this whole journey started out when I was 15 and wrote my first rock-star romance. I wasn't the only girl who wanted to marry a rockstar, I had two BFF's who were right there with me.

They are the inspiration behind Alex in LIMITLESS and now Ronni in FEARLESS.

The story in FEARLESS is very dear to my heart – for two reasons. One, I'm an avid pop-culture junkie, who is addicted to blind items. My favorite sites to get my gossip are Crazy Days & Nights and Alt Gossip

Celebrities (ALT). For years, I've been reading about these networks of creepy guys who exploit both men and women in Hollywood.

It sickened me. Fascinated me. And a couple of years ago when Harvey Weinstein was outed, I already knew all about all of the horrific things he had done – mainly because of these pages. He is not alone. It is pervasive. While FEARLESS was being edited, the entire story about Buffy the Vampire Slayer and the "toxic" set broke.

Another thing that I've followed for years is the "bearding" situation that so many actors/actresses and other celebrities turn to in order to navigate this world of celebrity. While many "couple" up to maximize publicity – others do it to rehab their image, or dirty up their image etc. This practice has been happening for decades and I thought it made a perfect pairing with the toxic set storyline.

Most of all, I wanted Ronni to be the one to find her power and bring things to a head. She may not solve everything, but her perseverance and focus gave her (and many others) a big payoff.

Now, onto Connor!

This book is a bit of a love-letter to my in-laws. My husband is Irish, really from Northern Ireland. He grew up during the Troubles, which was a really tough time to be a child during political warfare. It is one of the main reasons he moved to Seattle nearly 3 decades ago.

The issues he grew up with have largely resolved, and I've had the amazing fortune to spend many many months in the Emerald Isle. My family there is wonderful and I've been very sad not to be able to visit during this COVID-19 craziness. One day my husband and I hope to own a home like Connor's where I can while my days away writing more LTZ stories...

Any-hoooo— Connor's family is NOTHING like his family or him, but I hope that I've captured some of the dialogue in a way that isn't too annoying. As my husband likes to remind me, the Irish accent has been called the sexiest accent in the world!

I agree!

As far as Connor and Ronni's story goes, as often happens when people meet during the years their career is being established – it can be very difficult to join life force even when you love each other. When you are separated it is also difficult to build up the trust you need to share your deepest, darkest secrets.

I'm sure you've heard this from other authors, but somehow both Connor and Ronni wrote their own story. I got to know them as the words poured out and I hope you've fallen in love with the big gentle giant and the feisty girl who tamed him.

If you haven't received your free book, please make sure to sign up for my mailing list and get it free!

Until TIMELESS,

Love, Kaylene

ACKNOWLEDGEMENTS

This book was an absolute labor of love, and I couldn't have done it without the help and support of the following awesome rock stars:

Cover/Graphic Designer/Finder of hotties: Regina Wamba
https://www.reginawamba.com/

Editor: Grace Bradley
https://gracebradleyediting.com/

Proofreading: Letitia Delan

Formatting: Cat at TRC Designs

Photo Crew: Debbie Murphy, Elena Chavez

Connor: Ryan "Shorty" Vest Instagram: @shortyvest
Ronni: Christine Klein Instagram: @christine_klein

My VIPs/Readers/Alpha and Beta Readers Sheila, Kris, Laura, Amy, Tracy, Beth, Anna

OMG! To the ARC readers, bloggers, bookstagrammers & my Street Team – I can't do this without you.

Thank you thank you thank you for helping spread the word—I'm overwhelmed by your love, support, kindness, etc. Thank you for making my dream come true!

Please leave a review!

ABOUT THIS BOOK

Get ready for the gorgeous rockers of Less than Zero and the strong, feisty women who bring them to their knees.

FEARLESS

Family is everything, I protect mine with my life..

Connor McGloughlin had it all, a great family, a college scholarship and music.
Tragedy forced him to grow up too fast.
When his life finally is on track, Ronni Miller appears like a dream.
Kindred spirits in the most unlikely of circumstances.
There's only one thing in the way—
Her dark past he's determined to protect her from.

When your innocence is stolen, trust is a precious gift..

Actress Ronni Miller tasted fame at a young age.
But her path to stardom was riddled with tragedy.
She never imagined falling for Connor McGloughlin, a rogue, Irish rock star.
The thing is? Ronni's got revenge on her mind.
Regardless of the risk or the consequences—
Or losing the one thing in her life that makes her feel alive.

Connor has only ever asked Ronni for one thing: her heart.
But when her bravery is couched in lies?
She risks losing the man who would do anything for her.
Will she realize being fearless means trusting true love?

OTHER TITLES BY KAYLENE WINTER

ENDLESS – LESS THAN ZERO Book 1 (Ty & Zoey)
"An absolute Rockstar Masterpiece!" – Anna's Bookshelf

LIMITLESS – LESS THAN ZERO Book 2 (Jace & Alex)
"#Utterperfection!" – The Power of Three Readers

TIMELESS – LESS THAN ZERO Book 4 (Zane and Fiona) –
COMING FALL 2021

RESTLESS – LESS THAN ZERO PREQUEL NOVELLA (Carter &
Lianne)
"Rockstar Story, Rockstar Writer!" – Karen C

DEDICATION

G—you are my biggest supporter and push me to be better in everything that I do. Thank you for encouraging me to follow my dream.

To Kris, the inspiration for Ronni—I wanted to create a strong, beautiful woman you would be proud of.

To Blakely, thank you for all of your support. Your mama's the best.

Turn the page for a excerpt of ENDLESS!

ZOEY

CHAPTER 1
FIVE MONTHS PREVIOUS

"C'mon!" Alex pleaded with me. "We're going to be late!"

"I can't help it if I need extra time, you look amazing in a paper sack," I whined to my best friend since diaper-hood.

Even though my family had moved from Ballard to a big, renovated craftsman in the Wallingford neighborhood when I was eight, Alex and I spent time together most weekends and nearly every day during the summer. Our neighborhoods were close enough that we retained our sisterly bond, which was so tight we could finish each other's sentences. Now, with only a few weeks to go until graduation from our respective high schools, all we did was obsess over music and boys, sometimes not in that order.

Which meant on a Saturday night, as per our usual routine, we got ready at my house to go out for the evening.

"You look gorgeous, you always do." Alex surveyed my outfit, her hands on her hips. Tall and thin with supermodel beauty, my BFF looked fantastic in her simple getup of a black, V-neck fitted T-shirt, baggy boyfriend jeans with a beat-up brown belt holding them up, hoop earrings, a distressed, black motorcycle jacket, and black motorcycle boots. Her blonde hair styled with fringy bangs was effortlessly tussled as though she'd spent hours on it, when really all she did was run her fingers through it a few times.

I sighed, studying my image in the full-length mirror. As a short and slightly voluptuous girl, I tried to accentuate my curvy assets. Tonight, I wore a casual outfit of skinny black jeans with shredded knees, my favorite black, flat, suede knee-high boots, and a vintage Van Halen T-shirt with the sides and back cut out in a crisscross pattern, which gave a glimpse, but not full view, of my D-cup boobs.

"Well, this is as good as it's going to get." I shook out my long, thick blonde hair streaked in beachy waves, and turned to check out how my butt looked. I loved my curves, and thanks to the Kardashians normalizing a bit of tits and ass, I could hold my own even if I couldn't be bothered to paint on a perfect Instagram contour.

"Thank God, the Uber is here." Alex swooshed out of the room and bounded down the stairs, with me following close behind.

We had been waiting all week for tonight's show at The Mission, an iconic Seattle all-ages venue, which launched the grunge era over two decades ago. My parents had met there at a Limelight show, so they were surprisingly cool about my acute love of live music. The club, which lacked in charm, still featured an awesome lineup of up-and-coming bands and we loved nothing more than to experience live music up close and personal.

Even better, we were finally going to see Less Than Zero, a throw-back rock band that made actual real music and didn't rely on auto-tune or fancy production. We'd been obsessed with their YouTube channel and Instagram account because of all their hot pictures and crazy video snippets. Their music was amazing, driven by screaming guitar riffs, anthemic lyrics, and groovy beats. It also didn't hurt that all the guys in the band were tasty, tasty snacks.

"Are you staying over tonight, Alex?" my dad called out as we bounded past him in the living room.

"No, Mr. Pearson." Alex stopped to address him. "Mom and I have plans early tomorrow morning."

Alex's mom and dad were divorced, and she lived with her hilarious mother who had a successful mail-order pie business. If her sense of humor wasn't reason enough to hang out at her house, we were guinea pigs for her kitchen experiments, which turned out some delicious food. Her dad, a developer who had remarried, lived on Bainbridge Island, a suburb across Puget Sound.

"Alex, how many times do I need to tell you to call me Mike," Dad chastised good-naturedly. "Are you off to The Mission, then?"

"Yep!" I bopped over to give him a kiss on the forehead. "I'll be home by midnight."

"How are you getting home?"

"Jeez, Dad. Stop interrogating me like a lawyer. You know I'll take an Uber." I rolled my eyes. For God's sake, I was a dedicated 4.3 GPA student, it was annoying that he didn't think I could figure out a ride home.

"Zoey, I'm glad you're finally getting out of the house, you've earned some free time to go out and be more social." Dad hugged me. "I'm just happy you're not buried in books for a change."

"Is Mom home tonight?" I ignored his annoying comment. My

mom, Olivia, traveled a lot for her job as a pharmaceutical sales manager. She was flying in that night from a conference in Miami.

"Yes, I'm going to pick her up in an hour." Dad smiled cheekily. They were still so in love, I hoped to find that for myself someday. Maybe when I was thirty.

When we finally made it through the long line into the divey, dark club, Less Than Zero's melodic, guitar-driven, ass-kicking rock was already in full force. As was our usual M.O., we pushed our way to the front of the stage so we could see the band in action and, of course, dance. Our bodies couldn't resist moving to the music. LTZ was on point. By the time they launched into their third song, I felt electrified. The energy in the crowd was intense, as if we all knew we were witnessing something special.

All the guys in the band looked hot in the videos and pictures we had been poring over on YouTube and social. LTZ in person? Other-worldly.

Drummer, Jace Deveraux, played shirtless, lean with taut muscles, intense, piercing green bedroom eyes, and sexy dirty-blond hair that brushed just past his shoulders. He thrashed hard yet kept the most complicated groovy rhythm, his mouth moved in time to the beats he played.

Zane Rocks, a pretty boy with an infectious grin, dark-brown eyes, and a mop of jet-black, unruly hair that didn't quite reach his collar, played lead guitar. He bounced all over the stage but managed to make eye contact with everyone in the crowd, drawing them in. Effortlessly channeling classic Slash and Eddie Van Halen, his natural skill translated into his own unique sound.

Bassist Conner McLoughlin was the hottest ginger I'd ever seen, his thick, reddish-brown hair hung well past his jaw. He stared into the crowd with light, golden-brown eyes that were brooding and almost dangerous. Ropy, thick muscles bulged underneath his vintage Alice in Chains T-shirt. He was cool AF, popping and thumping in perfect rhythm with Jace's percussion.

As hot as the rest of the LTZ guys were, lead singer Tyson Rainier was the most magnificent-looking guy I'd ever seen in real life. His chiseled, square-jawed face with just a hint of stubble made him look like a young, rogue biker. His gorgeous long, brown hair hung in loose waves. He swung it wildly, scanning the crowd through sapphire-blue eyes rimmed with dark, long lashes. His lithe yet muscular body rocked tight skinny jeans and a frayed, fitted white V-neck. He stomped around the stage like a throw-back grunge rocker in duct-taped, forest-green Doc Martins. Ty's voice was mesmerizing—a mix of soaring range, complicated and unique lyrical phrasing, wolf-like growls, and passionate, emotional delivery.

He figuratively and literally mastered the stage and the audience, and I was hypnotized by him. There was no way not to stare. To me, he was passion personified. My body was consumed with what felt like an intense, gravitational pull.

While I was gaping at him, the beat changed to a slow, sultry low groove. At that moment, he looked down from the stage directly into my eyes. Like a lightning bolt, his look caused a *zap* straight to my core. My heart thumped so fast. I wouldn't have been surprised if it exploded. I glanced around and saw beautiful women everywhere having the same reaction to this magnificent rock god. Immediately, I felt foolish. He hadn't singled me out, specifically. I was nothing special. He just had that effect, which is why LTZ was destined for something bigger than a local club.

Throughout the rest of the show, I purposefully avoided looking at the sexy singer. Making eye contact was like looking directly into the sun. Smiling to myself at the ludicrous thought that I would ever have a chance in hell with Tyson Rainier, I immersed myself in the music. Alex and I swayed, danced, and cheered at LTZ's awesomeness. Hands down, they were the coolest band I'd ever seen.

After their encore, Alex and I were still a bit sweaty by the time we pushed through the crowd to find our friends, who were live-streaming their commentary about the show. Alex added to her Instagram story, and I flashed her some rock horns when she turned the camera phone on me. We couldn't stop squeeing about the band and how incredible they were. Despite my earlier insecurities, I couldn't shake the feeling that something about the lead singer had struck a chord deep inside me.

"I think he looked right at you." As if reading my mind, Alex nudged me and waggled her eyebrows.

"Uh-huh. There is no chance," I guffawed, "the lights were shining in his eyes, he couldn't see anyone in the crowd."

"No, I'm serious. He kept trying to catch your attention," she asserted. "You didn't see it? He was singing to you. My Gawd, you have to talk to him!"

"I can't do that." I wrapped my arms around myself protectively. "I'd die of embarrassment. I'd just be standing there looking completely basic."

The thought of it made me cringe.

"Holy fucking shit. Well, you better think fast because I'm pretty sure he's heading this way." Alex's eyes were wide with excitement.

I barely had the chance to turn around when a big hand clasped my shoulder and a distinctive, deep, husky voice asked, "Hey, um. Sorry to interrupt, but haven't I seen you before?"

Looking up into the deepest blue eyes I'd ever seen, for a beat too long, electricity once again crackled throughout my body. I managed to speak, if not eloquently, "Um—Umm. I just was watching your show."

I stared at his exquisite face, not able to help it. After a beat too long, I finally was able to look down at my shoulder where his hand rested. "You are amazing, I mean—the band was amazing— I mean— I loved it!" I stuttered, wanting to disappear through the floor at my ineptitude of being able to flirt.

"Oh, uh, cool. Thanks." Ty's cheeks visibly reddened and he looked at his boots almost bashfully. This took me by surprise, I hadn't expected any of the LTZ guys to be modest. Or nice. Or shy. They were all so, well, overwhelmingly hot. Brushing off the compliment, Ty looked at me intensely. "No, I mean it. I feel like we've met somewhere and it's driving me crazy trying to figure it out."

I couldn't find my words. With little dating experience, having such a powerful reaction to a guy was new. But then this was not just any guy—he was a fucking rock god, so maybe it was to be expected. "Oh-kay, but no, I think I'd remember you."

Realizing this came out somewhat snarky, I changed my tone, trying to be sexier and more confident. Unfortunately, instead, I sounded like a total nerd fangirl. "I mean, I'd for sure remember meeting you."

God, I'm an idiot. I blushed literally everywhere.

Some of the crowd swarmed around us when they noticed the singer of LTZ was among the masses. Ty didn't appear to be aware of his effect at all. His focus was solely on me, like I was the only person in the club. He moved closer in so he could hear me better. His fingers lightly stroked down my arm, almost like he was afraid to touch me but couldn't help it. "I'm not super good at this, um. Well, maybe I made up an excuse to say hello, so hello. I'm Ty."

Not good at it? How could this possibly be? Everyone wanted to talk to him as evidenced by the crowd of people pushing toward us.

"I'm Zoey," I answered, and then my mind emptied of all coherent thought because the world around us fell away and there was only me and him in the room.

We stared at each other, both of us with goofy grins on our faces, the silence between us embarrassingly long. I didn't know how to flirt with him. Apparently, he was in the same boat. Beautiful girls of every size, shape, and color surrounded us, batting their eyelashes, trying to catch his attention. Clearly wondering how to divert his attention from me.

"That's a pretty name for the prettiest girl here," he said before finally breaking eye contact to glance down at his phone.

My bullshit detector activated.

"Really? That's your line?" I cocked my hip and wrinkled my nose in dismay. Surprised, but internally cheering for myself, at my wariness. "I almost fell for it. This is actually how you meet girls after a show. Ty, I'm *not* a thirsty groupie, I actually genuinely loved your music."

A look of mortification passed through his eyes before changing into intrigue. His hand continued running up and down my arm slowly. "Hmmm, well, I admit—that sounded super cheesy." He looked back down at his phone but smiled up at me through his mane of brown waves, scrunching his nose slightly.

My arm was tingling, hyperaware of his touch. Could he feel the energy between us too? I studied him and challenged, "I was hoping you wouldn't be a pick-up-line guy."

His blue eyes snapped up from his phone, piercing mine again intensely. "I'm *not* a pick-up-line guy," he insisted.

A text lit up his phone that he read quickly before he shoved the device back into his pocket.

"I've gotta go help load out, Zo-ey." His deep voice drew my name out, which sent sparks to my girl-parts.

"I didn't mean—" I called out to Ty's back. He was already stalking back toward the stage where the rest of the band was packing up their gear. Feeling deflated, I traced my arm absently, immediately missing the warmth and zing of his hand rubbing it.

"OMG are you SERIOUS?" Alex whisper-squealed, interrupting my trance. "He is the most gorgeous man I've ever seen in real life. Although . . . No. The drummer is delicious, more my type."

"Alex, I just royally fucked that up." I pouted dramatically. "I'm such a tool, I basically put the hottest guy that ever talked to me on blast. No wonder he bailed. I totally just missed my chance."

"Shut the fuck up. Did you see the way he looked at you? He'll be back, trust me. Let's just chill and hang out for a bit more. Just look nonchalant, cool. As your dad would say, 'Be Fonzie.'" She laughed.

I tried to be Fonzie. Unsuccessfully. Keeping an eye where the band was loading out, I hoped to catch a glimpse of the gorgeous singer and maybe make amends. Waiting around while Alex chatted with friends, I prayed Ty would come back. After a while, there didn't appear to be any sign of LTZ, their gear, or Ty. Of course, I was so short it was hard to get a good look, even when I continuously stood on my tiptoes to assess the situation.

Dejectedly, when my curfew approached, I turned back to the group and pulled out my phone. After one more hopeful look, I opened my Uber app, tapped in the address of The Mission, and said my goodbyes. "Guys, I'm calling it. I'm heading home."

Because the club was in the heart of downtown Seattle, a car arrived in under two minutes. I was a wannabe Cinderella, and the hourglass had run out for any chance at talking to Ty ever again. I didn't exactly give up. I took one last, sad look around the club before dashing out the side exit to locate the car. When it pulled up, I jumped in and was closing the door when it suddenly flung back open.

"Hey, wait, did you forget about me?" Ty was nearly out of breath when he got into the car. "Can I catch a ride?"

"Tyson, uh, uh I-I— I'm going home. I have a curfew." I mentally thwacked my hand against my head, not wanting him to know that I was still some dumb high school kid for another month.

"Uhh, shoot. I had this great idea to ride home with you, Zoey. Maybe you'll give me your number and we can hang out sometime." Ty gave me a side look, his hair flopping over his eyes. "That's not a line. It's just what I hope will happen."

My smile stretched from ear to ear, and it felt like a thousand butterflies had been released from the top of my head. Holy shit, this was like a movie. Determined not to blow it again, I scooted over and patted the seat. Ty slid in next to me, pressing his long, lean thigh against mine in the tiny back seat of the car. He turned toward me and grinned, just a hint of white teeth peeking through his full lips. I turned toward him, my smile widening even more. The car sped off and I couldn't help but get lost in the depths of his piercing, blue eyes.

Crap, this guy's gonna break my heart.

I pushed the thought aside, beamed at him like a fool, and heard myself saying, "Pretty good comeback, rocker-boy."

TO READ MORE—GET ENDLESS
AVAILABLE NOW!

Made in the USA
Middletown, DE
17 April 2022

63996154R00223